"You'll pay for that, girl!" he snarled. "Just wait until we get back to *my* realm!"

I beat at his face with my left fist. Then I was covering that face and head with the shadow I had gathered with my right hand. Instead of letting go, he groped for my wrists, pulling them together and holding them, and then began brushing at the shadow. Without my touch it began to dissolve, the weaving falling apart.

He began pulling me toward the stuff of the Falls, toward a deep reddish-brown spot that pulsed more heavily than the rest. It was eight feet high and just as wide, all the beauty drawn out with nothing but sullen anger left. I stumbled along, fighting uselessly, being taken nearer and nearer.

Suddenly the man pulling me fell backward, still holding tight to my wrists. Back he went, toward the sullen red, drawing me with him. And then we were *into* it, falling into the color, spinning, spinning, down and down and down. . . .

Worlds of Fantasy from Avon Books

ALCHEMY UNLIMITED
by Douglas W. Clark

THE DRAGON WAITING
by John M. Ford

THE GRYPHON KING
by Tom Deitz

THE SHINING FALCON
by Josepha Sherman

THE WHITE RAVEN
by Diana L. Paxson

DAWN SONG

SHARON GREEN

AVON BOOKS ◆ NEW YORK

DAWN SONG is an original publication of Avon Books. This work has never before appeared in book form. This work is a novel. Any similarity to actual persons or events is purely coincidental.

AVON BOOKS
A division of
The Hearst Corporation
105 Madison Avenue
New York, New York 10016

Copyright © 1990 by Sharon Green
Front cover illustration by Keith Parkinson
Published by arrangement with the author
Library of Congress Catalog Card Number: 90-92994
ISBN: 0-380-75453-3

First Avon Books Printing: September 1990

AVON TRADEMARK REG. U.S. PAT. OFF. AND IN OTHER COUNTRIES, MARCA REGISTRADA, HECHO EN U.S.A.

Printed in the U.S.A.

RA 10 9 8 7 6 5 4 3 2

". . . all know of the time when Creation held no more than the Sun and the Moon and the Earth. Our own people were the Children of Toil, in fast bond to the Lord of the Earth, looked upon with pity by the Lord of the Sun and the Lady of the Moon. The Lord of the Earth was not the same, however, and when a son of the Sun Lord came to offer alliance with the Realm of the Moon Lady through marriage to one of her daughters, the Lord of the Earth was not pleased. Angrily he gathered his forces . . ."

—*The Beginning*,
ancient Keeper chant

Chapter 1

❦

THE WOODS WERE as beautiful as they always were, dark and lovely and far from silent. Night woods are truly alive, the heat and passion of their prowlers almost bright enough to light the shadows. I've always felt I could spend forever exploring them and never learn everything there was to learn, every secret they hid. Sometimes they revealed small mysteries, little things to delight, and as I moved through the brush under the trees I felt that this might be one of the nights they did.

Do you hear that? Sahrinth asked in a mind whisper, the wisps of his small, light gray body-shape almost clear in the dark where he hung in the air beside me. *The trees say there's a stranger in the woods.*

"A stranger to them has to be a stranger to us," I answered, now aware of the leaf-rustle that spoke as clearly as words. "I think we're about to have some fun."

Greaf's tiny blue flame-body glowed briefly in protest at that, his memory undoubtedly still full of the lectures we'd gotten after our last escapade. He was a good companion, and Sahrinth and I would never have gone out without him, but sometimes his faint-hearted panic was annoying. The three of us were lectured *every* time we did something someone else didn't care for, but so what? Taking the lectures to heart would have made for a very dull life.

1

Haliand, possibly we could simply see who it is, Sahrinth sent in a tone of diffident suggestion, his streamers of mist beginning to move ever so slightly in the center of his thin cloud. *Your Lady Mother was extremely angry with us the last time, and Greaf and I, as entities older than yourself, were specifically warned . . .*

"Oh, Sahrinth, not you, too," I grumbled, putting my fists to my hips as I looked back and forth between them. "Hasn't either of you gotten as tired as I am of being guilty for absolutely nothing? What's life for, if you don't do something with it? Anyone can be dull, as most people have no trouble proving. Isn't it better to prove something else—and have fun at the same time?"

There were no thoughts from Sahrinth and no blinkings from Greaf, as clear an attempt to avoid answering my question as I'd ever seen. I knew well enough that they had been sent to accompany me in order to keep me out of trouble, but with the passage of time we had all discovered the closeness of friendship to be found between those of like mind. They *wanted* to have a romp with me, I didn't doubt that for a minute, but the last one must have brought them a lot more trouble than I'd been given.

"On second thought, it just might be more fun doing this alone," I said, as though simply musing aloud. "And you two can spend the time watching to see how innocent it all is—and how difficult it would be for you to interfere even if you wanted to. I'm not a small child anymore, after all, and it really is time everyone understood that."

I ended my speech on a pleasant note before beginning to move away through the dark and greenery, letting my friends know I wasn't angry with them. Blaming them for what I did was patently unfair, and I would no longer allow it to happen. Once the point was made perfectly clear to everyone, the two could join me again without worrying about blame.

The trees still spoke with a whisper of leaves above my head, discussing the stranger riding through the woods. They considered everything that happened around them a different aspect of the philosophy of life, but that was, of course, the philosophy of *their* lives. I'd listened to discussions a few times, and had even been there once when they'd argued bitterly, but there's only so far a mobile life form can go in understanding a stationary one. Status from root spread is clear enough, and so is extra standing from extra height, but when it comes to primacy by number of offshoots and the conviction that everything coming by them in the woods has meaning and purpose in relation to the trees themselves, I'm definitely out of my depth.

With the trees' conversation to guide me, it wasn't difficult to find the place the stranger rode. The configuration of the trees themselves formed an aisle that was used by those who couldn't or didn't care to move more directly through the woods, not so much a trail or a road as a grassy highway. Above him my mother's light shone down brightly through the gap in the ceiling of branches and leaves, the warm circle of silver sharp against the black of the sky. The visitor to our realm seemed larger than our own men, but it was difficult to tell his exact size because of the horse he rode. I'd never seen a horse quite that big, and its easy lope covered more ground than another horse's gallop would have.

*Haliand, he's wearing a *sword*,* Sahrinth's whispered thought came to me, as though if he hadn't whispered someone might have overheard him. His light gray cloud-body had floated up to me without my having noticed, and I could feel the way he was staring at the stranger.

"So what?" I asked in a matching whisper, but one that was verbal. "My mother's guards wear swords, and that doesn't make them special. He must be a courier from someone's court, bringing a message to my mother or someone in the Circle. From the way he's looking around, I don't think he's ever come this way before."

That's why the trees speak of him as a stranger, Sahrinth pointed out in a distracted but still superior way. *If he'd been this way before, they would have recognized him.*

"Well, it looks to me like he's bored," I said, annoyed. "He must have had a long, tiring ride, and will probably be glad of a diversion. I wonder what kind he would prefer?"

Being showered with flower petals might not be so bad, Sahrinth suggested in a hesitant, slightly hopeful way. *He'd certainly be surprised, and his expression would be priceless. In fact, I'd really enjoy seeing something like that. I've never seen it done before, so . . .*

I moved away from my cloud friend without commenting, a gesture of friendship if I'd ever performed one. Sahrinth was trying to keep me out of trouble by suggesting a lark *no* one would get upset over, but if I'd been in the mood to be boring I could have accomplished it more easily by doing nothing at all. What fun is there in a lark that no one gets upset over?

The stranger had by that time ridden past me, so I took a shortcut through the woods to a point he would reach on the highway in just a few minutes. My mind had continued to ask what sort of diversion he would prefer, and Sahrinth's observation about his sword helped give me the answer. The stranger would certainly prefer an adventure, a little action that would wake him up and give him something interesting to think about. For my part, it would be fun to see how long it took him to catch on to what was happening.

I realized at once how useful the brightness of the highway would be to my plans, but I needed other things as well if everything was to work out properly. When my mother's ladies had first begun teaching me moonlight and shadow weaving I'd hated the whole idea, but after a short while I had discovered that more could be done with the skill than producing low-grade amateur works of art. I raised my arms and gathered strands of moonbeams to me, reached back and down for a mound of shadow, then quickly got to work.

By the time the highway brought the stranger to where I lay in wait, I was all ready for him. The woven moonbeam concealed the gossamer draperies I wore, making it seem I wore nothing at all, a touch the stranger was sure to appreciate. Men, I'd heard, liked the idea of naked females, and although I still didn't quite understand why, it seemed only fair that he be given some fun of his own for the fun he would give me. I'd used the mound of shadow to weave a very special shape, one that would, of course, move at my direction, and as soon as the man appeared around the curve of the highway I put my plan into action.

Which consisted of running lightly across the highway on a diagonal that put my back to him, appearing and disappearing in one leisurely moment. When his horse abruptly stopped I knew for certain that he'd seen me, and that meant I had to run through the undergrowth a good distance before it was safe to stop and look back. The hoofbeats had already resumed at a faster, more deter-mined pace by then, which made me grin as I peeked through the dozing bushes.

The man hadn't dismounted, but he'd drawn his sword and was using it energetically to move bushes and branches aside. An uninformed observer would have concluded that he seemed to have lost something. His head moved around as though he were trying to pierce the dark with his eyes, looking for what he *knew* he'd seen: a naked woman flitting through the woods, unaware of the black, slinking predator following her. My woven shadow-predator wasn't good enough to stand up to close inspection, but at that distance it had been more than adequate.

The poor man seems rather agitated. Sahrinth's thought came to me as he appeared beside me to my left, the direction in which the stranger still stood prodding bushes. *I'm pleased to see he has the good sense not to dismount and give chase into the dark. He could be hurt that way.*

"He won't be hurt," I whispered back. "He'll keep searching for the poor victim-to-be every time he sees her, until it suddenly dawns on him that *he's* the victim. That's when he'll start feeling really foolish . . . but he certainly won't be harmed."

I laughed softly before moving off through the under-growth, leaving Sahrinth and the stranger behind. I wanted to get to the next curve of the highway before the man did, in order to be ready for his appearance. This time I would cross the highway from right to left in front of him, and my woven predator would be just a little closer behind me. It might also help if I ran with a bit more desperation, as though I had discovered what came along behind me. The game wasn't one I could continue forever, but some imagination would certainly add to the length of it.

My second appearance went just as well as the first, and after the third the stranger was more than simply agitated. His frustration was so sharp it rivaled the edge of his sword, and even the big horse he rode was aware of his upset. It pawed the ground as its rider tried again and again to see into the place in the dark where I'd disappeared, his weapon all but hacking the woods apart—and that told me the game was nearly over. The trees would not care for being attacked, even though a sword did not upset them as much as an axe. One or two more times, and if he didn't understand by then I'd simply stroll across the highway with the "predator" trotting beside me. Or maybe I'd reverse the whole thing and end it with me chasing after the predator, the poor thing trying to get away from the vicious, pursuing victim. I liked the sound of that, and chuckled as I slipped toward the next curve of the highway.

It took a little longer that time for the sound of the stranger's horse to come, a delay that made me glad the game was almost over. Standing around waiting is boring even when you're waiting for a reason, and I was beginning to get hungry. High Moon Meal was due to be rung soon, and that would have ended the game anyway. For my last appearance, I would run across the highway one last time, wait until the stranger began getting violent with the place of my disappearance, then reappear a short distance away chasing my weaving after making some sort of noise to draw the man's attention. He would then probably be in the mood to get violent with me, but if he hadn't been able to follow me into the dark to save me, he'd find the same lack of success with murder in mind. After that I'd be gone, and he could be angry or not as he liked.

As the hoofbeats approached the curve I noticed that the horse was moving faster. I started off, right to left diagonally across, faster than the other times but not so fast that the stranger would miss seeing me. The grass of the highway was soft under my sandals, my hair flying out behind me, and then—

"Oh!" I yelped as the arms closed around my knees, sending me sprawling face down in the grass. The breath was knocked out of me, and before I could recover I was turned roughly onto my back. The stranger knelt across me, staring down, his eyes unusually bright in the moonlight.

"Well, well, what have we here?" he drawled. "I was ready to swear I'd been chasing one of those wraiths I've heard so much about, but you're a little too solid to be a shade. Did you have fun trying to drive me crazy?"

"As a matter of fact, it turned out to be more boring than fun," I said, annoyed that he wasn't making any attempt to apologize for knocking me down. "You'll have to move back a little before I can get up."

"Yes, I will, won't I?" he said, grinning as he leaned forward. "Which I *might* do as soon as you tell me what you were up to. Did someone send you to delay me, or was this all your own bright idea? If you'd prefer taking your time answering, go right ahead. If I start getting bored, I'm sure to find *something* to fill the time."

He was looking down at me with a good deal of amusement, but I didn't quite understand the joke. His face was broader than those of the men of my own land, and his skin seemed to be darker. Even kneeling it was fairly obvious he was larger as well, and his hair was a golden red color I'd never seen before. He was handsome in a stronger way than the men of my mother's Court, and I was suddenly very pleased that he'd caught me.

"Why would anyone send me to delay you?" I asked in turn, wondering if he could be carrying so important a message. "And what *sort* of something would you find to fill the time?"

I knew he was hinting at something deliciously improper, one of those things my sisters discussed together with wide grins, but he didn't give me any details. His grin faded to puzzlement and he parted his lips to speak, but he was interrupted.

Oh, please, sir, please don't hurt her! Sahrinth's agitated thoughts came, his mist-body suddenly floating between my face and the stranger's. *It wasn't her intention to do you harm, really it wasn't, she's just a child with no common sense at all! If you can find it within you to forgive her, we'll be eternally grateful!*

Greaf was hovering to Sahrinth's right, blinking fervent agreement with the plea, the blue of his shape more intense than it had been.

"But what if I'm not in the mood to forgive her?" the stranger asked Sahrinth and Greaf. "She's given me more than a little trouble, you know, first making me believe a woman was in need of help, and then making it necessary for me to run ahead of my stallion to catch her. She deserves more than a fall onto soft grass—*especially* if she's a child. Children need to be taught to behave themselves."

"I am *not* a child!" I protested, after blowing hard at Sahrinth's body to float him away from my face. "It may be true that I *used* to be a child, but everyone suffers from that at one time or another. He's not going to hurt me, Sahrinth, he's just angry that I made him look silly. Can't you tell when you're being teased?"

"What makes you think I'm not telling them exactly how I feel?" the stranger asked me, giving Sahrinth and Greaf no chance to comment. "You seem to believe you're perfectly safe no matter what you've done, safe enough not to feel the need to apologize. What will you do if it turns out you're not quite safe after all?"

He still hadn't raised his voice or lost any of the calm he'd been showing, but he was staring straight down at me, the most direct and unwavering stare I'd ever seen. A moment earlier I'd been sure he was teasing, but suddenly I wasn't quite as certain. He really was very big and wide, and he *was* a stranger, and he still wasn't letting me up, and— Very abruptly I wished I'd never started that stupid game.

"You're beginning to get the idea," he said as he continued to stare at me, his voice sounding faintly satisfied but still far too sober. "If you really were a child and did something like this, the worst you'd be faced with right now is a good, hard spanking. Since I can see without half trying that you're not a child at all, you're in line for something a good deal worse. Would you like to be given that something worse?"

All I could do was shake my head, wishing I could reach enough moonbeams to weave myself into invisibility. The men of my mother's Court never got as grim as this stranger was, and I didn't like it at all. He looked so—*dangerous,* and so terribly, awfully serious!

"Well, at least you're bright enough to know what not to want," he said, and again that satisfaction was in his voice. It was also in his eyes, which seemed to be dark but glowing gold. "If I let you go, will you ever do something like this again?"

I shook my head a second time, and that seemed to complete his satisfaction. He nodded slowly, as though he knew I was telling the truth, and finally got to his feet. After giving completely different nods to the hovering Greaf and Sahrinth, he turned and walked to his horse.

See there, Haliand? Sahrinth sent, an odd tenor to his thoughts. *He hung his swordbelt on his saddle when he came after you on foot, but he kept his dagger with him. I told you he was a dangerous man who shouldn't have been disturbed, and you're quite fortunate that he let you go. He could just as easily have . . ."

Since I had no interest at all in hearing what he might have done to me, I was already up on my feet and heading for the shadows under the trees. Once there I made no attempt to look back, instead taking myself directly and quickly home.

I didn't notice that High Moon Meal was late until it was rung, and only then discovered I'd lost all interest in it. I'd spent the time since getting home in my suite, shaking the moonbeams out of my gown and coaxing the grass and leaves out of my hair. And brooding. I stared at myself in the circle mirror, my hair bright and alive from having been brushed, a really strange expression on my face. It was an excellent representation of what I felt inside, a core of indecision with anger and uneasiness swirling around.

"And you were going to make *him* feel like a fool," I muttered to my reflection, trying not to look into the ice-green eyes. "It was going to be a lark, nothing but fun. If that's your idea of fun, there's something seriously wrong with you."

Which might well be the case anyway, I thought with a sigh. Why was it that I alone, out of all my sisters, couldn't seem to settle down to life at my mother's Court? Everyone else enjoyed it so much, was so willingly a part of it—they were all so happy with their lives. Even as a small child I hadn't been satisfied, and constantly getting into trouble had been the only way to avoid that terrible, stifling boredom it seemed I'd been wrapped in at birth. Most people envied me my place as a daughter to my Lady Mother, and she really was a wonderful mother with more patience than just about anyone else would have shown, but . . .

But I still had this overwhelming urge to do outrageous things, to break out of the mold my sisters were set in, to be *different*—

"And maybe end up finding out about those somethings that are worse than a hard spanking," I muttered again, seeing the faint flush in my cheeks that normally I could only feel. That stranger had been impossible, undoubtedly from some backward Realm where they did awful things to people all the time, and I had no intention of leaving my suite until he was well on his way back to wherever he'd come from. I was fairly certain he'd been serious about doing something terrible to me, and although the thought made me angry it also made me very uneasy. It was obvious he had no idea my mother considered spanking an inappropriate punishment for her daughters, and had blithely discussed doing something that was even worse. He was certainly handsome enough, and maybe if he'd just been teasing—

And it was possible he *had* just been teasing, getting even for what I'd been doing to him. He'd said something about knowing I wasn't a child, but he'd still tried frightening me as if I were. Tried and succeeded—in a way. I wasn't *really* afraid of him, but if it turned out he had been serious . . .

"I'm not leaving this suite," I told my reflection firmly, getting an equally firm nod in response. "I like being different, but being the first to have something horrible done to me isn't quite the different I had in mind. No doubt there's something wrong with me, but I'm not *that* far gone."

My reflection clearly approved of my decision, which was certainly wise of it, and that helped the turmoil inside me to settle down a bit. I had no intentions of changing my mind—and then my door chime sounded.

"Lady Haliand, you're going to be terribly late!" Renna exclaimed as soon as she was through the door, wringing her hands over her rounded middle. "Your Lady Mother will be very angry!"

"Why should my mother be angry over my taking the Meal here in my suite?" I asked, going back to brushing my hair as though nothing were bothering me. "It won't be the first time, and it's hardly likely to be the last."

"Oh, child, when will you learn to pay attention to the bells?" Renna asked impatiently. "It wasn't the Meal that was rung, it was a Gathering Feast, and you *know* all members of the Family are required to appear at a Gathering Feast. The Court has a very distinguished visitor, and your mother will want to present her daughters. If you leave right now and hurry, you still might be there on time."

"I'll be damned if I'll hurry to my own execution," I muttered, slamming my brush onto the mirror ledge. So he was a distinguished visitor, and my mother would introduce me to him and he would say we'd already met, and she would ask where we'd met and he would tell her, and then my life would be over—or at least I'd wish it was.

"Well, at least Sahrinth and Greaf won't be getting in

trouble with me this time,'' I said under my breath. Trying to avoid the mess would be useless, I knew that from experience, and I had just discovered I didn't *want* to avoid it. Let him tell my mother everything; at least that would keep me well away from him no matter how long he stayed.

Renna fussed and fluttered until I left her behind, her last words still telling me to hurry. She was as intense and conscientious as the rest of her kind, as chunky and thick of body as they all seemed to be, so very different from the people of my mother's Court. Children of Toil they were called, those like Renna, and everyone I knew felt sorry for them and their lack of grace and . . . spirit, you might say. They seemed to have no dreams besides serving, and no people can be free of chains without proper dreams. None of them apparently understood that, or toil would not have been their only destiny.

Most of the house was as cool and dim with moonglow as it usually was, but approaching the large, open, circular terrace used for Gathering Feasts, I saw that quite a few torches had been kindled to intensify the light. I remembered then how badly our distinguished visitor did in the dark, and began to seriously wonder who he was. Increasing the light level wasn't often done, and servants like Renna had long since gotten used to the moonglow preferred by the Court. I hadn't been in bright light for years, and hadn't enjoyed it the last time, which seemed to be an advance warning of how pleasant this Feasting was going to be. External light shed light on things previously kept in the dark, an omen that needed no further interpretation.

Everyone in the entire Realm seemed to be on the terrace. My mother stood in its very center, not far from her eating couch, all of her glowing more brightly silver in the strong torchlight. Her hair, inches longer than mine, floated around her gown at a point below where her knees would be, more of a silver sheen to it than the platinum of my own. Her eyes were also of a warmer green—as my sisters had so often pointed out—but she and I were almost exactly the same height. It had always bothered my sisters that they were all shorter, but for the life of me I couldn't understand why. As the youngest of nine I had absolutely no chance of succeeding our mother when she grew tired of being Lady of the House, and wouldn't have wanted the place even if it were offered to me. What I did want was another question entirely, and one that I expected to have some trouble answering.

"Ah, there she is," my mother's voice came, and I blinked back to where I stood to find that she was looking directly at me through an opening in the group around her. "My youngest daughter, who seems to have taken to heart the position of being last. Do join us a little more quickly, Hali, there's someone here I'd like you to meet."

The someone stood directly on her right, too big to be missed. His hair was definitely a golden red and his eyes were darker gold but very bright, and he had changed out of the leather and cloth traveling clothes I'd last seen him wearing. His tunic was a golden silk, his heavy leggings and boots a golden red to match his hair, and a thick-chained medallion of red gold hung around his neck and down onto his chest. It was no real surprise that he still wore a sword-belt, the leather of the original one having been replaced with a linked gold stand-in, and as I neared the group it was also no surprise to find that he recognized me.

"Prince Jentris, son of the Lord of the Sun, I would like to present my daughter, the Princess Haliand," my mother said with a smile, putting an arm around my shoulders to urge me closer to the man. "The prince comes with an unusual and unexpected proposal from his father, Hali, and for that reason wished to meet *all* of my daughters. Now that you're finally here, he has."

"And an admittedly pleasant chore it's been," the stranger said with a faint grin as he reached for my hand. "So very many young ladies and all so lovely—the choice will be an extremely difficult one. How delightful to meet you, Princess Haliand."

As he took my hand and raised it to his lips his golden eyes laughed at me, as though he were daring me to guess whether or not he would add "again" to the delight of our meeting. My hand was very pale in his large, tanned one, and I made no effort to match the warmth of his grip or to return his grin. If he was going to tell on me he would, and I wanted him to know I didn't care. I refused to be pleasant just to keep him quiet.

"Now that Hali is finally with us, Mother, we'd like to know why Prince Jentris had to meet us all," my oldest sister Dorithen said as he released my hand. I stepped back just a little, and my sisters promptly glided gracefully in front of me.

"The Lord of the Sun has proposed that he and I consider a very old geas put on our Houses," our mother said, smiling first at Dorithen and then at the rest of us. "Back in the very beginning, when our separate Houses were first established, it was understood that our Houses would remain separate only until there was a need to join them. No one knew when that would be, most especially since our Houses would have to be threatened, but apparently the time has come. The Lord of the Earth, having not long ago taken the place of his father who now travels elsewhere, is about to demand that our Realms be made vassals to his. He has gathered great armies, and means to attack us if we refuse."

"Loyal servants brought my father the word, warning us with the last breath left in them," Prince Jentris said into the mutter of shock and disbelief. "The Lord of the Earth means to attack our Realm first, and then expects to take yours with very little trouble. We none of us want to see that, so I'm here to find a bride and do my part in joining our Houses. At the ceremony, our Flames will also be joined."

The prince gestured then toward one of the arches leading from the terrace into the house and three servants appeared, two of them flanking the third, who carried a very small gold box in his hands. They made a procession of bringing the box to my mother and Prince Jentris, and when it got there our distinguished guest opened it with a flick of his finger. A combined sigh arose from everyone on the terrace at sight of the pure blue Flame burning inside the box, a Flame that needed nothing to consume in order to be. We had a similar Flame in a silver box, and it was said that when the Flames combined there would be born from the union something that had never before been known.

"So you see, young ladies and princesses, I'm here to ask for the hand of one of you," Prince Jentris said, turning away from the Flame. His faint grin was back as he let his glance move from one of my sisters to the next. "It's said that once our Houses are combined we'll be invincible, but after seeing how lovely you all are I'm feeling invincible already. I do hope at least one of you will take pity on me and help me see to what is, after all, a solemn duty to my House and yours. A duty, I should add, I can't wait to get to."

His grin widened at that, echoed by my mother's tinkling laughter, and then my sisters were all crowding around him, adding their own laughter and amusement and undersubtle attempts to get his attention. I turned away with a sigh, less than pleased to learn that the man would soon wed one of my sisters. If they settled in my mother's Realm . . . He hadn't told on me and didn't seem prepared to anytime in the near future, but matters like this were usually subject to change without notice.

The finger-table beside my couch already had a crystal of wine on it, so rather than cause a fuss by leaving the Feast, I went to the couch and took up the crystal of wine. Except for my sisters and mother the Court was already settling down on their own couches, and the three servants were trying to leave with the Flame sent by the Lord of the Sun. Out of the corner of my eye I noticed that they were having something of a problem, and when I turned to look I almost groaned. Sahrinth's mist was hanging back to one side of the terrace, but Greaf's little body was darting around and above the Flame in the golden box. From his movements he was clearly in ecstasy, as though he had found the love of his life, but that was more than silly. His sort of entity couldn't even communicate with one of the Great Flames, not to mention combine with it.

Since everyone knew he wouldn't have been there if not for my presence, I was going to be in trouble again if I didn't do something fast to stop it. Luckily, one of the servants reached over and closed the lid on the golden box. Greaf stiffened with disappointment, giving the three servants a chance to march away from him. I wanted to go to him and soothe his hurt if I could, but there was still that stupid Feast . . . Sahrinth saw my indecision, understood the situation, then rippled his mist to tell me to stay where I was before he moved off after those who were already out of sight. He would companion Greaf until I was free, and for that I was very grateful.

By that time my mother and sisters were beginning to move toward places of their own. Prince Jentris had been settled right next to my mother in the center of the terrace, and once they were down the food began coming. Three servants for my mother and the same for her guest, two each for my sisters and me, one for those members of the Court encouched, and circulating tray-bearers for the rest. Gathering Feasts were always the same—crowded, fattening, and boring.

But though my servants brought me samples of everything being offered, practically waving it under my nose, I just couldn't find much attraction in any of it. I lay back among the cushions of my couch, sipping my wine—golden, in honor of our guest, I assumed—and tried to figure out what prevented me from finding enjoyment the way other people did. I was my mother's daughter, just the same as my sisters, so why couldn't I . . .

"Princess—Haliand, I believe it was," a voice said above me. "Do you mind if I join you for a moment or two?"

I looked up to see Prince Jentris looming over me again, but not quite in the same way he'd done the first time. What was he doing near my couch?

"Your mother suggested I spend a short time with each of you girls, in an effort to know you as individuals," the man said as though reading my mind. He gestured to the side of my couch. "May I sit down?"

"No," I answered, deliberately ignoring the shocked looks on the faces of my servants. "I'm sure you'll find your time spent much more profitably elsewhere. Besides, I'm busy right now."

"Busy with what?" he asked, glancing to my servants with a reassuring smile before sending them away with a flick of his finger. Then he sat down facing me on the edge of the couch to my left, just as though I hadn't said no.

"I'm busy wondering what my mother would have done if you had hurt me for any reason at all," I said. "She wouldn't care what started it. All she'd care about was that I was hurt."

"I'm sure that's just the way she'd see it," he answered, those bright golden eyes softening. "But she won't have to see it that way, because I don't intend to hurt you. What happened earlier is over with now, so there's no reason we can't be friends. And I'll make a deal with you: I won't tell anyone you tried to ambush me, if you don't tell anyone I knocked you down and sat on you. Are you willing?"

He did everything but spit on his palms and rub them together, his expression warm and friendly as he offered me the best deal in creation. I sometimes wonder what it is about me that makes people think of me as a child, and what I can do to get rid of the blasted thing.

"You're not here to be friends with me, you're here to marry one of my sisters," I told him bluntly, wishing at the same time he wasn't sitting on quite so much of my gown skirt. "I didn't try to ambush you, I tried to make you look like a fool, and you may have knocked me down but you didn't sit on me. Not that anyone but my mother would care even if you had. You can tell everyone in the Realm what I did if you like, but don't expect to surprise anyone. They know me a good deal better than you do."

"Apparently so," he said, blinking with surprise. "From what you said I take it you're not interested in a deal, and

I'm sorry you don't want to be friends. There's just one thing— You said something that isn't quite true, and I'm afraid I'm going to have to correct you. I'm not here to marry one of your sisters.''

"If you marry all of them, you'll regret it," I said, unsure of what else there was to say. "I've heard some of the Court men talking, and I understand they're rather demanding.''

"That isn't what I meant," he said, grinning. "You seem to have a very unusual way of considering things. What I meant was, I'm here to marry one of the daughters of your Lady Mother, not one of your sisters. Do you see the difference?''

"If you're trying to make the point that *I'm* one of those daughters, don't make me laugh," I retorted, almost laughing anyway. "If you were ever silly enough to choose *me* as your bride, that invincibility you mentioned would immediately lose its 'in.' I tend to affect people and things like that—it's a talent I have. And now I think your moment is up.''

"I think you're right," he said with the same wide grin as he finally got off the couch and my gown. "I still have four of your sisters to visit with, and this Feast won't last forever. After that I'll be spending a full day with each of you, so you'd better start bracing yourself. When it's your turn, I'd like to see a change of mind on the subject of being friends.''

"It's possible by then I'll have changed my mind on lots of things," I said with a shrug, looking up at him to see the puzzlement I'd expected my comment to cause. "It may have slipped your mind, but there aren't many *days* in this Realm, although we have a few every now and then. If I have to wait for the ninth of them, I may not even remember who you are.''

"Then, by all means, let's change that word to *nights*," he came back, amusement in his eyes. "I don't mind admitting I like the sound of it more, and that way you'll have a much better chance of remembering me. Possibly in a way not far removed from the way I remember you.''

He put his left hand to his sword hilt as he bowed to me, and I wondered with annoyance if he knew I didn't really understand what he was talking about. I was very tempted to ask him to explain, when we were interrupted.

"Dearest Haliand, now that our illustrious guest is taking his leave of you, I shall replace him," Feledor said as he materialized from behind my couch, a cool smile for both the prince and me. Feledor was another thing I'd lately been afflicted with, a very high member of my mother's Court who had suddenly discovered a more than casual interest in me. I'd learned through devious means that he'd spoken to my mother about me, but just exactly what he wanted was unclear. He bothered me every chance he had, trying to engage me in clever conversation, trying even harder to get me to visit with him for a while on his estate. Though younger and more inexperienced than I liked to admit, I wasn't so young that I didn't know he had more than visiting in mind. Most of my sisters considered me an idiot for refusing, but I'd known right from the start that I wanted no part of whatever he was offering.

"Prince Jentris, this is Feledor," I said, wondering as I sat up why our big visitor no longer looked amused. His bright golden eyes moved over Feledor's smaller, more slender body, assessing the costly pale yellow silks Feledor wore, the richly jeweled dagger hung at his belt, the short, soft boots on his feet. If his concluding expression meant anything he wasn't impressed, not even by the fact that his size, next to the other man's elegant grace, made him seem like a gross, overgrown servant. Feledor, however, seemed aware of and pleased by the difference, and his pale green eyes were solid smirk.

"That's *Lord* Feledor, Your Highness," he said in his usual condescending way. "Haliand is completely lacking in an appreciation of all matters of class distinction, a quality I look upon as rather endearing despite its social awkwardness. Although my Court standing is quite high, I find nothing of the diminishment others undoubtedly would suffer due to such a slighting attitude. A diminishment, I might add, that others would be forced to accept in the sight of those about them, due to an involvement with her. I thought it best that Your Highness be fully informed, well before any irrevocable decisions are made."

"Why, that's extremely thoughtful of you, Lord Feledor," our guest said slowly. "I'll be certain to keep the information in mind when irrevocable decisions have to be made. Until then— We'll speak again, Princess Haliand."

He bowed to me a second time, nodded to Feledor, then moved on to the couch of my nearest sister without looking back. I didn't know if he was aware of the cultured scowl Feledor sent after him, but I had the feeling he wouldn't have cared even if he *had* known.

"I find myself filled with a complete dislike for that man," Feledor said softly. "He should have insisted that the rest of us not be subjected to all this light, he should have made a point of being introduced to members of the Court, and he should certainly take warnings a good deal more seriously. For your Lady Mother's sake, I do hope I don't find it necessary to resort to something other than words with him."

"And just what do you think you were warning him about?" I asked, the words turning his smoothly handsome face in my direction. "None of this is any of your business, so what do you think you're doing?"

"My dear child, there's no need for you to upset yourself," he said in that unctuous, supercilious way he had when he saw how annoyed I was. "You've been all but promised to me, and I have every right to protect what is meant to be mine. My House may be minor when compared with yours, but your Lady Mother is well aware of her need for my support. I'm sure the Lord of the Sun is firm in his belief that an alliance between the great Houses is necessary despite the more rational doubts of those like myself, but none of that needs to affect *us*. When one of your sisters is chosen for the purportedly high honor, we will commence our own, more modest, association. I find myself scarcely able to wait."

He stepped forward to bend for my hand and lift it to his lips, his light green gaze on me all the while, and then he strolled away to find someone else to bother. Bother. I looked down at the hand he'd kissed, shivering with a sudden chill as I abruptly remembered the full meaning of that word. I was bothered, all right, straight through to my insides, and confusion was no small part of it. Why did it have to be me he wanted, when most of my sisters would have been delighted to oblige him? He'd admitted my mother hadn't yet given me to him, but what was I going to do when she did? The only House in the Realm more powerful than his was ours, and to think he wouldn't get what he wanted was to live in a dream world.

And one of the things he *didn't* want was to see me chosen by that Prince Jentris. I looked over to the stranger where he sat on my sister's couch, his back to me, the faint sound of laughter floating away from the two of them. He probably hadn't been serious when he'd said I was as much under consideration as my sisters, but I almost wished he had been. There was very little I wouldn't have preferred to being claimed by Feledor, and abruptly I realized that included running away. If only I could find some place to run away *to* . . .

Suddenly there were two servants stumbling out of the house, bloody and disheveled. The two men made their way to my mother without anyone trying to stop them, then they fell to their knees in front of her.

"Greatest Lady, we must beg your forgiveness," one of them groaned, obviously in pain. "We have failed you, and our lives are yours to take. We fought with all our strength, but the strength and numbers of the thieves were greater. The Flame of the Lord of the Sun— They took it and fled, leaving us for dead. And so we should have been, before allowing so vile an act. We came as quickly as we could . . . but the time has not been short . . . none in the halls to pass the word to . . . all here at the Feast . . ."

Chaos erupted as the servant fell over senseless to join his companion on the floor. I was on my feet, just as most of the people on the terrace were. My mother was also standing, signaling frantically to other servants to see to the ones who were hurt, and Prince Jentris was already striding quickly toward her. Everyone was demanding to know how such a thing could have happened, how thieves could have entered the palace and taken an object of such importance, but no one was volunteering any answers. I stood there next to my couch, wondering if there was anything I could possibly do to help, then noticed Sahrinth making his way over to me. The thin cloud of mist that was one of my two best friends seemed agitated, and although he floated to me quickly there was also something of hesitation in his movement.

Haliand, something terrible has happened, he sent as soon as he was near enough, the thought-words trembling with upset. *I didn't want to disturb you, but now that the Feast has been interrupted I thought— Oh, dear, what are we going to do?*

"Sahrinth, there's very little we *can* do," I said, raising a hand for him to touch with the edges of his body. "The Flame is gone, and we don't even know who took it. How can we do any more than anybody . . ."

No, no, you don't understand, he protested, his agitation increasing. *It's not so much the Flame—but it is—or at least I think it is—Haliand, I think Greaf found a way into the box of the Flame! I searched for him when I heard about the theft, but I can't find him anywhere! If I'm right—then he's been stolen along with the Flame!*

I stood there staring at Sahrinth, too shocked to say a word, almost too frozen to think. Greaf had been in love, had tried to get closer to the object of his love, and now he could be gone and in terrible trouble. If that was so, if he really was stolen along with the Flame, what was I going to do?

Chapter 2

❦

B<small>Y THE TIME</small> Sahrinth and I, with the help of as many servants as we could gather, discovered that Greaf was nowhere to be found in the house, I'd decided what to do. I couldn't just stand back and hope that others would find the Flame and him with it, not when he was one of my two best friends, not when there was no reason *I* couldn't join in the search. The trees would know which way the thieves had gone, and once they told me I would go in the same direction.

I went back to my suite to pack a few things, more than relieved to find that everyone was too concerned with the theft to pay attention to me. I couldn't take much, but I didn't really have to; once I discovered the proper direction, I would ride moonbeams to follow faster than the thieves could travel. They were only servants, after all, and constrained to take the long way to wherever they were going. As my mother's daughter I didn't have that limitation, so it wouldn't take long before I recovered Greaf and the Flame in the golden box.

While my hands were busy with packing what I would take, my mind insisted on trying to understand why some people stole things. Thievery was so rare in my mother's Realm that I couldn't remember the last time it had happened, and although there was supposed to be a reason for this particular instance, I still couldn't understand why someone had done it. The Lord of the Earth Realm was trying to stop the merging of the two Houses he wanted to conquer, but it wasn't likely he was the one who had done the stealing.

It was the one who had actually come to our Realm and committed the act—he was the one I didn't understand. Hadn't anyone ever taught him what an admission of incompetence stealing is? If you're a fully capable person you earn what you want, and if for some reason you can't earn it, you do without. Doing without shows the same strength earning things does, and is usually harder to live with. Developing a strength like that keeps you from reaching out blindly.

Reaching out blindly. I sat down on the rim of my bed, the pack of clothes near my hand, a heaviness inside me. Everyone in our Realm was taught as a child not to reach out blindly, not to let the desirability of some particular thing blind us to the rest of life. The things we find most attractive are always balancing forces, able to tumble our lives toward success or disaster, whichever we're most prepared to accept and most believe we can accomplish. The story—

The story usually told young children was about the boy who noticed one day that his group of friends wasn't the only one at their university. Of course he'd known about the others all along, he just hadn't noticed them. That day he also noticed that one of the other groups wore bright and beautiful jewels, spun silk clothing in colors he'd never thought of, hand-tooled leather sandals—and the girls! The girls were the prettiest around, but one was the most beautiful he'd ever seen.

The boy decided right then and there to join that other group, the one that had everything he wanted. He left his friends, the ones whose company he'd so enjoyed for so long, and tried to become friends with those in the new group. He discovered after a while that no one in that group *had* friends, they were too busy competing with each other, but he didn't care. He did everything they did, and because of that got what they had, and at long last he reached the side of the most beautiful girl he'd ever seen.

He spent a lot more time winning the girl as his own, and once he had her he looked around at his total victory. He had the brightest jewels in the group, but they were nothing more than shining prettiness. He had the nicest and most colorful clothing in the group, but all it did was cause envy in those around him. He had the sturdiest sandals, but not a single friend to walk with. And he had the girl. She was really beautiful, and was even devoted to him, but it was in her nature to be devoted to the best in the group. If anyone ever surpassed him, she would have to be devoted to the new best.

It was then that the boy really understood what he'd done. He'd concentrated so hard on what it would take to get what he wanted, he'd never thought about what it would be like once he had it all. He was capable of keeping what he'd earned, he knew that well enough, but suddenly he didn't know if he *wanted* to keep it. Wanting to get something and being happy once you have it are two different conditions, but he'd never stopped to consider the point. And just how happy was he, really, after having spent so much time clawing for the things he'd thought he wanted?

The girl had been his ultimate turning point, just as human balancing forces always are. He'd wanted her so badly, but if at any point he hadn't been strong enough she would have turned all his luck against him. Human balancing forces are like that, and they don't necessarily do it on purpose. If he stayed with her he would have to really want to maintain his position, otherwise his lack of belief and desire would cause everything to crumble around his head. And all because he'd seen attractive things, and had reached out blindly before thinking about consequences . . .

Just as the thief had reached out blindly, thinking he was taking nothing but the Great Flame. But he had also taken one of my best friends, not knowing *I* was a balancing force who would be coming after him. Unless he was absolutely and completely determined in his own mind, causing his luck to strengthen because of the belief, one touch of my hand would give him exactly what he deserved. I stood up from the bed, and took my pack of clothes with a grim nod. Yes, I would be there, and he would get exactly what he deserved.

Slipping out of my suite with my belongings, I headed for the place outside the house where Sahrinth and I were to meet. He had insisted on going with me, of course, and I couldn't say I was sorry for his companionship. When Greaf was safe we would all consider the episode an unusual kind of lark, and laugh over the fact that one of our larks was finally doing some good.

I stepped through an arch into the true dark of night, heading for the beautiful, softly glowing fountain that was our rendezvous place, certain that Sahrinth had gotten there before me. He had nothing to pack, after all, so there was no reason . . .

"Princess Haliand," a soft voice came, startling me with the unexpectedness of it. I turned quickly to see two servants, one of them holding a small, transparent globe of water, and felt the pit of my stomach sink into my sandals. My preparations and attempt at departure hadn't been quite as unobserved as I'd thought, and I had no choice but to move closer to the globe the servant held.

"Hali, we've got to do something about speeding you up," my mother's image said to me from the center of the globe, not a ripple marring her image on the water. "You take forever to cover a distance of five feet. I want you here in my entertaining room, but I don't have all eternity to wait. Do you think you might make the effort to hurry?"

"Mother, I'm rather occupied with something at the moment," I said, holding my small bundle of belongings behind me in an attempt to keep her from seeing it. "As soon as I'm through I'll come to you immediately, and I'll try to make it as fast as—"

"Hali, it's what you're occupied with that I want to discuss," she interrupted. "I want you here *now*, young lady, without side trips of any sort, and at the moment I'm not speaking as your mother. Do you understand me?"

"Yes, Ma'am," I answered with very little grace, a subject of the Realm responding to her sovereign. Rarely did my mother choose to be Lady of the House rather than simply my mother, and there was no sense at all in arguing. She had the power and ability to enforce her wishes, and just because she seldom exercised those talents didn't mean she couldn't.

By the time I reached her entertaining room, I was striding along as briskly as anyone could have wanted. I also held my belongings in the crook of my left arm, right out where everyone could see them, no longer making an effort to hide what I was doing. If my mother tried ordering me not to go after Greaf I would refuse, and what happened after that would be entirely up to her. She was the one who had taught me that you never desert a friend, and if she was ready to change her mind on the point, I wasn't. I knew she still considered me a child, and it was more than time to correct that attitude.

I saw all the light in the entertaining room even before I stepped between the door guards, which told me my mother was entertaining company other than myself, and also who that other company was. I wasn't terribly pleased to have Prince Jentris as a witness to the discussion between my mother and me, but maybe his presence would keep her from insisting on anything dishonorable. I looked around the smallish room as I entered, seeing only the two of them, wondering what they were watching so intently on the top of the mirror table that stood in the center of everything. The room had silver couches and chairs, carved tables of pale wood, light yellow and delicate green hangings and drapes of silk, and the faintest lemon-white of a floor covering. Only the mirror table was made of dark wood and its polished top usually gleamed with that darkness, but as I drew nearer I could see that that top was now a glowing silver.

". . . shouldn't have known that," my mother was saying to the man beside her, anger clear in her voice. "They *must* have had help, and not only from *his* Realm. When I find out who it was . . ."

"You'll do what my father would," Prince Jentris finished for her, a grim satisfaction to his tone as he stared down at the tabletop. "Right now, though, our first order of business is recovery. If we fail at that, we can forget about the rest of it. We'll be too busy fighting invaders in our halls to worry about traitors."

"That's something I refuse to let happen," my mother said in a final way as she began to turn from the table. Then she saw me standing there, not five feet away. The anger in her face changed to a soft smile, and she put out a hand to me. "Hali, I'm glad you got here so quickly. Greaf seems to be missing along with the Great Flame, and I wanted you to know what's being done to recover them both. Prince Jentris will be starting after the thieves in just a few minutes, and he's promised to keep a special eye out for your friend. Greaf will be fine, I know he will, and he'll soon be back with you."

"I appreciate your consideration in telling me that, Mother, but it really isn't necessary," I answered, using my former resolve to keep me firm in the face of her unexpected gentleness and understanding. "I've decided to go after the thieves myself, and I'll certainly reach them before Prince Jentris does. Greaf is my friend, and he'll expect me to come after him. Which is what I mean to do."

I had the uncomfortable feeling I was repeating myself, but I did want her to know I'd made up my mind. More than once my mother had managed to talk me out of things, and I wanted it to be clear that that would not be happening again. If our positions had been reversed Greaf would have come after *me,* and if I failed him I'd never be able to live with myself.

"Hali, those men are dangerous," my mother said, some of the kindness fading as she glanced at the bundle I hadn't tried hiding from her. "What do you expect to be able to do against them even if you catch up to them? Do you want them to take you captive as well? How would something like that be of any help to Greaf?"

"They won't be able to catch me, Mother," I returned

with something very close to exasperation for her lack of faith. "They're only servants, after all, and you can't say I don't have experience avoiding servants. They've never been able to catch me when I didn't want to be caught."

"What if there's someone with them who isn't simply a servant?" Prince Jentris put in before my mother could get her growing annoyance vocalized, his golden eyes glowing with faint amusement. "If the Lord of the Earth sent one of his nobles with them, you might find yourself in a position that would—surprise you. I may be mistaken, but you just might have experience with that as well."

He was talking about the way he'd caught me in the woods, saying it straight out without actually telling on me. My mother showed a faint frown indicating her lack of understanding, but I didn't give her the time to ask any questions.

"But when you have experience with something and know it can happen, doesn't that usually mean you can't be surprised any longer?" I asked the man with none of the guilt or embarrassment he seemed to expect. "I like to think I'm capable of learning from my mistakes, if any learning experience really can be called a mistake. One of the things I've learned is that you don't leave it to others to help someone who's a friend of yours, not if you want to continue thinking of yourself as decent. I've generally liked myself until now, Mother, and I'd rather not do anything to change that."

I had moved my gaze back to her with the last of my words, just in time to see the frustration fill her lovely green eyes. She *couldn't* deny what I'd said, I could see, not and remain unchanged herself, and she didn't want to be something gross and ugly any more than I did. I smiled at her to show I understood her dilemma and truly appreciated her acceptance of the proper over personal preferences, then tightened my grip on my bundle.

"I think I'd better be on my way now," I said, reaching out a hand to touch her arm with gentle reassurance. "I'll be back before you know it, so please don't worry about me. Everything will be fine."

"Yes, it certainly will," she answered before I could turn away. "Your good opinion is important to me, daughter, but your survival is even more important. Prince Jentris will be going after the thieves, not you. You'll be staying here."

"And I refuse to stay here," I said, strangely enough feeling better now that I'd found the resistance I'd been anticipating. "This decision is mine to make, Mother, not yours. Prince Jentris is supposed to be here for the purpose of getting married. He can take care of that while I'm out helping a friend, and then everything really will be fine. "I'll probably be back in time for the ceremony, but definitely in time for the Feast."

"Hali, without the Great Flame there can't *be* a ceremony," my mother said in exasperation. "The only reason for a marriage in the first place, is to allow the Flames to be united at the same time our Houses are. This is far more important than you seem to realize, and the fate of two of the Three Realms can't be left in the hands of a girl. If you were waiting to be ordered to stay behind, consider it done."

"That's not a proper order, and you know it," I retorted, feeling my cheeks warm over the amusement I saw in our guest's eyes before he began turning back to the mirror table with my mother. "You can't simply dismiss me as though I were a child, ignoring everything I've said. I demand a Judgment from the Scales."

"Hali, why are you being so difficult just at *this* time!" my mother fumed as she turned toward me again, true anger now in her eyes. "Can't you see you're helping the enemy by distracting my attention from what's really important?"

"I'm trying to help a friend, not the enemy," I maintained doggedly, refusing to let myself be browbeaten. "It's my right, and you can't deny it."

"Very well then, young lady, we'll allow you your right," she agreed with a cool, regal nod, not at all pleased with me. "If the Judgment should go against you, however, as I believe it shall, you and I will have something of a discussion on the difference between firm resolve and stubbornness. An adult must truly know what she's about before she's capable of properly exercising firm resolve. Come with me."

My mother turned and led the way to the right of the mirror table, toward the Scales that stood on their own pedestal beside the wall. They were pure silver, of course, their pans eternally in balance, their patience endless as they waited to pronounce Judgment on matters that could not be decided without them. They weren't needed to tell right from wrong, not with powers as subtle as theirs. It was between two courses of right that they chose, indicating which course was more right under the circumstances then obtaining, and no one ever argued with their decision. It wasn't impossible to disagree, just an excellent way of making a fool of yourself, and although I'd seen Judgments rendered a few times, I'd never before been one of the petitioners.

"You may take the side to the left," my mother said, moving to the right. "Do you know what's required of you?"

I nodded, mostly to keep from having to use a voice I wasn't sure would hold steady. I'd demanded the Judgment to keep from being put to one side like an unimportant distraction, not because I was all that convinced I was right. Oh, *I* thought I was right, but that didn't mean the Scales would see it the same way. I considered putting my bundle down, changed my mind and held it more tightly instead, then raised my right hand to the slender cone above the left-hand pan. There was a fleetingly brief, almost painless prick in my palm, and then I stepped back from the Scales to find that my mother had done the same on her side.

"Well, it seems that we're ready now," she said, smiling with an assurance I wished I had even a small part of. "Since this is your Judgment, it's your place to ask the question."

"And just my luck," I muttered, but couldn't deny that that was the way it was usually done. I cleared my throat, tried to stand straighter, told myself sternly to stop wasting time, then managed to get out, "My friend is in trouble and I want to go and help him, but my mother thinks I'll be jeopardizing more important matters and wants me to stay home. Which of us is right?"

The Scales sounded a clear, crystal chime, letting us know that it heard the question and was considering it, and then a single drop of blood appeared at the mouth of each of the slender cones over the pans. The drops quivered briefly, then fell to the pans, my mother's blood to the right, mine to the left, at first both of them continuing to keep the pans in balance. Two tiny drops of living red surrounded by shining silver, more than simply the symbol of the Judgment that had been asked for. No one can expect to demand their beliefs be upheld without paying for the request in blood, directly or indirectly, one way or the other. Sometimes, if the demand is made by a large enough group, it's the blood of followers and friends that does the paying, but the cost is always met. Whether you turn out to be right, or not quite as right as the one opposing you, the need to pay a price remains.

Since the Judgment I'd asked for was a first request and concerned only a small number of people, my price hadn't been very large. I watched the pans holding the single drops of blood, close to holding my breath at the same time, and then there was a second chime. It told us that a decision had been made, and then slowly, slowly, the balance began to shift—to the pan on the *left!* The Scales had rendered their Judgment in my favor, and now my mother *couldn't* make me stay home!

"Incredible," she murmured with a small, lovely frown, staring at the Scales as our guest moved nearer. "Their advice has always been absolutely correct, but this time—! Why should it be necessary for *her* to go? She's little more than a child who has barely begun on her life. Why must she be risked, when there are so many others who would gladly face the jeopardy in her place? How can a child alone do what has to be done?"

"Are you sure she's meant to go alone?" Prince Jentris

asked, his tone half compassionate and half musing. "Some of our scholars believe the Scales are able to see all possibilities to their inevitable end, and for that reason can tell us the proper road to travel. Her question covered nothing more than whether or not she's to go; ask now if she's to go alone."

"You're right, of course," my mother answered with great relief, sending a smile to the prince before looking at the Scales again. I didn't quite understand what they were talking about, but I also didn't particularly care for the sound of it. The Judgment had been in my favor, but they didn't seem to be accepting it as completely as they should have been doing.

"You've said my daughter is to go where I have no wish to see her go," my mother addressed the Scales. "Is she to go alone into danger, with none to protect and direct her? She feels the mission is hers alone; is this the way it's meant to be?"

Again a crystal chime sounded, the Scales acknowledging that they'd heard, and I looked to the pans to see that the first drops of blood had disappeared. In another moment second drops were falling to the pans, but this time I wasn't at all anxious to have a decision made. The first decision had been in my favor; why couldn't that be enough?

When the Scales chimed again and the pans tilted, I could see that I'd been right in not wanting a second decision. This time the balance went in my mother's favor, and she laughed with relief while I scowled. I was free to go and do what I felt had to be done, but not without a nursemaid to look after me. I hated the thought of that, and decided not to accept it.

"I don't need anyone trailing after me and getting in my way," I said quickly. "Since it's clear that I'm meant to go, it should also be clear that I get to choose who will go with me. Sahrinth is the only one who won't be a drag and a burden, so that's who my companion will be. Him and no one else."

"Young lady, you're beginning to try my patience,"

my mother said with annoyance. "No one gets her way in everything in this life, and it's about time you learned that. Sahrinth can't even keep you out of trouble here at home; as a companion into danger, he'd be absolutely loyal and equally as useless. I say it's Prince Jentris who will accompany you—with him in charge and you accepting his orders. Since we're permitted to ask one more question, let's make it that one."

She turned to look at the Scales then, wanting to know if it would be necessary to repeat the question, but of course it wasn't. The chime came almost at once, as though the Scales couldn't wait to rid themselves of the third and last drops of blood they'd taken. Although few people asked for more than one decision, it was possible to ask for three at the same time. After that another set of three could be requested, but the price for the second set was considerably higher. It seemed to be a matter of complexity that governed the Scales' working; initial questions were of necessity simple and therefore cheap in price; the more questions you asked the more complex things became, and the price rose correspondingly.

If it takes talent to learn to anticipate the decisions of the Scales, then I must be very talented. I had no doubt that they would agree with my mother again, and it turned out I was absolutely correct. When the pans tilted to the right my mother sighed happily, but my response was somewhat different.

"Now I know why most people don't ask for more than one decision," I remarked, shifting my bundle to get a better grip on it. "Answers after the first tend to be more emotional than objective. I seem to be the only one around here able to believe I'm not an incompetent child, so I guess it's time the rest of you were shown. I'll see you when I get back, Mother."

I turned away from the Scales and began to march out of the room, but three steps of marching was all I accomplished. Our very large guest had planted himself four steps behind me, and it was either stop where I was or crash right into him. I chose the wiser course of stopping, but before I could navigate a path around the obstruction, my mother was beside me and putting an arm about my shoulders.

"Hali, no one is trying to make you feel like an incompetent," she said, her previous anger gone behind gentle compassion. "Being young and inexperienced isn't the same thing at all, but it *is* something that can't be ignored. The Scales have said that you're right in wanting to go along on the rescue mission, but wrong in thinking you can do it all yourself. If the decision were mine you wouldn't be going at all, but unfortunately as Lady of the Realm I *have* to let you go for the good of two of the Three Realms. But there are limits to the extent of the sacrifice I'm willing to make. If you don't do it the way the Scales say is best, I won't let you do it at all. I think you know I can keep you here if I wish, so the choice has become yours. Will you go with Prince Jentris as you're meant to, or do I have to forbid you to go at all?"

I turned my head to see the seriousness in her expression, the sober look that said she wasn't joking or threatening. She meant exactly what she said, and if I didn't agree Greaf would be saved or not without me. It wasn't fair for her to be able to do that to me, and I was about to tell her precisely how I felt when our guest joined in the discussion.

"Oh, I'm sure she'll cooperate when she realizes she'll also be doing me a favor," he said, drawing both our attention. "She already knows I need to spend a day with her and each of her sisters, so the time we'll be together can count as the day. As soon as we recover the Great Flame and her friend we'll come back here, and I can continue the much more pleasant chore of courting. I know I can count on you for the help I need, Princess Haliand, so why don't we all go back to the mirror table and see what sort of trail we'll be following?"

Between the two of them I was urged over to the mirror table, to see that there was now an image of our Realm imposed on the top of it. Tiny sparks shone brighter than the silver of the image, probably an indication of where the thieves were in the forest, but though discussion began again between my mother and Prince Jentris, I paid very little attention to their words. They both thought they were being so clever, trying to distract me from the fact that I would only be along for the ride, but they had a surprise coming. I hadn't agreed to do things their way, which meant I was still free to do them mine, in whatever manner I found to be most expedient. Let them believe Prince Jentris would be giving the orders; by the time he found out I wasn't taking them, Greaf would be safe and I'd have proven the Scales were right only the first time. After that, things would be much more pleasant for me at home.

Only another few minutes were spent in discussing the whereabouts of the thieves, and a short time thereafter found us in an outer court, taking and mounting the horses that had been saddled for us. Quite a few palace guards were going with us, armed men of the Realm wearing grim looks of outrage. The horses, of course, were also of our Realm. Prince Jentris had wanted to take his own mount, but his giant horse wouldn't have been able to take the shortcuts ours could. Horses had to be native to a Realm in order to do really well in it, and his horse couldn't see in the dark any better than he could. He was given the largest mount available, and once he was in the saddle he seemed satisfied. My horse was one I'd ridden before, and being mounted meant I could leave behind the bundle I'd thought I'd need. We'd be back in a very short time—*with* Greaf and the Great Flame.

As soon as we entered the woods, the trees began speaking to me. My mother had told them what was happening, and they were keeping track of the thieves while guiding us through their domain by the shortest, fastest route possible. The mirror table had shown that the thieves seemed to be heading toward the Silent Falls just beyond the far edge of the woods, so that was where we were heading. If they changed direction, we would know almost as soon as they did it.

We rode for quite a while at a very fast pace, me in the lead as we followed the directions given by the trees. At times we were forced to go single file through very narrow avenues, at others we could have ridden three abreast without feeling crowded. I hadn't realized at first that I was the only one who could understand the trees, but then I remembered hearing something about that from one of my sisters. We of the Family could speak to and understand the trees—but those of lesser human Houses could not. That didn't go for nonhuman Houses, of course, as Sahrinth had proven more than once. Thinking of Sahrinth made me wonder where he could be, but the thought was only a fleeting one. I didn't have the time to do anything more than pay attention to the trees and stay in the saddle, so wondering would have to wait.

Between our horses' swiftness and the help from the trees, we reached the Silent Falls before the thieves did. As we emerged from the woods and onto the rock plain our horses slowed to a walk, and the men stared ahead with mouths open and awe in their gazes.

"That has to be one of the most beautiful things I've ever seen," Prince Jentris breathed. "Was it always like that?"

"I understand it wasn't," I answered, smiling as I looked at the Falls. "At one time it was supposed to have been a real falls, with water and noise and everything, but then somehow it was touched by the ice of Eternity. Ever since, it's been as you see it."

Which was frozen in midfall, an unmoving but still rippling sheet of the most delicate crystal ever created. Even the spray thrown off by the living falls was stopped midmotion, forever suspended over the drop it would never complete. My mother's light from above touched it lovingly and turned it into coruscating fire, the silver becoming every color there was, its burning glow almost as blinding as its previous roar must have been deafening. We rode across what had once been the bed of its river, and it rose up before us like flaming legend.

"I'm glad we were given the chance to get used to it before our quarry gets here," the big man said with a sigh, pulling his eyes away from the Falls. "And come to think of it, shouldn't we be stopping as close to the woods as possible, so that the trees will be able to warn us when the thieves are almost here?"

"I could still hear the trees even if we rode to the base of the Falls," I answered with a shrug, wondering if his Realm had no vegetation of its own. "You should be able to hear them too, even if you can't understand them. There's really no need to stop here, but if you're tired of course we can stop."

He turned his head quickly and somewhat sharply, looking at me with those bright golden eyes, but kept himself from putting his annoyance into words. I had very little practice at being condescending, but the way he and my mother had been treating me had given me the urge to see how well I could do. My first try didn't seem to have gone over too badly, especially when the big man made his own try at changing the angle of our conversation.

"With saddles like these, riding is anything but tiring," he said, bringing his mount to a complete halt and beginning to dismount. "They're so soft and comfortable no one could have trouble with them, not even a woman in a gown. That must be the reason they were made in the first place—so women could keep up with men."

With that he was at the side of my horse, putting his hands to my waist to help me out of the saddle. I didn't want or need his help but I got it anyway, just as though I were helpless. He set me down on my feet with a faint grin, pretending I wasn't looking daggers at him, then left me to go and talk to the men he was leading.

I spent some time just staring at the Falls, for once not really seeing them. I had a lot of things to think about, not the least of which was what would happen once I got Greaf back. It would then be time to talk to my mother about Feledor, and I couldn't help but remember what she'd said about sometimes needing to be the Lady of the Realm instead of simply my mother. If she needed the support of his House badly enough . . .

"Any word yet on how close they are?" a voice broke into my brooding, the voice of Prince Jentris. He had stopped beside me on my left, and was looking at me rather than at the Falls.

"It won't be much longer," I told him, rubbing my arms to chase away the faint chill that had crept up on me. "Trees have almost no sense of time except in the sense of seasons, you know, so asking them 'how long' is a waste of effort. What they've told me is that the thieves' position will soon match ours, and they'll let me know when the riders are a stand's distance away from us. That should give us a couple of minutes to get ready."

"Good enough," he said, still looking down at me. "And while we're waiting, let's spend the time to good purpose. I *am* supposed to be getting to know you, remember."

"I don't think there's really enough time for me to make us a tent," I said, still partially distracted with my previous thoughts. "If we were alone we wouldn't need the tent, but with all those men around my mother will be very unhappy if we don't use one."

"A tent," he repeated, sounding totally confused. "What in the Three Realms would you make a tent out of, and why would we need one in the first place?"

"I'd weave it out of moonbeams and shadow, of course, and we need it for *privacy*," I answered with a sigh, speaking slowly and carefully so that he would have less trouble understanding. "Don't you think I got what you meant when you said you wanted to know us all better? My sisters say that only a fool would accept a lover before trying him out, and that should go double for someone you're going to marry. You want to try us all to see who's best, but there really isn't enough time now."

"I see you have it all figured out," he said, and for some reason he sounded amused. "You must have quite a lot of experience with lovers in order to have seen the truth this quickly. I hadn't realized I was speaking to so worldly a woman."

"I told you I wasn't a child," I returned, making sure I looked away from him to hide the warmth I could feel in my cheeks. In strictest fact I hadn't yet had *any* lovers, but since somebody had to be first there was no reason it shouldn't be the man who had come to marry one of my sisters. Once he realized I wasn't someone who could hold his interest, he would stop bothering me with the pretense of consideration and leave me alone to worry out my real problems.

"Oh, I was able to see right from the first that you weren't a child," he said, the words sober but still sounding odd. "The only thing is—hasn't it ever occurred to you that a man and woman can only spend so much time in bed? And even in bed, there are occasions when you actually have to speak to one another. Making love to someone who delights you out of bed is a lot more pleasant than doing the same with someone you can't stand to hear a word out of. It's a point even worldly women would be wise to consider."

"In a situation like this?" I asked, turning back to face him while wondering what he was trying to convince me of this time. "You don't know my sisters and they don't know you, so why pretend there's anything more to it than a matter of state? And are you trying to say you don't intend inviting my sisters to bed? Look straight at me, and say it to my face."

"Whether I do or don't has no bearing on what we're discussing," he hedged, and this time it was his golden eyes searching for something else to look at. "You and I will be *talking* to get to know each other better, which is, after all, just as important as—"

"You don't want to take me to bed?" I asked, surprised that his skin actually seemed a bit ruddier than it had been. "You're going to take them to bed but not me?"

"Haliand, it has nothing to do with wanting," he said, and now he seemed more desperate than amused, his gaze back to me, trying to make me believe him. "As I said, I know you're not a child, but I also know you haven't—really had much experience. It wouldn't be right for me to simply—drop in—for what would actually be a very special occasion for you. Of course I *want* to, but . . ."

"Then we'll do it," I said with a shrug, having no idea

why he seemed to be so embarrassed. "We'll have plenty of time when we get back to my mother's house. You said yourself that you had to get to know *all* of us, and that's really the best way. I'll arrange everything."

"Now, you wait just a minute," he said, and I could have sworn he was more flustered than exasperated as he ran a hand through his golden red hair. "I like making my *own* arrangements, and right now I'm not ready to do anything of the—"

His protests broke off when he heard the voice of the trees, a voice he couldn't understand but one he couldn't miss. It sounded like the wildest of windstorms, but that was only because the trees were excited.

"They're almost here and moving fast," I interpreted, turning to look back toward the woods. "No more than twenty tree widths away from emerging, so we'd better get ready."

"The guardsmen and I will get ready," he contradicted, taking my arm as I tried to move past him. "You'll stay here with your horse, and keep well out of the way. If any of them get past us and seem to be heading for you, get mounted fast and go back into the woods. Since you do so well hiding in the dark, you shouldn't have any trouble once you're in there. Ask the trees to tell you when it's all over, and then you can come out again."

He turned and hurried away to the others without giving me a chance to argue or even to say a word, but that didn't make me as angry as it might have. He didn't yet know that I wasn't taking his orders.

I went to my horse and mounted up instead of simply waiting beside him, but there wasn't anyone left around to see me do it. The others were already on their way back toward the woods, watching the place where the trees said the thieves would emerge. They were putting themselves between the woods and the Falls, meaning to force the thieves into facing them if they wanted to go on, but I hadn't yet decided what I was going to do. I urged my horse into motion after the rest of our group, moving slowly over the uneven ground as I considered the question, and then—

And then the thieves were suddenly out of the woods and riding fast toward the Falls, most of them mounted on horses that weren't from our Realm. They were following three men who *were* properly mounted, and when the three quickly slowed the others weren't alert enough to do the same. Two of the heavy-bodied, thick-legged out-Realm horses went down screaming before the others were able to pull up, and then our group was into theirs and my mother's light gleamed off swinging blades. After that the noise came, the clash of metal, the squealing of horses, the shouts of men, the screams of the hurt and dying. In a way it was like the dance of the night predators, the song before dawn that spoke of the need of some to die so that others might live. In a way it was like that, but the fact that it was deliberately planned took the edge of beauty from it. Those who stalked the night killed so that they might live; those who walked everywhere else killed because they chose to.

The fact that I still hadn't been able to decide how to help kept me from riding too close to the melee, and for that reason I was able to see it when one of the thieves broke free of the fight. He rode away without looking back, heading toward the foot of the Falls, moving as fast as he could over the treacherous footing of the rock plain. He was one of those mounted on a horse from our Realm, I saw, and I was wondering how he had managed to get away when suddenly a thin mist appeared in front of my face.

Haliand, we mustn't let him get away! Sahrinth sent, his agitation so thick the air fairly shimmered around him. *We must do something, we simply must!*

"Sahrinth, what makes you think he's so important?" I asked, trying to project calming thoughts. "And where have you been all this time?"

When I saw those servants approaching the fountain with a globe, I knew your mother had found out what we were about to do, he answered, the thought-words practi-

cally falling over one another. *I left alone then, and with
the help of the trees was able to catch up to the thieves.
I've been following them ever since, trying to think of
something I could do, but Haliand—he's the one who has
the Great Flame, and he's getting away!*

The one who had the Great Flame—and Greaf! I turned
my mount and started after him, Sahrinth floating along
beside and keeping pace with ease. The footing on the
rock plain was horrible, translating frantic hurry into an
agonizing crawl, but at least the problem wasn't mine
alone. The man ahead of me was doing even worse, his
horse obviously not as familiar with the terrain as mine
was. As the minutes passed the gap between us began to
close, and then Sahrinth brought up a point I hadn't wanted
to think about as yet.

*Haliand, what are we going to do when we catch up to
him?* he asked. *He's closer to the size of that Prince
Jentris than to one of ours, and he's wearing a sword and
dagger. How are we going to get Greaf away from him?*

"We'll do whatever we have to," I answered, trying to
sound as though there were all sorts of options available.
"If he refuses to be reasonable and give us what we want,
we just won't be responsible. It will all be on his head, so
don't spend any time worrying about it."

Sahrinth's silence felt somewhat open-mouthed and confused rather than simply quiet, but it had come to me that
I'd told the absolute truth. Whatever we did to the thief
would be his problem, and he couldn't say he hadn't asked
for it. He had our friend, after all, and wasn't it up to us to
get him back?

The silent flame of the Falls rose higher and higher
above us the closer we got to the base of it, and the closer
we got the smaller the gap between us and the thief grew.
The sounds of our horses hooves were just about swallowed up by the thick—nonsound—emanating from the
Falls, as though they were being absorbed by something
we couldn't see. I hadn't ever been quite that close to the
base of the Falls before, and I couldn't imagine where the
thief could be heading. He made no effort to turn either

right or left, just kept going straight ahead, and then it came to me that he was slowing down. He acted as though he had almost reached the place he wanted to get to, but there was nothing there *to* reach! I felt annoyed, but used the opportunity to close the gap between us even more.

When he came to a complete halt and began to dismount, I was only steps behind him. I decided to move just a little closer before dismounting, and then I discovered what had told him he'd reached his destination. Between one step and another normal sound returned, just as though I'd ridden out from under a blanket, and that very last step caused the man to whirl around, finally aware that he'd been followed. His hand went to his swordhilt, his dark eyes narrowed, but he straightened without drawing the weapon.

"Now where in the Three Realms did *you* come from?" he asked, more annoyed than frightened or guilty, apparently squinting in order to see me more clearly. "Wherever it was you'd better get back there, girl. This is no time or place for kiddie games."

"I'm glad I didn't have to explain that to you," I returned, completely disliking his attitude. "Give me what you stole and you can go wherever it is you're going, without anyone trying to stop you. Refuse and I won't be responsible for what happens to you."

"You won't be responsible for what happens to me," he repeated, then began walking toward me. "Have you any idea who you're saying that to? If I weren't in so much of a hurry, I'd— Or maybe I shouldn't be in that much of a hurry. From what I can see of you, you ought to afford a man quite a lot of entertainment. And once you grow tiresome, you can always be sold. Yes, I think I *will* take you with me."

He had reached the side of my horse by then, and without any further warning reached up to pull me from the saddle. I yelped as I was yanked down, startled and upset by the abruptness of it all, but not quite as helpless as he seemed to think. I beat at his face with my left fist, making him jerk his head back, and then I was covering

that face and head with the shadow I had gathered with my
right hand. There was certainly plenty of shadow there to
gather, and a muffled shout came from him as I continued
to wind it around his head. In a matter of minutes I would
have had him helpless, I know I would have, but instead
of standing still or letting me go he groped for my wrists,
pulled them together and held them, and then began brushing at the shadow. Without my touch the thickened shadow
began to dissolve, the weaving falling apart, and I couldn't
even reach to the box-shaped lump I could see in his tunic
above his swordbelt. I was so *close,* to Greaf and the Great
Flame both, and I couldn't do *anything!*

"Oh, you'll pay for that, girl," he quavered once he
was free of the shadow, the unsteadiness of his voice
showing how frightened he'd been. "I don't know what
you did, but you'll pay for it ten times over. Just wait until
we get back to my Realm."

He began pulling me with him then, toward the stuff of
the Falls itself, specifically toward a spot that pulsed more
heavily than all the rest of it. A deep reddish brown that
spot was, eight feet high and just as wide, all the beauty
drawn out of it with nothing but sullen anger left. I didn't
want to go with him, and certainly not closer to that awful
part of the Falls, but struggling wasn't getting me loose
and he was forcing me with him. I stumbled along, fighting uselessly, being taken nearer and nearer—

And then there was a shout and the sound of running,
and suddenly a big body crashed into the man holding me.
From the thud of the contact I thought I would be immediately free, but somehow it didn't happen that way. Somehow, instead of falling down, the man pulling me fell
backward, thrown by the force of the attack and still
holding tight to my wrists. Back he went, toward the
sullen red, drawing me and his attacker with him, and then
we were *into* it, falling into the color, spinning, spinning,
down and down and down and down and—

Chapter 3

I DISCOVERED I WAS AWAKE when I noticed my head was throbbing. Opening my eyes brought to view what looked like a cave, gray and streaked with brown behind the shadows, hard under my back. For an instant I wondered what I was doing there, and then I remembered what had happened just before everything went dark.

Sitting up fast almost always causes dizziness, but for some reason you never remember that until it's too late. I waited impatiently for the dizziness to pass, then half slid, half crawled to where Prince Jentris lay. He was still unconscious but otherwise seemed unhurt, and that was all there was in the way of people in the cave. Me and him, and not a single sign of the man who had the Great Flame and Greaf.

I settled down on the cave floor beside my companion with a sigh of disgust, and stared at the wide silver glow coming from the back of the cave. That dark red area beneath the Silent Falls had obviously been a Realm Threshold, something I'd never before seen but had certainly heard about. All of the Doors between the Realms were well known and used on a regular basis, and took no more effort to go through than a doorway in a house. Tresholds, on the other hand, seemed to be incomplete or incorrectly made Doors, difficult to use and usually almost as difficult

46

to find. They always took you between the Realms, but the transition wasn't pleasant.

"To say the least," I muttered to myself, a hand to my head as I remembered that sensation of endlessly falling into chaos. It was no wonder we had come through unconscious, but there was nothing to explain why there weren't three of us on the cave floor. And if the dark-haired man *had* been the first to come out of it, why had he simply left? I wasn't in any way disappointed that he hadn't taken me with him the way he'd said he would, but I didn't understand what had made him change his mind. Or why he hadn't at least hurt Prince Jentris before leaving.

Oh, Hali, thank the Far Reaches you're finally awake! Sahrinth's thought came to me, and then he was floating only inches from my face. *That man and the people who were waiting for him—they're getting farther and farther away even though they've stopped now for a short while!*

"There were people waiting?" I asked, finally understanding what had happened. "They must have awakened him, and then taken him out of the cave while he was still groggy."

Oh, no, Hali, they took him while he was still unconscious, Sahrinth corrected, his cloud-body bobbing in the air in front of me. *That transition was so terrible it almost took *my* senses, and they probably wouldn't have been able to awaken him. They glanced at you and Prince Jentris, but apparently only had orders about the thief. They carried him outside and down to the flat ground below, put him in a wagon, and then they all left. I followed, of course, and came back here each of the two times they stopped.*

"Then the Great Flame and Greaf aren't lost to us after all!" I exclaimed, getting quickly to my feet. "Come on, Sahrinth, you lead the way and I'll follow."

But Haliand, you can't do that! Sahrinth sent, his agitation suddenly greater. *Just as the thief is still unconscious, so is Prince Jentris. If you simply leave the prince here, there's no telling *what* could happen to him. This isn't your Lady Mother's Realm, you know. It's the Realm of the Lord of the Earth.*

"But we can't just let the thieves get away!" I protested, turning to look at the unconscious body of the man who would marry one of my sisters. I'd heard stories about the things that sometimes happened to people in this Realm, which meant Sahrinth was right. I couldn't simply walk away and leave Prince Jentris all alone.

There's no question of their getting away with me right behind them, Sahrinth pointed out, and I could feel his anxiety to get back to that position. *I'll follow the thieves, and once Prince Jentris is awake and able to travel, you two will follow me. I'll leave word as I can with the trees of this Realm, and will seek you out whenever I'm given the opportunity. The trees are not like ours, but you should have no trouble speaking with them.*

"I suppose we really have no choice but to do it that way," I said with very little enthusiasm as I finally looked away from the man my mother had thought would take care of *me*. If I'd left alone as I'd wanted to, I would have been able to go and do instead of having to sit and wait. "Be careful, Sahrinth, and make sure they don't catch you. If the ones who were waiting are anything like the one carrying the Flame . . ."

Well, of course I'll be careful, my friend returned indignantly, bobbing up and down where he hung. *You just be certain you do the same, as you're a much easier life form to capture and hold. I'll see you again at the first opportunity.*

And then he was gone, no more than a streak of mist quickly disappearing from the cave. I stood there for a moment, wishing I could have gone with him, but that sort of wish is a waste of time. If you do it right wishes will come true, but even proper wishing won't get rid of a millstone around your neck.

I spent a few minutes wandering around inspecting the cave, but as far as caves went it was very dull. Caves in my mother's Realm are often fun to explore, what with the different sorts of life forms usually found in them, but that cave had nothing that even came close. Tiny crawling life forms that ignore you and slightly larger flyers that also ignore you come in a poor second to singing rock, glowing, molten crawlers, and flying, chattering crystal chips. Even the silver glow of the Threshold was on the uninspired side, but as I turned away from it in boredom I received a surprise: the unmoving body of Prince Jentris was no longer unmoving, and was in fact struggling to sit up.

"Well, at last!" I said, beginning to move toward him as he put a hand to his head and looked up at me with a frown. "Now that you're awake we can leave, and probably not a minute too soon. I don't know the size of this Realm, but it would be nice to catch up to that thief before he loses himself somewhere on the far side of it."

"Will you please slow down?" Prince Jentris said as I began to turn toward the cave mouth, sounding annoyed. "I'm going to need more than a handful of seconds before I'm in any shape to go racing off in all directions. Right now this cave is spinning slowly around me. Why don't you tell me what happened while I'm waiting for it to stop. Or don't you know?"

"Why would I be trying to hurry you if I didn't know what happened?" I asked, trying to sound more reasonable than I was feeling. The man now had his hands over his eyes, probably in an effort to banish the dizziness, but I was too filled with impatience to be terribly sympathetic. "We all fell through the Threshold and ended up here in the Realm of the Lord of the Earth. The thief had men waiting to carry him away, so by the time I woke up he was gone. I would have followed almost immediately, but I couldn't leave you here all unconscious and unprotected. Now that you're awake I can leave, so if you want to come along you'd better hurry up and pull yourself together. I've already waited as long as I intend to."

"If you're in that much of a rush to get lost in this Realm, go right ahead," he came back, lowering his hands from his eyes so that he might give me a cool, uncaring look. "You have no idea what direction your quarry has gone in, and you don't know enough about the things and people you'll be coming across to keep yourself safe. Since I've been to this Realm before I won't have those problems, but that's probably not a good enough reason for you to wait for me, so go ahead. Run right out and get yourself lost—and maybe eaten.''

His golden-eyed stare was very uninvolved and uninterested as he carefully raised himself to his feet and brushed at his clothing. I could see he thought he was being terribly clever, telling me I was free to walk out into something horrible, but that sort of line hadn't worked on me in years. It was true I didn't know the Realm, but with Sahrinth leaving word for me with the trees, getting lost wasn't likely to be a problem.

"Oh, getting eaten by predators isn't that bad," I told the man in a wide-eyed, offhand way that should have made me look and sound as simple as he obviously thought I was. "I've had it happen to me dozens of times, and after the first time or three you tend to get used to it. As for getting lost, that's just plain impossible. Nobody I know has *ever* gotten lost."

I gave his immediate confusion a pleasant, simpleminded smile, then turned away from him and began walking toward the cave mouth. I was really hoping he would be held in place long enough for me to be gone, but I'd forgotten that truism about wishes and millstones. I was still a good six feet away from escape, when a big hand closed around my left arm.

"All right, I can see I was wrong trying to frighten you," he said, his tone telling me he'd decided to try another way of manipulating me, his hand swinging me back to face him. "The truth of the matter is, this would be a really bad time for us to separate. If there actually were people waiting here to help the thief, it was pure luck he couldn't tell them to disarm me at the very least, maybe even kill us both. By now he's probably awake, which means our luck on that score has run out. Even low-class servants or slaves who aren't bright enough to make decisions on their own are capable of following orders, or they wouldn't have been chosen to be here waiting. If you and I separate, we'll just make it that much easier for them to defeat us."

"If you're still not certain there were people here waiting for the man, how can you be so certain those alleged people will defeat us if we separate?" I asked, adding only the mildest curiosity as I looked up at him with very heavy innocence. "And if you're that easy to defeat when you're by yourself, don't you think you ought to go back for some of my mother's Guard instead of relying on *me* to look after you? I mean, I know I can take care of myself, but I've never had to be responsible for someone else before, so . . ."

"Okay, okay, you've made your point," he growled, very unhappy with the way I'd chosen to highlight the flaws in his argument. "I was trying to smooth things over for the sake of your dignity, but you've insisted on the truth so I'll give it to you. If you leave this cave at all it will be with me, following my instructions exactly, and forgetting about doing anything at all on your own. If you don't agree to that right now, the only place you'll be going is back through that Threshold. I told your Lady Mother I'd be responsible for your safety, and I don't believe in breaking my word."

"Then you should be more careful about giving that word," I returned stiffly, only faintly surprised that he was the sort to believe *I* was bound by *his* given word. "I'm not a child who needs a nursemaid, and I refuse to be treated like one. You claim to have understood the point I was trying to make a moment ago, but there are still a couple of others that seem to have gotten by you. Point one is that forcing me back through the Threshold won't do you any good, not unless you intend staying here from now on to be sure I don't simply come right through again. Point two is that without me, none of the messages Sahrinth leaves with the trees about where the thieves are will do you any good. Or am I wrong in believing you don't speak the language of the trees?"

"Sahrinth is out there following the thieves?" he asked in

surprise, then shook his head in annoyance. "Of course, I should have seen it sooner. He was there with us on the other side of the Threshold, and how else would you have known about the people who were waiting for our former third? That's a break for our side and probably one of the reasons the Scales gave their approval of your coming along, but it doesn't change anything. You still won't be taking off on your own, and if you give me any trouble I'll just tie you hand and foot before tossing you back through the Threshold. Do we understand each other?"

"Probably better than you know," I murmured as he turned away from me to take a typical last look around the cave before we left. According to him nothing had changed, but he'd gone from demanding my agreement to his terms to talking about nothing but mutual understanding in an awfully short space of time. Of course, if he wanted to take advantage of that "break for our side" there wasn't much else he could do, and I didn't really mind that he refused to admit his defeat out loud. The simple fact of winning had always been enough for me, an attitude that had never failed to annoy my sisters.

My companion discovered rather quickly that there was nothing in the cave but what we'd brought across the Threshold with us, so it wasn't long before we were outside and beginning to work our way down to the road waiting below. It seemed to be darker outside than it had been in the cave—not to mention cooler—but climbing down a slope covered with boulders, pebbles, and uneven footing tends to take your mind off temperature levels.

Prince Jentris insisted on going first even though he couldn't see more than an inch or two beyond his unbearably stiff neck, and I was all ready to argue until I saw the faint trail hidden in shadow to our left. I slipped and slid to it without mentioning the discovery to the man who felt he was the better leader, and the descent suddenly became a good deal easier. We continued on like that for a couple of minutes, me practically strolling downhill, Prince Jentris struggling to keep from killing himself, and then he managed to notice I wasn't behind him any longer.

"What are you doing over there?" he asked, giving more attention to where he put his feet than to looking at me. "If you aren't behind me I can't help if you fall. It's darker than Blackfire this close to dawn. Give me your hand, and I'll help you get back."

He stopped to reach out gingerly in my direction, and then it came to him that I was standing still with no difficulty whatsoever, while he was keeping himself upright only by holding tight to a boulder. He blinked at me with a frown while I tried to think of something to say, but nothing in the way of inspired conversation wanted to come. Not only hadn't he been nasty about my changing position, he was actually putting himself in more danger by offering to help me get back to what he thought was safety. I'd known all along he couldn't see very well in the dark, and I suddenly felt very guilty about not having mentioned the trail.

"Maybe we'd be better off if you came over here," I finally managed to get out, not quite looking at him. "I think the footing's more reliable than where you are. Would you like me to help you?"

"Thanks anyway, but I think I can make it," he muttered, beginning to scramble over the boulder he'd been hanging on to. "Just to satisfy my curiosity, though, is there anything else you can do besides see in the dark and talk to trees? If there is, I promise to remember for next time—which might save us both some trouble."

By that time he was standing on the narrow trail beside me, and the fact that he was being sarcastic rather than yelling only made me feel worse. It had come to me that I might have been taking my annoyance with my mother out on him, which wasn't exactly fair; my mother had undoubtedly forced him to give his word about keeping me safe, and that made none of it his fault.

"I think we can move a little faster now," I said, still not looking at him as I started down the trail again. "The sooner we get the Flame and Greaf back, you know, the sooner you can get on with courting my sisters."

He didn't say anything to that and he didn't argue about

my going first, so he probably realized I was right. We
made it all the way down to the bottom of the slope
without any other mishaps, but reaching the road Sahrinth
had mentioned wasn't the accomplishment I'd been expecting it to be.

"The only difference between this road and the slope
we just came down seems to be direction," I said, looking
around at some pretty desolate landscape. If there was
anything but rock and dirt I couldn't see it, and even the
trees were too far away to speak to. "I know it matters
which direction we go in, but except for the thief it
wouldn't matter."

"Other parts of the Realm are a good deal more hospita-
ble than this one," my companion assured me, at the same
time trying to peer up and down the road. "Well, I was
hoping we weren't risking our necks coming down that
slope in the dark for nothing, but it looks like we'll have to
wait for daylight after all. With nothing to tell us which
way our quarry went, we'll have to hope there are tracks to
see in the morning. If there aren't, we'll have to pick a
direction and ask the trees—once we reach trees to ask."

"Uh . . . we have to go that way," I offered, pointing
to the right. "You may not be able to see it, but Sahrinth
turned some of the dust of the road into an arrow cloud,
and that's where the arrow's pointing. Can you see the
cloud now, hanging over the road on the other side, just
opposite the trail we just came down?"

"Not really," he answered with a sigh, no longer even
trying to peer into the heavy darkness. "What I *can* see,
though, is that it really is a good thing I'm with you. If
you'd left alone, we'd both be remembering now what I
said about getting hopelessly lost."

With that he started walking up the road, his left hand
resting on his sword hilt, his shoulders trying to straighten
out of the depression his voice had held. He seemed to be
feeling embarrassed and incompetant, and it was all my
fault. What I'd said about having to take care of him—I'd
only been trying to annoy him, but it was turning out to be
true. I really felt terrible then, but there was no way to call

back the words. All I could do was hurry to catch up with him, and ask the first question I could think of to distract him.

"Did you say it will be daylight soon?" I asked, making no effort to keep the distaste out of my voice. "We don't often *have* daylight in my mother's Realm, and most of us are very pleased to have it like that. I suppose it's simply our bad luck to get to this Realm just when a time like that is due."

"Haliand, I think you'd better brace yourself," he said, pulling himself out of the low mood to slow a little and put his arm around my shoulders. "Your mother's Realm has mostly dark just as my father's Realm has mostly light, but this Realm has the same amount of both. All the time, on a regular basis. There are hours and hours of daylight ahead before dark comes again, and the dark won't last. While we're here you'll have to put up with it, and be as brave as possible."

"I'll try," I answered with the dejection he had lost, carefully controlling my expression just in case he could see better in the dark than I believed. "I'll probably hate it, but for the sake of the Great Flame and Greaf, I'll try."

"Good girl," he said with approval, squeezing my shoulders just a little. "I knew I could count on you. We'll keep going as long as we can, and keep our eyes open for a town. Our first order of business is getting ourselves mounted with decent supplies, or we'll never catch up to the people we're chasing. They already have too much of a head start, so we can't afford to stop until we really have to. That time may come sooner for you than for me, so if it does you just let me know. All right?"

I made a sound of agreement that seemed to satisfy him, as he took my hand so that we might walk together up the trail. I was equally satisfied, having suddenly understood more of what the Scales had undoubtedly seen. I was there to take care of my companion Prince Jentris, but letting him know it would ruin everything. I'd once heard that the pride of a man was more delicate than the thinnest crystal, and once shattered it was just as impossible to repair. If

Prince Jentris thought he was taking care of me instead of the other way around, his pride would be safe and our mission would be more effectively seen to. Remembering how easily that thief had overpowered me showed that my companion *did* have a reason for being there; his size and strength would cope with those things I couldn't, but ultimately our protection lay in my hands alone. Knowing that it had to be my secret didn't stop me from feeling happily warm inside; I would take care of us, and everything would be fine.

Walking along a dirt road in the dark surrounded by stone gives new meaning to the word *boring*, but at the pace we kept to at least I wasn't chilly as well. For a time the dark was the same as it always was when my mother no longer rode the skies in argent glory, and then, almost before I noticed, the dark began to change. Rather than being a true velvet black the way it was supposed to be, it shifted to heavy dark gray, then lighter dark gray, and then a bluish gray. Outcroppings and the trees we were nearing began separating themselves from everything else, as though a unity were being withdrawn from the landscape, and then I heard Prince Jentris make a sound of satisfaction.

"It won't be long now," he said, looking around the way I was doing. "Once it's full daylight we should even have some color to brighten up this landscape, and then we'll both feel better. When we reach the trees and you ask about any messages Sahrinth left, ask also about the nearest town."

"I don't really know what a town is," I admitted, more curious than embarrassed over the lack. "Maybe it's what those people call a court or an estate."

"No, towns are where large numbers of people live and work together," Prince Jentris said, turning his head to look down at me. "My Realm doesn't have them either, but this Realm really needs them. You may remember I said that the current Lord of the Earth only recently took over from his father, who has now gone Traveling. Well, word has it that when the former Lord took over from his father, the first thing he did was forbid his people to Travel."

"The people of this Realm aren't allowed to Travel?" I asked in disbelief, more shocked than I could ever remember being. "But that's outrageous! Why would he do such a terrible thing, and why did the people stand for it?"

"My father tells us he tried talking him and your mother into doing the same thing once they had taken their places," Prince Jentris said, tugging at my hand to get me moving at our previous pace again. "His position was that Traveling should be reserved for Noble and High Houses alone, that the common people had no business going to the same places their betters did. He wanted them all to stay in the Realm of their birth, and do nothing but work for the betterment of that Realm."

"Work to make *him* feel more important, you mean," I said in disgust, letting anger move me faster. "I know my mother didn't listen to him, and your father obviously didn't either. And I still don't understand how people could allow themselves to be shut into one place for all of forever. If nothing else, the overcrowding should have driven them crazy."

"Haliand, Traveling wasn't the only thing the Lord of the Earth took away from his people," Prince Jentris said carefully, and he slowed to a stop as he looked down at me with serious golden eyes. "If he had simply announced his people weren't to Travel anymore, they would have stalked away in insult and shortly thereafter his Realm would have been empty. After all, being common born doesn't mean anything other than being a member of a commonly known family rather than a High or Noble one. High Families have heads and members who are highly interested in helping the Realm to run smoothly, and if you happen to be common born but find your life interest high, you simply join one of the High families through adoption or marriage."

"And Noble families just happen to have more Founder blood and talents in them than anyone else," I said impatiently, annoyed that he would lecture me as though I'd never heard any of that before. "Those who have higher than average Founder blood themselves consider it a duty to present themselves at Court and become a part of it, no matter what their birth was. If they didn't, how would my mother have found adequate consorts to give her fully talented daughters? I know all that, Prince Jentris, and can't see what it has to do with why people stayed in this Realm."

"At first they stayed because of the sickness," he said, so quietly and gently I felt a chill run through me in the brightening light. "No one has ever been able to prove the sickness was the doing of the old Lord of the Earth, but my father has said he knows that working with the unseen life of this Realm is one of its Lord's talents. Whatever the real truth, the sickness swept over every part of this Realm and touched almost everyone in it. People took to their beds with an illness worse than anything they'd ever experienced, and when they were finally able to rise again they found their Realm entirely changed.

"To begin with, none of the elders of any common family and no more than a few of those of the High families had managed to survive. By elders, of course, I mean those with experience in life and with talents fully developed through having exercised them. You know how rare it is for even a single someone to fail to survive accident or illness in your Realm, and mine is the same, so you can imagine how devastated the people of *this* Realm were. They had no one left to teach them the Way, no one to pass on the Words that were their birthright from the Founders. They didn't know what to do, and could find no one to ask."

"Why didn't they ask us?" I blurted out, knowing I was interrupting but finding it impossible not to. "My mother would have sent them help, I know she would! I'll bet half our Realm would have volunteered to go!"

"Let's keep moving," he said as he tightened his grip on my hand, and then, once we were walking again, shook his head. "At first they decided they *couldn't* ask another Realm for help, not when they didn't know what had caused the sickness. They weren't about to give others the same agony they themselves were suffering, especially not

when the Lord of their Realm wasn't at his Court. He had
gone Traveling just before the sickness hit, and they decided that the best thing they could do was wait for him to
get back. They didn't know the other Realms had no idea
that anything at all had happened, because they didn't
know it was an Interlude that barred each Realm from the
others. Interludes happen every now and again and most
people make sure to be home for them, but that's because
our elders know when they're coming and warn us. The
elders in this Realm died before they could speak about it,
and the last one had happened so long before, none of
those left alive knew about it.

"The people waited and waited for their Lord to get
back, but when he didn't they decided they had to try one
of the other Realms. They went to a Doorway, but since it
was Interlude the Doorways weren't working. Once again
they didn't understand what was happening, and then they
got another shock. Those who had become the eldest of
them through the deaths of the true elders, men and women
who were no more than a few Earth Realm centuries old,
began dying in turn. By ones and twos they showed signs
of a terrible disease, one that turned them frail and dried
up, sickly and weak, and then, for no apparent reason,
they just stopped living. We know a little something about
this because of journals found later, after the Interlude. At
the time no one but the people here knew what was
happening, and they were helpless to stop it."

He grew silent for a moment as we trudged along, the
day waxing bright and gold around us, but there was no
more gladness in him than there was in me. It was a
terrible story I was hearing for the first time, and I had the
awful conviction there was more and worse to come.

"By the time the Interlude was over, this Realm was
completely changed," he continued after the pause, his
tone now more than a little reluctant. "Except for some of
the High families and the Lord's Noble House, all of the
people here had become incredibly ephemeral. The eldest
left alive were no more than decades-old infants, all of
them having been born during the Interlude. They knew

nothing about the blood or the talents or the Way or the Words; all of that had become distant folklore for them, distorted to half-remembered myths and twisted superstition. All they did was work to stay alive, breed to keep their lines going, and die long before they reached the age of even a single century. They were almost a race apart, and their Lord was very pleased to have them that way. He no longer had to complain about their Traveling, because none of them remembered there even was such a thing.''

"I don't know about your father, but I refuse to believe my mother just stood by and let him get away with it," I stated, stopping to look directly up into the face of Prince Jentris. "I've never heard of such a travesty against humanity, turning the people of your Realm into little more than animals just because you felt like it. How did they get it turned back, and what did they do to that so-called Lord to make him pay for his crime?"

"Haliand, both your mother and my father tried, but there wasn't anything they *could* do to change things back," he said regretfully but calmly, trying to soothe away the growing fury inside me. "You know it's against one of the most basic Founders' Laws for one or more Realms to interfere with the goings-on in another, but even that didn't stop them. People were sent here from both of our Realms, trying to tell the poor, ignorant ephemerals the truth of their beginnings and heritage, but it didn't work. The Lord of the Earth had done something to make sure none of his new people would listen."

"You don't mean he made them deaf as well as ephemeral," I said with as much sarcasm as I could, getting the distinct feeling more had been done in the way of excuse-making than in efforts to help. "If they weren't deaf, all they had to be told was that their Lord had betrayed them and they could have back what they'd lost if they wanted to take it. Even if only a few tried, when the others saw them succeed they would all learn the truth."

"Even if only a few tried *what?*" he countered, no more than very faintly annoyed with the tone I'd used. "If they tried living as long as they should have been able to?

If they tried learning to use talents they didn't even know they had? Suppose someone came up to you and told you you could breathe underwater; would you believe it? Especially if you and all your people before you had been told for generations that you mustn't even go near water? People don't listen to strangers when they have trusted advisers who tell them something else entirely."

I didn't think it was the time to tell him I *could* breathe underwater, at least for a little while. That had nothing to do with what he was trying to say, and his true point was what I didn't understand.

"Where could advisers have come from?" I asked, disliking and distrusting the whole idea. "If all their elders were gone and no one had come from the other Realms, who—"

"I think you just got it," he said when my voice trailed off, his expression now grim. "We've pretty much established that these advisers appeared when the first generation of ephemerals were grown to adulthood and had taken charge. They told those babe-innocent people that their Lord wanted to love them, but they had to do certain things to earn that love. There were a whole lot of things they had to do, and the advisers chose and trained surrogates from among the ephemerals to remind them of all the things and make sure they did them. The surrogates became the new advisers, and by the time our people tried to let everyone know what had really happened, those new advisers and their trainee staffs had too tight a grip on their victims. The ephemerals were actually too afraid to listen to our people."

"Afraid?" I echoed, distantly surprised that my jaw had come back up off the ground far enough for me to say that. If I'd thought I was shocked earlier, I was beginning to learn the true meaning of the word.

"They were afraid that if they even thought about what they were being told, their Lord would stop loving them," he answered, his grimness increasing. "If that happened they would then be unprotected against all sorts of evil things that wanted an inner, eternal part of them. What gets me angriest is the fact that they *do* have an inner eternal part—from the blood of the Founders that we all share—but it isn't anything anyone can use to cause them harm. All they do now is work their fleeting lives away, trying to please a Lord who stole their heritage from them, bowing first to his whims and now to those of his son—!''

His words broke off as his face worked, a terrible blaze of anger showing in his golden eyes. Then he regained control of himself and took a deep breath.

''And that, in case you were wondering, is the reason why the current Lord of the Earth has enough of an army to pose a real threat to our Realms,'' he said, reaching a hand out to smooth my hair. ''I didn't want to frighten you or get you angry, but you have to know what we'll be running into with the people of this Realm. We'll have to stay out of sight as much as we can, and we'll have to take what we need and simply leave payment for it. If we try walking straight up to people they'll know us immediately as strangers and run to report us to their advisers—or maybe worse.''

''I think I'm afraid to ask what 'worse' would come to,'' I said, feeling as though I had stumbled into a nightmare. ''No wonder people call those from the Earth Realm the Children of Toil. They don't mean the ones in our Realms, they mean the ones here. How can you dream for the right things, when those you trust lie about what there is to dream for?''

''You can't,'' Prince Jentris answered, putting his arm around my shoulders again. ''When those you trust lie to you, all you can do is grovel on your knees instead of standing straight and tall to demand your heritage. We'd better get moving again, or we'll lose even more time than we already have.''

I knew he was right so I let him urge me forward again, but I couldn't stop thinking about what I'd been told. It was so bizarre I kept expecting to hear it was all made up, nothing but a story told to frighten small children into behaving themselves. It was also something that made me furious, so furious that I barely noticed the daylight that didn't seem prepared to stop brightening.

"There has to be something that can be done for them," I muttered, refusing to consider the idea of being totally helpless. "There has to be some way of freeing them to be whole again, and at the same time making the Lord of the Earth pay for what he and his father have done."

"We can make the Lord of the Earth pay by ruining his plans to overrun our Realms," Prince Jentris replied. "And it's been said by certain of the elders of my Realm that now only the victims of the injustice can do anything to regain what's been lost. Their longevity will begin to return, and once it does they must begin to question what they've been told and reject it *themselves*. Until then, all we can do is mind our own business and leave them alone to go their own ways."

"How can you be so cruel and uncaring?" I demanded, looking up at him as he pulled me along by one hand. "Doesn't it bother you that these people should be enjoying the same things we have and do, but aren't being allowed to? Don't you have any—"

"Hold it!" he ordered, returning my stare with a good deal of annoyance. "You're making it sound as though I'm personally responsible for what's happening here, which is probably why no one told you about it sooner. I am *not* responsible for what happened, none of us are; we can't even *prove* the old Lord of the Earth did what we think was done. When you're a little older you'll understand—"

"What do you mean, 'when I'm a little older'?" I demanded. "Do people turn cowardly when they get to be as ancient as you are? If saying there's nothing to be done and then turning your back is supposed to be wise, I hope I never reach the point of wisdom."

"I don't think you have anything to worry about on that score," he retorted, his golden eyes beginning to look as hard as they had in the woods when we'd first met. "Judging from the way you act, you probably have a natural immunity against wisdom. And although I can see it's difficult for you to tell from the position of your tender years, I don't happen to be 'ancient.' My state of life is called *maturity,* another thing you won't be understanding from personal experience for quite some time—if ever.''

I gave him a stare that told him he was too low and vile to argue with, then I pulled my hand out of his and continued up the road alone, only faster. If it had still been dark I would have stalked off into the shadows and left him to take care of himself, but the only shadows still around were mere . . . shadows . . . of their former selves. It was also getting warmer as well as lighter, which added to the enjoyment I was experiencing over everything else.

Silence kept me company awhile, a much more pleasant companion than the one who kept pace just behind me, but it wasn't destined to last much longer. The first of the trees weren't too far ahead, and then I'd be asking for Sahrinth's messages. I could have spoken to them from where I was, of course, but that wouldn't have been very polite. I'd never met those particular trees, and when you introduce yourself to someone new, you don't do it from a mile away.

When I finally stepped in under the first of the trees, I took a moment to enjoy the cooler green they provided, at the same time simply listening to what they were discussing. I expected it to be some philosophical point similar to what the trees in my own Realm would be talking about, but I was entirely wrong. The trees were talking about the people who were around them, and they actually sounded as excited as saplings. I was standing still, confusedly wondering if the old Lord of the Earth had made the trees as ephemeral as the people, when one of the objects of my conjecture spoke directly to me.

"You must surely be the out-Realm unrooted we were told we would soon sense," the tree above me said, sounding as excited as the rest. "Your off-shoot life form has spread the most interesting word. Would you care to hear it?"

"Yes, I would," I answered, trying not to show how odd I felt. I'd introduced myself to any number of stands of trees in my lifetime, but none of them had ever gone so far as to acknowledge me. When the trees discussed you among themselves you considered yourself noticed and acknowledged, and thereafter were free to listen to what they said to each other. Only my mother had ever had a direct answer from them, but as Lady of the Realm that was her right. And as for describing Sahrinth as my "off-shoot life form" . . . ?

"The noise and tremor producer you all have interest in has experienced a small natural disaster," the tree said, all chatty and warmly friendly. "It apparently suffered a sudden separation from one of its limbs, and because of that the unsensing unrooted within was thrown about with the force of a gale wind. The unrooted is now even more deeply unsensing, and those unrooteds accompanying it have halted and are attempting to replace the limb. It has not been told us what season the regrowth is expected for."

"I must take a moment for consideration," I told the tree, and as strange as it was it still had no trouble understanding and accepting the standard excuse mobile life forms made when they were faced with deciphering what they'd just been told. Sometimes understanding trees was easy, but then there were other times . . .

"What's the matter?" my almost-forgotten companion asked. "Did the trees have bad news?"

"I'm not sure," I answered in a mutter, making no effort to look at him. "The noise and tremor producer suffered a sudden limb separation. What sort of limbs would a wagon have, and why would it matter if one of them came off?"

"It would matter if the limb was a wheel," he said, almost as excited as the trees, and then the excitement disappeared. "No, if they said limb instead of root, it couldn't be a wheel. Are you sure they did say limb?"

"I'm positive," I answered, turning triumphantly into his frown. "And limb *has* to mean wheel. Limbs move but roots don't, and if you lose a root you start to die. The wagon obviously isn't getting ready to die, so it must be only a limb that was lost. The unrooteds with it are trying to regrow the limb, but the trees don't know what season to expect the regrowth.''

"They're trying to fix the wheel, but they're having trouble," Prince Jentris translated with a grin, putting a little more optimism into it than I would have done. "Our former third must be having a fit over the delay—unless there are saddle horses he can use to go on without the wagon. By the golden blaze of noon, he could be well on his way right now!''

"I doubt if he's on his way anywhere," I interrupted, wondering if everyone in Prince Jentris's Realm jumped from one emotional conclusion to the next the way he did. "The unsensing unrooted inside the noise producer was thrown around when the limb was lost, and now is even more deeply unsensing—which has to mean he hit his head and is now unconscious from that rather than the transition. If they're having trouble replacing the wheel— something we don't know for certain—there's no one standing around having a fit over the delay.''

"Yet," Prince Jentris qualified, looking grimly satisfied, "if we can get ourselves mounted before there is, we may not need to follow all the way into the Lord of the Earth's private keep to get the Flame and Greaf back. Have you asked about the town?''

"Not yet," I said, trying to hide a grimace. Asking about something I didn't understand very well in a way the trees would be able to understand—well, I wasn't looking forward to it. I considered explaining that to my companion, sighed as I decided against it, then looked up at the tree I'd been speaking with.

"I thank you for the word you've passed on to me, Ancient One," I said, putting as much polite respect as possible into the whooshing, whispering sounds. "Should it be discovered that the limb has been replaced or regrown, I would be grateful to be told of it. At this juncture, I must ask the favor of referencing your wisdom on another point: Is there a—gathering place of unrooteds at some small distance ahead of us?''

"Unrooteds gather and then disperse in many places,''

the tree answered, and unfortunately for me there was a puzzled tone to the words. "They come among us without speaking, indeed have not spoken to us for many seasons, nor do they hear our words. At times they gather beneath our branches and among our roots, and still they fail to address or heed us. Also do they take many of our bodies, without first inquiring which of us has come to the desire for seeking the next higher slope on the mountain. We find the entire matter extremely upsetting."

"I don't wonder why!" I exclaimed in outrage, only then beginning to understand exactly how much had been taken from the people of that Realm. None of them could speak the language of the trees any longer, and that had caused them to become murderers without even knowing it! "I'm sure if they knew—but of course they don't know, and no one is taking the trouble to tell them. But the gathering I'm inquiring about—I believe the unrooteds may leave the place, but tend to return there over and over again. They gather in numbers, and many also remain there."

"Ah, now I truly hear the words you speak," the tree answered, all sense of puzzlement gone. "The gathering you seek is in the direction the life-warmth takes as it departs to make place for the time of lessened activity. We sense a good deal less during times of lessened activity, no more than what occurs immediately about each of us, yet do we discuss these happenings with the return of the life-warmth. We are then also able to speak with unrooteds."

"I, too, hear words more clearly now," I said, surprised by what the tree had told me. So *that* was why the trees of my own Realm had never spoken to me. In our Realm they were *always* in a state of lessened activity. I wondered if that was also why they discussed philosophy so much, but the point wasn't one that needed to be brought up right then. "Again I offer my thanks for your help, and will seek an opportunity to repay the favors."

"Well?" Prince Jentris said as I looked down and away from my new conversational companion. "Do they know where the nearest town is?"

"It said there's a gathering of the sort I described in the direction the life-warmth takes when it departs," I said, giving him a shrug to show I'd done the best I could. "Since I doubt we'll be getting anything more detailed even if I ask again, it looks like we'll have to wait until the daylight starts fading. Considering how bright it's grown out there, it shouldn't be much longer before the fading starts."

"Haliand, the *day* is only just starting," he answered, the words gentle and considerably less impatient than his previous ones. "Sundown is many hours away, but happily we won't have to wait for it. My father leaves these skies to the west, and west lies in that direction, off through the trees. Are you able to start now, or do you need to rest a short while?"

"Oh, I'm much too young to need a rest now," I answered, suddenly resenting his patience and solicitous condescension. "You adults may tire quickly, but we ignorant, silly children don't. You said it's this way?"

I started off in the direction he'd pointed to without waiting for any kind of an answer, brushing unnecessarily at my draperies. With the amount of dust that had settled on me brushing was just about useless, but it seemed the better alternative to asking the trees for a branch to use on Prince Jentris's head. There seems to be a law that the youngest in a family isn't supposed to be allowed to grow up, no matter what, and it had been annoying enough when my family went along with it. Having a total stranger doing the same was two steps above annoying, and I'd already had more of it than I'd ever intended to take.

"Haliand, wait," Prince Jentris called, hurrying a few steps to catch up with me, his hand coming gently to my arm. "I wasn't trying to insult you, and I apologize. Do you forgive me?"

"No," I answered shortly, pulling my arm out of his hand without looking at him, then resuming my original pace. He was still being so disgustingly patient with my poor, injured, and youthful pride that I was beginning to think more seriously about asking for that branch.

"You don't forgive me," he stated, sounding as though he was beginning to climb to my level of annoyance. "I do absolutely nothing and then, because I'm a gentleman, I apologize for that nothing, and you won't accept the apology. Do you make a habit of getting offended over nothing, or are you just doing it as a special entertainment for me?"

"If you didn't do anything, why worry about whether or not I'm offended?" I shot back, still looking only straight ahead, through the trees I was threading among. "You're an innocent adult and I'm an unreasonable child, and that's all that needs to be said."

"I never said I thought you were a child," he ground out through partially clenched teeth, or at least that's what it sounded like. "I was trying to be thoughtful and considerate, but maybe you *are* too young to tell the difference. Maybe you *are* younger than I thought."

"A virtual infant," I agreed with a curt nod, slitting my eyes against a ray of impossibly bright light streaming down through a gap in the branches. "Now that we're in complete accord, there's nothing left to talk about."

His following silence seemed to be filled with soundless growls and rumbles, and I couldn't understand what was bothering him. Most people are pleased to have others agree with them, but maybe in his Realm they did things differently. Whatever his reasons, he went on like that for a moment or two, and then I heard the sound of a forced deep breath.

"Women!" he muttered low. "All the same no matter what age they are." Then he raised his voice back to normal level and said, "Okay, let's get this all out into the open. We'll be finding danger ahead of us no matter how careful we are, so there's no sense in making it worse by allowing ourselves to get bogged down in an argument. I told you I wanted to be friends, and I meant it. What did I say or do that got you so fired up?"

"I think I'll ask the trees if there's any free-running water in this area," I mused aloud, in reality talking only to myself. "The brighter that light gets, the thirstier I get."

"Oh, no," he said at once, closing his hand on my arm and pulling me around to face him. "None of that 'I'm ignoring you because you're too low to be worth noticing' nonsense. We're going to talk this out like two adults, even though one of us may not qualify."

"I think you're being too hard on yourself," I said into his golden-eyed glare, ignoring the less-than-gentle grip on my arm. "I'm just as sure you qualify as an adult as I am that you weren't referring to me with that remark. After all, you're the considerate gentleman who wouldn't dream of saying anything insulting."

The stare coming from those golden eyes suddenly shifted to another level, and the hand wrapped around my arm loosened just enough to remove the discomfort. I was stared down at for another moment, and then he came up with a small sigh.

"All right, that's one part of the answer I was looking for," he said, this time sounding unhappy but determined. "What else am I doing that I hadn't even noticed I was doing?"

"You keep acting as though you don't have to get upset with me, because you know my nurse will be along soon to take me to my suite for a nap," I said, wondering if he would understand what I meant. "Since I haven't had a nurse for years it won't be happening, no matter how much you obviously want it to. I'm here for a reason, but that reason isn't to give you a chance to practice being patient."

"So what you'd like me to do is watch the casual comments and beat you when you annoy me," he said with pursed lips and a judicial nod, something of a gleam now in his eyes. "I think I can manage that without too much trouble. After all, we *are* supposed to be cooperating with each other."

I made a sound of exasperation and pulled away from his grip again, blaming myself for having answered him in the first place, but this time both of his hands came to my arms from behind, keeping me from moving more than a step or two.

"I was just kidding, so don't get mad at me again," he said with a laugh, pulling me back up against him. "Since you were right to be insulted I'm going to apologize again, but this time I really mean it. If the Scales of Judgment think you need to be here, I have no business treating you like a helpless burden. And that's the way I was seeing you, as a burden rather than a child. Do you believe me?"

"I don't know," I answered, feeling his hard body pressed so casually into my back. "Maybe if you stop what you were doing, Prince Jentris, no matter what the reason behind it was, the question won't come up."

"You've got a deal," he said, squeezing my shoulders just a little before stepping beside me to the right and taking my hand. "No more of whatever I was doing. And the first step is telling you we don't have to be so formal. I'll call you Hali the way your mother does, and you can call me Jiss."

"Is that what *your* mother calls *you?*" I asked, letting him head us through the trees again. "It sounds as much like a child's name as mine does."

"As a matter of fact, that's exactly what it is," he answered with a chuckle. "Mothers seem to give out those names without stopping to think that their child will one day be grown. I haven't told anyone that name in years, so I'd appreciate your keeping it just between the two of us."

"It's not all that bad, but I will if you want me to," I said, suddenly finding it a lot easier to match his smile. He seemed to understand more about how I felt than I had expected, and I wasn't often asked to keep someone's secret. I was good at keeping secrets, but most people didn't know that.

"Now we each know something about the other that we wouldn't want mentioned around," he said, looking at me with only part of his attention as he watched the forest we moved through. "That should be a good enough basis on which to build a friendship, especially since we have a common goal. Do you have any idea how far it is to that town? I know we're not likely to round a tree and suddenly find it there in front of us, but we ought to know when we're getting close so we can watch out for people who might happen by.''

''Well, I asked about a gathering that was a small distance ahead of us,'' I said, wishing I could tell him more. ''How small that distance turns out to be depends on how large this forest is. Trees tend to measure things by the size of their own surroundings, which means we could be right on top of the town without knowing it, or we could have hours of walking ahead of us.''

''I think we can be sure we aren't right on top of it,'' he said, flashing me a brief but very warm smile. ''Since you've never been in this Realm before, you can't be expected to know it, but there's usually a good deal of empty space between a town and the nearest stand of trees. The townspeople don't want anyone to be able to sneak up on them, so they clear the ground for quite a distance in all directions.''

''With people who have forgotten how to speak to trees, I'm not surprised,'' I said with a sniff of disapproval. ''It isn't their fault, of course, but that doesn't make it right. I'm just glad we're not going into that town thing.''

''*You're* not going in,'' he corrected, ''which makes you the lucky one. If we're going to get horses I'll have to go in, but I'll be back out again as fast as I can manage it. You don't like towns without ever having seen one; try imagining how much *I* dislike them.''

''It doesn't seem fair that you have to be the one to go, then,'' I said, looking up at him where he walked beside me. ''If you hate it all that much, there's no reason why I can't—''

''No, now, don't you worry about it,'' he said really fast, turning his head to look down at me with another smile and a hand squeeze. ''It's no more unfair for me to do that, than for you to do all the talking to the trees. We'll each do what we're best suited to do, and that way we'll have no trouble regaining what was stolen from us.

And since we have some time now, why don't we work on getting to know each other?''

He seemed anxious to change subjects, and there was really no reason not to go along with him. In my mother's Realm, when you wanted to get to know someone well, one of the first things you did was go to bed with them. Human beings have a sense of physical attraction they feel toward one another, and too often the physical interferes with how well the personalities involved would blend together. Having sex lets you put the physical aside for a while, at least long enough to be aware of the other factors involved, and then you can *really* know if you like a particular person.

Which was why I didn't understand the reluctance Jiss was showing. There was nothing *wrong* with having sex, not when it was not only extremely enjoyable, but also the way human beings kept themselves from dying out. Of course, I didn't know from personal experience just how enjoyable bed activity was, but that was only because I hadn't had much interest in it. I'd known for a while that my attitudes were changing, but just hadn't found anyone I was interested in starting with. Jiss would be the first man I got to know that way . . .

For an instant I thought *that* might be the reason he was so reluctant, but then I realized how silly the idea was. Granted I would be clumsy and awkward compared to my sisters, but they would be expecting quite a lot in the way of technique from Jiss, whereas I would not. My sisters never minded speaking about the men they enjoyed, but when they got to what they considered details, I was usually lost. It was something you had to experience to really understand, and I wouldn't mind experiencing it with Jiss. He was very handsome and physically well made, the sort of man a girl was encouraged to look for when she first decided she was ready for bed activity. Once she got the experience with perfection out of her system, she would then be free to consider more important things than physical attributes.

So my best bet was to get things rolling as quickly as

possible. I still didn't believe there would be anything
deep developing between Jiss and me, but arranging the
exchange in a properly calm, businesslike manner would
let us put it behind us, and then we could go on from
there. To the point of really getting to know each other.

"All right," I agreed with his previous suggestion. "I
suppose these woods are private enough so that we don't
need a tent. Since we're in a hurry I'm assuming it won't
take very long, but if—"

"Wait a minute," he said in a strange voice, the tug on
my hand not letting me stop. "I think I already told you
that people don't get to know each other only in bed. You
and I are going to talk, remember? Which is a good thing,
because we don't have enough time to stop. Why don't
you start by telling me about the things you most enjoy
doing."

"You really *don't* want to take me to bed, do you?" I
said, feeling a little hurt over the way he was making sure
we didn't even slow, not to mention stop. "Well, I guess
that takes care of your decision where I'm concerned. At
least now you can't correct me when I say you've come to
marry one of my sisters."

"Hali, you're making this all much more complicated
than it is," the big man said, sounding really upset. "Just
because I want to talk to you to get to know you, doesn't
mean I don't want to take you to bed. That would mean I
didn't like you, and nothing could be farther from the
truth. You're a beautiful young woman, and talented as
well, but I . . ."

"Then you do want to take me to bed," I concluded,
privately wondering why he used such a roundabout way
to state a natural desire. "You're right about our not
having the time to stop for it now, so we'll do it first thing
when we do stop and get it out of the way. Then maybe
you won't have so much trouble talking about it."

"*Me* have trouble talking about it?" he demanded with
a look of total outrage. Then he regained control of himself. "Hali, I think it's time we got this settled once and
for all, in a way we'll both understand. You may not know

it, but when a man and a woman are friends, it's bad manners for one of them to try forcing the other into going to bed. Unless *both* of them are willing it just doesn't work out, and right now I don't happen to be willing. My reasons have nothing to do with how much I like you, they only relate to me. If you keep on trying to force me into bed, I'll be very embarrassed.''

By that time he seemed completely calm and was looking at me with a very sober expression. I didn't know what to say, not when he'd talked about being embarrassed. I'd overheard my sisters a few times, discussing various men who looked hale and hardy enough, but who just couldn't seem to cut it. I didn't know what it was they were supposed to cut, and so had assumed they were simply unable. I knew how terrible it was for a man to be unable, and if that was Prince Jentris's problem I could have kicked myself for having made him admit it.

"Oh, Jiss, I'm so sorry," I blurted out, tightening my grip on the hand that still held mine. "I didn't mean to force you into anything, or embarrass you, or— I won't bother you about it again, really I won't. And I'll leave it to you to tell my sisters in whatever way you think best."

"Tell your sisters what?" he asked, now pretending to be puzzled while at the same time looking totally relieved. "And I don't want you feeling bad about this, especially not when we both know it isn't your fault. You're not responsible for my problems, so I don't want you thinking you are. You and I will talk to get to know each other, and one day you'll learn how much better an idea that is than simply jumping into bed."

Because he couldn't do anything in bed, I realized, trying not to show how terrible I felt on his behalf. If he was accepting the tragedy calmly and unemotionally, the least I could do was the same. For his sake, then, I would pretend there was nothing wrong at all.

"Talking should make us really good friends, so obviously talking is the best thing we can do," I said, working for a smile to match his. "Sahrinth and Greaf and I became best friends through talking, and maybe you and I will too. When we stop to rest, we can have a really good conversation.''

"And pay attention to each other rather than to what we're walking through," he said, suddenly remembering he hadn't been watching the woods as we moved. His attention immediately returned to it, his eyes examining the low-hanging branches and bushes we were passing. Then just as suddenly his right hand was blurring toward his sword and he was pushing me behind him. I didn't understand what was happening—until a large group of men stepped out of the greenery around us.

"Don't do it, friend," one of the strangers said to Jiss, causing my companion's hand to go motionless on his hilt. "Those boys're real good with the bows they're holdin', an' they won't mind diggin' their arrows outa your carcass later on. Move yer hand from off that pig-sticker real careful-like, an' maybe y'll live t'see our camp."

"Camp?" Jiss echoed, his hand still unmoving, his eyes on the man who had spoken. "Who are you people, and why are you stopping us?"

"Let's jest say we're men in business," the stranger drawled with a grin, causing the others to chuckle. "We took a look at you an' that pretty girl there, an' right off we knowed we c'd do lotsa business. First off we'll do business f'r whatever y'got on ya, an' then we'll do more f'r whatever you two bring. Or f'r whatever she brings, if y'don't move that hand right now."

The stranger's grin had grown hard and his dark eyes glittered. Jiss muttered something furious under his breath and then withdrew his hand from his sword, and I couldn't keep quiet any longer.

"Jiss, what is it?" I whispered from where I stood half behind him. "Who are they, and what do they want?"

"They want us and whatever we happen to have of value," Jiss answered low as the strangers slowly approached us, his voice disgusted. "It wasn't a town the trees directed us toward, Hali, it was an outlaw camp, and we walked right into it. Since they apparently intend to sell us as slaves, I think it's safe to say our biggest problem will be walking away again.''

Chapter 4

🍎

THE STRANGERS MOVED slowly and carefully until they'd taken Jiss's sword and dagger and had tied his wrists behind him, and then they relaxed, laughing and joking with one another. They were typical Earth Realm natives, of course, heavy moving and stolid looking and mostly dark of hair and eye, and only one or two of them were even as tall as I was. The rest were a lot shorter, which meant they stared up at Jiss as though he were the one who was odd. They wore rough-woven clothing in many colors that neither matched nor looked particularly well cared for, and their leather boots were downright dirty. When they finished with Jiss they turned their attention to me, and the one who had done all the talking began grinning again.

"If she don't bring twice 'r three times what he does, I'm a bald-faced talker," he said to a man standing next to him who was also grinning. In point of fact neither of them was bald-faced, not with the dark, dirty, and uneven hair all over their cheeks and chins, but that was the least of what I didn't understand. "Just look at 'er, Gid, an' tell me I'm wrong."

"Druther lay m'hands on 'er thin m'eyes, Tander," the second man answered, the words so garbled I almost couldn't understand them. "Whin we gonna git t'taste 'er?"

"We can't do nothin' till Reff gets back frum leadin' them trackers off in another direction," Tander replied.

78

"Once we don't have that fool tracker group ready t'crawl in our blankets with us, we c'n think about takin' somethin' else in there. Reff'll want firsts, o' course, an' then he'll say who goes after 'im."

"I'll kill any man who puts a hand on her," Jiss said, his words only just loud enough for everyone to hear. His arms were still tied behind him and the three men guarding him wore swords and daggers, but there was such quiet assurance in his voice that grins and laughter disappeared together.

"Sure you will," the man Tander said after the briefest hesitation, forcing a grin back to his face before turning to look at Jiss over his shoulder. "Just as soon as we turn y' loose, y'll do lotsa things. Till that happens though, y'll keep yer mouth shut. Okay, men, let's get 'em back t' camp. Him first, an' if he makes any trouble put some arrows 'r a blade in 'im."

The three men near Jiss began pushing him in the direction they wanted him to go, and all he could do was give me a final glance before they got their way. There was reassurance in that glance, and an insistence that everything would be all right, but if he'd said it out loud I probably would have argued. I'd never seen anyone as primitive and backward as those Earth Realm ephemerals, and looking at them it was hard to believe their ancestors were as civilized and talented as anyone else.

"Okay, pretty, now it's y'r turn," Tander said, staring at me. "Y' just follow right along, 'cause we're gonna take real good care a ya. You two'll bring us more 'n the last town we stripped, 'cause there ain't gonna be nobody who ever saw y'r like b'fore. An' speakin' a strippin', y' just let me know when y' want t' take that dress off. I'll be right there t' help."

"I don't need anybody's help with anything," I said into the men's laughter, trying to keep my voice steady as I moved away from the arm Tander was putting around me. "And aren't any of you curious about why my companion and I look so different? Don't you even wonder where we come from?"

"The only thing I'm wonderin' about is how y'll look with that dress off," Tander replied, his grin wide. "I been partial to fair-skinned women f'r as long as I c'n remember, but I never seen anythin' that comes even close t' bein' as fair as you. I'm gonna have you, girly, one way 'r another I'm gonna have a real good taste a you."

He shoved my back to get me walking then, and the renewed laughter simply added to the chill that shouldn't have been part of the rising warmth of the day. Tander's attitude reminded me very strongly of Feledor, back in my own Realm, and that in turn showed me the ephemerals hadn't lost *every* link to what they'd once been.

It only took a few minutes of walking before we reached what they called their camp, a wide area of cloth tents spread out over a partial clearing in the woods. The tents were all of dark colors, brown or green or very dirty yellowish tan, and there seemed to be the remnants of cooking fires in front of most of them. The trees in the area were oddly silent, and then I realized they weren't just silent, they were actually withdrawn. Trees disliked doing that, withdrawing into themselves so deeply that they lost all contact with the outer world, but they never hesitated when conditions around them were terrible enough. I could imagine how bad it was for them with the ephemerals constantly committing casual horrors, and wished briefly but intensely that I could help.

Right after I figured out a way to help Jiss and me. I sighed as I saw the men forcing Jiss toward a small green tent, while I was being directed toward a larger brown one. They weren't even going to keep us in the same place, which meant we couldn't even discuss an escape plan—not that it needed much discussion. Jiss was tied tight and his weapons were in the possession of one of his guards, while I was still free even though I was being watched. That seemed to mean it was up to me to do what had to be done, but I was faced with one major problem.

It was getting brighter out, not darker, and whatever talents I had were meant to be used in the dark.

"And if we just sit around waiting until night, the

thieves will get away," I muttered to myself, too low for the men around me to hear. I had to do something to get us loose as soon as possible—even though I couldn't think of anything *to* do.

"Inside that tent with you, girly," Tander said, and his hand reached in front of me to pull aside the tent flap. "Won't be too long b'fore Reff gets back, an' then we'll have us some fun."

His other hand tried to touch me as he said that, but I avoided the contact by slipping quickly inside the tent. That, of course, marked the occasion for more laughter from the others, as though what Tander had said and had tried to do was the height of original wit. I was beginning to get very tired of the way they were acting, as though bed-sharing was something special and important. Only very small children—and, apparently, Prince Jentris—thought of it like that, before they grew old enough to understand how minor a thing it really was. Jiss had a reason for being strange on the subject, but the strangers were adults, and shouldn't have acted like that.

Since the tent flap had been closed behind me, I glanced around then went to the back of the tent to sit down. There was nothing in the thing but stained rugs scattered around, a dim lantern hanging on the wall to the right of the entrance, and the heaviest, most sickening smell I'd ever come across in all the years of my life. The air smelled as though it had died ages earlier, and had spent the time since its death slowly decomposing. I settled down on a patch of bare ground between two rugs, wondering how people could live like this, and then remembered my thoughts about their being adults. Maybe they *weren't* adult, and that was why they made such a fuss over bed-sharing and seemed never to have bothered cleaning up after themselves. It takes time to learn to think and act in a way that doesn't impose your beliefs and doings on others, and time was something ephemerals had very little of. The Lord of the Earth had taken away their time, and most of their humanity had gone with it.

I spent a good chunk of my own time sitting and thinking and trying to fight off depression, but none of it was particularly successful. Sitting on the ground was uncomfortable, especially since my hair insisted on piling up under me no matter how many times I tried moving it out of the way. Thinking about escape was producing nothing in the way of brilliant ideas, and with all four sides of the tent tied down tight, I couldn't even figure out a way of leaving there. Every now and again I remembered about the ephemerals' plans for us, and the depression I was trying to fight off crept nearer and nearer. Along with the depression was a fear I couldn't afford to acknowledge, and that simply added to the depression.

After what seemed like ages I got to my feet to walk back and forth, no longer able to sit still. I'd been thinking and thinking without coming up with any ideas, and on top of that I was thirsty and beginning to be really hungry. How I could be thirsty and hungry at a time like this I didn't know, but it didn't change the fact that I was. I was disgusted with myself, and beginning to be worried; I needed something to distract my anxiety—

"Whatsa matter, girly, y' gettin' tired a waitin'?" a voice said suddenly from behind me, at the tent entrance. I turned quickly and saw that it was Tander, just as I'd thought, and he was alone. A grin covered his hairy face and he stood there with his fingertips resting on his swordbelt, looking like nothing more than someone who had just dropped by for a friendly visit.

"Summa us decided Reff was takin' too long gettin' back," he said, beginning to walk slowly toward me. "We thought we oughta get acquainted with the new merchandise, b'fore she's sent off t' be sold. Wouldn't wanna miss knowin' one like you, girly."

"If you hurt me, my mother will make you regret it!" I blurted, backing away toward the corner of the rear of the tent, feeling my heart pound. "And even before that, *I'll* make you regret it!"

"Will you, now?" he asked with a grin, still coming toward me. "An' how do y' spect t' do that, girly? Th' same way y'r momma's gonna do it, maybe by not talkin' t' me no more? That'll hurt me real bad, I gotta tell ya, real bad.''

He began chuckling as he came closer, his hands reaching for me, but I was already doing the only thing I could. He and I were blocking off the lanternlight, turning the shadows thicker and more substantial in that back corner than what could be found in the rest of the tent. I'd begun fashioning a shadow-stick with the hand held behind me, and just before he reached me I turned away to finish it faster by using two hands. Shadow-sticks can be used for more than games and tie posts for spun-moonlight tents— I hoped.

I was just smoothing the last of the roundness into the stick when the man's arms closed around me, but not in a way that had ever happened before. In my mother's Realm touching and being touched were things all children were encouraged to do, so that when they grew to adulthood they were already comfortably familiar with the sensations. It was considered proper to ask before touching anyone, but since no one really minded, refusals were rare. It was a sharing thing that had never bothered me— and nothing at all like what that ephemeral did right then.

I'd known Tander's touch would be unpleasant, but it was even worse. I'd expected to be hurt, probably even hit, but instead he wrapped his arms around me and spread his hands over my breasts, at the same time pushing at me from behind with his body. For an instant it seemed as though he was an infant, doing things he didn't understand but liked because they felt good, as though he had never been granted permission to touch a woman before in his entire life. I was so surprised I just stood there with the shadow-stick in my hand, trying to understand what was happening.

"That's right, girly, no screamin'," the man panted in a low, rough voice, his hands and body moving together. "Them others don't need t' know what we're doin' in here, an' y'r really gonna like what I got t' give ya. We're gonna have fun, you 'n me, lots 'n lots a fun.''

Clumsy and unpleasant groping seemed to be his idea of

fun, but it certainly wasn't mine. His actions were as rude
as simply shoving someone out of your path, and I'd never
been able to stand bad manners. I closed my hand really
tight around the shadow-stick and struck at his face where
it rested on my left shoulder, the blow not as hard as I'd
wanted it to be because of the way Tander's right arm lay
above mine. He shouted when the blow landed, then shouted
again when I hit him a second time, but instead of letting
me go he simply pulled his head back. I struggled to get
loose, intent on beating at him until he ended up on the
floor. He'd said he didn't want anyone to know what he
was doing in my tent, which meant he had to have come
inside when no one was watching. If I could just get
loose—!

But I couldn't, even though I was struggling with all my
strength. The man had shifted from touching me to holding
on to me, and his growl matched his angry grip. He
snarled something about making me sorry I'd even thought
about trying to stop him, but as he pulled me back out of
the corner I was more frantic than sorry. My shadow-stick
began fading as soon as stronger light started touching it,
and I knew in another minute it would be completely
dissolved. I fought to get free soon enough to use my one
weapon, succeeded only in tightening the hold on me to
the point of pain, and then suddenly Tander grunted and
stiffened, and an instant later I was free.

I stumbled around to face the man who had finally let
me go. Tander stood there with his arms at his sides, a thin
stream of blood coming from one of his nostrils, his eyes
completely glazed and clouded over. Even as I watched he
began to fall face down, making no effort to catch himself,
forcing me to get hurriedly out of the way. When he was
flat on the ground I could see the wide red stain wetting
the back of his shirt, and because of that finally moved my
eyes to the stranger who now stood in the tent with us. He
was a good deal larger than Tander or any of his men, and
he held a dagger that wore a sheen of wetly glistening red.

"I'm glad I got here in time," the man said lightly, a
smile warming his dark brown eyes. He wiped the dagger

on his pants before resheathing it. "I wouldn't have used a blade in the back if he hadn't been armed and holding you, but I know that slime. He wouldn't have minded hurting you to save his own worthless neck, and I wasn't about to let that happen. Not that he was doing all that well against you. From what I could see when I first came in here, you probably would have beaten him without my help."

"Me?" I said in an unfortunately squeaky voice, more than aware of the grin he was now giving me. Having Tander drop at my feet had upset me, and the look of that newcomer was almost as bad. He wore a heavy cloth tunic in a dark blue with cloth trousers and leather boots of black, all of it seeming of better quality than what the rest of the men around there wore. In addition to the dagger he also had a sword belted around him, and his longish dark brown hair somehow gave him an air of adventure. His clean-shaven face was quite handsome, something I didn't think an enemy should be. Ugly, dirty, ill-mannered people make the best enemies, a consideration that helped me pull myself together.

"How silly of me," I said with a small, cool smile, the sort I'd seen my mother use often and very effectively. "Of course I could have taken care of myself against that—lowlife. Just as I can take care of myself against you."

"Hey, now, don't start attacking *me*," he said hurriedly with widened eyes that nevertheless seemed to have a faint twinkle in them, both hands held palm outward in front of him. "I'm not here to do you harm. All I want is to help you and your friend to get out of here as fast as possible. I'll get you mounts and show you how to get away from this place—if I can go with you."

"Why do you want to go with *us*?" I asked, genuinely surprised. "If you want to leave, why don't you just go ahead and do it?"

"I have my reasons and they're good ones, but we don't have time to discuss that now," he answered, looking more serious. "First let's get ourselves out of here, and once we're clear we can stop to talk. Is it a deal?"

"Until we can stop to talk," I agreed with a half-reluctant nod. There was no other response to make. We needed a way out of there, and I couldn't come up with an escape plan of my own.

I quickly followed the newcomer out of my tent. Just as I'd suspected there was no one in the camp watching from the outside, but as we hurried toward the tent they'd taken Jiss to, we had to avoid an unmoving body on the ground. The dead man had been holding a bow with an arrow loose in the string, but there wasn't a trace of blood on him anywhere. I had the impression his head was twisted into a very odd position as I hurried past, and then he was behind me and I didn't look back. I'd once seen someone with a broken neck, and knew that staring didn't make the sight easier to take.

The large, deserted camp was silent behind us when we reached Jiss's tent, but it wasn't the pleasant silence I was used to in the forest dark at home. For that reason, among others, I hurried into the tent after the stranger, then nearly ran into him when he stopped short. Beyond him I could see Jiss straightening out of a crouch, his left hand holding the swordbelt he'd just taken from one of the two unmoving figures on the ground, his right hand beginning to unsheathe the sword. Toward the back of the tent was a small pile of still-smoldering leather, very much like the leather Jiss had been tied with.

"I'm starting to feel as though I'm wasting my time," the stranger said pleasantly to Jiss, who had stopped drawing his sword with a frown when he saw me next to the man. "First the girl beats Tander half to death before I can put him out of his misery, and now you've done for these two. If I thought you also knew the best way out of here, I'd throw my hands up and just go back to what I was doing."

"Who are you?" Jiss demanded. "If you expect to use the girl against me . . ."

"I know, I know," the stranger interrupted, once again holding his hands up, palms outward. "You'll have no trouble handling me, especially since I don't happen to

have a bow. I'm just glad there are only two of you, so
this should be the last time I have to say it: *I'm on your
side*. We can stand around discussing details once we're
out of here. Are you ready to leave?''

Jiss looked as though he wanted to demand more in the
way of answers, but he nodded curtly and strapped on his
swordbelt. A breath later we were leaving the tent.

"All right, here's how we have to do it," the stranger
said to Jiss once we were outside. "There are seven or
eight men standing sentry in the path through the forest we
need to take, so our first plan of action is to eliminate
them. I've already saddled three horses, and once the
sentries are out of the way we can leave. Are you willing
to go along with that?"

"If that's the only way we can escape, of course I am,"
Jiss answered with a shrug, still looking less than friendly
and trusting. "We didn't come after these people, they
came after us. If they find more trouble than they expected, it's no one's fault but theirs."

"That's right," I agreed. "Which way do we go?"

"Now, Hali," Jiss began, but the stranger didn't give
him a chance to finish whatever he'd been going to say.

"Taking out the sentries is a job for me and your big
friend there," he said, his eyes directly on me. "He and I
are the ones with the swords, which means you get to
collect the horses I saddled and then you bring them after
us. If there's still any fighting going on when you get
there, you'll stay well out of the way until it's over. Do
you understand?"

"Who appointed *you* leader?" I demanded, disliking his
entire attitude. "I'm not as helpless as you seem to think I
am, which means you can assign someone else the very
exciting job of fetching the horses. If there's going to be a
fight, I want to be in it."

"You can't be in it," he answered flatly, interrupting
Jiss for the second time without even knowing it. "Those
men are dangerous to face even for someone who's armed;
barehanded you'd have less than no chance against them,
and they could catch you and use you against us. And who

else do you think I can get to bring the horses after us? It's the three of us against all of them, and if we make a mistake we've had it.''

"Hali, we all have to do the job we're best suited to, remember?" Jiss asked smoothly while I stared at the stranger. "We need to be mounted more than we need a hand in the fight, and this way I won't have to go into a town. You did say you were willing to save me that trouble, didn't you?"

"We really don't have the time for this," the stranger said, this time interrupting me as I was about to argue with Jiss. "The horses are tied to a line behind that light green tent over there, girl. Once you have them, look for the faint trail leading through the woods that lies just beyond those two brown tents over that way. By the time you find it, you should have the sound of fighting to guide you the rest of the way. Come on, friend, let's see to it."

Jiss seemed reluctant to leave without saying anything else, but the stranger was already striding away and my companion didn't want to be left behind. I stood there with my fists on my hips as I watched them go, really annoyed at being treated like that even if much of what had been said was true. That savage had been rude on purpose, and I really do dislike bad manners. As I turned away to search for those stupid horses we needed, I decided Jiss and I would separate from that stranger just as soon as we possibly could.

More than three horses were tied to the line, but only three of them were saddled. The line itself was heavy braided leather stretching between half a dozen trees, and seemed to have been placed there to hold a good many more horses than it did just then. I untied the reins of the three horses and led them toward the trail I was supposed to find next, unimpressed with the choice in mounts. The man who had chosen them was just as common, and probably wouldn't have known a decent horse if it galloped over him.

By the time I found the footpath that had been complimented with the name of trail, I was sure there was more jackass in our mounts than horse. They didn't seem to like being led at a walking pace, and kept trying to pull out of my grip on their reins and move faster. They were big bodied and clumsy looking, almost completely devoid of the grace and intelligence to be found in the sort of horse I was used to, and after the third time I was nearly knocked out of the way I discovered it was the big red bay who was instigating insurrection in the two brown geldings. At that point I stopped and tied his rein really tight to the saddle horn of one of the browns, and then I was able to continue on in peace. The bay hated the idea and was really unhappy, but I liked it fine.

When I'd first started up the trail I'd heard something that must have been the clash of steel, but by the time I reached the scene of battle the action was over. There were bodies everywhere, covered in one way or another with spreading red. I swallowed quickly and moved my eyes instead to Jiss. He was cleaning his sword on a piece of cloth that looked like it had been ripped from the clothing of one of the victims, and when he glanced up to see me he grinned.

"Adequate transportation, and right on time," he said, sounding and looking happier than he had. "Since we're all finished here, we can be on our way."

"We can be on our way as soon as we relieve these men of what they don't need any longer," the stranger said, rising from the side of one of the bodies to jingle something in his left hand. "We will be needing it, and it can't be considered stealing. Whatever coins this bunch has came from people who never intended to give them up. Our taking them isn't— Hey, what have you done to my stallion?"

The last part of his speech was directed toward me, his eyes on the bay where it still tried to pull loose from where I'd tied it. He strode over, his previous task apparently forgotten.

"I should have known that stupid beast was yours," I said. "It kept trying to pull out of my hand and run me down, so I tied it up. If you like the idea of getting run down better, by all means untie it as quickly as you please.''

"He probably heard the sounds of fighting, and was trying to get to me to help,'' the stranger answered while his hands went to the rein tied to the saddle after his eyes had moved over the blood bay horse. "If he wasn't trained to be very gentle when being handled by a woman, you wouldn't have gotten away with doing this to him. If something like this ever comes up again, turn him loose instead of tying him. He won't run away.''

"If he does, don't forget you're the one who asked for it,'' I said, then felt curiosity getting the better of me. "Why was he trained to be more gentle when handled by a woman?''

"My sister used to spend a lot of time around him,'' the man answered, giving his attention to running his hands over the bay. "She wasn't allowed a horse of her own and wasn't even supposed to be near mine, but she really loved horses and I loved her. I taught her how to handle and ride Deel here, and taught him to be very gentle with her. She's been married and gone for years now, but Deel hasn't forgotten what he was taught. And now I think we'd better collect what coins we can and be on our way. If we're not out of here before Reff and the others get back—or before that sky decides to go all the way over to dark and stormy—we won't make it at all.''

He left the horse to go back to bending over the unmoving bodies on the ground, and I took a minute out to look up through the trees at the sky. I hadn't noticed sooner but the brightening light of the day had stopped brightening, due mainly to the large gray clouds that were gathering above. I wasn't about to admit I didn't know what stormy meant, but decided fairly quickly that it couldn't be very important. If it was linked to dark it couldn't be bad, after all, especially since it seemed like a very long time since it had last been dark. Then I realized there was something else I didn't understand, but it also wasn't a passing comment I could afford to ignore.

"What are these coins you keep talking about?'' I asked,

moving forward a few steps with the two horses I still held. "What are we going to need them for that it's so important we waste time looking for them?"

"You consider food and shelter unimportant?" the dark-haired stranger asked, glancing at me with faint ridicule as he moved on to the next nearest body. "Without gold and silver we won't get anything of what we need, and so far I've found more copper than gold. Where can you be from that you don't know about coins and what they're used for?"

"She was raised very sheltered," Jiss put in quickly before I could say anything. "This is the first time she's been off a very large, very well-guarded estate, so there are a lot of things she doesn't know about. If she says anything strange, just ignore her."

The stranger grunted noncommittally and moved on to the last of the bodies, either not noticing the way I was looking at Jiss, or simply not caring. Jiss was silently returning my stare with a warning look that told me I had to keep quiet and go along with his story. I agreed there was no need to tell that stranger anything about what we were after, but I couldn't see a single reason not to mention how backward it was to trade metal for necessities. Metal itself has no real value except when creativity is used to form it into trinkets and decorations, so . . .

"Okay, that's it," the stranger said, straightening from the last of the dead outlaws. "There isn't as much as I'd hoped to find, but it ought to last us for a few days anyhow. Now let's get out of here."

Jiss had already sheathed his sword, so all he had to do was come over to take one set of the reins I held. As soon as he did I circled my own horse, intending to mount—but discovered immediately that I wasn't considered capable of doing something that complex.

"Once you're mounted I'll adjust those stirrups for you," the stranger said from behind me while Jiss held my horse's head, and then the stranger's hands were on my waist, giving me help up I hadn't asked for and didn't need. "And we have to do something about replacing this gown you're wearing. Pretty is for ballrooms; what you need is an outfit that's both durable and practical.''

"I don't remember asking your opinion about my clothing," I said when I was in the saddle, looking down in annoyance at the man who had decided I couldn't adjust my own stirrups—or pick out the proper clothes.

"Now, Hali, the man's only trying to be helpful," Jiss said over his shoulder while he lengthened the stirrups on his own saddle as far down as they would go. "Since we probably have a lot of riding ahead of us, it might be a good idea to take his advice.''

"I'll certainly think about it, Jentris, and just as certainly will let you know what I decide," I answered very sweetly, which made Jiss sigh without turning again. The stranger, almost finished with my stirrup, glanced up at me with an unreadable expression, but I didn't care *what* he thought. The man brought out the absolute worst in me, and I couldn't wait to part company with him.

It only took another couple of minutes before all the adjustments were finished, and then we rode off through the woods, following the stranger. He seemed to have a specific destination in mind, which wasn't the road Jiss and I had originally been following. When we finally got to the road he crossed it and kept going into the woods on the far side, and didn't even slow until it was well behind us.

"Unless our luck turns very bad, we should be all right now," the man said at that point, falling back to ride on the far side of Jiss, to the left. "Reff and his bunch were supposed to have led the searchers off to the northeast, and then west of there before splitting up into smaller groups and making their way back on the slink to a rendezvous point. That would put them on the other side of the road from here, and also out of our way.''

"Then that means it's time to thank you for your help," Jiss said with a warm smile. "I still don't know why you helped us, but that doesn't change the fact that you did. Do you care to tell us where you'll be going now?''

"I'll be glad to tell you," the man said, his grin some-how very appropriate. "Now I'll be going with you two."

Jiss was silent for a moment, and then he shook his head slightly.

"I don't understand," he said, trying very hard to be reasonable. "We appreciate your help in getting out of there, but that doesn't mean we— That is, Hali and I have a destination to reach, and the trip won't be easy or safe. There's no need for you to expose yourself to our enemies."

"But there's every reason," the stranger interrupted, still maintaining his air of friendliness and pleasance. "We don't even need to mention the fact that your lady has already agreed to most of my request. What we do need to mention is the painful truth that if you don't let me go with you and help all I can, I won't be able to go home again."

"Now I really don't understand," Jiss said before I could correct the stranger about what I'd supposedly agreed to. "What could helping us possibly have to do with your going home again?"

"I come from a very well-to-do, very important fam-ily," the stranger said, now into a sad, heavy sigh. "The kindest thing to say might be that I did something ex-tremely stupid because I was young. My family very reasonably grew upset with me—not for the first time, I must admit—and finally decided they'd had enough. I was handed my belongings, given the reins of my horse, and escorted off the estate. I was told I could come home again when I'd proven I was no longer a child, no longer some-one who thought only of himself. I had to help someone and really mean it, do it because that someone needed me more than I needed them. I know you two are runaway lovers, and I really do want to see you both safe before I take the road home."

That time Jiss and I just stared at the man, and if my companion understood what he was talking about, I cer-tainly didn't. What I did get, though, was some idea of what our expressions were like when the stranger looked from one to the other of us and then laughed.

"You're wondering how I could possibly know?" he

asked, his wide grin back again as he guided his mount around the far side of a very young tree. "I've been out in the world for a number of years now, and the weeks I spent with those outlaws only hardened me, they didn't blind me. A girl who has led a very sheltered life, a young man who tries to protect her even after he's been captured, the two of them with a long way to go and enemies who might have to be faced— You wanted to marry her, her family refused, so the two of you ran away. Now they're after you and trying to get her back, but you're heading for someplace you think will be safe. I'll bet everything I own you're taking her to your family's estate, or at least to their part of the country. Isn't that right?"

"I—hadn't realized anyone had noticed so much," Jiss said, an answer that didn't quite match the question, and then he turned just a little to put a big hand against my shoulder where I rode beside him. "I doubt if I can say how much this girl means to me, and without that, saying what lies ahead of us would be meaningless. I don't feel right about embroiling a passerby in our troubles, especially since I can't discuss any more of our biggest problem than to say this: Something has been stolen from us, and we need to recover it. As soon as we do that we really will need more help. Why don't we arrange to meet somewhere afterward, and then—"

"Why afterward?" the stranger asked, apparently believing everything he hadn't quite been told. "I can help you get back whatever's been stolen, and then we won't have to bother meeting somewhere. And you can't tell me you don't need someone who knows this area a lot better than you do. You're strangers around here, which I'm not, and I'm also someone who realizes it takes a real man to accept help when he needs it as well as give it when he's asked. I've been thinking of you as a real man, my friend; was I wrong?"

I felt a surge of annoyance when Jiss simply stirred in his saddle without answering, apparently caught in a corner he couldn't get out of again. The stranger was acting terribly mature and superior, ages older than everyone around him, in wisdom and experience if nothing else. Physically he seemed to be no older than Jiss, which meant he was probably younger than both of us by quite a lot. It was bad enough being patronized and manipulated by people who were older than me; I wasn't about to accept the same from an infant ephemeral.

"Jentris, why try to spare feelings he obviously doesn't have?" I said, letting a good deal of the annoyance show in my voice. "He had his own reasons for helping us get out of that outlaw camp, and we've already thanked him for it. I never told him he could ride with us forever, only until we were free and could talk about the matter. Now that we've talked about it, just tell him no, he can't continue on with us, and then we can get on with our own concerns in peace. You can see he won't take a hint, so just say it straight out."

"In the same delicate way you just did?" the stranger asked with a very bright smile. "Some people have better manners than that, girl, especially when the man who just saved their lives asks a favor in return. Did you miss hearing the favor I asked, or are you ignoring it as not worth paying attention to?"

"Oh, I heard it, all right," I answered. "You're trying to force your help on people who don't want it, just so you can go home telling yourself how selfless you've learned to be. If that's your idea of selflessness, I would suggest you look for help of your own—in redefining the word."

"Is it selfish to want to help people who have troubles so serious they feel it would be unfair to embroil a stranger in them?" the man demanded, his dark eyes hardening as his bright smile disappeared. "If I only wanted to be able to say I'd helped someone, I'd already be able to say that. I can lie to myself and others as easily as the next man, but you seem to be missing the point that I don't want to lie. I want to really do what I'll be claiming I did, and if that's too difficult for you to understand—"

"All right, let's all calm down," Jiss said suddenly. "Exchanging insults doesn't help to settle differences. And if you think about it, Hali, the man has a point. We

don't know this area, and he does. You could be turning
down help we'll need very badly.''

"We already have help, or have you forgotten that?" I
came back, trying to remind him about Sahrinth and the
trees without mentioning them aloud. "Our—friends—can
give us all the information we need about the area, and we
won't have to worry about their motives. Can you say the
same about him?"

"Hali, have you forgotten that it was the information we
got from our friends that sent us walking into the hands of
outlaws?" he countered, his voice still very calm and
reasonable. "Our friends mean well, but they don't really
understand everything going on around them, and we have
trouble understanding them. I'll bet if you checked with
them right now, they'd tell you very little of real use."

"And I'll bet they'd give us more help than he could,"
I returned, using my chin to gesture toward the stranger. I
had the feeling Jiss wanted me to check with the trees
again, but the way he'd said it suggested he didn't want
me to do it in front of our noble rescuer. I knew if he
expected me to turn invisible in order to do it privately
he'd have to wait until nightfall, but it turned out he had
something else in mind.

"Well, why don't you think about it for a couple of
minutes, while I ride ahead with our new friend for some
private conversation?" he said, reaching over to pat one of
my hands. "The temporary separation will do both of you
good, not to mention that it will also get me out from
between you. We'll just be a few feet ahead, so if you
need me all you have to do is call."

He smiled fatuously and gestured to the stranger, then
the two of them were pulling ahead to ride through the
forest about fifteen feet in front of me, angling to move
parallel to the road. I made sure my expression didn't
show it, but I was feeling very impressed with Jiss's
cleverness. By pretending he was the one who wanted
privacy, that was what he'd gotten for me. I could ask the
trees anything I cared to, and when I had what I needed I
could "call" him to share what I'd learned. All of it

would be done directly under the stranger's nose, but the man would never notice a thing. I liked the idea so much I chuckled to myself.

The trees around us already knew about my first conversation with a member of their forest, which made things a good deal easier. They told me what had happened since the first time I'd asked, answered all the questions I tried to use to clarify the information, then went back to discussing their own topics of interest when I thanked them. After that I spent a few minutes thinking over what I'd heard, then looked toward the two broad backs now riding more than twenty feet ahead of me.

"Jentris, can I speak to you for a moment?" I called. The two of them turned in their saddles. "Privately?"

Which comment, happily, kept the stranger where he was when Jiss said a final few words to him then dropped back to where I rode. His patient brown horse made no objection to slowing almost to a complete stop, and then I was riding beside him again.

"I think they managed to get the wagon fixed, even though it might not be the best of repairs," I said very low, keeping my eyes on the stranger's back to make sure he was staying where we wanted him. "Apparently the 'limb' is still obviously broken, but the noise and tremor producer is moving again. The previously unsensing unrooted is no longer unsensing, but the sap seems to be flowing rather slowly within it. The trees believe the unrooteds are trying to reach a shame-place before the life-blessing arrives, but have chosen the longer on-path over the shorter back-line. My offshoot life form is still following, and sends word that it will merge roots with me as soon as possible. If your friend over there can help us make sense out of *that*, you won't ever hear me utter another syllable against him."

"Unfortunately for the sake of peace, we're going to have to try deciphering it ourselves," he answered with a sigh, glancing at the stranger. "I wasn't joking about our needing that man's help, but that doesn't mean I want him to know who we are and where we're from. There are too

many things about this Realm we're not familiar with—
like this area—while our enemy has at the least been
through it. Do you want to see Greaf lost along with the
Great Flame simply because you can't get along with
someone?''

"I have no trouble getting along with people," I pointed
out reasonably, dismissing the thought that I would let
anything keep me from saving Greaf. "That ephemeral's
the one who can't be gotten along with, not unless you
don't mind being treated like a thing. And I also don't
trust him, no matter what story he cares to come up with.
He has sneaky eyes."

"Sneaky eyes," Jiss repeated, his own eyes looking
amused, and then he reached out to touch my hand. "Hali,
you're being hard on our new friend because of what the
others said they were going to do with us, and that's not
very fair. He isn't the one who captured us; he's the one
who freed us. I'm not saying we have to trust him, only
that we have to accept his help. I know you don't like it,
but will you go along with it?''

"Only as long as he doesn't try telling me what to do
again," I said with a slow headshake, wondering if Jiss
made a practice of looking for trouble. "Nothing he can
say will convince me he doesn't have unmentioned reasons
for wanting to stay with us, and if you intend to trust him
you can make that mistake alone. I'll be happiest if I don't
even talk to him."

"Hali, you need to understand something," Jiss said
slowly, disturbance now in his eyes. "I agree that our
friend has unmentioned reasons for wanting to stay with
us, and it's possible his most pressing reason is something
that could cause us trouble. I don't quite know how to say
this, but— Hasn't it occurred to you that *you* might be the
reason he helped us in the first place?''

My eyebrows rose as I looked at Jiss, but there didn't
seem to be any words to go along with the gesture. I knew
my mother and sisters were considered very beautiful and
aside from individual differences my looks weren't far

from theirs, but I had never considered the possibility that a stranger might be attracted to me.

"Jiss, that doesn't make any sense," I finally managed to get out, shaking my head again. "If he felt any interest he would have said so right at the beginning, to give me a chance to think about whatever proposal he was planning to make. Since he hasn't said anything, you have to be mistaken."

"People in this Realm don't behave the way they do in yours, Hali," he answered. He seemed to be searching for the right words. "To begin with, the man believes you and I are runaway lovers being chased by your family. That would mean we had certain agreements between us, the sort your people don't make unless and until they marry. I'm sure he thinks he would have to face me with weapons if he did make you a proposal, so he's not saying anything that would start the fight. Most likely he's trying to find out if you really do love me. If you do then he doesn't have a chance, but if you don't he'll be right here and handy to take my place. I felt you had to know this, to make sure you don't accidentally do anything to encourage him."

"If you think I would encourage someone like him, accidentally or otherwise, you're not very observant, Jiss," I said, letting a small amount of my exasperated confusion through in the look I gave him. "I don't understand anything of how they live in this Realm, don't really want to know, and don't want anything to do with that ephemeral. As far as he'll be concerned, you're the one and only love of my life."

"I'm sure we'll all be better off like that," Jiss said with a smile, reaching over to pat one of my hands again. "And now let's try to understand what the trees were saying. Would you like to start the guesswork?"

"Well, some of it is obvious," I said. "We already know the wagon is fixed but not well, and is moving erratically. That part about the sap flowing slowly in the unrooted who's no longer unsensing—our former companion isn't unconscious, but he hasn't recovered. He's probably still dazed and isn't thinking clearly or moving very well."

"That makes sense," Jiss said with a distracted nod. "If it's true then luck is with us, and I only hope it stays. What about the 'shame-place' they're heading for, and all the rest of that?"

"The shame-place has to be something made of wood," I said, pleased with having gotten that particular point. "The trees think that anyone who takes something without permission is shaming himself, and the people of this Realm take wood without asking. The on-path is going ahead, so the back-line must be the opposite direction, toward us. It's too bad our luck didn't extend to having them decide to turn back."

"They probably decided to go on instead of back because they know this area," he fretted, frowning. "That shame-place of wood is either a large inn or a town, most likely with the facilities to fix the wagon. They knew they couldn't get the repairs done by going back, so they went on. I understood the part about Sahrinth joining you when he could, but there's still one thing I couldn't get. What's a life-blessing, and why are they trying to get to the inn or town before it arrives?"

"That's the part I can't figure out either," I admitted with a headshake of annoyance. "I don't think I've ever heard trees say that before. Maybe it's important to them and the trees, but won't matter to us."

"Because we're not from this Realm?" he said, considering the idea with raised brows. "I suppose it's possible, but I don't think we ought to assume that. There may be a way to ask our new friend without going into details."

"Ask your new friend what?" a voice said with unashamed nosiness, and we both looked up to see that the stranger now rode only a few feet in front of us. "I told you you'd need me, so why not take advantage of the fact that I'm here?"

"Isn't it enough that *one* of us is into taking advantage?" I couldn't help saying, annoyed with myself for having forgotten to keep watching the man. "This was supposed to be a private conversation, and if you try claiming you didn't know, I'm going to find something hard to throw at you."

"Now, Hali, we were just about through anyway," Jiss said. His soothing tone of voice was wasted because of the stranger's arrogant grin. "In all fairness you have to admit our conversation wasn't particularly short, so we can't really blame our friend there for getting impatient. In his place, we probably would have done the same."

"In his place I *didn't* do the same," I contradicted, even more annoyed with Jiss for trying to excuse his new friend's rudeness. "When I decided the conversation you two were having had gone on long enough I didn't ride up and listen, I called to you. But that's because I was taught manners, which he obviously never was."

"At least you don't claim to have been taught *good* manners," the miserable ephemeral returned in a drawl, looking at me over his shoulder. "When I glanced at you two a minute ago I could see you were discussing something that bothered you, so I came back to offer my help again. Taking help is often harder than giving it, but if the person you have to take it from keeps insisting on giving it, that makes it a little easier. Even if one of the two needing that help is badly in need of something else as well."

"Meaning what?" I demanded, ready to argue anything he cared to put forward. I'd met people with a lot of nerve before, including powerful ones like Feledor, but never had I met anyone like that ephemeral.

"Suppose we change subjects before I need a weapon to protect my life," Jiss put in very quickly, holding one hand up to silence the stranger. "I keep ending up between you two even when you aren't to either side of me, and I really don't care to become your war's first casualty."

"You know, you're absolutely right," the stranger said, too quickly for me to get my say in first. "If I were in your position, I'd be short-tempered and unreasonable, too. Why don't we just start over from the beginning, and pretend we're meeting for the first time?"

"Why not?" I said to the grinning idiot, managing to nudge Jiss's comments aside. "And this time *you* can go and fetch the horses—if the job won't tax your intelligence and abilities too far."

"Hali, I told you I wanted a truce," Jiss said in a growl as the stranger finished maneuvering to ride to his left again. "This man is making an effort to be civil, and I expect the same from you. If we spend all our time fighting among ourselves, our enemies can just sit back and let us defeat ourselves. Is that what you want?"

"What I want is him to go his way alone," I pronounced, furious with Jiss for speaking to me in a way that put a shadow of amusement in the stranger's dark eyes. "If you're not prepared to join me in that, don't bother asking again."

With which words I deliberately turned my face from him, letting him know that if he was unhappy with what I'd said so far, he'd have nothing further to listen to. He and his idiot friend could talk to each other, and if I felt the need for conversation I'd talk to the trees again. Who made more sense than that ephemeral did.

"I'm sorry about that," Jiss said to the stranger with a sigh. "As I told you, she isn't used to dealing with people she doesn't know. Starting over sounds like a fine idea to me, and the best way to accomplish that, I think, is for us to introduce ourselves. I'm Jentris, and the lady is Haliand."

"It's a pleasure to finally meet you, Jentris," the stranger said with a chuckle. "I must admit that because of my upbringing I'm most comfortable with formal introductions, but unfortunately I can't reciprocate in full. Even my given name is too familiar to too many people, and to use it would embarrass my family in a way that's entirely unnecessary. For that reason I'm called the Skyhawk, and will usually answer to Skyhawk or even Hawk. The choice of the name wasn't mine, but it's better than being called 'hey, you!' "

"I would say so," Jiss answered with a chuckle. "And I've always believed that it isn't what a man calls himself that's important, it's what he does under the name that counts. I did have a question for you, Skyhawk, and now that we've been properly introduced I can ask it: What can you tell me about any inns or towns along the road we're paralleling?"

"You didn't have to wait until we were introduced to ask that," the stranger responded. "It's not exactly a personal question. There's an inn not too far ahead and a town named Rackford about half a day's ride beyond it, and if you intend to continue following the road, we'll have to push on to the town."

"Why?" Jiss asked, only faintly curious. "The lady and I have been on the move since before dawn, and unless they gave her something in the camp back there, she hasn't had anything to eat or drink in longer than that. For both our sakes I intended to stop at any inn we came to."

"If we stop, we may get more rest than we're prepared to appreciate," the outlaw Skyhawk said, his voice now grimly sober. "When Reff and the others get back to their camp, they'll find out about the escaped captives from the approach guards who helped take you two. Since they were on the perimeter on the other side of camp, I didn't think it was necessary to silence them. Reff will also figure out that you two had help in escaping, which just may convince him he won't be wasting his time trying to get you back. And the first place they'll look is that inn. Which means, of course, that if the weather holds we have no choice but to keep on going to the town."

For a moment Jiss grew silent, obviously considering Skyhawk's words. "You think this Reff is likely to come after us even with all the dead bodies we left behind?" he asked carefully. "You know the man better than I do, of course, but that strikes me as rather strange. And what does the weather have to do with the decision on stopping? Do outlaws make a practice of staying in camp unless the weather is exactly to their liking?"

"In a manner of speaking, that's precisely what they do," the stranger answered, chuckling. "I'll explain that in a minute. But first—under normal circumstances, Reff and the others would *not* try to retake escaped captives. There isn't enough loyalty in him for him to want to avenge the men we killed, and the bodies themselves would be a good argument against tangling with us a second time. The one thing that's very likely to change his mind, though, is what you two look like."

Jiss had no immediate comment on that, but I was curious enough over what the stranger meant to turn my head to look at him. He, in turn, examined Jiss, and all amusement was once more gone from him.

"A man with hair the shade of red yours is would be unusual enough, but your eyes are so oddly light they look more gold than brown," Skyhawk said, his tone suggesting he was listing the good points of a prize animal. "No one looking at you could doubt that the slavers would pay two or three times what they do for a more ordinary man, which means you're worth as much as raiding a small village would bring. On top of that the girl is the most beautiful female I've ever seen, and I've traveled rather widely in my time. That long, pale hair and those green eyes, a body that had every man in camp at attention— she's easily worth double what you are. Stop for a moment and consider what I've said, and then tell me Reff isn't likely to come after you two if he can."

"You've made a point that can't be argued," Jiss said with a sigh, not even glancing in my direction. "If Reff believes what his men tell him, he'll decide to come after us. What they think they can do with me isn't very important, but I can't let them get their hands on Hali. I think the very first thing I have to do is get her back where she belongs, and then go on alone."

"Absolutely not," I stated, ignoring the flash of approval in the stranger's eyes. "Even if I agree to it, what do you think the thieves are going to be doing while you calmly retrace our steps? Taking their ease and waiting for you? You'd be throwing away everything luck has brought us so far, and I won't allow that. Just the way I won't allow myself to be sent home like a burdensome child. I have just as much reason to be here as you do, and it's about time you remembered that."

"Now, Hali, you can't be stubborn about something as important as this," Jiss said, pulling his horse to a stop. "With the thieves ahead of us and the outlaws behind, we could find ourselves trapped; what good will your being there do then? If I take you back I'll be giving the outlaws time to know they've lost us, and at the same time I can get my own horse. He and I can keep going a long time without rest, which means the thieves won't find it possible to maintain their lead. The more I think about it the better the plan sounds. We'll just turn around right here and—"

"No," I said again, kicking my horse to keep him from stopping. "We're only a little more than half a day behind those thieves, and if we keep going we can catch them now. It isn't a guarantee that those outlaws will be coming after us, only a possibility. And I flatly refuse to go back under any circumstances but success. If you're that afraid of what might happen, you go back."

"If you like, Jentris, I'll take her back to wherever you want her to go," the stranger said with heavy annoyance as his horse and Jiss's hurried to catch up to mine. "That would leave you free to go on; you would, of course, have my word that I'd see her there safely or give my life trying. You'd find it easier keeping yourself out of sight without her anyway."

"How wonderful, Jentris, you'd have his *word*," I said as Jiss reached my side. "You could let him hit me over the head, tie me up, then drag me back all alone, secure in the knowledge that he'd given his word about my safety. That should let you go on with nothing but the thieves to worry about."

The expression on Jiss's broad face didn't change even when the stranger growled wordlessly under his breath, but I knew that the idea of sending me back with protection would tempt Jiss, so I'd had to quickly negate the offer. I wouldn't have had to bother if not for that outlaw, which meant I was even more fond of him than I'd been to begin with.

"The girl knows nothing about the value a man puts on his word, Skyhawk, so don't let what she said bother you," Jiss said after the briefest hesitation. "Normally, I would be more than happy to accept your offer of help, but this situation is far from normal. I gave my word to protect her personally. If anyone takes her back, it has to be me."

"Each and every time," I said. "Which means, of course, that even if you took me home, I'd simply leave again as soon as you were gone. If you found me following you and took me home a second time, I'd leave again as soon as you did. Try to remember that I was granted the *right* to be here, which isn't as meaningless to me as it obviously is to you."

"I don't remember you being granted the right to be sold into slavery!" he snapped, reaching over fast to put a big hand on my reins. "This danger is real, not something to be dismissed without a second thought."

"So I *have* to continue on," I finished for him, meeting that golden-eyed air of stubbornness with plenty of my own. "I know you won't like this, Jentris, and I'm sorry I have to say it out loud, but our mission is too important to mess up simply in an effort to spare your feelings. I'm also here to protect *you*, just the way I did when we left that cave this morning, and you can't deny you need that protection even if it embarrasses you. It's *my* protection you need, not his, not when knowing where we're going isn't half as important as being able to do what's necessary when we get there. If I go back we just might lose, and what we're doing happens to be more important than I am."

When I had it all said I just sat there waiting for him to get angry, but the expression on his face wasn't one of anger. He looked gently bothered, very frustrated, and completely incapable of immediate answer, but he didn't look angry. His friend the outlaw seemed very surprised for some reason, but a bare glance was all the attention I cared to spend on him. A cool, unexpectedly uncomfortable breeze had grown up there beneath the trees, and that was what I had to ignore as I waited for Jiss to respond.

"Hali, I'm not sure about how to answer you," he said after another moment, his sigh more than clear. "I want you to know that I very much appreciate your willingness to protect me, and your decision that our mission is more important than you are. Being ready to sacrifice yourself for the greater good is one of the most noble outlooks a human being can have, but sometimes the sacrifice just isn't necessary."

"How can you say it's unnecessary?" I demanded, immediately outraged, but he held up a calming hand, silencing me.

"I said *sometimes* the sacrifice is unnecessary," he corrected, his voice and expression sympathetic and soothing. "If there's no other choice than to put yourself in danger then you do it, but doing it when there is another choice turns a noble act into a meaningless gesture. Only *one* of us has to go on no matter what, and that one of us is me. Not having your protection will be a great loss, but I will survive because I have to. What *you* have to do is go back to where you'll be safe even if you don't want to be, to leave me free to do as we both know I must."

Of course I began arguing with him, trying to make him understand that he could *not* get along without me, but an unexpected interruption came. The stranger hadn't said anything at all for a while, but suddenly he held out a hand and made a sound that silenced both Jiss and me.

"Be quiet, both of you," he ordered softly, his head up and cocked to one side as though he were listening to something. "I could have sworn— Just give me a minute, and try not to make any noise at all."

At first I couldn't understand what he thought he was doing, but then I heard what the trees were saying. It wasn't the stiffening breeze that was causing their agitation, it was the warning being passed along from another part of the forest. Those who lived in the area where trees dreamed unwillingly had spread out from that area in numbers, and now were moving toward us. The trees were worried that some of them would be cruelly cut or broken and that fires would be lit, but those two things weren't precisely our concern.

Our biggest problem seemed to be that the outlaws had already begun searching for us, and they weren't very far away.

Chapter 5

"ALL RIGHT, NOW we have to move fast as well as silently, but at least we don't have far to go," Skyhawk said briskly, gathering up his reins. "Follow me. Reff and his men are in the forest, and none of us will get a polite thank-you if we help them find us."

I was tempted to ask him how *he* knew the outlaws were after us, but unfortunately he was right about making unnecessary noise. As Jiss gestured to me to ride directly behind our own outlaw, who had already begun moving, I decided to put the question away for a more appropriate time, and simply followed.

Only the sound of hoofbeats accompanied us through the forest, and those were muffled to an extent by patches of thick grass and fallen needles. Skyhawk seemed to know exactly where he was going and the best way to get there. We rode for several minutes, still paralleling the road but farther from it, and then the stranger slowed and abruptly stopped to dismount.

As soon as I pulled up behind his bay, I could see the tangled wall of thorns directly in our path. It was the kind of area even the animals of the forest avoided, but the stranger wasn't that smart. Pulling on a pair of leather gloves, he strode right up to the thorns, then reached into the middle of the wall. Very carefully he pulled back on the thorns, and abruptly there was an opening into and through the tangle that looked wide enough even for our horses.

"Well, what are you waiting for?" the outlaw hissed after he had set the section of wall to one side of the opening. "Get off those horses and get in there, so I can do the same and close it again."

Jiss made a sound of self-annoyance and immediately dismounted, with me not far behind him but without the same sound. I found it much more pleasant being annoyed at the stranger, whose abrasive manner was enough to annoy living rock. If there was a pleasant way to say something and a nasty way, Skyhawk seemed destined to always choose the nasty.

Jiss led his horse through the opening in the thorns, and after he was well out of the way I followed with my own mount. The brown geldings seemed indifferent to where they were being led, and I wished I could have said the same. I've never liked thorn catches, not even from a distance, and not only because they mutter among themselves and refuse to speak to anyone else, including the trees. Thorn vines are mean, through and through, and always try to hurt anyone or anything coming near them. They didn't have much chance at my draperies as I walked the aisle cleared in the middle of their catch, but that doesn't mean they didn't try.

I could see the slope in the ground when Jiss's horse began going down it, and a moment later I was going down the same way. From the outside, the catch had seemed to spread uninterrupted for quite a way in all directions, but after little more than fifteen feet the ground fell away into a depression that the vines didn't seem interested in filling. Jiss led his horse into the depression and I followed with mine, but there was still plenty of room for the stranger and his bay. The bottom of the gullylike depression was broad and flat, easy for standing or sitting on and deep enough to hide the horses from outside observation.

The stranger brought his bay down and left him with us, hurried back up the slope, and disappeared for a few moments. When he came back he moved quickly down the slope, then grinned at Jiss and me.

"Now they can search all they like," he said quietly, his gloved fists on his hips. "I prepared this place against emergencies a long time ago, and since then have only had to maintain it. Once they've given up and left the area, we can be on our way in peace."

"And how long do you think that will take?" I asked, refraining from looking around at the muttering vines above us and from rubbing my arms against the growing chill. "If anyone knows how outlaws do things, you're certainly the one."

"Well, of course I am," he answered with a pleasant smile. "There's no denying I was an outlaw for a while, so who would know better than me?"

"Maybe that's a topic we ought to take a couple of minutes to discuss," Jiss said, sounding more serious than conciliatory. "We appreciate what you did for us, Skyhawk, but nothing you've said so far tells us why you were in that outlaw camp to begin with. I'll admit I've been wondering how you came to be so handily available."

The stranger looked from one to the other of us, started to say something, then shook his head.

"Okay, no more stories like the last one," he said, as serious as Jiss. "My popping up out of nowhere does need explaining, and with more than a passing word or two. The truth of the matter is I've been riding this area for years, and my family didn't throw me out, I ran away. My father approves of the way people are treated and I don't, so I took off on my own."

"To do what?" Jiss asked, but gently. "Embarrass them into listening to you?"

"If they were going to listen, they would have done it years ago," the stranger said with a shake of his head. "They know I won't use the family name because I'm the one who's ashamed, so they just keep going their merry way, squeezing everything they can out of the helpless. I've been doing everything I can to counter them, but it isn't easy. They have more wealth and power than most people would believe.''

"So you ride around helping people," Jiss said with a thoughtful nod. "Did you think you could do a better job of it by joining the outlaws?"

"I'm not *that* naïve," the stranger answered, his short laugh harsh. "Reff was the one who decided I should be recruited into his outlaw gang, to give them better pickings. People around here trust me, and will tell me things they won't tell anyone else. Reff thought he could use me to find out where any valuables might be hidden, and told me I could join his bunch or be run down and have my throat cut. I pretended to go along with him while I got this place ready again—I started preparing it a long time ago, in case my father sent his guardsmen out after me— and was just about up to giving Reff my answer by disappearing. That was when you two showed up, so I took the time to free you. I couldn't very well just leave you there, not and continue to tell myself I wasn't anything like my father. Is that so hard to understand?"

"No," Jiss answered with a warm smile. "That's not hard to understand at all. Is it, Hali?"

Jiss seemed very impressed by what he'd heard, but I couldn't quite say the same for myself. This second story had come off a lot more sincere than the first one had, but there was nothing to prove it wasn't just that: another story. Since I already knew I was there to protect Jiss, I could see I would have to be the one to be skeptical of what we were told. If I left it to Jiss, that outlaw would be able to turn on us anytime he pleased. Which I was still far from convinced he wouldn't do in any case.

"You still haven't told us how long it will take the outlaws to give up on looking for us," I pointed out instead of agreeing with Jiss. "Weren't you with them long enough to learn at least that?"

"How long they take will depend on how long the weather holds, which shouldn't be much longer," the outlaw said after the briefest hesitation, as though disappointed he hadn't convinced me as easily as Jiss. He also seemed to want to say something else as well, but then he changed his mind and added, "Why don't we all sit down and be comfortable while we wait?"

He gestured toward the flat, pebbled ground and then folded down on it, making no effort to see if the rest of us were prepared to go along with the suggestion. Jiss didn't even glance at me as he joined his friend, but he did look around at what he was sitting on.

"The horses won't enjoy the lack of grass in this place," he remarked, lifting a handful of dirt and stones. "Do you have any idea why this depression is so barren?"

"I think there used to be a pool of poisoned water here," the stranger answered, picking up a pebble of his own to play with. "Water like that ruins the ground for quite a distance around its location, which is probably why only the thorn vines grow close. They can stand it more easily than other vegetation, but even they can't live in the bed of the pool. Aren't you going to sit with us, Hali?"

"I don't feel like sitting down," I answered, suddenly annoyed that the man would talk to me that way, as though he'd fooled me as well as Jiss. "And don't call me Hali. To you, I'm Lady Haliand."

"Oh, I do beg your pardon, my lady," he said as I turned away from him, definite mockery in his tone. "It wasn't my intention to be guilty of familiarity with a noble of your obviously high station. I do hope you'll forgive me, and will defer the lashing due me for such presumption. I'll try not to let it happen again."

"Of course you will" was all I said as I walked away from him and Jiss, not even bothering to give my antagonist a last glance. It was getting darker and colder even in the shelter of the thorn catch. I was very hungry and thirsty and tired, and was beginning to be seriously worried about Greaf. The longer we sat there doing nothing, the farther away the thieves were getting. If the gap became wide enough we might never catch them, at least not until they got where they were going. The Great Flame might be stolen but it couldn't be harmed, while Greaf—

"Hali, are you all right?" Jiss's voice came softly and

suddenly from behind me, his hands touching my upper
arms in the same way. "I don't want you worrying about
those brigands out there, not even for a moment. I won't
let them take you again, and I certainly won't let them hurt
you. That's a promise I'm making you, and when you get
to know me better you'll learn I always keep my promises."

"I believe you, Jiss," I said just as softly, leaning back
against him as I closed my eyes, trying to get more of the
warmth I could feel in the big hands still on my arms. "I
was thinking about Greaf, and what they might do if they
find him with the Great Flame. He's a fairly hard life form
to hurt, but that doesn't mean it can't be done. We've got
to get out of here and after them again, we just have to!"

"We will, Hali, we will," he immediately assured me,
his tone soothing as his grip tightened just a little. "Try to
remember that Greaf isn't alone, not with Sahrinth following just behind. I'll get him *and* the Flame back, that's
another thing I promise."

"Jiss, *we* have to get them back," I said intensely,
turning to put my hands to his chest as I looked up directly
into his eyes. "If it wasn't necessary for me to be here, the
Scales would never have agreed to my going in the first
place. I couldn't say that with *him* listening, but now I can
and you know it's the truth. If you try taking me back,
we'll never save either of them."

"But, Hali, it's so dangerous," he said with real concern, his words, like mine, intense despite their lack of
volume, his arms coming up to circle me. "Skyhawk
wasn't lying about the way you affect men, and if the
wrong people get their hands on you they'll hurt you very
badly. I promised to keep you safe, but the longer you stay
in this Realm the harder it will be for me to keep that
promise."

"Is a guarantee of my safety more important than recov-
ering the Great Flame, Jiss?" I asked with all the sobriety
I'd learned to show when I'd needed to defend myself to
my mother. "If you can say yes and really mean it, then
I'll go back without another word of argument. And I'm
sure you realize I'll have to go back alone. You can't spare

the time to take me, and I won't have that outlaw with me no matter how many solemn words he gives. I don't trust him not to sell me to the first slavers he can find, and you can't afford to trust him that way either. Can you?''

The two questions silenced him, just as I'd known they would. In battle, always attack to the weak side, I'd been taught, which seemed so obvious I'd wondered why they'd bothered mentioning it. It had taken a while to understand that many people had trouble finding the weak side, not to mention knowing one was almost always there. I'd practiced attacking to the weak side for quite a few years, and because of that had become rather adept.

Jiss's gaze turned inward while he considered how to counter my arguments without lying, so I moved closer to him and rested my cheek against his chest. He was so delightfully warm, especially with his arms around me, that I had no desire to move away again. I just stood there quietly, waiting for him to come to the only decision he could.

"Excuse me for intruding, Jentris, but this would be a good time for us to discuss what we'll do once we leave here," the stranger said, his approach having been so silent that neither of us had heard him. "If we're taking the girl back to her home, I have to know where it is before I can decide on the best way to get there."

"We won't be taking her back, Skyhawk," Jiss answered with a sigh, causing his friend to look somewhat surprised. "It may be dangerous for her to stay with me, but she convinced me she would, ah, suffer if we were separated. We'll just have to make sure she isn't seen and taken by the wrong people."

"The decision is yours, of course," the outlaw said with a shrug. He seemed annoyed by the smile of triumph I wasn't quite showing. "If she were mine I would rather have her suffer from separation than slavery, and would take her home even if I had to carry her kicking and screaming over my shoulder. Some women don't have enough sense to know what's good for them, and it's up to their men to decide things for them. Since I'll be helping you anyway it doesn't matter to me, but I hope you don't find yourself regretting the choice.''

He gave Jiss a comradely smile and began turning away, very likely missing the way Jiss also turned, to put himself between me and that miserable outlaw. I wasn't sure how Jiss knew I was about to tell that ephemeral exactly how much I thought his opinions were worth, and it's possible Jiss didn't know. As he moved he tightened his arms around me, and then his lips were next to my ear.

"Since we're supposed to be lovers, I think it's time we showed some evidence of it," he murmured, holding me close against his very warm body. "Instead of snapping at me you're going to give me a kiss, which I hope will convince Skyhawk we really can't bear to be separated. If you intend staying you have to do your part—unless you don't know how to kiss a man."

"Don't be ridiculous," I whispered, glad he couldn't see the flush in my cheeks. "Of course I know how to kiss."

"I'm glad to hear that," he answered in the same murmur, sounding amused. "I don't have to tell you, then, that the first step is for you to raise your face to me."

Since I'd been whispering into his chest, his last comment increased the warmth in my cheeks to a point that was very uncomfortable. He was teasing me on purpose, but I wasn't about to give him an excuse to talk about taking me home again. With resolution, then, I raised my face to him, ignored the smile that brightened his eyes and curved his lips, and then . . .

And then he lowered his head and kissed me. It wasn't the first kiss I'd ever had, or even the second or third, but somehow it felt different from anything I'd ever experienced. His lips were so warm and sure, touching mine gently at first, then with more and more strength and attention. One of his hands was on my hair and the other held me tight against him with its place in the middle of my back, and I could feel his warmth and strength with all of my body, not just the hands I had pressed to his chest.

His heat passed through his lips and into me, making me want to get even closer, making me join in the kiss I was getting. Jiss was the first *man* I'd ever kissed, and I could feel the tingling difference racing up and down through me.

I paid no attention whatsoever to the passing time, but it couldn't have been very long before an annoying noise began to intrude. It took a moment to identify the noise as throat clearing, which meant the intrusion was being caused by that stranger; although I was more than ready to ignore him, Jiss slowly but deliberately let the kiss end. Then he turned his head toward the intruder.

"I seem to be developing the habit of interrupting, Jentris," the stranger said, looking more amused than sorry. "I apologize again, of course, but this interruption is necessary. We should be able to leave here in a relatively short while."

"We can leave?" Jiss said with sudden eagerness, letting me go.

Suddenly I became aware of a different distraction. Drops of something were falling on me, apparently out of the empty air. I looked up to see nothing that would account for the phenomenon, but even as I looked the fall grew heavier, quickly beginning to soak me and my companions and everything around us. Whatever was happening I knew I didn't like it, but the stranger seemed delighted.

"Now that the storm has begun, we can leave as soon as Reff and the others have had time to pull out of the area," Skyhawk told Jiss, a grin on his soon-to-be-streaming face. "You asked if the outlaws made a practice of staying in camp if the weather wasn't to their liking, and I said yes but didn't explain the attitude. Now I have the time to explain, so here it is: Every once in a while, when outlaw raids get to be too annoying and costly, the High families in this area get together and hire trackers. The trackers lead a large number of professional guardsmen from the various households, and if they manage to locate the outlaw camp not many outlaws are left to talk about it afterward. That's why Reff and most of the others were gone, in an effort to lead the trackers as far away from their camp as possible.''

"Wait a minute, I think I understand," Jiss said, using one big hand to push back a dripping lock of hair. "If they stay out in a storm like this and miscalculate how long the storm will last, they could leave tracks in the mud that will lead their enemies right to them. Either they go back to camp fast and let the rain wipe out their tracks, or they can't go back except in small groups that all take different approaches.''

"And the more small groups they break into, the more likely one of them will be found by the trackers," the stranger said, nodding as he ignored the unbelievable amount of water pouring down on him. "If even one of those groups is taken or followed, the camp and almost everyone in it are done for. You have to be able to tell the guardsmen with the trackers exactly who you are and where you come from, and if they have any reason to disbelieve you they'll use torture to learn the truth. Which means, of course, that we have to avoid them too, if at all possible. For that reason I've decided the inn is the best place for us to go.''

"I thought you said we *couldn't* go to the inn," Jiss responded, and I wondered if his narrowed eyes were indications of suspicion or the presence of too much water. "Why is it suddenly the answer to all our problems?''

"It's only the answer to one of our problems, not all of them," the stranger replied. His explanations were still as smooth and easy as a slide across cave ice. "Before the storm, Reff and his bunch were guaranteed to check the inn to see if we were there. Now they won't have the time—and they would never consider doing it even with all the time there was. Only strangers will stop at that inn during a storm, and for their own sakes they'd better not be outlaws.''

"I may be the cause of all of us drowning by saying this, but I'll need a few more details before I understand what you're talking about," Jiss said, trying to wipe the torrent from his face with an equally wet hand. For my own part I'd been noticing distant rumbling sounds, and there seemed to be flashes of light appearing high above. I stood there with water pouring down on me, telling myself I hated the thing called storm, but it was more than that. I'd never seen anything like it before, and if Greaf hadn't needed me to be strong and brave, I might have begun to be frightened.

"During storms like this one, that inn is haunted," the stranger said, his grin not far from being a grimace. "There was a raid on it once, years ago, and innocent people were killed. The raid took place during a storm, and a year later, when new people reopened the inn, Reff's predecessor decided to try the same thing again. He sent five of his people in to pretend to be travelers, to find out who had what before the raid took place, but the attack never came off. His five men were found by the outlaw sent in to call them out before the raid, all of them horribly murdered and mutilated. When the leader heard about it he stormed inside with his three killer bodyguards to discover who had done it, not noticing that the rest of his followers were too frightened to go in with him. Those waiting heard screams of terror—from the guilty, they thought—and then there was nothing but silence. It took them a few minutes to realize the screams had come from their leader and his bodyguards, and that they weren't coming back; a minute later they were racing back to their camp as fast as they could ride. Every few years someone doubts the story and volunteers to spend a stormy night at the inn checking to see if a raid's worthwhile, but none of them have ever come back with an answer. Most of the men in the camp would rather be hanged than go anywhere near it."

"I can understand why," Jiss said in an odd voice, his left hand on his sword hilt. "I've heard of things like that before, but I've never been in a position to see it for myself. Considering how safe the inn must be for honest travelers, I expect it's packed full in weather like this."

"Not exactly," the stranger said, appearing slightly uncomfortable. "Local people prefer to avoid the place even if they're honest, and that goes for the guardsmen riding with the trackers as well. Since some of them weren't guardsmen all their lives I can't blame them, but that means the inn is the one place you and the girl can rest for a while without worrying. We'll stay only long enough for you two to get something to eat and a little sleep, and then we'll move on.''

"When you say 'we,' do you mean all three of us?" Jiss asked, frowning. "If outlaws don't live to leave that place again, and even former outlaws don't care to take the chance of going near it, you obviously can't go in with us. If you think I'm going to relax where it's warm and dry, while you wait outside with rain dripping down the back of your neck—"

"No, Jentris, you misunderstand," the stranger said warmly, stepping forward to put a hand to Jiss's shoulder. "I appreciate your concern for me, but I'll be inside with you. Since I never became an outlaw voluntarily, I firmly believe the inn won't be a danger to me. And now I think it's time I went to see if we can be on our way."

He gave Jiss's shoulder a final slap of friendship, then turned away to climb out of the depression. Jiss watched him until he disappeared over the top, apparently not reassured, but I had better things to do than worry about an outlaw. The depression already had enough water in its bottom to cover my feet, and on top of that there was something I'd been wanting to ask, and now finally could.

"Jiss, what does haunted mean?" I asked in a whisper when I'd sloshed over to him, putting my hand to his arm. I was colder than I'd been before the water falling had started, and really would have enjoyed being held by him again.

"Haunted means—having the spirits of the dead remain where they were while they were living," he answered, pulling himself away from his thoughts to turn and look down at me. "People in your Realm and mine cease living when they feel themselves ready to go on to the next form of existence, but these people don't have the same choice. Their lives are terribly short even when they live them to the end, and all too often they aren't allowed to live even that long. When they're ended before they should be, usually by murder, their spirits sometimes remain after their bodies are gone. The spirits in this case seem to be the vengeful sort, but it's nothing for you to worry about. They certainly won't be going after us.''

He reached out then and did put his arms around me, but what he'd told me took all the pleasure out of the gesture. Spirits of the dead, staying around to avenge the murder of their bodies? And we were going into that place with the sort of someone they tended to choose as a victim? I shuddered in Jiss's arms, knowing I had to go inside the inn if I was going to protect him the way I was supposed to, but I liked that necessity even less than the water falling with its noise and light.

''And at least now we know what the trees were telling you,'' Jiss said, holding me more tightly. ''The life-blessing they said was on the way was this rainstorm, something we should have guessed sooner. Water is one of the things trees need for life, so they would certainly consider rain a blessing.''

''I don't know how *I* was supposed to see that sooner,'' I replied. ''I've never seen anything like this in my entire life, and I hope I'll never see it again. They may have water falling out of the skies in *your* Realm, but I can't imagine my mother ever allowing something this awful where we live.''

''Well, we don't have rain like this in my Realm either,'' Jiss admitted. ''I've experienced it before here, though, and after a while you get used to it. In a way. Just think about how good it will feel to get out of it, and then you might not mind it as much. They don't have people with talents, Hali, so we have to make allowances.''

I was too wet and miserable to want to make allowances, but I was also too wet and miserable to argue. It might have been true that there were people in my mother's Realm who had the talent to see that it never rained on people, only on vegetation, but that didn't mean I liked what was happening. Where I came from rain was practically a fairy tale, and I would have been happier keeping it like that.

We waited in silence until the stranger came back to say he'd opened the thorn wall again, and then we got our horses and followed him out.

Riding through a dripping forest in sopping wet draperies on a very hard leather saddle isn't an experience I would heartily recommend to those who haven't tried it. It was dim rather than dark, chilly cold rather than comfortably cool, silent beyond the sound of falling water, without sign of life other than ours. I had never experienced a forest so alien and unsharing, where even the trees were wrapped up in a wordless song of welcome to the life-essence that precluded all conversation. We moved so slowly that the misery was doubled if not tripled, and for the first time it came to me to wonder if I wouldn't have been wiser staying home.

But, of course, I couldn't have stayed home, I told myself with a sigh, feeling as though my weight had doubled because of the amount of water in my hair. I had to be there to save Greaf, and Jiss needed my protection if he was to recover the Great Flame. Uncomfortable or not, miserable or not, I couldn't simply decide I hated that Realm and wanted to go home.

Even though I was beginning to wish I could.

It couldn't have taken all that long to reach the large house that was undoubtedly the inn about which we'd heard so much, but by the time we dismounted in the big connecting stable it felt as though ages had passed. Once we were under a roof the water had stopped falling on us, but that still left us drenched to the skin and me, at least, flinching every time the overcast skies rumbled menacingly. A slow, bent man with grayish hair and beard appeared out of nowhere to take our horses, and his eyes never really touched any of us. He gathered our reins in a gnarled and spotted hand, accepted the metal coin the outlaw gave him without a word of acknowledgment, then led our mounts away. I stood there staring after him, wondering what was wrong with him and why someone didn't fix it, and then Jiss was right beside me.

"Hali, I've given Skyhawk some of the gold coins they'll accept in this Realm," he told me very softly as he put an arm around my shoulders. "It was our good luck that the outlaws hadn't gotten around to searching me, so they never found my gold. He's going to get us three rooms and all we can eat and drink, and after that we'll sleep for a while. We intend to leave here as soon as the storm is over, but in the meantime we'll let him do the ordering and negotiating."

"He'll hate that," I said as I let the arm around me urge me after the stranger who, carrying a pair of saddle-bags, was already near a door that presumably led into the inn. "Giving all the orders, I mean. And I don't think I'm thirsty any longer."

"Now, Hali, you'll soon be dry so I want you to cheer up," Jiss said, trying to sound stern, but in a kindly way. "You're going to be as pleasant as I know you can be, and there aren't going to be any more arguments with Skyhawk. When you have to travel with someone, bickering makes the trip longer and harder."

"I'm not the one who thinks we *have* to travel with that man," I answered with a shrug, making no effort to meet his golden eyes. "If he tries to order me around again, you can expect a lot more than bickering. I don't like him as well as you seem to, so we'll have to settle for you being sweet enough for the both of us."

By then we were passing through the door and into a room that seemed dimmer than the stable, despite the fire blazing in a large hearth in the opposite wall. To the right were double wooden doors that didn't look particularly heavy, most likely the doors we would have come through if we hadn't ridden into the stable, and to the left was a long counter with a thin man behind it. Nothing in the way of furnishings was visible, not even a painting on the tessellated wooden walls, and the sound of Skyhawk's voice broke a silence that was heavier and yet more delicate than the one we'd ridden through in the forest.

"I bid you a goodday, sir," he said to the man behind the counter, his cheerful friendliness about as well accepted as it would have been by me. "My friends and I would like three rooms, and we'll also take a meal in your fine establishment as soon as we're no longer dripping all over your floors."

"The rooms we have, an' the meal'll be cooked," the thin man replied softly, his eyes on Skyhawk. "This's a fine inn t' stop at—f'r some. Payment in advance by th' day 'r night, dependin' on how long you mean t'stay. Baths 'n girls extra over th' price a th' room, same as th' meals."

"We'll take the rooms and order the meals, and work our way from there," Skyhawk said, his left arm curled around the saddlebags now draped over his shoulder. "We'll probably ask for the baths, but I think we'll want to get dry before we're ready to get wet again. As for the girls, even if we decide to be interested, at most we'll only be needing two of them."

At that point the man's face turned toward Jiss and me, and despite the fact that we were standing in moderately deep shadow I had the feeling he could see us as well as I saw him. He reached to his right, raised a small bronze bell and rang it, then set the bell down again. By putting it down he also silenced it, but somehow I could both hear and feel the bell still ringing elsewhere in the house. Then he turned back to Skyhawk and put his hand out, and a discussion of prices began.

"That's called haggling," Jiss said to me in a murmur, his arm still around my shoulders. "It isn't considered proper to accept the first price offered, but I hope they don't drag it out too long. I feel wetter now than I did while we were still being rained on, and I'd like to get out of these clothes. I can dry them once I'm dry, but I can't get dry until I'm out of them. You know, that man behind the counter has skin almost as pale as yours."

Since I'd already noticed that I didn't say anything, but I couldn't help feeling bothered. Judging by the Earth Realm people I'd already seen, they tended to be darker skinned than anyone in my own Realm, although they weren't quite as dark as Jiss. Looking at the man behind the counter reminded me of what haunted meant, and also reminded me of the dead bodies I'd seen earlier that day. I discovered then that I wasn't enjoying being in out of the water falling as much as I should have done, which came as no surprise whatsoever.

The haggling took less time than it could have, and Skyhawk came away from the counter looking pleased. The man behind the counter just stood there, looking neither pleased nor displeased, but the third of our party was too unconcerned to find that disturbing.

"We're all set, so let's go find our rooms," he said to Jiss and me, holding up three keys with round metal tags attached to them. "I don't expect them to be the best we've ever seen, but they'll be dry and warm and aren't costing us everything we have. That gold piece is covering the rooms, the meals, baths, oats for the horses, and as much ale as we care to drink. Not knowing what plans you had I didn't include anything about the girls, but if the night gets too chilly we can always change that. Meanwhile, we go this way."

He turned again and walked to the right of the counter, where a door stood silent in the shadows blanketing the wall. As we passed, the thin man at the counter followed us with his dark, deep-set eyes, a wordless inspection that sent tiny tremors skittering through the wetness on my skin. There was a chill in that place, but not one that being dry would chase away.

The door brought us into another large room, but this one wasn't empty. Another fire blazed in a wide hearth, but this one was on the wall to the right of the doorway we passed through. A neat arrangement of tables and chairs broke up the expanse of the polished wood floor, but the tables were bare, the chairs unpainted and ancient looking, and there weren't enough of either to give the room the feeling of being really filled. Possibly half a dozen people sat at some of the tables, two men together and the rest by themselves, but none of them sat near the long windows filling most of the wall opposite our entrance. The windows were curtained but not yet draped, and the rain beat against them in a way that negated the warmth of the fire. A few lamps had been lit, but mostly by the doors in the left-hand wall and the area surrounding the wide staircase there.

"Our rooms are on the second floor, but this is where we'll be taking our meal," the outlaw told Jiss and me, gesturing at the room before continuing toward the stairs. "By the time we're dry the food should be ready, and the ale will certainly be. I don't know about you two, but that's what I'm looking forward to."

He grinned again and began climbing the stairs, but I couldn't help noticing that even *his* voice wasn't as loud as it had been. If there had been any conversation among the people in the dining hall, it had stopped at our appearance and didn't resume again even as we followed our guide up the stairs. I raised the skirt of my water-heavy draperies with both hands as we climbed, and spent no time wondering if anyone spoke normally in that place. The house didn't seem to *want* anything of the normal, and the people in it obviously knew that.

The next floor of the house spread out a short distance ahead of us to the foot of another stairway, but also curved around to the right and behind the stairs we had just come up. Jiss and I waited while Skyhawk checked door numbers, then we followed again around to the right and up the hall. The further away from the stairs we went the darker it became, and then Skyhawk stopped to peer closely up at a door number.

"This is the first of them, I think," he said, sounding faintly annoyed. "I don't expect them to hang lamps enough to rival the sun, but a single candle on the wall down there doesn't help much when you have to read numbers."

"That number is thirteen," I supplied. The candlelight was more than adequate for my sight. "If you couldn't see where you were going, you should have told us."

"I didn't know you could do better," he answered,

separating the keys he held rather than turning to look at me. "If I were you I'd have me well whipped later, to teach me not to repeat such mindless oversights. If this is room thirteen, then it's the second of our rooms rather than the first. Why don't you go down and take number fourteen, Jentris, and I'll go back for number twelve. Your lady can have this one, which will put us to either side of her."

"That's a good idea," Jiss said before I could find a basis for disagreement, any basis just for the sake of disagreement. Everything that outlaw said made me want to disagree with him, but being soaking wet apparently affects the creative process. No logical-sounding reason for refusing came to me, and then the door was unlocked and being swung inward. By then the opportunity had passed into the next life, so I gave it up by leaving Jiss and walking silently into the waiting room.

The waiting and somehow expectant room. I looked around as I closed the door—hopefully in the outlaw's face—and the scene shown by the wall lamps seemed to have a double personality. Outwardly the room was larger and better furnished than I had expected, with a fireplace, a big bed set on an intricate floor weaving, two stuffed chairs, a settle that matched the chairs, paintings on two of the walls, a washstand with ewer and basin, a mirrored wardrobe—all of it painfully neat despite the toll taken from color and shape by the passage of time. The curtains and drapes on the long windows were the same, and so was the bedcover, and the lace furniture protectors, and the weaving the bed stood on—

Outwardly neat but achingly hungry on the inside. Quiet and well behaved and precisely in place, much like the way a predator is just before it attacks. I could feel the sense of waiting where I stood, still right in front of the door, wondering if my next step deeper into the room would be my last. I stood dripping on the polished wooden floor, searching for the source of the hunger, trying to locate the heart of it, just short of trembling at the thought that I would—

And then it was gone. Just the way pulling the windows shut would have closed out the falling water, just that quickly and abruptly was the sense of hunger shut off, beyond the point of my being able to feel it. The room was no more than a neat, shabby room, and I was standing backed against a door for no reason at all.

"Unless it's only pretending to be harmless," I muttered to myself, still looking around for . . . I hadn't the faintest idea what. If the ceiling had grown teeth or the furniture claws I probably would have felt better, but neither of those things happened. It all just stood or lay there, continuing to be harmless, which meant I became aware again of just how wet I was.

"I have to get out of these things," I muttered a second time, the sound of my own voice helping to settle me down. It was possible my first impressions of the room had been nothing more than imagination, so unless or until it happened again, I would ignore it. In the meantime it could only help if I got myself dry.

The logic to that line of reasoning might not have been sound, but at least it got me moving away from the door and toward the washstand. The bed stood out from the wall to the left, opposite the fireplace to the right, and the washstand was positioned between the bed and the wardrobe, also to the left. I circled the bed to the right and reached the stand, saw that a thick, dry towel was folded next to the empty basin, and didn't wait a moment longer.

Stripping off my sodden draperies was pure pleasure, and once they lay in a puddled heap I used the towel to rub some warmth back into my body. My sandals had come off right after the draperies, so once my body was reasonably dry I was able to walk to the fireplace without leaving large, wet footprints behind me. I had left drying my hair for last, and knew I would need the help of the fire if it was ever to get done.

I used the towel to blot as much of the droplets from my hair as possible, then pulled the mass of soggy hair over my right shoulder and stood with that side to the fire as I stared out one of the windows. Using the towel to rub at the strands was something I could do without thinking, and as I watched shadows of the rain crash against the window I considered something that did need thinking about. Sahrinth was supposed to come and find me and tell me what was happening as soon as he could, but with that storm going on and on, it would be a while before I saw him. Sahrinth didn't dissolve in the presence of water, but he did dissipate to the point where he couldn't draw himself together again until the water was gone. Being made of mist had its drawbacks as well as benefits, and that gave me something else to worry about.

"I don't think I've ever seen hair quite that long before," a voice said suddenly from behind me, a voice I had in no manner been expecting to hear. I dropped the towel—and the hair as well—and whirled around without thinking, and Skyhawk's grin widened as he looked at me. The door was closed behind him, he had changed into dry trousers and shirt, and he stood with a bundle of something cradled in his left arm.

"Who told you you could just walk in here?" I demanded, for the first time in many years feeling embarrassment over being seen without clothing. "How dare you barge in and— And how did you get in here?"

"The door was unlocked because you forgot to take your key," he said, holding up the item in question without moving his eyes from me. "And as for barging in, you can't possibly consider this an intrusion. Slaves are required to come and go as their duties take them, without stopping to ask for permission the way the free do out of courtesy. Slaves aren't allowed to knock before entering, and since you've been treating me like a slave ever since we met, I didn't think you'd mind my walking right in just like any other slave."

"Since I've never had any slaves, I don't know as much about them as you seem to," I returned in a not-quite-steady voice, finding it impossible not to spread my wet hair like a blanket over the front of me. His dark-eyed stare made me feel naked rather than simply unclothed, and I wished Jiss were there to stand behind. The stranger wasn't as large as Prince Jentris of the Sun Realm, but he was far larger than the other ephemerals I'd seen and I didn't trust him. I wasn't afraid of him, of course, not the way I'd been of Jiss when I'd first met him, but that was because Jiss was real and whole. Earth ephemerals were neither, a fact that helped me stand up to the one who was trying to violate my privacy.

"Slaves are also something I never intend to have," I continued to the brute, raising my chin just a little. "If I ever did have a slave like you, though, I wouldn't wait to sell him, I'd give him away to the first person silly enough to accept the gift. I didn't mean to treat you like a slave, I meant to treat you like the intrusive boor you are, and if my intentions fell short of the mark you have my apologies. Now you can get out of here the same way you came in—like a sneak."

"You know, there's one part of your bratty, abrasive personality that I'm forced to admire," he said, the words deliberately calm over the anger I could see in his eyes. "When you have something to say you say it, without caring what might happen to you because of it. You obviously believe speaking the truth as you see it is more important than whatever consequences might come, and most people don't have the courage for that. Personally, I find the practice offensive, but I do admire your courage. I brought these clothes for you to wear, at least until yours are dry, and now I *will* get out."

He threw the bundle to the floor at my feet, sent the key after the bundle, then turned toward the door. He strode the few steps, reached for the knob, then stopped as though he'd remembered something and turned to look at me again.

"I didn't intend to say this, but since you think so much of the truth I'm sure you won't mind," he told me, his gaze as sober and steady as it had been for the last minute or two. "If you intend keeping Jentris interested in you, you'd better start treating him better than you've been doing. The way he says, 'Now, Hali,' tells me he has lots of experience in soothing that temper of yours, but I can also hear the growing exasperation in the words. One of these days he'll find he's tired of repeating himself, and shortly after that you'll look around to find him gone. If you don't learn to behave yourself, you might have to learn instead how to live alone. And in case you're wondering, I'm telling you this for his sake, not yours.''

His speech completed he finished opening the door, went through it, then pulled it shut behind him, leaving me to stare silently at where he'd been. Over the years I'd met many strange life forms, but none of them had been half as strange as the ephemeral who called himself Skyhawk. The man had come to bring me clothing, but instead of simply saying that, he used the occasion to start another argument. And then, after he finally got around to the real reason for being in my room, he stood there and lectured me about the way I treated Jiss!

I shook my head at the closed and unresponsive door, threw my hair back over my shoulder, then bent to see what had been brought for me to wear. Unfolding the bundle showed a cloth-shirt of green and a pair of dark brown trousers, neither item new and both just this side of not-quite-clean-enough. I didn't like the idea of having to wear trousers, but it was either that or put on wet draperies again or go naked. It occurred to me then that the clothing might well belong to the outlaw, and once I straightened and held the trousers up to me, the possibility became a near certainty. He and Jiss were the only ones I knew in that Realm whose trousers would be long on me, and Jiss hadn't brought extra clothing.

I sighed and began to get into the clothing. The rough fabric of the trousers bagged around my feet and hung wide around my hips, just as though they didn't want to be on me any more than I wanted them on, apparently saying without words that I might have no choice but they certainly did. It seemed rather fitting that the outlaw's items of clothing would be as uncooperative as their owner. I took a tie from one of the room's drapes and threaded it through the loops of the trousers. Knotting the tie kept the trousers up, and simple folding took care of their length and the shirt sleeves both. It was neither comfortable nor stylish, but at least I was covered and dry.

Once dressed I took my sandals over to the fire, and with the help of the towel they were quickly wearable again. Woven cloth over terma leather is good that way, and many people in my mother's Realm swam without taking off their sandals. The fact that they were very light also helped, and I wondered why those of the Earth Realm didn't wear the same. Then I remembered that their saddles were just as hard and stiff as their boots, as clumsy and uncomfortable as most of the things in that Realm, and understood what it meant. The Children of Toil preferred suffering, as though suffering would replace the dream they lacked, as though suffering was a good thing all by itself. If they ever found their dream they would realize that suffering never benefited anyone but those who told them how good it was, those who only pretended to suffer with them. The Children of Toil were slaves in everything but name, and hopefully one day they would understand that.

It seemed impossible to keep my thoughts away from topics both dark and depressing, which is why the knock at my door was welcome even though I didn't know who it was. I rose from the floor in front of the fire and went to the door, then opened it to find Jiss.

"Oh, good, you're ready," he said, eyeing the clothing I had on. "I'm two steps away from eating the carpeting raw and you can't be doing much better, so let's get going to that meal. Where did you find those clothes?"

"Your friend Skyhawk brought them," I answered, stepping out into the hall and locking the door behind me. Jiss wore the same leather he'd had on all along, but now his garments were dry and fresh, looking as though they were completely new.

"I think it's time you admitted you misjudged him," Jiss said as we walked along the hall toward the stairs. "If he was as self-centered as you claim, he never would have given you his own clothes to wear."

"And I think you'll find he did it for you rather than for

me," I countered. "He knew you were hungry, so he gave me something dry to wear. If he hadn't I would have needed to wait until my own draperies were dry, and you might have decided you had no choice but to wait with me. If it wasn't so impossible, I'd think he liked you the way men usually like only women."

Jiss stopped short so suddenly I almost left him behind, and when I paused to look back at him it was almost as though he'd gone pale under his tan. He was briefly silent as his mind worked behind those golden eyes, and then he shook his head a shade too firmly.

"No, it can't possibly be that way," he said, speaking more to himself than to me. "Skyhawk knows I have no interest in other men, so no matter how many stories there are about what they sometimes do in outlaw camps, he'd never think that I— No, Hali, you have to be mistaken. I know they do that sort of thing in this Realm, but I don't believe it of Skyhawk."

"Then why did he give me that lecture?" I asked, somehow not very surprised that his good friend might be one of those who wasted their time finding interest in a member of their own sex. "He told me I'd better treat you nicely or I would lose you, and then he said the advice was for your sake rather than mine. I may have an active imagination, Jiss, but I don't use it to fabricate conversations."

"Well, there are ways of finding out without putting my foot in it," he said after another moment. He gave a small, very unamused laugh before starting to walk again, and I went with him without commenting further.

When we reached the bottom of the stairs we found that our third had already claimed a table, and sat waiting for us with a large flagon in his hand. There were only four other people in the dining room, each at a separate table, and none of them looked up from their food or drink when Jiss directed me by a hand on my elbow to Skyhawk's table. The outlaw, however, made up for the lack of response from the others by looking directly at Jiss with a hidden grin.

"There's plenty of food in this inn, Jentris, you didn't

have to bring along a sack of potatoes," the miserable
beast said, and then he moved his eyes to my face and
pretended to be surprised. "Oh, I'm sorry, Haliand," he
drawled, leaning back in his chair. "For the moment I
didn't recognize you, but those clothes do look familiar. Is
your hair dry yet?"

"Not quite," I answered, sitting in the chair Jiss held
for me without even glancing at the outlaw. "If I knew
you would be that interested, I would have issued formal
statements."

"She was drying her hair when I walked in on her," the
outlaw confided to Jiss as my real companion took his own
seat. "I had to tell her that I'd never seen hair as long as
hers, but her hair wasn't precisely what I was looking at.
You might do well explaining to her about locking doors
before taking off her clothes, my friend. If it had been
someone else walking in, she could have had a problem."

"But of course she didn't have a problem with you,"
Jiss said in a very strange but neutral way, his eyes on
Skyhawk. "All you did was comment on her hair, and
give her dry clothes to put on."

"I don't believe in intruding in another man's terri-
tory," the outlaw replied, his gaze meeting Jiss's. "You'll
never have to worry about what I'm doing behind your
back, my friend. It will never be more or different from
what I'd do with you watching."

"I had the feeling that would be the case," Jiss said,
obviously working to sound warm and approving. "When
two men are friends, each of them knows they can count
on the other's discretion. But they do act differently when
they're involved with a woman who doesn't belong to a
friend, don't they? I remember the last time I walked in on
a woman who wasn't wearing anything, and her hair wasn't
the main topic discussed. I'll bet you could tell a story or
two of your own on the subject."

"I was raised to watch what stories I told in mixed
company," the outlaw said with a rather unsteady smile,
his glance in my direction verging on embarrassment.

"We can swap tales on the subject later, if you like, after your lady has retired to her room."

Jiss's lack of agreement with that suggestion was concealed by the arrival of a girl carrying a large tray of food, but I noticed it even if the outlaw didn't. Jiss didn't seem very happy with the idea of meeting with Skyhawk later without me, which probably meant his tests, whatever they'd consisted of, hadn't been passed. I, myself, had no idea whether there was anything unusually unusual about the outlaw, but I also didn't care. If Jiss became uncomfortable enough we would leave the man behind, which meant I would do well to keep my eyes open against the further possibility of helping things along toward that very desirable end.

The food the girl brought signaled the beginning of our meal, and I was surprised at how tasty the various dishes were. We had meat and fish and fowl, bread and cheese, fruit and soup, puddings and pastries, all of it well seasoned and expertly prepared. The three of us stuffed ourselves so completely an observer would have thought we were making up for a week of no eating rather than only a day's worth, but that's not all an observer would have noticed. He might also have seen how the outlaw tried to start a conversation with Jiss and keep it going, but apparently Jiss was too hungry to uphold his end of the attempt.

The one thing I disliked about the meal was the ale we were given to drink, a beverage of the Earth Realm I hated after a single taste. It was strong and bitter, perfectly fitting for the people who had made it, but Jiss joined Skyhawk in drinking it as though he hadn't noticed its taste. I, on the other hand, after forcing down the smallest of sips, pushed the glass aside and made no effort to try it a second time. Under other circumstances I would have asked for wine, but I really had no interest in being disappointed—or poisoned. I had the serving girl bring me a goblet of water, and made do with that.

The meal wound along to its end as most meals do, and by then Jiss was talking more and Skyhawk less. The serving girl had been very good about refilling their flagons as soon as they'd been emptied, but they'd both taken to sipping their latest refill, as though they knew they'd finished the last of the ale and would not be getting any more. Jiss swirled the tawny liquid in his flagon, then looked over toward the outlaw.

"This could well be the strongest brew I've tasted away from home, brother," he said, his voice and smile containing matching laziness. "I think it's doing me more good than the food did."

"I don't remember the ale being quite this strong," the outlaw answered, aiming a faint frown at the drink in question. "I'm enjoying it at least as much as you are, but it seems strange that— Well, possibly I'm misremembering, after all the time it's been. And speaking of time, I think it's time we made our final arrangements for the night. That rain doesn't sound as though it intends letting up until morning, so we might as well get comfortable. Do you and the lady have—plans, or do you want me to check on the availability of inn girls? With everyone else already gone to their rooms, we'll have to take what's left."

"If you're asking whether I'll be sharing Haliand's bed, the answer is no," Jiss said with a smile, sending only a lazy glance in my direction. "She's already been told how I feel about that, and understands that her first experience should be more special than casual. After we escort her to her room, we can inspect the girls together."

The outlaw immediately looked over toward me with a sober, dark-eyed gaze I couldn't quite interpret, and I just as immediately looked away. I could feel my cheeks burning over how easily Jiss had made his announcement, how effortlessly he had told my privacies to a stranger I detested. I wondered then how I could have considered Jiss attractive, how I could have kept from hating him as I did that very moment. Prince Jentris of the Sun Realm had nothing wrong with him that kept him from taking women to bed; what he had was no interest in taking *me* there.

"Your lady seems to be feeling the weariness of her very long day, Jentris," the outlaw said after a heavy moment, the weight of his eyes still clearly on me. "I think it would be a good idea if we took her back to her room now.''

''Before we get on to other choices, eh, Skyhawk?'' Jiss said with an amiable chuckle, having a small amount of trouble pushing away from the table. ''A man enjoys having another man's company at a time like that, a *real* man's company. And a friend, nothing but a friend.''

Jiss was apparently in a very good mood, and Skyhawk gave him an odd, curious look as they both got to their feet. I rose silently without really looking at either of them.

The two men walked slightly ahead of me going up the stairs, and the only sound breaking the silence of the inn was Jiss's voice, murmuring something to his good friend that he couldn't keep from chuckling over. The other guests had completely disappeared from sight, as had the serving girl, making me feel as though we three were the last people in the house left alive. Earlier I would have been bothered by that, but just then I barely noticed.

When I reached the top of the stairs I circled right after the two who had gone ahead of me, but after no more than a couple of steps almost ran directly into them. They had stopped to stare down the hall in the direction of our rooms, where even the few wall candles that had been lit were now extinguished. Nothing but deep blackness loomed ahead, in a way that gave new meaning to the word ''loomed,'' most especially since I could see something in that darkness. Over the shoulders of the men ahead of me I could see the forms of other men, shadows that stood waiting in the deep, dark black.

''If they think I'm simply walking into that, they're out of their minds,'' Skyhawk said to Jiss, staring into the pitch blackness ahead of us. ''I usually make a habit of seeing what I'm getting into before doing anything, and I don't like to break old habits.''

''Come on, Skyhawk, you're not afraid of a little dark, are you?'' Jiss countered with an amused laugh, as blind to the men waiting only a few steps away as the outlaw obviously was. ''It's not as if we don't know what's down that hall. If you want to make absolutely sure we're ready for whatever comes, we can always go down there with our swords in our fists.''

Just as I was about to tell them what was really waiting in the dark Jiss began drawing his sword, and that became the signal for everything that followed. The shadows that had been so motionless immediately began to stir, and then they raised dark bars of arms and threw something toward us, something that became more than one something as the objects landed at our feet with the tinkle of breaking glass. A thin, greenish mist floated upward as we stared down in confusion, but the confusion didn't last long for Jiss and Skyhawk. They couldn't have taken more than a single breath before they were crumpling to the floor, senses gone along with their surprise.

Leaving only me to stand there and stare at the shadow forms now moving toward me.

Once again I remembered about hauntings and what the word meant, and realized that those coming toward me didn't necessarily have to be alive. My heart went chill and cold in my chest, trying to freeze me in place, but I was too frightened for that. Without being aware of how it had started, I suddenly found myself turned and running as fast as I could for the stairs leading up. It came to me then to scream at myself silently for not going down instead, but it was much too late. I was heading upward and they were right behind me.

Chapter 6

THE FLOOR ABOVE had two sections, rooms to the right and an unpartitioned jumble of what seemed to be storage items to the left. Without breaking stride I ran to the left, hoping to lose myself in the forest of silhouettes in the new darkness I'd entered, and strangely enough I seemed to be successful. The footsteps pounding behind me faltered as they reached the top of the stairs, causing me to stop dead where I was in the jumble to keep from making any noise. As I stood there in the musty dark, I wondered how much good not moving would do; my heart had unfrozen with so much enthusiasm that its pounding should have been audible for miles. I waited for those who were chasing me to hear it, waited for them to start right for me—and then I heard the sound of footsteps slowly descending the stairs.

"Don't jiggle the web yet, there's still one there," a very tiny voice whispered to me just as I was about to collapse with relief. "My mother can see it clearly, and she says it's waiting for you to let it know where you are."

"There are spiders living in this house?" I whispered back in the language I'd been spoken to, every bit of the relief and delight I felt coming through in the words. "I saw nothing of webs down below, so I assumed— But why are you on my side rather than theirs? If you share the same house, you have to be their partners."

"You mean the old stories are true?" the tiny newcomer whispered in surprise, lowering itself just a little more on its invisible line. "I could never quite believe that humans and spiders were once partners, and wasn't even expecting you to understand me. Tradition demands that we talk to every human we come upon, but none of them ever understands or answers."

"The humans in this Realm don't understand the trees either," I told the young spider, wanting it to know there were others being treated the same. I'd always had trouble telling male from female in young spiders, and at that point it didn't really make much difference. "I'm not surprised that you and the others keep trying to communicate, though. The humans here don't know what a wonderful partnership they're missing."

"But we know, and I don't think we'll ever give up trying to get it back," my new friend said with a sigh. "The old stories say we spun our webs only where we and our partners wanted them, and then we protected our joint home from invasion by those things that were harmful to our partners. In turn our partners protected us and our webs and provided nourishment when pickings were lean, and everyone was happy. Now—now they tear down our webs no matter where we put them, kill us when they see us as though *we* were the harmful ones. I can't tell you how awful it is, and how many of our people have turned bitter and uncaring."

"Which explains why there were no webs down below, and why you warned me," I said with a sigh of my own. "You and your people are hiding out up here, and the humans of this house are as much your enemies as mine. Or maybe it's the spirits who are our mutual enemies, I just don't know any longer. Oh, I wish I'd never come into this house!"

"Ssh, not so loud," the tiny messenger hissed, bobbing on its line. "My mother said the waiting one almost heard that, and we don't want it to catch you. Move back behind that big box over there, and then sit down and wait. As

soon as the other leaves this section of world-area, we'll
let you know.''

It began rising on its thread then, going back where it
came from, knowing I'd have no trouble finding the box it
had been talking about. There was only one box amid the
clutter of old furniture and piled sacks and stacks of moldy
linen, and a narrow but clear path led around behind it. Or
possibly I should say the path was clear to me; Jiss wouldn't
have been able to see it, and hopefully whatever was
waiting would have the same trouble.

I moved very slowly and silently until I was behind the
box, and then I lowered myself to the dust-covered floor
with the same care. It was my mother's luck that the
spiders I'd found still spoke the language they and humans
had worked out together, or I never would have understood them even if I understood their words. I'd once been
given an example of spider-thought by a friend living in
my mother's house, and although I'd understood every
word I hadn't been able to make the least sense of it. Trees
may have their own way of looking at things that colors
their speech patterns, but humans can understand them if
they try. Spiders begin at a totally different point, and
many believe that that's the reason our partnerships are so
successful. We're so different from one another, there's
nothing for us to argue about.

I leaned back against the box carefully, making sure it
wouldn't squeak or shift with my weight, very glad I was
no longer wearing my draperies. That entire storage area
was absolutely filthy, and I'd even accidently pulled down
some webs. Once I got out of there it would take me a
week to get my hair clean again, and . . . and . . .

And what difference did any of that make, with Jiss
captured by someone or some *thing*? The fact that the
outlaw was with him also made no difference at all, not
with both of them completely unconscious. It was necessary to admit that they could both be dead by now, and
even if they weren't, there was no one but me to save
them. I raised my hands to my face and then bent forward,
wishing I could moan aloud. If they didn't find me I would

have to do something, but once again, just like in the outlaw camp, I couldn't think of anything! It was all up to me, and I just sat there in the dark and trembled!

And tried to tell myself that I shouldn't care what happened to Jiss and his good friend. I hadn't exchanged even two pleasant words with that outlaw, and Jiss had said—openly and in front of the stranger—that he preferred taking just about anybody to his bed rather than me—and it had been so embarrassing—and I hated him for it—

But not as much as I'd been beginning to like him. The way he'd kissed me that time, and the way it had made me want him to do it again; the way he never really lost his patience over the constant arguing between me and the outlaw; the way he was able to see reason and do things he didn't like for the sake of our quest, like not taking me home. Even before that he'd offered to be friends with me, which was something very few others had offered before him. If I wanted to be angry with him there was no reason not to be—*after* I figured out some way to get us out of there.

If we both lived long enough for me to figure out something. I sighed without sound, took my hands from my face, then began weaving some of the darkness into a pillow. If I was going to have to wait I might as well do it in comfort, and once the watcher was gone I would check with the spiders. It was just possible that they would think of something, and then I could get started with the rescue.

As soon as I opened my eyes, I realized I should never have laid down on the cushion I'd made. As tired as I was I'd fallen asleep almost immediately, and because of that had no idea how much time had passed. I sat up quickly but silently, wondering if the watcher was still there, and had my question answered almost before I'd thought of it.

"The one who waited is gone," a spider voice informed me, different from the first voice that had spoken. "My webling told me you do speak our language, so when your enemy left I came down to talk with you myself."

"How long ago did the watcher leave?" I asked the female spider, rubbing sleep out of my eyes with one hand. "It was stupid of me to lie down like that, I don't know where my mind could have been . . ."

"Be calm, young human," the spider said, and there was almost a tinge of amusement in her voice, something that worried me. Spiders and humans don't consider the same things funny, and when a spider finds humor in a situation, you can be fairly certain you won't. "The watcher was only just called away from its post by another of its kind, so there was no reason for you not to take all the rest you could. Do you intend to leave here now?"

"I can't leave until I free my friend—and the other one too, I suppose," I answered, wishing I had a choice in the matter. "Those—whatever they are—knocked the others out with a green mist, and then tried to catch me. Do you happen to know if they really are . . . spirits?"

"I've never heard that word, so I have no idea," the spider said, hanging motionless at the end of her thread. "The one who came for the watcher spoke to it, but not in this language so I don't know what was said. What are you going to do to free your friend?"

"I wish I knew," I muttered, pulling a large section of my hair out from under me. The shirt and trousers I wore were rough and uncomfortable, I felt filthy and rumpled, but I was still supposed to come up with a plan of escape for me and two others. Two others who might already be dead.

"The first thing I'm going to do is have a look around," I told the spider, straightening where I sat. "It's silly to make plans when you don't know what you're fighting against, and this is no time to be silly. Is there any chance you or one of your weblings or copartners know where my friend is being kept? I doubt if they simply left the two bodies lying there in the hall below."

"It's possible those of us in the lower world-areas know what was done," she said, now sounding thoughtful. "They're the ones who enjoy a life of adventure, spinning webs they know will be torn down as soon as they're discovered, constantly at risk of discovery, trying to be as invisible as possible. We up here prefer a more sedate life so we don't associate with them much, but we can ask. I'll have you told as soon as we find out. And I'd like you to know how pleasant this conversation has been.''

With that she immediately began rising up her thread, and in seconds she was lost in the upper darkness. Spiders were usually like that, having their say and then leaving without giving you a chance to say anything of your own, and they saw nothing wrong with it. If you wanted to say something of your own, they contended, you should have done it while you had the chance, just the way they did. They weren't wrong, of course, but I still sighed and shook my head as I rose to my feet.

I moved out of the storage jumble very slowly, trying to keep from pulling down webs and especially trying to be very, very quiet. I didn't know why those who had chased me hadn't come back with lanterns and greater numbers, but it might have been they had more important things to do first. They'd trapped me on that upper floor, had left someone to see if I would make enough noise to give away my position, and when I hadn't they'd decided against immediate pursuit. That didn't mean they wouldn't be after me eventually, which was why I was best off leaving the floor as soon as I could. If they hadn't left anyone watching from below. If spirits needed to leave someone watching from below.

''Of course they need to have someone watching,'' I told myself firmly in a very low whisper as I approached the top of the stairs. The watcher they'd left earlier proved it, and also proved they weren't all-powerful. They hadn't been able to catch me, they hadn't been able to hear me, and they hadn't been able to see well enough in the dark to follow my trail through the dust. I had been able to see that trail, as clearly as if my mother's glow had illuminated the scuffings, but they hadn't. That meant they couldn't see in the dark even if they did enjoy skulking in it, which definitely gave me an advantage.

I started down the stairs feeling considerably heartened,

but not so overconfident that I strode rather than tiptoed. That house was so quiet, so thickly silent that the continuing rain could be heard beyond the windows, so heavily without even the smallest of noises that it seemed unnatural.

I reached the bottom of the stairway without having produced any creaking sounds worthy of notice, but no one was there to hear even if I had. The candles were lit again at the far end, providing the feeble glow that helped most people not at all, and the two bodies that had been on the floor just beyond the stairs leading downward were nowhere to be seen.

I stood there for a moment thinking hard, trying to figure out what they would have done with their captives, but not knowing why they had taken the two men to begin with meant I didn't get very far. I would have to do some searching, and hope I didn't run into whoever it was I was trying to avoid.

The first and most obvious places to check were our rooms. Creeping up the hall while looking in all directions at once, I kept expecting something to come jumping out at me with a scream, but I peeked into Skyhawk's room, my own, and then Jiss's. Skyhawk's room held his saddlebags in plain sight and mine had my draperies spread out near the fire, but the third room might never have been tenanted.

"Psst!" The sound came not a foot from my ear as I was closing the third door, startling me so badly that my heart nearly stopped. "Are you the human looking for its friends?"

"I was almost the late human looking for its friends," I whispered to the small spider hanging on its thread, trying to stop trembling. "Couldn't you have given me some sort of warning you were there?"

"How could I have given warning without doing exactly as I did?" the spider asked, far too reasonable and logical for my taste. "I was told you would want to know where those others were taken, but if all you're interested in doing is complaining . . ."

"No, no, I am interested," I interrupted hurriedly, knowing the spider would be less bothered by that than by what I'd previously said. Since it would have left as soon as it was finished speaking, my getting my own say in while I could would be considered nothing more than making use of an opportunity.

"I'm glad to hear I'm not wasting my time," the spider acknowledged with unspiderlike sarcasm, the soft words accompanied by a lowering on the thread. "The two who fell to the floor in this world-area were lifted by those of this place and carried below. Certain of us below saw them being taken through the doorway behind the stairs, a place others have been taken before this. Many of those others were kept there until wagons were brought to remove them from this major world-area altogether, but some were taken out rather quickly. Those taken quickly were spoiled forever for the partnership, and those of us below believe at least one of the two they have now will soon be spoiled in just that way."

"They're going to kill one of them?" I asked in agitation, not at all amused to remember that this was the place that was supposed to be so safe. "Have you any idea how soon they intend doing that?"

"It might be possible to spin a three-layered web in the interval," the spider answered, the shrug in its voice as clear as any gesture. "I suppose it would depend on how fast a spinner you were."

"All right, all right, I know we don't perceive the passage of time in the same way," I grumbled. "I asked the question without thinking, mainly because I'm worried. I'm the only one who can stop what's going on, but I'm all alone and don't have much of a plan."

"The best we can do is get information for you," my small friend said, regret in its voice. "We would much rather have you and your friends here to partner with us, but we can't do anything to help make that happen. Even if all of us attacked at once, we would be no more than an annoyance to them and then we would be spoiled. If it means anything, I hope your plan is better than you think it is."

The small being took itself up the thread with that, leaving me with all the help I was likely to get in that place: information, words of encouragement, and a hasty farewell. Not that I blamed the spiders. I wouldn't have been going up against the inhabitants of that place if I hadn't had to.

And I might not have very much time to do it. I turned and began moving back up the hall at a faster pace than I'd used coming down, intent now on getting the rescue over with as soon as possible. If I found the two men and woke them, released them from where they were being held and located their weapons, the problem should be solved without undue fuss and fury. All I had to do was stay out of the way of their captors while I did all that, and incidently make sure I wasn't captured myself. Nothing more than that . . .

I told myself disgustedly to forget about planning and just pay attention to sneaking down the stairs to the ground floor. The first thing I had to do was locate the two captives, and then I could worry about what came next.

Somehow the ground floor seemed even quieter than the upper ones, the fire in the dining room's hearth doing nothing to warm or cheer the large empty room. I quickly circled the staircase I had just come down, and stepped behind it to find the door I'd been told about but hadn't noticed myself while we were eating. The door was metal-braced wood that stood in deep shadow, but as heavy as it looked a single push opened it easily and smoothly. No scrapes or screechings announced my presence to the world, and once I stepped through I closed it just as quietly behind me. Three steps ahead there was a stone stairway leading down into the deep dark, but at the very bottom I could make out the pale glow of a candle or torch somewhere ahead.

"I understand I'm supposed to announce myself before telling you anything," a tiny, very soft voice said from the vicinity of my right shoulder, startling me only a little. I was beginning to get used to being snuck up on by spiders, and the truth was I felt better having them around even if they couldn't help.

"On behalf of my nerves, I thank you for the announcement," I answered, really working hard at keeping my voice down. "What is it you're supposed to tell me?"

"There are three of this major world-place's beings down there with the two you're looking for," the spider said, the words so soft as to be almost inaudible. "I've been asked to tell you to be very careful, and to make a good deal less noise than you've been making. If you don't, they'll find you."

I waited a moment to see if there would be more, but the spider's voice didn't continue, which probably meant it had left. I started down the stone stairway on my toes, holding my breath until my foot was entirely on a step, trying to decide which part of the spider's message had upset me more. My heart beat harder at the thought of the enemy being where I had to go, but a cold chill touched me when I realized I hadn't been as quiet as I'd thought. I didn't know if I *could* move more quietly, but I had to try.

The bottom of the staircase brought me to the beginning of a narrow stone corridor, and the light I'd seen came all the way from the left, the only way it was possible to go. The corridor stretched to the left about thirty feet and then turned sharply right, and all I could see from where I stood was another heavy, metal-bound door at the end of the thirty feet. It was in the far wall just before the turn, and there was a torch on the wall beside it. There was also an area of really deep shadow just under the stone stairway, but nothing and no one was in it, not even another door. I took what I hoped was a silent deep breath, got a better grip on my quivering courage, then began moving up the corridor toward the only door I could see. I must have moved three or four steps, and then—

And then I heard the sound of boots, coming from the corridor around the turn to the right! Since I couldn't yet see anything they couldn't see me, but if I continued to stand frozen in fear where I was, discovery would come in no more than minutes. Getting myself moving was one of the hardest things I'd ever done, but the deep dark under the stone stairway was just wrapping itself around me when three men turned the corner and walked briskly in my direction.

". . . came out of it too damned fast," one of the three was saying, annoyance plain in his voice. "They probably didn't put enough in his ale, so the mist only knocked him out for a little while. That other one was also starting to come around, and I don't like that any better."

"I'll sure talk to th' girl in th' kitchens," a second one said, sounding faintly nervous. "We ain't never had this trouble b'fore, an' I'll see as it don't happen agin. We ain't—"

"Stop making excuses," the third man interrupted with a sharp movement of his hand, then came to a stop, which forced the other two to do the same. "It doesn't matter that those two aren't staying unconscious as long as our—guests—normally do; they won't be getting out of that cell until we want them out. What I'm more concerned about is that girl, and how soon I can get her. Your men were fools for letting her run in the first place."

"Would you have preferred having her scream her pretty head off?" the first man answered the accusation, his tone now stiff from insult. "Our other guests are keeping quiet and minding their own business because they think this inn is haunted, but if they all come out of their rooms together because they hear a girl screaming, they could stand together long enough to learn the truth. We knew the girl didn't like the ale so she didn't drink it, but we didn't expect her to run upstairs and lose herself so close to the rooms we have guests in. Once those guests are gone we can tear the storage section apart until we find her, and then she's all yours."

"There better not be any problem with that," the third man said with a growl, his shadowy face turned directly toward the other two. "I'd curse this weather for bringing so many travelers here that they're interfering with our primary business, but it was probably the weather that also brought those men and the girl. Even you two should understand what she'll be worth in gold, so make sure nothing goes wrong in catching her. If you find her sooner than you expect to, bring her directly to me no matter when it is."

He turned away from the others, strode to the stairs, then went up them with the scuffing steps of heavy boots. The first and second men stood where they were until they heard the soft sound of the upper door closing, and then the first man shook his shadowed head.

"Who does he think he's fooling?" he asked with heavy scorn, his words fairly low. "The amount of gold that girl is worth has nothing to do with why he wants her so badly. You can bet he'll get our gold when he eventually sells her, but that won't be until he gets tired of using her himself. He was watching through the peephole when she first entered her room, and ever since then he's been pawing the ground like a stallion forced to do without."

"Can't say I blame him much," the second man ventured, and it finally came to me that he was the one who had given us our rooms. "When I registered them three, I had t' work real hard not t' stare at that female like I wanted t'. He's the boss an' all so he gets firsts, but maybe he won't mind if'n summa us do some tastin' after he's done. You ain't seen her, sir, but once you do maybe you could sorta speak up f'r . . ."

"I think you'll have enough to do for a while without worrying about bedding a female," the first man told the second, a dry superiority now tingeing his scorn. "That outlaw will have to turn up very gorily dead, an object lesson to the others, proving again that they'd better not try coming anywhere near this inn, and then the other will need to be readied for the wagon that's coming. We'll have the gold from his sale quickly enough, and although he won't bring the same as the girl it won't be a sum you'd throw to beggars. And before we leave the subject, are you sure that girl is boxed in the way we think she is? If she happens to get away from us, our glorious leader will probably see to it you lose the ability to bed females for the rest of your life."

"She can't go nowhere," the second man assured the first with a laugh, but a laugh that sounded more frightened than amused. "I had t' pull my man offa the floor up there t' keep anybody from wonderin', but I got men at every door, an' th' windows 'r locked tight. We'll have a real good look around b'fore dawn just in case she come down without us seein', an' if she did we'll have 'er then."

"For your sake, I hope so," the first man said, finally beginning to move again toward the stairs. "Now, there are still a few hours before we have to arrange the gory ending of the miserable lowlife of a forest outlaw that your man so kindly recognized for us, and possibly we can use the performance to rid ourselves of unwanted guests. If the death screams come close enough to dawn, those awakened by them just might decide not to go back to . . ."

The man's voice trailed off as the two got closer to the top of the stairs, but even the sound of the door shutting behind them didn't cause me to stir from my hiding place. I stood backed up against the damp stone of the wall, my arms wrapped around my body but doing nothing to stop the trembling that would have had my teeth chattering as well if they hadn't been clenched tight. It had come to me that I hadn't quite believed the outlaw Skyhawk when he'd described how desirable he thought men would find me, but right then I had no choice about believing him. It was terribly frightening to think that men intended using you even if you didn't want them to, and I wished harder than ever that I'd stayed home. Back there even Feledor had accepted a refusal without making a fuss, but in *this* terrible place—

"The two you want are behind the fourth door around the turn," a tiny voice said out of the darkness, this time from my left. "You weren't as quiet as one of us would have been, but those beings were too deaf to hear you anyway. Was all that noise they made really talking?"

"Yes, that's human language," I answered, trying to use the words to unfreeze myself from where I stood. "One of them was mangling what he said so badly it's starting to sound like a different language entirely, but of course that's silly. Humans won't ever speak anything but the tongue we all share, not unless we're speaking to beings who aren't human. The fourth door along, you said?''

''Yes, with its opening device on the wall to its right,'' the spider agreed. ''Humans need the opening device to get through the door, but spiders don't. I wonder if that makes spiders better than humans, or just smaller. I'll have to think about it.''

This time I caught a glimpse of the spider rising up and away from me, undoubtedly on its way to think. Spiders found great pleasure in spending time thinking, but I'd done enough of it for a while. I pushed myself out of the shadows and moved up the stone corridor, knowing if I let myself do any more thinking I'd never come out of the shadows again.

Turning the bend in the corridor brought to view the doors the spider had mentioned, but they didn't look like the one I'd been able to see from the bottom of the stairs. That first one was solid and metal bound, but the three beyond it had even more metal with small barred openings in their tops, and I could see that that man had been right about how well held Jiss and Skyhawk were. That man. I shivered as I remembered the sound of his voice, wished briefly but fervently that the enemy *had* turned out to be spirits rather than living humans, then pushed the thoughts away and got on with my purpose for being there.

The ''opening device'' I'd been told about was a key, of course, and I took it down from the wall to the right of the door, then returned to the lock with it. Only that single torch lit the entire area, which meant the fourth door would be rather poorly illuminated for someone without my vision, but dimness wasn't any part of my worries. More to the point was the fact that I heard nothing from the much thicker darkness behind the door, not even when the scraping squeak of the key turning in the lock broke the heavy local silence. If the three who had just left had done anything to their prisoners—

But I couldn't let myself think like that. I finished turning the key and then pulled on the heavy door, opening it wide enough for me to slip through amid the faint odor of burned leather. If the two men were unconscious again and I couldn't rouse them, that would end everything. There was nothing I could think of that I would be able to do alone against the enemy, which meant—

I tried to cry out when an arm circled my body and tightened hard around me, but a big hand clapped itself over my mouth to muffle the sound down to a grunt. I struggled wildly, kicking frantically against I-had-no-idea-what, and then I was released as suddenly as I'd been grabbed.

"You might not believe this, Jentris, but it seems we've just overpowered your lady," the outlaw's voice came from behind me, the tone soft but still fully thickened with amusement. "She won't do well as the hostage we were hoping for, but at least the cell door's open. Shall we wait to ask her what she's doing here until after we're out of this dungeon?"

"Good idea," Jiss muttered, not sharing his companion's amusement. "I prefer holding conversations in less formal surroundings. Any ideas on where a place like that might be found?"

"Since this has to be a basement level, let's go back up and take a look," the outlaw suggested, leading the way out of the cell. "There are lots of doors on the ground floor I never looked behind, and one of them should do us. But until we find a place, let's be very quiet."

That made the outlaw sound like a spider, but he wasn't as cute as a spider and certainly couldn't be as silent as one. The boots he and Jiss wore made sounds like the pounding of a drum as we hurried to the steps and up them, but there wasn't anything to be done about that. They couldn't very well carry the boots when there was a chance they might have to fight; all *I* could do was cringe on the inside, and hope there was no one around to hear the muted clatter.

But at least the hope was a good one. When Skyhawk

eased open the door to the upper floor and peeked out, no one and nothing was in sight. The three of us slid through the doorway, closed it fast behind us, then followed the outlaw to another door not far away. I hadn't seen anyone using the new doorway while we'd been eating, and once we had opened it we found out why. Behind was an L-shaped storage room that didn't seem much used any longer, with a small pile of wood for the dining room's fireplace stacked to the left, a shelf with candles and small brass candleholders, and not much else. We got inside fast, closed that door, then took a moment to breathe.

"Hali, can you see well enough in this ink to get me one of those candles?" Jiss asked in a whisper when the moment was up. "If we light it and then take it around the corner of the el, no one should be able to see it from outside."

The faint trickle of light coming from under the door was enough for me to see by, but obviously not enough for my companions. Rather than answer in words I circled around the outlaw, reached for a candle, then brought it back to Jiss. I had to press it into his hands before he knew I'd gotten it, but then he took it and turned away. Another breath of time went by before he turned back, and when he did the candle was lit.

"Ah, now that's what I call a welcome sight," the outlaw whispered, following after Jiss as he led the way toward the back of the room and around the corner. "I don't know where you're carrying flint that they missed it, Jentris, but I'm glad they did. First the leather down in our cell, and now the candle. Remind me not to get captured again with anyone but you."

"I enjoy your company, Skyhawk, but if it's all the same to you I'll pass on getting captured again," Jiss answered with a soft chuckle, but as soon as his eyes came to me the amusement disappeared. "And now that we're out of *this* capture, we have the time for a few questions. If you weren't in their clutches, Hali, why in the name of everything sane didn't you get out of the inn and wait for us in the forest? Were you feeling so left out you needed to try getting captured yourself?"

"What I was *trying* to do was free two fools I never should have given a second thought to," I answered, close to being open-mouthed in shock that Jiss would say that to me. His attitude also hurt, making me feel as though I wasn't good enough to have helped them. "If I had simply left the inn, I could have waited until your friend there was made into a gory corpse and you were packed off to the slave markets, and then I could have gotten on with important matters. Next time I'll do exactly that."

"You don't have to bite his head off for saying he doesn't want you hurt" the outlaw put in, shifting to my right and slightly behind me, from where he could watch the door. "If you hadn't shown up we would have found some way out of that cell. And since the subject has come up, how did you get away from them and find out where we were being held?"

"The mist that knocked you out didn't work on me because I didn't drink any of that ale," I answered, still staring at a Jiss who wasn't in the least sorry for what he'd said. "When you went down I turned and ran, and was able to hide in the litter that half of the third floor is covered with. It was too dark for them to find me, so they decided to wait until their guests were gone before they came back with torches and hunting dogs."

"And when they left, you snuck down to their dungeons," Jiss said, grim over the conclusion. "That still doesn't explain how you found us. You weren't foolish enough to follow one of them, were you?"

"Foolish!" I repeated in total disbelief, remembering just in time that we were trying to be quiet. The memory kept my voice down, but did nothing to bring my temper down with it. "I can't seem to do *anything* to suit your taste, can I, O Marvelous One? Well, it so happens I *didn't* follow the ones you call 'them,' so that makes it all right, doesn't it? Now I think I'll take your advice and get out of here."

I turned to stalk away from him and back toward the

door, intending to get out of that place even if I had to unravel the shadows of a dark corner and crawl through the resulting hole. I was absolutely determined, but as I took one step past the outlaw his arm circled me, and I was pulled around to face Jiss again.

"Now, now, children, this isn't the time or the place for hasty words or actions," Skyhawk said before I could even begin to pull away, speaking to Jiss as well as to me. "Jentris, I think it's time we remembered your lady was trying to *help* us. Shouldn't she be thanked instead of scolded?"

"Yes, I can see you're right, Skyhawk," Jiss answered, suddenly looking ashamed. "Hali, I was being too hard on you and I apologize. It's just that those men—they thanked us for bringing you here. It was very unselfish of you to try freeing us rather than simply thinking of yourself and running away, and I'd like you to know I really am grateful. We're both grateful."

"Oh, you're quite welcome," I answered coldly with my arms folded, having already shaken off the hold the outlaw had had on me. "I'm touched by your obvious sincerity—which someone else had to prompt you into. Was there anything else you wanted to say?"

"Now, Hali," Jiss began as he flinched, obviously scored on by the truth. "I wasn't trying to blame you for anything, I was simply trying to caution you about being more careful. And speaking about being more careful, we'll do a lot better at taking care of ourselves if we can get our weapons back. You don't happen to know where they've been put, do you?"

"No, I don't happen to know," I answered as flatly as I'd been speaking the entire time, not about to make any attempt to ask the spiders. Jiss had made it very clear my help was unwelcome; I was in no mood to garnish my previous idiocy by offering that help again.

"Haliand, playing stubborn in a situation like this can get us all recaptured or killed," the outlaw put in softly from behind me, his tone trying very hard for sober reason. "This bunch found themselves in a position to take advantage of the inn's reputation for being haunted, and we three aren't the only ones in danger. Some of the other people staying here will be sent along with you and Jentris into slavery if our enemy isn't stopped. We're all victims in common here, and if we don't work together the enemy will have us. Is there any way for you to find out where our weapons are?''

Jiss watched me without expression as the question hung in the air behind me, the words refusing to fade until they were answered. I would have been much happier simply going off by myself somewhere, even if it were back out into that rain, but something in my life-fate refused to allow for such an easy solution.

"It might be possible to find out," I said grudgingly, without turning to look at the outlaw, a man who kept coming up with reasons why I had to do things his way. "Wait here, and I'll look into it."

Jiss's face suddenly showed a faint expression as I turned away from him, as though he had been about to say something about my not going alone, and then had remembered we had an outsider with us. He might not have known exactly what I was up to, but it wasn't possible for him to have forgotten about the trees. If I was telling them to wait there, I intended consulting a life form humans in that Realm usually didn't.

A chore that didn't take long once I'd reached the deep blackness around the corner and toward the front of the storeroom. Another spider came quickly when I called, left for a moment to consult someone else, then returned with the answer and additional information besides. When I had it all I thanked the spider, then went back to the two men who were waiting.

"Your weapons are in the next room over, behind that counter in the entrance hall," I told them, seeing how pleased they were to learn that. "This floor also happens to be free of the enemy just now, so if you want the things this is the time to get them."

"I don't think I'll ask how you found that out," Skyhawk said, immediately gesturing us into following him toward the door. "If we have the time later I'll ask, but right now we have more pressing matters to attend to. Like breaking up this cozy nest of slavers."

Jiss blew out the candle as the two of us followed again, but not before he exchanged glances with me behind Skyhawk's back. If the time came later when questions were asked, I was clearly supposed to leave the answering of them to my partner. At that point I wouldn't have dreamed of arguing, but I couldn't help wondering how much experience he'd had in being evasive. I'd had lots of experience, but I'd also learned a lesson about offering help where it wasn't wanted.

We made it through the dining room and into the entrance hall without meeting anyone or disturbing the still heavy silence, and the weapons we were looking for were right where we'd been told they'd be. While Jiss and Skyhawk were strapping swordbelts around their middles I looked at the door leading to the stable, but decided against going anywhere near it. If the doors were all being guarded that meant someone was out in the stable waiting, and in that Realm I had no need to go looking for trouble. Just being there seemed to bring me trouble in a way I'd never experienced at home.

"Okay, let's get started," Skyhawk whispered, bringing my attention back to the two men who now stood outside the counter. "What we have to do is rouse as many of the guests in this place as possible, while at the same time not alerting the slavers who are now probably in the middle of gathering up their other prechosen victims. We can begin with the rooms on the next floor up, and try to get as far as we can before they find out what we're doing."

"That's not a very good idea," I said as I walked closer to them, interrupting Jiss's nod of agreement over what his friend had suggested. "If we don't start with the third floor, we're wasting our time."

"While you were up there you saw a sign on the wall that said, 'Start waking guests here'?" the outlaw inquired with brows raised. "The third floor struck me as a good place to withdraw to in the event of discovery, most especially since Jentris and I and our recruits could then hold the stairs while you went from room to room adding to our ranks. If we start on the third floor and get discovered there, we'll be cut off from any possible second-floor guest assistance. You see the matter differently?''

''We helpless female burdens often do,'' I said, folding my arms as I looked up at him. ''Hasn't it come to you yet that we were given rooms on the second floor, and even though there are supposed to be a lot of guests at the inn, they still made their move against you two on that very same floor? They obviously had no objections to a small amount of noise there, but when it came to searching for me on the third floor, they put it off for the time when the guests up there would be gone. Don't those two things together provide the smallest hint that *all* the guests on the second floor, even the unchosen, might be drugged to keep them from hearing what they shouldn't?''

''How do you know about them putting off the search for you?'' the outlaw asked, his interest real, but then he shook his head. ''You must have overheard them talking about it, of course, just before you opened our cell. Your objection is good and your point is made, so let's not waste the cleverness of the deduction. Our starting point is the third floor rather than the second, and we'd better not waste any more time getting there.''

He gave Jiss and me a friendly grin, and then led off back in the direction of the dining room. Jiss followed immediately and I hurried after them both, but I was having trouble understanding what the outlaw was up to. I had expected him to dismiss everything I told him, but rather than dismiss it he had adopted the plan at once and had even tried to compliment me. He had to be up to something, I was certain of that, but I just didn't know what it could be.

We went halfway up the steps to the second floor with the two men leading the way, and then Jiss stopped Skyhawk and gestured *me* into going ahead of them. For an instant I didn't understand, and then it became very obvious: I was supposed to be free and running around the inn, so if I was seen no one would sound any alarms. All they would do was chase me—right into the waiting daggers clasped tight in the fists of two men who were supposed to be safely locked up. Another benefit they might not be counting on was my ability to see well in the dark; if the second floor was still being kept dim, I had the best chance of discovering what, if anything, lay waiting in the shadows. I had to stop to take a deep breath, but then I began climbing the stairs.

Chapter 7

🍂

I KEPT LOW as I reached the top of the steps and peeked around the newel to look up the hall, but there was nothing to be seen nor anyone to see me. One of the doors down at the other end of the hall stood open, but no more than soft scrapes and muffled grunts came from inside. I waved a hand toward the two behind me without looking at them, kept watch while Jiss and the outlaw made their nearly silent way to the stairs leading to the third floor, then crept across the wooden flooring after them. We hadn't been seen, and that meant we had a chance of making our plan work.

The third floor was very dark, even in comparison to the floor below, but Skyhawk and Jiss didn't hesitate. They groped their way to the room farthest from the stairway, then Jiss whispered to me that I was to stay outside on guard while he and the outlaw went in to recruit help. If anyone started up the stairs I was to knock once on the door to let them know, and then lose no time hiding myself in the forest of debris littering the other side of the floor. I began to ask how they intended getting past a door that was probably locked when I saw Skyhawk straighten up from crouching in front of the door, and then turn the knob. Since the door opened without even a squeak of protest I didn't bother with the question, but I had the distinct feeling I was missing something.

161

I stood myself in front of the door that had been left open a crack, and after a moment I was able to hear soft words being spoken inside. A brief conversation was engaged in, I heard the sound of movement, and then three forms rather than two came through the door. The third man was as small as most of the other Earth Realm people I'd seen, looked rumpled and hastily half dressed, and reached for his sword when he caught sight of me.

"It's all right, she's with us," Jiss whispered at once, calming the man. "You stay outside the next room with her, but if anyone shows up you'll come in to tell us while she hides herself out here. Do you understand?"

The man nodded without saying anything, the hand he pulled through his hair the only indication of his unease, and by that time Skyhawk was straightening up in front of the second door. Jiss joined him in entering the room, the newcomer joined me in standing in front of it, and again we waited.

It took a small amount of time waking the eight men on the third floor, and all of them joined us but one. That one was a merchant traveling with a guard, but he made no objections to his guard joining our effort. The rooms on that floor were a good deal smaller than the ones on the floor below, so we gathered in the hall rather than crowding into one of them.

"All right, here's the whole story," Skyhawk said softly to the men around us, leaving it to the merchant to watch the stairs while we planned in the dark. "When Jentris and I woke up in the cell belowground, we were visited by three of the ones who are running this trap. They laughed over the fact that everyone thought this inn was haunted, and told us the truth of the story that originated the belief. The ones who reopened the inn after the original massacre by outlaws weren't just businessmen trying to make their fortunes, they were relatives of the people who had been killed. When they opened their doors they weren't simply expecting another attack, they were hoping for one and were completely prepared."

A low mutter ran through his audience, mostly vocalized surprise, but he quickly held a hand up to silence them.

"Let's remember how quiet we're trying to be," he said in warning as he glanced toward the stairs, and immediately got the silence he wanted. "That's better. Now, the relatives of the murdered people kept a close watch, and when they saw another raid was just about to be executed they set their plan in motion. The five men who had aroused their suspicions were drugged, one was revived and questioned, and when their suspicions were confirmed all five were put to death. They let the advance scout come in and find the bodies and then leave again, and when the outlaw leader and his bodyguards stormed in they snagged them with steel-mesh slave nets."

"No wonder the stories say they screamed with terror," one of the men there put in with a snort of scorn. "I never believed it happened, but if they were netted I believe it. Gettin' killed is bad enough, but knowin' you're gonna be sold instead of killed is worse. But I don't understand the rest of this. How did they get to go from doin' outlaws to doin' folk who never harmed them?"

"They didn't," Skyhawk said with a shrug. "Once they had their revenge they didn't want the inn any longer, so they looked around for a buyer who would let them go back to the lives they'd left for what was only supposed to be a short while. I suppose it never occurred to them to wonder when their buyer turned out to be the slaver they'd sold their captives to. A buyer is a buyer, after all, and slavers have enough gold to need to spend it on something. They'd built the perfect traveler trap, one that would even be safe from outlaw raids, and the slavers had no trouble seeing that."

"But it's more than time the game was ended," Jiss said, taking his turn addressing the others. "If we don't stop them now, while we can, the next victim they decide on could be one of you or a member of your families. The plan is to work our way down from here, waking or freeing everyone we can, killing or capturing anyone who opposes us. If this inn isn't in our hands by dawn, we could be in their hands for the rest of our lives. Now that we know what's happening they can't afford to let any of us go, so we have nothing to lose. Is there anyone who thinks he would be safer by not joining us? . . . No? You're smart men, and it will be an honor to fight beside you. Let's go.''

From the way the merchant stared at us I knew he'd heard what had been said, and when he darted into his room and came out again with a dagger in his trembling hands, he made the decision unanimous. I was called forward to descend the steps first to see what was going on, and everyone came somewhat quietly behind me to help in getting us started.

Creeping down the stairway the second time was easier than the first; knowing you're not alone makes a big difference, in outlook and attitude if nothing else. I reached the bottom and peered around, saw that a different door was open toward the far end of the hall, but there was still no one in sight. I turned and gestured for those waiting to come down slowly and quietly, and once they had, Jiss took my arm and drew me to one side.

"Most of us are going to see what's happening in that room," he whispered, the greatest part of his eyes and attention on the open door. "Two of the men will be staying with you, helping you check the other rooms to see if you can wake the people in them. If a fight starts, the men with you will jump in to do what they can, but you'll get back out of the way and stay there. Everyone around you will be armed while you aren't, and I don't want to see you getting hurt. Do you understand?"

"Do I understand that you'd still rather not have my help unless there's no other choice?" I said as I looked away from him, giving a small shrug. "Of course I do, Jiss, why would you even bother asking? And now that you mention it, why don't you find someone else to do the job of waking? Being allowed to come down the stairs first was enough to make me feel included rather than left out. Besides, I have things of my own to do."

I began moving away from him then, toward the room

where I'd left my draperies, not about to walk out of there without my clothes. If they were still wet I'd bundle them up and carry them, but they and I were getting out of that place as soon as I could manage it. Further up the hall on the right I could see Skyhawk and his contingent almost up to the opened door, their swords out and ready, their steps noiseless as they moved. They were too intent on what they were doing to pay attention to the rest of us, even when Jiss caught up to me and pulled me to a stop by one arm.

"Hali, this is no time to go storming off on your own!" he hissed very low, the look in his golden eyes showing his displeasure. "Once this trouble is settled I'll be able to explain how wrong you are, but just now I can't. These men are waiting to get to work with you, and that job has to come first. Every guest you wake will be another sword on our side, and I shouldn't have to tell you how badly we need those additions. We don't yet know how many men they can throw against us, but it's at least as many as we have right now, and theirs are most likely better with a sword than ours. Will you please stop wasting time being temperamental, and get on with what has to be done?"

One of the two men standing behind him really did seem anxious to be starting that oh-so-important job, but that was completely understandable. The man was the frightened merchant holding no more than a dagger, and even the presence of his bodyguard beside him wasn't giving him much in the way of reassurance. It obviously hadn't occurred to him that even if we were able to rouse the guests on that floor, they would be too drowsy from whatever they'd been drugged with to be of much use. I opened my mouth to tell Jiss exactly what I thought of his make-work project, but never got the chance. The rest of our group had gone through that opened door, and suddenly everything began happening at once.

The clash of swords in the open room, I gathered, indicated more of a fight than had originally been expected; Jiss frowned at the sudden sound as he gave it all his attention, and even went so far as to start in that direction with his hand reaching for his sword hilt. He was able to take no more than two or three steps, though, before the sound of swords being drawn came from the direction of the stairs leading up from the floor below, accompanying the sound of hurrying footsteps. We turned to see three men coming up, obviously having heard the fight in the room; they were readying themselves to join it, but a closer fight was quickly brought to them.

Without a word spoken between them, Jiss and the merchant's bodyguard both drew their weapons and moved toward the three newcomers, engaging them as soon as they came around the newel. I blinked in surprise at how fast they moved, and also over the fact that neither side said a word. One minute they were approaching each other and the next they were fighting, five men trying very hard to reach each other with edged and pointed steel. The merchant came quickly to stand next to me, his dagger held tremblingly between him and the battle, but despite his very obvious fear I had the distinct impression he was there to protect me rather than himself.

Which was utterly ridiculous. For some reason everyone around me seemed to think I needed protection, but that didn't happen to be so. I knew well enough I could take care of myself—as long as nothing like spirits was involved—but I missed my chance to prove it.

Even as I watched, Jiss beat aside the blade of one of the two men facing him and then ran him through. The second man cut at Jiss in an attempt to take advantage of his friend's death by cleaving the head of the man who had killed him, but Jiss ducked the swing while yanking his blade free of his first victim. The survivor's second attack found a weapon there to stop it, and then he was busy with defense while Jiss took his turn at attacking.

At about that time the merchant's bodyguard brought his blade down into his own opponent, striking the man at the juncture of his neck and shoulder. The sword didn't go very deep at all, no more than four or five inches into the slaver's body, but that was deep enough. The slaver dropped his sword as he spasmed, opened his mouth in an effort to scream, then fell to the floor as the weapon was slid out of his body. He felt nothing of the last of it, of course, and a moment later Jiss's opponent landed on top of him, also no longer feeling things. The fight was over, and without my having even started to get involved.

"Well, that tears it," Jiss said to the man who had been fighting beside him, annoyance heavy in his voice. "Those running footsteps down below have to mean someone heard us, and that someone is now in the middle of spreading the word. We'd better alert the others before every slaver in this house gets up here."

The bodyguard nodded without saying anything, simply coming along as Jiss returned up the hall to where the merchant and I stood. They held their blood-streaked swords down and away from things, but made no effort to put them away.

"You did exactly right, Hali," Jiss said as he came up, at the same time taking my arm to urge me along with him. "Keeping back out of the way is how to keep yourself safe. Now let's see if Skyhawk was able to achieve the same end without using the same means."

I was more than ready to be furious with Jiss over the condescending way he kept talking to me, but I didn't have the time. Just as I decided on exactly what words I wanted to use we moved through the open doorway into the room where the others had gone, and the shambles brought a temporary end to extraneous conversation.

Five bodies were scattered here and there amid the shards and tatters of the room's threadbare furnishings, splashes of blood covering them and their surroundings alike. The bed held an unmoving body that wasn't the same, not with the way its chest moved up and down in rhythm with its gentle snoring. That one must have been the intended victim, a young man broadly built who would most likely be no stranger to heavy physical labor, and the bedcovers had been pulled back to allow the slavers access to him. That they had started lifting him out of the bed was clear in the lopsided way he lay there, which also showed there had been an interruption.

An interruption that had culminated in five dead bodies. Four of the bodies were fully dressed in a way that suggested prior preparation, but one of them seemed hastily assembled, with shirt half in and half out of his trousers, hair disarranged from sleep, boots jammed quickly over otherwise bare feet. It came with a shock that the man had been one of ours, and despite the fact that he'd been on the side of right, he was still dead. I stood just inside the doorway and stared at him, in some way not understanding, and then I heard Jiss's voice.

". . . means we'll have to do what we can for him as fast as possible, Skyhawk," he said. "The rest of them will be up here in no time, and we have to be ready."

"Yes, our getting taken or killed won't do him any good at all," the outlaw answered with a sigh, one that made me look at him. I saw then that he was crouched over another body on the floor, but that one wasn't yet dead despite whatever was under the red-stained cloth being held to his chest. Another of ours had been hurt, then, showing the first hadn't been some sort of fluke, and again I felt that odd confusion.

"All right, we have to get out of here," Skyhawk said, reaching to the sword on the floor beside him before straightening to his full height. "Jentris and I will head this contingent, along with any of you who really know how to use those weapons you're carrying. The rest of you will follow along behind us, and once we've engaged the enemy you'll start looking for your chance. Don't try fighting fairly and honorably against scum who outnumber you and are better with a blade than you are. We'll engage and do the blade-to-blade fighting, you'll come up from behind if you can and lower the odds against us in any way you're able. Just remember what these people do to the innocent and helpless, and you shouldn't have any trouble over using their backs as targets. Any questions? . . . Then let's go, and Lady Haliand—I'd count it a personal favor if you would see if there's anything you can do for our brother here. If there isn't, just make him as comfortable as possible."

He gestured toward the wounded man on the floor, then he and Jiss led the others out of the room. The merchant's bodyguard moved directly behind them along with another man, and the remaining three trailed out last, looking frightened but determined. The merchant himself stayed in the room, agonized indecision on his face, but he wasn't the last of them. The wounded man was, and his eyes rested on me with a good deal of pain showing in them. It took that long for me to register the fact that I'd been asked to do something, and also that it was far too late to refuse. As I moved nearer the wounded man and knelt beside him, I knew I'd much rather be out there fighting.

"You and me both," the wounded man said, making the effort to send me the shadow of a grin. He was a mature man with dark hair, eyes, and beard, but his skin seemed paler than it should be. His clothes were no better than the ones I wore, and I didn't understand what he was talking about.

"You and me both—what?" I asked, wondering how he had gotten hurt. He looked as though he should have been able to take care of himself.

"I'd rather be out there fighting, myself," he said, the words weaker and less accented than some I'd heard. "That's what you were thinking, wasn't it? That you'd rather be out in the hall fighting than in here taking care of me? I was just trying to say I don't blame you."

"Then you're the only one who doesn't," I answered, feeling the tug of disturbance again. "If you were on your feet they'd welcome you, but they have no interest in any help I'd try to give. I think they think there's something wrong with me, and if they let me help the something will rub off on them."

"No man with eyes could think there was something wrong with you," he said, amusement strengthening in him as he stared up at me. "It was almost worth getting wounded to have you this close, and if you'll let me hold your hand, I'll be as comfortable as it's possible to be."

He raised his arm a little, possibly as high as he could just then, and after the briefest hesitation I gave him my hand. His broad, blunt fingers closed gently around my more slender ones, and he smiled as his eyes came back to my face.

"That's a good deal better," he said, his hand already beginning to warm where it touched mine. "And as I said, lovely lady, no man with eyes could think there was something wrong with you. They don't want you out there fighting with them because they're afraid you'll be hurt, and no man at all could bear the thought of you being hurt. Men would rather be hurt themselves than allow harm to come to someone like you."

"But that's ridiculous," I said, trying to ignore the sounds of new fighting that had just begun in the hall. "It's nothing but blindness that doesn't let them see I can take care of myself, a condescending, voluntary, self-serving blindness. They'll keep the victory all to themselves, denying me the least part of it, just because they're more comfortable that way."

"Victory?" the standing merchant said, obviously having overheard my comment, his words trembling with what he felt. "Does that sound like victory to you, girl? A man just screamed as he died out there! I should be fighting with them, helping to save my own life, but the shame of my existence is that I can't bring myself to do it. Be glad they've relieved you of the burden of such shame— and be glad you're in here, out of reach of the weapons that could end you forever."

He turned his head back toward the doorway then, his dagger still held out in front of him, his whole body quivering with fear and self-hatred and a longing for something that was just beyond his reach. I felt all of that very clearly, and then I felt the fingers of the wounded man close a bit more tightly on my hand.

"What he means, lovely lady, is that victory is never quite as certain as you just put it," he said, his smile stronger now. "We hope for victory, and they're fighting as hard as they can for it, but there's no guarantee we won't find defeat instead. It's defeat and death they want to keep you from, not a share in victory."

"But of course we'll win," I said as patiently as I could, wondering why he pretended he didn't understand. "They're the ones who are wrong, and we're the ones who are right. Don't you know that right always wins?"

The man's lips parted as he looked up at me and I saw out of the corner of my eye that the merchant turned back in my direction as well, but neither of them said anything. It was as though they couldn't find the proper words, and then the wounded man smiled very gently.

"Dear girl, I would truly enjoy living in a world where right always wins," he said, the words as soft as his smile. "Unfortunately, however, we live in a different sort of world entirely. You must remember that although we consider our cause right, those slavers believe themselves just as right. In their opinion they have the right to trap and sell any person who isn't sufficiently careful of his safety, and the gold they amass through the exercise of that right proves to them that they're justified. If we were to ask one of those slavers, he would insist *he* fought on the side of right."

"Then he would sound as foolish as you do now," I told the man, trying to be as gentle as possible without making any attempt to disguise the truth. "Right doesn't depend on individual peoples' opinions of it, it depends on how well it matches to life as it's lived. That slaver who would insist he was acting in the right—would he still consider the doing right if it was applied to him or those he loved? Could it be applied to everyone around him without changing their circumstances and his own? If something is right for everyone else but not you and yours, you'd better take another look at your definition."

"And yet the concept of 'right' is a rather slippery commodity," the man said, somewhat startled at my comeback. "Some things are right for people to do because, in one way or another, they benefit from doing them, but for some reason they must be forced into the doing. Right now we're trying to force our concept of right on the slavers, and we're right in doing it. Doesn't that mean we'd be just as right forcing others to do what's good for them?"

"You're confusing two sorts of rights," I said, wondering why the man seemed never to have been exposed to the points in childhood, when he should have been. "We're right to stop the slavers, because what they do affects not only themselves but us as well. If they wanted to enslave each other, we'd have no right to interfere even if we disapproved; if what other people do affects no more than your sensibilities and opinions, you have no right telling them they shouldn't be doing it. The other sort of right you're talking about, though, is even easier to decide on. If you think somebody should be doing something because it's good for them and you believe you have the right to force them to it, just turn the question around. Would you enjoy being forced to do what *they* do because *they* think it's right? If the answer is no, your best move is to mind your own business."

"That, young woman, goes counter to every concept of duty I've ever been taught," the merchant said, having moved closer to the wounded man and me and away from the opened door. "If you know the right of something, it's your duty to teach it to those around you. The good fortune of being able to see right isn't something meant to be hoarded and kept secret. It's meant to be shared, and anyone who doesn't share it is more than selfish."

"There's no special fortune or ability involved in being able to see what's right," I disagreed, aware of the heavy frown on the man's face. "Even the smallest child can tell you right from wrong—according to his or her own point of view. Eating sweets is right, because it brings pleasure; eating sweets is wrong, because too many of them will make you sick. If duty is involved anywhere, it's your duty to make yourself understand that what's good for you isn't necessarily good for the next person, and that what you dislike doesn't have to be disliked by everyone in order for you to justify the dislike. Is it right or wrong for you to be here in this room while the others are out there fighting to save our lives?"

The abrupt question brought a look of pain to the merchant's face, and once again I could feel the roiling inside him. His hands began trembling again as his shoulders slumped, and he shook his head from side to side.

"That, child, shows how truly innocent you are," he said, his voice low, his eyes haunted. "How can it be anything but wrong for a man to hide himself while others fight his battles for him? Cowardice is wrong, and nothing can excuse it."

"That sounds like something you heard from someone who was never troubled by fear, and therefore thought *nobody* should be," I answered, working very hard to keep the pity out of my voice. "Rather than tackling the broad topic of bravery, why don't we ask a few smaller, more practical questions? The first one would be this, I think: which action does more for the general good, a frightened man who forces himself to fight with everyone else and thereby gets in the way, or one who accepts the personal humiliation of taking himself out from underfoot? The second choice is harder to make, but it gives everyone else a better chance to survive."

The merchant frowned again and parted his lips to argue, but the proper words didn't seem to want to come to him. He knew what he was doing was wrong, but he was having trouble explaining it to me.

"And let's consider the second question," I said without waiting, shifting just a little where I knelt. "If a man is wise enough to know that he lacks the ability to defend himself and therefore hires someone to do the job for him, how can he be considered a coward when he leaves himself unprotected for the sake of the group? That *was* you who gave his bodyguard permission to fight with the others, wasn't it? If you really were a coward you would have kept him beside you no matter how badly the others needed his ability, or you would have used him to get you out of this place without worrying about the rest of us. Admitting his limitations is something only a very brave man can do, and you've even done something better than that."

"What?" the merchant asked, wide-eyed with confusion. His hands no longer shook, but I didn't think he was aware of it.

"You didn't decide that it was wrong for other people to do what you couldn't or didn't want to," I answered with a smile. "Some people who are afraid to fight and die justify their fears by saying no one should do what they're afraid to do themselves. They make a virtue of their fears and attack those who don't have them by calling them evil names, and that's where the wrong comes in. They have no idea that the people they're insulting feel as much fear as they do; the only difference between them is that the second group of people have learned to control their fear. Bravery isn't the absence of fear, it's the controlling of fear in order to do what has to be done. Someone who feels no fear can never ever know the true meaning of bravery."

The merchant simply stood and stared at me, beyond even wanting to say anything in response, and I really did feel very sorry for him. What I'd been saying was nothing more than what children were taught in my mother's Realm, ideas that were discussed again and again while they grew to adulthood. If you don't get used to the ideas as a child, how are you supposed to be able to handle them as an adult?

"I can see you're as wise as you are lovely," the wounded man said. "You have less difficulty seeing to the heart of things than anyone I've ever met. You tempt me to the belief that right always does win."

"Maybe I should have said right always wins if you're willing to fight for it," I qualified, seeing his smile and remembering that he and the others seemed to need to hear things on a child's level. "Being right doesn't guarantee anything at all, not unless you're willing to oppose those who are wrong—and I'm not referring to a matter of opinion. Right is a balance that can be demonstrated, and if your concept of right has that balance, you'll win if you fight. We're fighting on the side of balance—on the side that says you're harming me and those around me and therefore you *cannot* be right—so we'll win. It isn't our opinions that are being harmed, and we can't protect ourselves simply by not indulging, so we're right to try stopping them. It's demanded by the balance of everything there is, and that gives us the edge. Our best will in that way be better than their best, and so we'll win."

"I certainly hope you're right," the wounded man said with a wry smile, then began moving around where he lay. "What doesn't seem quite right, however, or even particularly comfortable, is lying here on the floor any longer. Do you think you can help me to sit up?"

He began struggling erect without waiting for the help he'd requested, which wasn't terribly surprising. He'd been holding my hand long enough not to need the help, something he should have realized.

"Damned if I don't think the wound has stopped bleeding," he said, dropping my hand while trying to peer under the cloth on his chest. "If that isn't the last thing I expected to happen, it has to be the next to last."

"I do wish you would stop saying things like that," I told him with a sigh of half attention, more aware of the fighting still going on in the hall and upset that I wasn't helping. "When you took my hand you *had* to be convinced you were going to heal, or you wouldn't have touched me. Not unless you were in a hurry to get on to the next level, of course."

"What . . . are you talking about?" the man asked, his tone so odd that he drew my attention back. He was staring at me now in a very peculiar way, and I didn't understand.

"You can't possibly not have known that I'm a balancing force in my own right," I said, sharing his obvious confusion. "When there are two ways something can go, my touch will add strength to the side that's most firmly convinced of its right to be. If you weren't absolutely convinced you were going to survive your wound, touching me would have tumbled you over to the side of ending."

"That isn't possible," he said with a forced laugh, one that seemed to be trying to convince him I was joking. "No one can be a—*balancing force;* there is no such thing. When you're wounded the way I was, either it's so bad you die, or it's not too bad and you live. It's nothing that can be controlled by an outside force—unless you're talking about the will of the Highest Lord, or of Fate.''

"I'm talking about a situation in which there's an equal chance for more than one outcome," I said, feeling a very strong need to make him understand. "With something like your wound, it was bad enough that you could have ended from it, but it was also short of the point where ending was unavoidable. The Highest Lord has nothing to do with that, and there *is* no such thing as Fate the way *you're* saying it. The only one involved was you, which is the way it should be. Would you rather have your life depend on someone else's strength of determination?''

"But it just isn't possible!" he insisted, an odd fear in his eyes. "How could my life depend on determination? It's not like choosing what color shirt to wear, or which pair of shoes! It's a choice between living and dying!''

"And a choice we sometimes have to make," I agreed with a nod. "If you know the choice is yours rather than belonging to some outside force, you can summon the necessary belief when the time comes. My role is as an extra bit of help, something to focus your own strength on while you do what you have to. All humans have the ability to decide their own fate, and the tool they use to accomplish it is belief. What else would belief be good for? What I do is reinforce that belief—one way or the other.''

"Maybe . . . maybe I was distracted by the conversation," he said, suddenly looking pale and shaken. "And by your beauty— But how could you *be* something like that? The whole idea is— And you didn't say a word, not a single word! Touching your hand could have killed me, but you didn't speak a single word in warning! How could you do something like that?''

"I . . . thought you knew," I said, tangling with my hair as I moved back from the terrible accusation on his face and in his eyes. "You kept talking about how beautiful I was—I thought everyone knew. The things we find most beautiful and desirable are always balance points, people or objects that are capable of affecting our ultimate fate either positively or negatively. We're all taught as children not to reach out blindly . . .''

"So it's supposed to be my fault for not learning some vague fairy tale as a child?" he demanded, his face ugly as he began forcing himself to his feet. "You could have killed me and knew it, but you still didn't make any attempt to stop me! I could have died, and it would have been no one's fault but yours! So much for the things that are right.''

"But the choice was yours," I whispered, feeling horribly cold and almost trembling. "No one has the right to tell you what to do with your life . . ."

I let the quivering words trail off, and didn't start them up again. He had turned away and was moving heavily toward the other side of the room, having heard nothing beyond the end of his own speaking. It was almost as though he were looking for someone else to blame for what his own decisions had brought him to, but that didn't make any sense. If someone else makes your decisions you're nothing but a shadow of that other person, and who would want to be nothing but a shadow?

After a moment or two I got to my own feet, but couldn't think of anything to do or anywhere to go. It finally came to me that the merchant was no longer in the room, and then I noticed that the sounds of fighting had stopped coming from the hall. I could hear soft voices, and people moving around, but the battle itself seemed to be over. I thought about going to the open doorway and looking out, but before I could take the first step the wounded man was already doing that. That didn't mean I couldn't do the same, of course, but the way he looked at me as he crossed the room froze me in place with the same chill I'd felt earlier. The man didn't hate me, he was disgusted by me, and that was a terrible feeling to get from another person.

I had turned away from the doorway and was trying to find something to look at that wasn't dead or covered with blood, when I heard Jiss's voice. I looked around to see him talking to the wounded man just outside the room, then the man walked off without a backward glance and Jiss came in with a smile.

"I think you'll be glad to hear that it's just about over, Hali," he said, walking toward me. "Most of the ones who chose to fight us are dead, and only a couple of them managed to get away. Skyhawk and two of our men went below after some of the runners, took care of them, and then looked around in the kitchens where they'd fought. They found the herbs that had been used to drug the guests, and then they found some to counter the first. We're getting ready to wake up everyone in the house, and once those who have had their sleep are settled into watchposts, the rest of us can relax a little. Right now I want you to come with me."

He put his arm around my shoulders and began leading me out of the room, and I didn't speak a word in protest. I wanted to be out of that room, wanted it very much, but when he led me across the hall and over toward his own room I was confused.

"Your room is too close to where they'll be trying to clean up what we dropped on the floors," Jiss told me as he opened his door, most likely answering the question he could see on my face. "You may remember that we have some conversation to exchange, and I'll be free to join you in just a little while. Go on in and rest while you're waiting, and I'll be back in no time at all."

He urged me inside with another smile, and then he pulled the door closed to make the privacy complete. I knew that earlier I would have resented being treated like that, but just then privacy held a great deal of appeal. Especially in a room that would hopefully not allow someone to look at me from behind the walls. I remembered what the slavers had said about the way that first slaver had inspected me, which meant they had known Jiss and Skyhawk would put me in the middle room, the one between them, for added safety. Being that safe made me shiver just a little, but I pushed the thought away and went over to the settle to sit down.

After the nap I'd had earlier in the evening I wasn't tired

enough to fall asleep, but whatever time passed seemed to float by in a mist of upset. I wasn't used to fully grown adults having so little understanding of the way things really were, or of being blamed for the reality they didn't care for. It made me feel unwanted and ugly, more like an alien intruder than I sometimes felt at home. I had the urge to curl up smaller against the settle back and hide myself with my hair, but until Greaf and the Great Flame were found and returned I couldn't afford to hide. Maybe afterward, though . . .

"See, that didn't take very long, and now I'm all yours," Jiss said, startling me as he came through the door. "Everything is going just the way we want it to, and we even have prisoners to turn over to the authorities in this area."

He closed the door behind himself and walked over to the settle, opening his swordbelt as he came. By the time he reached the table just before the settle the swordbelt was off, so he put it on the table then moved closer to sit down beside me.

"You won't believe the unexpected help we had, just at the end of the fighting and also afterward," he said, his face covered with amusement. "That merchant we left in the room with you and our wounded man—for some reason he decided to join the rest of us. He was really frightened, as anyone with eyes could see, but he moved into the fight and actually used that dagger he was holding to ease the pressure of three blades against his bodyguard. That act could very well have been the turning point of the entire fight, winning it for us rather than the enemy. Afterward the little man noticed he had somehow gotten wounded—a cut on the arm that wasn't serious but had to be painful—but all he did was laugh when he found it. He said it hurt terribly, but not as badly as not hurting at all. None of us could understand what he was talking about, but we didn't mind having him along to help mop up."

"I think you could say he finally found the peace he wanted, and wasn't surprised to discover it in the middle of a fight," I answered, suddenly feeling a good deal better. "Now that he knows what it looks like, he won't have trouble recognizing it when there is no battle. I'm really happy for him.''

"And *I'm* happy for *you*," Jiss said with a smile, moving just a little closer. "I kept expecting you to suddenly appear in the middle of the fighting, making things a thousand times harder for us. You have to understand that it isn't that we don't want your help, Hali, it's that we don't want to see you getting hurt. How much do you think we would have enjoyed our victory, if yours was one of the unmoving bodies we found on the floor afterward?''

"Honestly, Jiss, don't you think I would have been willing to stay out of it if I couldn't take care of myself?" I asked in turn, beginning to feel annoyed again. "I may not have your sort of weapon to swing in all directions, but that doesn't make me helpless. I'll admit I don't do very well when I'm surprised, but that fight wouldn't have been a surprise in—"

"Hali, let's not argue," he interrupted, looking down at me with smiling golden eyes that glowed in the firelight. "You added to our victory by going along with something you didn't agree with, and I'd like to thank you for that. In a way I hope you *will* agree with."

Without any further warning he put his arms around me, and then he was leaning down to kiss me the way he had in the thornbush clearing. I wasn't used to being held and kissed like that, but the experience is too pleasant to need very much in the way of adjustment. In a moment I was leaning closer to his chest, my hands spread out against the leather of his shirt, my lips returning the warm interest they were being given.

I think I expected us to be interrupted again, specifically by that outlaw, but the kiss continued on and on with nothing happening to ruin it. When Jiss decided to end it there was nothing of an unfinished feeling to the experience, and he looked down at me with a smile that was warmer than ever.

"Have you been practicing?" he asked, gentle teasing lightening the words. "That was a lot better than the first time, and the first time wasn't exactly a wasted effort."

"I told you you weren't the first one I'd ever kissed," I answered with a small laugh, feeling my cheeks warm with a blush of pleasure. "Did you really like it?"

"Very much," he said, his smile adding more warmth to the words than the fire in the hearth added to the room. "So much so, in fact, that I'd like to do it again. Would you mind?"

I shook my head to show that I didn't mind, then leaned toward him as his arms went around me again. When his lips came back to mine I realized that not only didn't I mind, I actually wanted him to hold me and kiss me like that. It was more than pleasant, more than delightful—and then it became more than I was expecting. Jiss had begun moving his hands around on me, gently but without hesitation, and then one of his hands went to the front of the shirt I was wearing.

"Don't be afraid," he said with soft reassurance when I ended the kiss rather abruptly, confusion pulling my face back away from his. "I'm not going to hurt you, Hali, I just want to show you how desirable a woman I think you are. And it's also what you've been insisting on since before we came through the Realm Threshold. Have you changed your mind?"

His hand had stopped opening the shirt as he waited for me to answer his question, but for a moment I didn't know what to say. I'd always thought bed activity was something you decided on in a cool and rational way, then got to in a businesslike manner. I hadn't realized that some people preferred kissing and touching first, and that might well have been why Jiss hadn't been willing earlier. It wasn't that he didn't find me attractive and adult enough, it was just that it hadn't started in the right way.

"No, I haven't changed my mind," I said after the hesitation I wished had never happened, trying to give him a smile that showed more conviction than nervousness. "I'd very much like you to show me how desirable you think I am."

"That will definitely be my pleasure," he said with the smile returned, his hands now urging me to lie back on the settle. Then he leaned down and began kissing me again, and only after it was well started did his hand go back to what it had almost done before with my shirt. He opened it slowly but deliberately, his other arm holding me comfortably, his lips taking most of my attention. I could feel my heart beating a little faster as each button was opened in turn, and once there were no buttons left Jiss's hand slipped inside the shirt. I closed my fingers on his arm to hold back a gasp of very great pleasure, and my companion raised his head to chuckle.

"You're even more desirable to touch than to look at," he murmured, giving me not-quite-brief kisses between the words. His hand was so warm on my breast, his fingers so gentle and sure as they stroked my flesh, the sense of a current flowing into me from it—all that tingled every part I had.

And then he parted my shirt and began kissing me elsewhere than on the lips, and my gasp turned into a moan. The sensation was exquisite, like nothing I'd ever felt before, and I clutched at the leather of his shirt knowing I would never forget it. It came to me faintly in passing that I should be embarrassed, but I was feeling too marvelous to even consider embarrassment. I wanted more of those new feelings, more of the wonder Jiss was creating for me, and then I got it.

His hands went to my trousers as his lips trailed down my body, and then he was opening them and pushing them down to my knees. The movement of his fingers paralyzed me, and then his face was back and touching his lips to mine. He kissed me lightly, quickly, letting me know there was something else he was about to do, and when I threw my arms around his neck to keep him from moving away he chuckled.

"Don't worry, I'm not going anywhere," he whispered, his breathing heavier than it had been. "He was absolutely right, and I'm glad this is necessary. You need a normal first time in case something happens, and in just a little while you'll have it."

Once again his lips came to mine, but that didn't stop

the movement of his hands that brought me feelings that turned me limp. Most of me was well on the way to being overwhelmed, but a small, round central core of deepdown me was listening again to what Jiss had said, and wasn't quite understanding. For some reason understanding was very important, so important that I was able to pull away from a kiss that was slowly growing more demanding.

"Jiss, wait," I pleaded, my voice trembling despite the near whisper I used, my hands flat to the leather of his shirt. "What did you mean, *he* was right? Who were you talking about?"

"Why, Skyhawk, of course," he answered as though it didn't mean a thing, his lips at my neck and throat, his hands stroking and gently tickling. "I hadn't realized how much danger I was leaving you in, but once he pointed it out to me I could see it clearly enough. If I wasn't going to take you home, there was only one other thing I could honorably do. Here, let me help you get those trousers off all the way."

He let go of me to reach down toward my trousers, which made it possible for me to push against him with all my strength. If the settle had been wider or Jiss smaller I would have accomplished nothing at all, but the man was already more than half over the edge, so the push I gave him sent him the rest of the way with a yell of surprise. Even as he hit the floor with a thump I was pulling my clothing back around me, and then I was standing up to finish the job properly.

"Hali, what's wrong with you?" Jiss demanded as he looked up at me, not very pleased with having been knocked to the floor. "You're supposed to be taking those things off, not putting them on again. Just lie down, and this time I'll be more careful of— "

"Of what you say?" I finished for him, absolutely furious. "You don't want to take me to bed, you're just seeing to a matter of honor! And once again you weren't even the one who thought of it! I hate you, *Prince* Jentris, and I'd rather be untouched for the rest of my life than go to bed with *you!*"

I'd finished knotting the tie closed on my trousers and had managed a button or two on the shirt, and that was more than enough to let me get out of there. I began striding toward the door that had been closed so cozily on our privacy, but Jiss just couldn't leave it like that.

"Now, Hali, don't be angry," he coaxed as he arose from the floor. "I'll admit I was blind not to see how really desirable you are, but now that I *can* see, what difference does it make whose idea it was? I'm the one who wants you, and I have no intention of simply letting you walk away from me."

"Try and stop me," I snapped over my shoulder with a glance for his bright-eyed stare, then I was yanking the door open and moving out into the hall. I could hear talk and movement coming from the floor below, but everyone, living or dead, was gone from the floor I was on.

"We're not through talking about this, Hali," Jiss said from his doorway as I neared mine. "If you need a little time to calm down you can have it, but right after that I'll be with you again, and then we'll finish what we started."

"You come near me again, and the only thing finished will be you," I said in a growl, then shoved my way into my room and slammed the door behind me. The idiot had grinned at the solemn promise I'd given him, as though he had nothing at all to worry about from me, and didn't *that* help to improve my mood!

I stalked back and forth an uncounted number of minutes, but the movement didn't do much to calm me down. I was furious at myself for believing even briefly that Jiss had changed his mind about finding me attractive, that he had suddenly and magically opened his eyes to the fact that I was a woman rather than a child. He had done nothing of the sort no matter *what* he insisted on, and foolishly I felt hurt that he would lie to me like that. I wasn't any more attractive to him than I was to that wounded man who had been so upset, and if he thought I was too much of an infant to understand that, he was as wrong as I had been.

And that miserable outlaw! I stopped short to clench my

fists, feeling how good it would be to beat at his face with those fists. Why do you want to take me to bed, Jiss? Because Skyhawk told me to, Hali, why else? Don't I do everything Skyhawk tells me to? There was no doubt Jiss did exactly that, but this time the outlaw had meddled too far. I'd had more than enough of both good friends, and from then on if they were interested in bed play, they could use each other. I would no longer be around to give them practice in order giving or advantage taking.

Never in my life had I made a decision that fast or that firm, and I was on my way over to my draperies so quickly that under other circumstances I would have been surprised. That time I felt no surprise whatsoever, only faint disappointment when my clothing proved to be still damp. That meant I would have to take it with me rather than wear it, but the problem was easily solved. I rolled the draperies up, tucked them under my arm, then left the room for the very last time. I was going after Greaf and the Great Flame alone, just the way I should have to begin with.

Chapter 8

THE FOREST WAS STILL very wet and the air was too cool because of that, but it had stopped raining. My horse moved at a decent pace along the road, rested well enough that he didn't mind being on the way again, and the continuing darkness was even soothing me to a certain extent. I still wished the Earth Realm were more like my mother's, where rain only fell at carefully designated times, when no one would be around to be bothered by it. I'd never seen rain before passing the Realm Threshold, and couldn't say I would have missed the experience if I hadn't seen it then either. There seemed to be quite a lot of things I wouldn't have minded missing, but it was a little too late to try avoiding them.

Or avoiding them entirely. I sighed as I shifted on that very hard saddle, tugging my hair out from under me again, glad at least that I'd left my largest difficulties behind me. With all the people moving around the inn it hadn't been easy getting out without being seen, but the spiders had acted as lookouts for me, and had let me know when everyone's attention was enough occupied with other things that I could slip behind them all into the stables. Whoever had been on guard out there was no longer around to be worried about, and the shadows had been thick enough that I hadn't been seen even when someone had come out to look around. I'd waited until he left, finished saddling my horse and stuffing my draperies into a saddlebag, and then I had ridden away.

"Without getting the chance to thank that outlaw for being so concerned about me," I muttered aloud, regretting that lack most of all. The man called Skyhawk had been too busy sending everyone in different directions when I'd left, which meant I hadn't been able to reach him without letting everyone know I was going. I'd never known people could be that cruel, to resent someone so much they wanted to hurt them, but not in a face-to-face exchange. He had used Jiss to hurt me, making it worse than anything he could have done himself, and I would never forgive him even if he lived as long as I would.

The trees murmured sleepily all around me, doing more dreaming aloud than actually saying anything, which meant my thoughts and planning went on uninterrupted. Not that I had that much in the way of thoughts to interrupt once I turned my attention to planning. I'd gotten as far as deciding to chase the thieves all alone, and now that I'd accomplished the beginning of that decision all I could see beyond it was a large blank area. The thieves were somewhere up ahead of me, but I didn't know exactly where; they would soon be starting to move again, but I didn't know exactly when; if I managed to catch up I'd have to stop them, but I didn't know exactly how. I had the feeling I couldn't have done worse even if I'd tried, a conclusion that was designed to lower my spirits even more than—

Haliand! a thought suddenly came out of the dark, a thought I hadn't heard in far too long. *I'm so glad I've finally found you!*

"Oh, Sahrinth, how I've missed you!" I laughed in answer as I pulled my horse to a halt, wishing I could hug my friend's small, delicate cloud-body with all my strength. "I was beginning to think we'd never see each other again. Are you all right?"

It's rather difficult to cause me hardship, Haliand, Sahrinth answered, and I had the distinct impression I was being closely inspected. *The question is how you are. Wherever did you get those outlandish clothes?*

"My draperies were soaked in the rainstorm, and this was all that was available," I explained, not bothering to glance down at myself. "What about Greaf and the Great Flame? Are they all right too, or have those thieves done something else?"

Aside from being held captive, they haven't been harmed, he answered, bobbing just a little in front of my face. *The one who carried them across the Realm Threshold can't quite say the same, though. He was still unconscious when they put him in the wagon and that seemed to be part of their plan, but having him get hurt when the wagon wheel broke off certainly wasn't. He hit his head rather sharply, and hasn't really come back to himself since. The ones traveling with him are frantic, but there's nothing they can do aside from continuing to return him to where he came from. I overheard them talking more than once, and he was supposed to leave the wagon when he awoke and take what he was carrying to some special place as fast as it was possible to ride. At this point, the man barely knows who he is; going somewhere alone is completely beyond him.*

"Thieves deserve whatever happens to them," I said, feeling no sympathy at all for the man I had spoken to so briefly. "Most things in the worlds want to balance, and I'd say that man was being given a good taste of balance. If he's hurt that badly, maybe the ones with him will decide to stay longer in the place where they are."

They decided against that, and are already back on the road, Sahrinth replied, still moving with suppressed agitation. *They're going to take him where they're supposed to go, and let their superiors decide what to do next. They're very much afraid of making the wrong decision, so they're not really making any at all.*

"That's what happens when you depend on terrorized slaves to do your work," I said, feeling quite a lot of grim satisfaction. "You don't just deserve what happens, you've asked for it and earned it. Do you know where they're going?"

Not precisely, but I know how they're getting there,

Sahrinth answered. *They're going to continue up this road to a crossroad, turn east at the crossroad, pass two small villages, then follow a fork northwest toward a river. Wherever they're going is near that river. One of the group, the one who had been driving the wagon, made sure all the rest knew the way when he had to let someone else drive while he took care of the man who was hurt. Once they were on the road again I came back to look for you and Prince Jentris, but I wasn't able to find you. Where were you, and where is the prince?*

"We stopped at an inn because of the rain," I said, letting nothing of how I felt show on my face. "There was some trouble there, and the prince stayed behind to help while I came ahead. East at the crossroad, you say, then past two villages to a fork, and then turn northwest toward a river? Are they moving really fast, or are they taking it slow out of concern for their passenger?"

They've compromised on moving as quickly as they can without causing the man too much discomfort, he said, the whitish gray of his body beginning to roil darker. *Haliand, I don't like the idea of you traveling alone in this Realm. It isn't safe, and the humans are— Well, let's just say they're strange. How long do you think it will take Prince Jentris to catch up to you?*

"Sahrinth, don't you think Prince Jentris wants to recover Greaf and the Great Flame as badly as we do?" I asked in turn, hoping he would miss the fact that I wasn't really answering his question. "He'll be back on the road after the thieves as soon as he possibly can, and that's something you simply can't doubt."

Of course I don't doubt that, he quickly assured me, his tone going faintly defensive. *I do know what sort of being the prince is, and I have every confidence in him. I'll return to the wagon now, and you can be sure I'll be back again to report at the first opportunity. By then the prince should be with you, so I won't need to repeat myself.*

I smiled and nodded without saying anything, and happily Sahrinth took that to mean full agreement. He bobbed quickly in his version of a wave good-bye, waited until I waved back, and then melted away into the dark again.

"I'm sorry, Sahrinth, but I'd rather you have the need to repeat yourself, than that I have the prince with me," I murmured, patting my mount as I glanced back up the road. I didn't know how long it would take before Jiss knew I was gone, but whenever he found out he would also discover he had a choice to make. He could search actively for me, simply follow the thieves of the Great Flame, or be on the alert for me while he tried to recover the Great Flame. If I knew Jiss he would go for the third choice, especially since he was well enough aware of the fact that I would not go wandering off somewhere while Greaf was still a prisoner. No, he would expect to find me on the trail ahead of him, which meant I could avoid him if I simply stayed out of sight.

Which I fully intended doing. I looked around at the dark again and I noticed the softening quality to it, a presence that spoke as clearly as words of the approaching dawn. Jiss did best in his father's strong light, and I in my mother's bright glow; I should have remembered that and stayed away from him, no matter how handsome the man was. I turned my horse toward the woods and kicked him gently, then guided him around things once he was moving. Jiss had come to my Realm to marry one of my sisters, not one of my mother's daughters, and from then on I would keep that fact firmly in mind—even if it did hurt.

I rode on through the woods until the sun was high and hot, and then I found a stream to drink from and a place to sleep until it was dark again. The trees helped me find the stream and the sleeping place, and also kept me going on a course parallel to the road. I didn't stop until I was beyond that town place, of course, and also asked the trees to warn me if any enemies came toward me or I rode toward them. That part, at least, was simple enough; all the people of that Realm were enemies—nonfriends—to the trees, and they were the same to me.

The grassy little hideaway the trees found for me to sleep in was very pleasant, for my horse as well as me. He was able to graze while I spread my draperies in a slant of sunshine to dry them the rest of the way, and then I lay down to sleep in the shadow of some bushes. It would have helped if I could have grazed first myself, but I had no food and that was that. Once I was on my way again I'd have to see what I could do about the problem, but there was nothing I could do right then.

I slept deeply for what felt like a long time, and when I awoke it was just about full dark. I stretched hard and then lay where I was for a moment, wondering how much of the gap I'd be able to close between me and the thieves. I'd continued on for half of the time they'd been moving as well, but I intended to keep going all through the night, the time they would be sleeping. It wasn't beyond reason to think I might even catch up with them, and if I did I might be able to take back Greaf and the Great Flame without their knowing it. They were only ephemerals who couldn't even see in the dark, after all; maybe having someone along with a weapon would prove less necessary than—

"It looks to me as though you're awake," a voice said suddenly, startling me into twisting around. "With this little light it's hard to tell, though. If you're not really ready to get up, by all means go back to sleep."

"How did you find me?" I demanded, sitting up as I stared at the calm face of that miserable outlaw, Skyhawk. "And even above that, what do you think you're doing here?"

"I tracked you to make sure you were all right," he answered, sitting up and away from the tree he'd been leaning against. "When Jentris found you gone he was frantic, and that was when he told me what had happened between you. He wanted to ride after you but didn't know where to begin looking, and also had that mission he had to finish seeing to. I volunteered to come after you while he took care of his business, and now that I've found you we can go looking for him. He'll be leaving trail signs for me to follow, so . . .''

His words cut off as I climbed quickly to my feet, my intentions straightforward enough even for someone like him to understand. I'd heard all I had interest in hearing, and now I was going to get ready to leave—alone.

"Haliand, don't be angry with Jentris," the man said gently as I moved to my now dry draperies and began folding them again, the sounds of his rising accompanying the words. "What happened between you was my fault rather than his, and even I wasn't trying to hurt you. For some reason Jentris wasn't seeing you in the right way, but all that has changed. He told me how much he wants you now, and if you give him the chance he'll make you want him just as deeply.''

I was tempted to tell that ephemeral exactly how much of a chance I would be giving his good friend Jentris, but for once I had no interest in speaking to the man, not even to explain the truth about things. I had nothing to say to him and even less to say to Jiss, so all I did was take my folded draperies over to my horse, where I stuffed them back into a saddlebag. With that done I shifted over a little to begin tightening the saddle girth I'd loosened before going to sleep, but the outlaw was very much like his good friend. He too had no idea when to leave an abandoned topic to lie undisturbed, and this time his voice came from close behind me.

"It bothers me that you're not screaming and yelling and telling me how wrong I am," he said, his voice still gentle. "That has to mean you were hurt very badly, which in turn makes me wish Jentris had had the sense to keep his mouth shut. I don't know what's the matter with you two, but I've never seen two people more determined to tell the truth no matter what it costs them. You should both be old enough to understand the benefits of discretion and occasional dishonesty, especially when members of the opposite sex are involved. The practice is called tact around here, and really isn't very difficult to learn.''

Lying never is, I thought to myself as I finished with the

girth, then brought the stirrup back down to where it belonged. I knew how to be evasive, how to be tactful, and even how to lie outright, but I'd never thought any of that should be used when it came to bed activity. I'd always thought that would be a time for complete honesty, but it didn't surprise me that Skyhawk and other ephemerals saw it differently. It was probably true that I was innocent, but Earth Realm people were worse in that they were predictable.

"Haliand, you're not riding off alone again," the outlaw said as I went to take the grazing lead from my horse's neck and the other end from the tree it had been tied to. "Even if you never say another word to me, I'm still not about to let you disappear into the night. We'll stay together until we find Jentris, and then I'll leave you two alone for as long a time as you need to work things out between you. Running away from problems doesn't solve them, all it does is give them time to grow to an even more unmanageable size."

I nearly told him he was seeing only one side of a truth, but instead coiled the grazing lead and put it into the saddlebag with my draperies. Most problems did have to be faced before they could be solved, but in some instances simply admitting there was a problem took care of the facing part. If a particular food disagrees with you, you don't keep eating it in the hopes that you'll get used to it. You stop eating it no matter how good it tastes, and solve your problem that way.

"Now look, you have to be hungry," he said in a coaxing tone, practically reading my mind. I hadn't realized I shouldn't have used a food analogy, not until it was too late. "Let's sit down and have something to eat, and afterward I'm sure you'll feel better. And you'll also be able to accept the fact that you aren't going anywhere except with me."

His voice went flat with finality when he reached the point he refused to argue, but I really couldn't have cared less. I would rather have starved than share anything with that man, and if I ever rode with anyone, it most certainly would not be with him. Walking back and forth taking care of details had given me time to think about what I could do to get rid of him, and the answer had been both simple and obvious. As soon as everything was ready for me to leave, I turned from my horse and walked away into the darkness.

It took no more than half a dozen steps before the blackness swallowed me up, and then I was able to turn back to watch the outlaw as I circled around to the far side of the resting place. My hands were busy as I moved, weaving myself a thick cover of shadow, one that would turn me invisible even to close-up inspection. The only uncertain part of my very simple plan had been whether or not the outlaw would just let me walk away from him, but I needn't have bothered worrying. Since I'd left on foot he'd obviously taken my abrupt departure as a need for privacy, which it certainly had been, but not in the way he thought.

I stood and watched Skyhawk as he waited, and saw at once when he shifted from calm patience to growing suspicion. He was beginning to realize I'd been gone for quite some time, and that moved him to face more fully the section of dark I'd disappeared into. That put his back to me, of course, but the shift didn't become a handicap. He waited no more than another brief moment, and then the waiting ended.

"Haliand, are you all right out there?" he called, letting no more than casual concern color his tone. "I'm not asking you to talk to me, just to let me know you're all right. If you don't answer, I'm going to have to come out there to see for myself."

The darkness he faced gave him nothing of the answer he'd demanded, which in turn made him shift in place before straightening his shoulders.

"If that's the way you want it, then it's all right with me," he called again, this time sounding firm and determined. "I didn't mind the first time, so I certainly won't mind a repeat performance. If you don't like that idea, you can stop it immediately by answering me."

He hesitated very briefly to give the answer he wanted its chance to come, but when it didn't he moved off into the bushes and trees with a very determined stride. How he thought he would find me in the dark I had no idea, but I also had no time to waste thinking about it. My circling around had put me only a few feet from his horse, and as soon as he left the clearing I stepped over to his saddlebags. He'd offered to share food with me earlier and I'd decided to take him up on it, but in my way rather than his.

He seemed to have taken quite a lot of edibles from the inn, but I didn't have the time to examine everything and then pick and choose. One of the cloth-wrapped packages had bread and cheese and another had meat, so I took those over to my horse, thrust them into the empty saddlebag, then circled my horse again and mounted. Both of the horses were faintly uneasy over the fact that they could smell and hear me but couldn't make me out with their eyes, and that gave me an idea. The outlaw's stallion wasn't tied, not even on a grazing tether; once I was mounted I rode close to the beast, moaned eerily in its ear, then watched it take off into the forest. Horses hate that particular sound, and I chuckled to myself as I rode off in a different direction entirely. The magnificent Skyhawk was the one who had said his horse would never run away; when he got back to the clearing, he might decide it was time to have second thoughts about not having tied his mount.

I made sure of the location of the road before continuing on through the night, and kept going for quite a while before stopping for a meal. After eating some of the bread, meat, and cheese I discovered I didn't need the trees to help me find water; the air of the night dark fairly shouted the location of many things, in a way the daytime sunshine didn't. I'd put away my woven cover of shadow when I'd stopped to eat, so after my horse and I had drunk our fill from the lovely brook we'd come to, I mounted again and we went on.

I had time to wonder how that outlaw had found me

with the trees supposedly on guard against intruders, but with no chance to find out by asking, I let the matter drift away. Only dawn would bring the trees out of their dreaming and to a point where I could speak to them again, and by then I'd probably discover they'd tried to wake me but I'd been sleeping too soundly. As long as it didn't happen again it really wouldn't matter, and I'd taken my own steps to be sure it didn't.

I was able to keep to a good pace as I rode through the night, and I didn't even have to fight really hard to keep from thinking about where Jiss might be. He'd probably stopped to camp at sundown, and was just then sound asleep. He didn't know where the thieves were or where they were heading, and when I came to the crossroad and traversed it to head east, I realized he would probably never find them. It really was up to me to get Greaf and the Great Flame back, and being alone while I did it wasn't going to bother me at all. I'd do what I had to and then I could go home—*without* Prince Jentris of the Sun Realm.

It was almost that time of the very early morning that causes birds to begin stirring and chirping, when I saw something in the woods a short distance off the road. I was still keeping the road to my right, just as I'd done before I reached and passed the crossroad, and the large, out-of-place shadow there attracted my attention. I stopped to look at it more directly, then caught my breath and immediately began to dismount. The strange shadow had the outline of a wagon, which definitely called for a closer, on-foot investigation.

As soon as my horse was tied to a tree I began moving as silently as I could around bushes and other trees, hoping hard that the thud of my heartbeat really wasn't loud enough to be heard from the outside. I'd thought about the possibility of catching up to the thieves and had even told myself I was expecting it, but from the way I felt I apparently hadn't believed I would. When I rounded one tree and saw a small, previously hidden campfire I swallowed, and then had to be very firm with myself. Those people couldn't see me, and even if they did they couldn't hurt me. So why was I so nervous?

I couldn't think of an answer to fit that question, and waiting around until I did wasn't something I was prepared to do, so I pushed away the upset in my mind and simply crept a little nearer to the wagon. The closer I got the more I could see, and once the fire was well in view so were the sleeping bodies ranged around it. At least six men were rolled in blankets against the cool of the night, and none of them seemed ready to wake up. If those were the thieves I'd found them at the best possible time, but I still didn't know if they were the ones I was looking for. The one face I would find it possible to recognize was probably inside the wagon, so how was I supposed to—

Right then was when I saw the left rear wagon wheel, and I was delighted to notice how much better that observation made me feel. The wheel was as mud-splashed as the rest of the wagon—and the other wheel I could see— but under the mud the wood and metal looked new and barely used rather than old and worn. The likeliest explanation was that I had found the thieves, and as far as I could see they were all asleep.

As far as I could see. I stirred where I crouched beside the body of a large tree, knowing I couldn't be certain they were all asleep until I looked in the wagon. I had to get into the wagon anyway since that was where the box of the Great Flame probably was, and then it occurred to me to look around again, only more carefully. I was as certain as I could be that that was the wagon of the thieves, but if it was, where was Sahrinth? He would know exactly where the box was and could also look around for anyone still awake without our worrying that he would be seen, but there wasn't the least trace of his cloud-body anywhere. I searched again, really straining into the dark to see as much as possible, but the second attempt was as successful as the first.

"That's the trouble with cloud life forms," I muttered under my breath as I gave up on the search. "They're never around when you need them. I guess it really is all up to me.''

I straightened up and stepped behind the tree, then began making my way back to where I'd left my horse. It would have been nice having Sahrinth to do my looking for me, but the truth of the matter was that I didn't need him. That cover of darkness I'd woven earlier in the night was all ready and waiting, and once I had it over me I would be even more invisible than Sahrinth. I'd have to circle around to the other side of the wagon to avoid the firelight, but once that was done the Great Flame and my close friend would be as good as in my hands.

By the time I reached my horse I was wondering if it wouldn't have been faster weaving a new cover rather than going back for the old one, but it was already done. I reached to the saddlebag with a shrug, knowing my circling would have to be accomplished from that far out anyway, and then—

And then I was seized from behind, an arm around my waist, a hand over my mouth, the arm pressing me back against the hard body it was attached to. I let out a yell and tried to struggle, but the yell was muffled down to nothing and the struggling proved totally ineffective. I was lifted clear off the ground and carried a short distance away from my horse, and then was forced facedown into the grass. With the body I'd been held against now holding me down I couldn't even try pulling away, and then the hand over my mouth was replaced by a cloth held in the other hand, which was then tied down with a long strip of cloth. Once that was done, my wrists were brought behind me and tied with another strip of cloth, and lastly the same was done to my ankles.

Needless to say, by that time I was almost frantic. I didn't know who it was who had done that to me, and even beyond that I was losing my chance to rescue Greaf and the Great Flame! With the weight gone from my back I struggled over onto my right side, wild to know who had attacked me like that. It was still very dark in the forest and the light of that campfire didn't reach where I lay, but when the man came back leading his horse I had no trouble seeing his face. The sight was so much of a shock I lay still on the ground, trying to understand how it was possible. The man who had captured and tied me was none other than Skyhawk!

By the time that miserable outlaw decided we'd come far enough from where we'd been, it was full daylight. He pulled his horse to a stop and dismounted, then reached up to lift me down from where I hung draped over his saddle like a sack. I was so furious I would have tried killing him if I hadn't been tied, and when he put me down in the grass on my back the look in his dark eyes said he knew it.

"Why don't you try to calm down while I take care of the horses?" he said, his voice even and reasonable in a disgustingly superior way. "They can graze while you and I talk."

Talk! I wanted to talk to him, all right, and as I watched him walk away I began choosing the words and phrases I intended using. Of course, the calm he wanted was nowhere in sight, but that was just too bad. His idiocy had ruined everything, and I intended letting him know it.

It didn't take very long before he had detached the lead rope from my horse and had retied it in a place that let the gelding reach the grass, and then he came back toward me. Once again he'd left his own horse to do as it pleased, and that added to my annoyance. By rights he should have still been searching the forest for the beast, but instead he was right there, completely in my way.

"Now that it's light out, I think we can dispense with keeping you tied," the outlaw said, bending first to my ankles. "You disappear too easily in the dark, but I don't think you can do the same in broad daylight. Just in case, though, I don't intend letting you out of my sight."

Once my ankles were free he moved to my wrists, but that was all the help I had interest in taking from him. As soon as the cloth came loose I pulled my arms away, then yanked the gag out of my mouth.

"If you aren't the stupidest being ever created, I'd have

to see one worse before I believed it," I began at once, twisting around to glare at him. "Have you any idea what you've done? But of course you don't, how could you? You'd have to have a *mind* to understand, and on that score you simply don't qualify."

"Is that so?" he said, anger beginning to show in his eyes as he looked back at me from the crouch he remained in. "*I'm* the one who doesn't have a mind? Since I'm not the one who was about to commit the greatest stupidity I've ever come across, I think you'll have to reexamine your statements. That *was* you who was preparing to sneak up on the campsite with the wagon, wasn't it?"

"No, not just 'the campsite and the wagon,'" I mimicked, really angry that someone like him would have the nerve to try criticizing me. "I was preparing to sneak up on the *thieves* Jentris and I have been chasing, and if not for you and your interference, I would have had our property back! Now, what was that you were saying about me reexamining my statements?"

"I'm not surprised you don't remember," he returned, unbelievably not in the least taken aback. "I know Jentris said you were raised very sheltered, but that's not supposed to be a euphemism for thickheaded and blind. Didn't you see the device on the side of the wagon, or did you simply decide to ignore it? That wasn't your thieves you found, it was a group belonging to the household of the Highest Lord of Lords! You're just lucky the four sentries they had out missed seeing you the first time you got close, or you'd be holding this conversation now with someone other than me. You made a *mistake*, girl, and refusing to admit it just shows how badly you do need to have someone keep his eye on you."

I was so angry I almost told him what a complete fool he was, but that wouldn't have been very wise. His mentioning the strange design on the side of the wagon, a mud-spattered painting of a closed fist in a bronze glove, simply confirmed what I already knew: the thieves were in the hire of the Lord of the Earth. Or were owned by him, a much more accurate description of things as they were. If I said his precious Highest Lord of Lords followers *were* the thieves I was after, the outlaw was bound to ask more questions than I would care to answer. I wouldn't have put it past the creature called Skyhawk to decide to steal the Great Flame for himself, which meant that the last thing I could do was tell him the truth.

"If there's anything I *don't* need, it's having *you* around to keep an eye on me," I said with the smallest hesitation I could manage, knowing I had to get rid of the man before I'd be able to go after the thieves again. "What I do or don't do is none of your business, and I insist that you leave me alone. And now that I have the time to ask, how did you find me? I know how well you can see in the dark, so don't try telling me again that you tracked me."

"I'll tell you how I found you just as soon as you tell me how you found out the location of my sword and Jentris's back at the inn," he countered, finally straightening out of his crouch. "You're not the only one who can pull tricks others can't, little girl, and it so happens that what you do *is* my business. Jentris asked me to look after you and keep you safe, and that's exactly what I intend doing. Even if he would have been wiser asking me to protect everyone else from you."

The look he gave me as he turned away said very clearly that he didn't think much of me, and the feeling was certainly mutual. I got to my feet even angrier than I had been, my teeth and fists clenched over the way he'd called me "little girl." He thought he was so good, so utterly superior, when all he was was a fool of an ephemeral outlaw who knew nothing but the stunted learnings and outlooks of a twisted, backward Realm. As things stood he probably had no *right* to treat me like a child, since we of the other Realms most certainly aged a good deal more slowly than ephemerals. Under those circumstances it stood to reason that I was quite a lot older than the man, and the way he'd been acting finally convinced me that I really should start behaving like it.

"Jentris has no more right interfering with my life than you do," I told his back as I straightened where I stood, letting true maturity calm me the way it was meant to. "He and I are nothing to each other, not even friends any longer, and you and I were never even that much. If you two think I need looking after and protecting, that's your opinion and you're entitled to it. My opinion is the exact opposite, and since I'm the one involved it's my opinion that counts. You're now free to go and protect everyone else, because as soon as my horse gets in a little more grazing, I'm leaving. Alone."

I turned then and began to walk away from him, certain that I'd made my position clear enough for anyone to understand, but there are some people in the Realms who don't care to understand. All they're interested in are their own points of view, and understanding is always a matter of will or won't, not can or can't.

"Look, Haliand, maybe I shouldn't have said that about everyone else needing protection more," the outlaw's voice came from behind me, grudging concession. "Anger sometimes makes us say things we don't quite mean, like what you just said about Jentris. You know as well as I do that everything isn't over between you, not because of one foolish argument. Once I take you back to him the two of you will talk, and then everything will be straightened out."

"You really should do something about your hearing problem," I answered, turning to look at him with the cool, controlled regard my mother usually used. "I have nothing to say to Jentris, and have no interest in anything he might want to say to me. I'm not a slave who can be taken where others want her to go, so you're not taking me anywhere. I'm interested in no one's company but my own, so you're not even staying with me. Is all that stated clearly enough for you, young man, or do I need to go over it again?"

"Young man?" he said, and suddenly a grin showed on his face as well as amusement in his eyes. "I beg your pardon, ma'am, but I didn't realize I was dealing with someone so much older than me. If I had, I certainly would have shown more respect. Will you do me the honor of joining me for a meal? I don't have much, only odds and ends brought from the inn, but your sharing them will make them seem like a feast."

"You have no intention of listening to me, do you," I stated, ignoring the way he suddenly seemed to be enjoying himself. "You think you're going to let me say anything I care to, and after a while I'll get so tired of repeating myself you won't have any trouble diverting me to something else entirely. That's only to be expected from someone like you, and it pains me deeply to have to disillusion you, but it isn't going to work. Go away and leave me alone."

"But, my dear elder lady, I can't!" he protested with completely insincere upset, hurrying around to stand himself in my way. I'd begun walking away from him again, but he didn't seem prepared to allow that. "I really am very hungry, and it wouldn't be proper for me to eat without you. A lady of your advanced years needs all the nourishment she can get, after all, so you can't refuse to join me."

"But I do refuse," I returned, not even a fraction as amused as he was. "I'd rather starve than eat with you, and if you won't eat unless I do, I hope *you* starve. It will serve you right. *Boy*."

This time I turned away in another direction—after pretending I was going back the way I'd just come—so my path was finally clear. The outlaw had jumped to block the route he thought I was going to take, which ended him up behind me to my left instead of in front of me. I really expected that to make him angry, but surprisingly it started him laughing instead.

"You move too fast for so elderly a lady," he said, scrambling to catch up to me and then following just behind. "And you don't really want to see me starve; older ladies are much kinder than that. Just join me for one small meal, and after that I promise not to bother you about it again. What do you say?"

I stopped to stare at the scattering of thin trees ahead of me, part of the clearing in the midst of larger, wider trees.

I could remember how sorry I'd been for trees when I was small, thinking how much luckier humans were, not to be forced to spend all their lives in one place. It had been a while before I'd found out that trees felt sorry for humans, pitying them for not being able to set their roots in one place and never having to move again, but that hadn't changed my outlook. I still felt sorry for trees—and hated the idea of being kept where I didn't want to be.

"What I say is what I've been saying all along," I answered after the briefest pause, making no effort to look at him. "I don't want to eat with you, I don't want to talk to you, and I don't want to be near you. What I do want to do is leave here, which I intend doing in just another few minutes. Save your deliberately ambiguous promises for someone who has no experience with that sort of thing."

"What do you mean, deliberately ambiguous promises?" he asked after a pause of his own, no longer sounding quite as amused as he had. "And what's this about experiences with them?"

"You tried to make me believe that if I ate with you, you would stop bothering me," I said, not at all reluctant to show he hadn't fooled me the way he'd thought he would. "What you really said was that you would stop bothering me about *it*, meaning the meal, which means absolutely nothing. Once I had the meal with you there would no longer be anything to bother me *about*, and the precedent of my having given in would already have been established. Well, it's not going to *be* established, so you might as well stop wasting your time."

"That's a very observant analysis," he said, no more than a comment as he moved along behind me. I'd begun walking again, in truth strolling, but he refused to be left behind. "It looks like you really do have experience to call on, but you've made me curious. How does one get experience in something like that?"

"One grows up with a large number of older sisters," I commented, more interested in looking around at the calm peace of the forest than in what I was saying. "When one of them tells you she'll play a game with you as soon as she finishes the book she's reading, you learn that that means she just started the book and isn't a particularly fast reader. It also means she's counting on your having forgotten the promise by the time she *is* finished, and if you haven't she'll be sure to find something else that needs to be done first. The same applies to promises that you'll have something incomparably wonderful if you run a dozen errands, or don't interrupt a conversation about a really fascinating man, or lend your newest gown and not complain when you get it back stained and ruined. The incomparably wonderful thing you get is your sisters' gratitude, which lasts all the way until the next time they want something. If you don't happen to be there to supply it, the wonderful gift you've earned tends to dissolve and disappear from sight forever.''

''Older brothers and sisters can be rather cruel, can't they?'' he said, now sounding completely sober. ''Most of the time it's just thoughtlessness, but some people take great pleasure in hurting others. My oldest brother—he and I never got along even for a minute, especially since the day I grew big enough to stand up to him. . . . Well, that isn't important now. What is important is that I owe you a really sincere apology. I appreciate your pointing it out to me and promise not to do it again, and that's one promise you *can* rely on.''

I just kept strolling along, preferring the pleasure found in looking at the forest to finding pain in old memories. As a matter of fact there wasn't anything I cared to talk about, but some people seem to think there's a Realms law prohibiting silence.

''Didn't you hear me?'' the outlaw asked after a good ten heartbeats worth of quiet, the words rather concerned. ''I said I apologize for what I did, and won't do it again.''

''Does your persistence mean that this is where I'm supposed to congratulate you?'' I asked in turn, still not making any effort to look at him. ''If it does, then consider it said. You're a good little boy, and everyone is very proud of you.''

''What in the name of all that's good is wrong with

you?'' he growled, and then I was being pulled around by the arm to see the anger blazing out of his dark eyes. "You can't even be bothered to treat me like a human being when I'm trying to apologize! Do you think your beauty and the accident of your birth into a wealthy family give you the right to treat people like dirt? If you do, then I have news for you: *no* one is that beautiful, or that nobly born.''

"That's funny, but I could have sworn you were one of those who thought exactly the opposite," I countered, refusing to let him see how much his grip on my arms was hurting. "*You* were born into a wealthy family, and that seems to give you the right to interfere in my life however you please. Until you came along Jentris and I were starting to be friends, friendship being the only thing he had any interest in from me. Then, suddenly, he decided he wanted to take me to bed after all. I can't tell you how that made me feel, how wanted and appreciated and really beautiful—until I found out he was doing it only because *you* had suggested it. I knew you didn't like the things I'd said to you and were interested in getting even, but you could have chosen a less painful way, like using one of those weapons you carry. You want me to treat you like a human being? Well, I'm sorry, but I'm much too beautiful and desirable to sink quite that low.''

His grip had loosened enough by then to let me pull away, and I didn't even care that the anger had also faded from his eyes. He'd really thought he had something to be angry about, and I believed I understood why that was. A man as handsome as he was couldn't possibly be used to having women ignore his apologies, but he'd apparently forgotten something. I wasn't really a woman, only a little girl, and little girls weren't as susceptible to his charms as their older sisters.

"Haliand, please, you have to let me explain," he said from behind me, a position that was rapidly becoming his usual place near me. "I didn't make that suggestion to Jentris to hurt you, only to protect you! You *are* a very beautiful and desirable woman, and that's why the subject came up in the first place. I never dreamed he would tell you it was someone else's idea—he's the man you ran away with, after all— Isn't he?''

"What he is or isn't is none of your business," I returned harshly, completely unimpressed with the painful protest I'd heard in his voice. Some of my sisters were really good at offering sincere apologies when they found they'd gone too far, but I'd learned they couldn't be believed any more than the man behind me.

"But it *is* my business," he insisted immediately, once again moving around to block my path. "You two said you were lovers, and sometimes you even acted like it. Why else do you think I—I mean, why else was Jentris so upset when you ran away? And he really does want you now, I'm absolutely certain of it. You may not be interested in apologies from me, but you can't refuse to listen to his.''

"I can do or refuse to do anything I like," I told the very anxious look coming down at me, still speaking mostly at the urging of the roiling deep in my middle. "Jentris was upset at my disappearance because he thinks he's responsible for me, but he's just as wrong about that as he is to believe I'd ever share a bed with him. At this point, I'd rather share a bed with *you*.''

I was sure putting it like that would make my point about how I felt about Jiss, but it seemed to do something else as well. The oddest look came into Skyhawk's dark eyes, and he almost began a step toward me with his arms starting to rise. I say almost because the action was ended so abruptly it was the next thing to a figment of the imagination, and then the outlaw shook his head hard, turning partially away to run his hand through his hair.

"I wasn't joking about being hungry," he said abruptly. "I'd enjoy having you join me, but even if you don't I'm getting something to eat. We'll continue this discussion when I can uphold my end in a more reasonable fashion.''

He turned then and walked off toward his horse, leaving me with something really strange to think about. Unless I was very much mistaken, Jiss had been right in saying that the outlaw was attracted to me. His unexplained reaction a moment earlier—he really did consider himself a man of honor, and that despite what he'd been doing to me. As soon as I'd realized that, it had come to me how I might get even with him and Jiss both, in a way I'd heard some of my sisters talking about. Although I'd never done anything even remotely like it, it hadn't sounded as though it would be hard; the only thing I couldn't decide was whether I wanted to go quite that far.

The outlaw reached his stallion, paused to pat it to let it know he was there, then moved a couple of steps over and began rummaging in one of his saddlebags. I stared at him without truly seeing him, remembering how my sisters had laughed at what one of them had done, considering how really fitting my doing the same thing would be. It would also be distasteful, but probably not as bad as it would be for those who didn't care how they hurt others, not as long as they got what they wanted. By rights I should have done it right then, but a moment of thought convinced me the only fair thing was to give my intended victim one last chance to avoid his due.

Without saying anything I began walking toward my horse, at least half of me hoping there would be nothing happening to keep me from leaving. The idea that had come to me was one I was sure would work, but the longer I thought about what my part of it would have to be, the less attractive the idea became. All I really wanted was to be on my way out of there, alone and able to continue with finding those thieves. That wasn't so much to ask, not when it was the reason for my being in that Realm in the first place.

"Haliand, where are you going?" a calm and quiet voice said from behind me, its tone suggesting it already knew the answer to its question. "Your horse isn't ready to stop grazing yet, so there's no sense in bothering him. If you want to watch someone eat, you can come and watch me."

"Horses are ready to stop grazing when their riders say they're ready," I countered without turning, still moving toward my mount. "I have places to go and things to do, and I've already wasted enough time. Enjoy your meal."

I really did want that to be the end of it, but there must have been some balance in the universe that had no intentions of being cheated. I was still about eight feet away from my horse when the hand closed on my arm, a hand that made sure I wasn't going to be getting any closer to my objective. I immediately tried to pull loose, but that was something else the hand disagreed with.

"Haliand, please don't make this any harder than it has to be," that miserable outlaw said, his voice gentle but firm as he began forcing me back to the place beyond the horses. "You know I'm not going to let you ride off alone, and it has nothing to do with thinking less of you. Jentris and I have to know you're safe, and the only way we can do that is if I'm around to protect you."

"I don't need your protection," I said through my teeth, still trying to get my arm loose. "You have no right to force your version of safety on me, not when I don't want anything to do with it. I have the right to refuse your protection, and I do refuse it!"

I was expecting his anger to come flaring out as usual to meet mine, but apparently he'd decided on a change of tactics. He sighed as he looked down at me, and then he showed a faint smile as he shrugged.

"All right, then it won't be you I'm protecting," he said as he finally released my arm, his tone of voice lighter than it had been. "I'm the one who took that horse for you, so that makes me responsible for his well-being until I can return him. And those clothes you're wearing—if you stop to think about it you'll remember they're *my* clothes, and that makes them my responsibility as well. Why don't we just say I'm here to protect your horse and your clothes, and that way you, personally, won't enter into it at all, which just might make you feel a little better."

The wider smile he gave me then was nothing short of insulting, considering the nonsense he had just been spouting. He was treating me like a small child who could be told anything at all, with complete certainty that the anything would be accepted and believed. His attitude would have gotten me absolutely furious, except for the fact that he had outsmarted himself without knowing it. He had given me the perfect opening for getting my sister's plan started, and he couldn't say my being there to do it was anyone's fault but his own.

"So, it's my horse and clothes you're going to be protecting, is it?" I said with a growl as he began moving toward the small wrapped packages he'd obviously taken out of his saddlebags and put on the ground. "Then suppose I make things easier for you, not to mention more pleasant for the both of us. If the horse is meant to be returned when it's no longer needed, then consider it no longer needed. I'd rather walk than keep something someone else is responsible for."

"No one said you had to give the horse back *now*," he answered at once without looking around, then settled himself on the ground near the packages. "I didn't even hint that something like that would be necessary, so you can forget about claiming I did. The horse is completely yours, except for the fact that I get to protect it. Since the arrangement isn't unreasonable, *you* have no grounds for being unreasonable. Now, why don't you come over here and join me in finishing up some of this—"

At that point his words ended very abruptly, due, no doubt, to his finally looking up at me. By that time I'd opened his shirt and had slipped it off, and tugging at the tie around my waist had loosened his trousers enough to let them fall around my ankles. Stepping out of them took only another moment, and then I had gathered up both shirt and trousers and was able to throw them together in his open-mouthed, staring direction.

"And as far as those clothes go, I'm only too glad to be rid of them," I said as though he hadn't uttered a word to interrupt my previous speech, my own stare a good deal colder than the one I was getting. "As costly and well-made as they obviously are, you should never have parted with them to begin with. Now that they're safely returned

to their owner, though, I have nothing more to concern
myself with."

"Hey, get back here!" he squawked as I turned and
began walking away, the sounds of his scrambling to his
feet coming only just before his hand closed around my
arm again. "You can't march off into the woods wearing
nothing but those sandals, and as a matter of fact you can't
even stay here like that. Get back into those clothes, and
then we'll talk this out."

"I don't have anything I care to talk to you about," I
said, tossing my head to get the hair back over my right
shoulder. "As far as I'm concerned everything's been
said, especially about those clothes. If you like them so
much, you put them on."

"I'm not the one who's standing around stark naked,"
he came back, and I noticed then that his dark eyes were on
nothing but my face. "Didn't you have enough men panting after you when you were dressed? Anyone who sees
you like that won't waste an instant coming after you, and
he won't even have to be a slaver. Most of the men in this
area will consider a naked woman an open invitation, and
no one will even think of blaming them for it."

"And I'm supposed to believe that," I said, just as
though I didn't know what I looked like—or hadn't had
enough proof about how attractive men were beginning to
find me. "Jentris has to have someone else talk him into
touching me, someone who was without doubt delighted
he'd be getting out of having to do it himself, and that's
supposed to prove how devastatingly beautiful I am? You
may not have a very high opinion of my intelligence, but
kindly grant me a little more than that."

"Haliand, you're not seeing any of this the way it really
is," he protested, making sure, as I'd known he would,
not to let me turn from him again. "You heard me tell
Jentris you're the most beautiful woman I've ever seen,
and you have my word that I wasn't lying. When they first
brought you into camp— Hey, that's the proof you wanted!
If you weren't beautiful, why would those men have been
so eager to get their hands on you?"

"You mean my being chosen ahead of the hundreds of other women they had available was supposed to mean something?" I asked, not about to be out-maneuvered quite that easily. "I hadn't thought much about it before, but now I can see I should have been considering it quite an honor."

"Now look, your having been the only woman in camp has nothing to do with how badly they wanted you," he came back, the expression in his eyes now saying he was determined to make me see the truth. "A man would have to be dead not to feel something when he looked at you, and Jentris is no exception to that. I promise you he'll say exactly the same thing as soon as I've gotten you back to him."

"Back to him," I echoed, letting a desolate look show on my face before lowering my gaze to my hands. "All the pretty words ever created won't change the fact that it's you who came after me rather than him. I know that what was stolen from us is important, but if I really meant something to him it wouldn't have been more important than me. If you were the one who supposedly wanted me so badly, would you consider other things more important than me?"

I looked back up at him with the question, only this time I was using an expression I'd practiced a few times in front of my mirror. I'd heard more than a couple of my sisters say at various times how useful looking wide-eyed, innocent, and helpless was when dealing with men, but even though I'd practiced the expression I'd never expected to use it. Now I was using it on the outlaw Skyhawk, and if I'd felt faintly silly to begin with, his reaction quickly drove all thoughts of silliness away.

"No, if you were mine I'd never consider anything more important," he whispered, his arms raising and about to go around me, his face and eyes filled so full with desire that it was only a shade less than frightening. Then, with what seemed like great effort, he had control of himself again, and his arms withdrew without having touched me. "But you aren't mine," he said, calmly and evenly.

"I'm finding it hard to remember that, but hard doesn't mean impossible . . ."

He let the words trail off as he turned partially away from me to run one hand through his dark hair, and I was so frustrated I could have screamed. From what my sisters had said seducing a man was never much trouble, but Skyhawk was the second man I'd tried who found it completely possible to resist me. It could have been that he and Jiss both had superhuman willpower—or it could have been that they really were only trying to make me feel better by telling me how beautiful I was. That particular consideration really did make me feel desolate, and suddenly the idea I'd had to get even wasn't such a good idea after all.

"Hey, now don't start looking like that again," the outlaw's voice came, and then there was an arm around me, but an entirely neutral one. "You have to understand that some men have a very strong sense of duty, but that doesn't mean they don't care about the women who are involved with them. They do care, very much, and they aren't always pleased that their duty has to come first."

"Of course," I agreed tonelessly, once again not believing a word he said. "Jentris has this overpowering sense of duty and you have the self control of a boulder, and none of that changes the fact that I'm exquisitely lovely. No man anywhere will be able to keep himself from coming after me—except for the two who have actually had the opportunity. If you'll excuse me now, I think I'd like to get back into my clothes."

I moved away from that very neutral arm without making any attempt to look at the man, feeling more humiliated than I ever had in my life. I'd actually stripped myself naked in an effort to seduce him, and afterward I would have waited until he said how good it had been for him, and then I would have laughed. I would also have been able to laugh at Jiss, for having missed the enjoyment another man had taken in his place, but I wasn't the one who would be laughing. Jiss and Skyhawk would be laughing, and I couldn't say I didn't deserve it.

"I've had enough of this," a voice growled from behind me, and before I'd taken more than two steps I was pulled around and suddenly held by two very strong arms. The body I was being held to was harder than I'd earlier thought, and the dark eyes looking down at me were blazing.

"I don't have the self control of a boulder, and I can't stand any more of this," Skyhawk said, his words tempered steel from the flame in his gaze. "It's killing me to see the most desirable woman I've ever met picturing herself as ugly and unwanted because of the stupidity of the man who had the incredible luck to meet her before me. I want you, Haliand, more than I want to continue breathing, but you happen to belong to another man. If I could I would take you right here, right now, but—"

I looked away from his eyes with the second of his "buts," too familiar with the word not to know exactly what it meant. Of course I'd like to play that game with you, Haliand, but— Of course it would be fun to go riding with you, Haliand, but— Of course I'd replace that gown for you, Haliand, but— It was really the only word in its sentence that mattered, the one word that told you exactly how things stood.

"I want to get dressed," I whispered toward his chest, meaning it even more than I had earlier. "Please let me go."

"You don't believe me," he said, his arms not loosening in the least. "No matter what I say you won't believe me, not when it's all nothing but words. Anyone can string a bunch of words together, but by the roaring heat of the Dark Realm I'm not just anyone. Now I have to show you."

I gasped in surprise when he shifted and then lifted me in his arms, and then I tried to tell him to forget about it. I was feeling too miserable to want to seduce him any longer, but he changed that. He carried me over to a patch of sunlight coming through the leaves overhead and put me down in it, and although I tried to tell him I didn't want anything proven to me, he did it anyway.

Chapter 9

❦

I'D ALWAYS WONDERED what "afterward" would be like, and as I lay there in the grass wrapped in a wide, warm smile, I realized I finally knew. The stream of sunlight through the leaves had shifted its position by then, but I really wasn't lying in shadow. Not that I needed shadow to be more comfortable. I was very comfortable curled just a little on my left side, comfortable and contented and surprisingly satisfied. I hadn't expected to be feeling any of that, not after the reactions I'd seen in my sisters. I'd expected to feel smug, or faintly bored, or in the mood to babble or criticize, or maybe just relieved that it was over, but the only thing I was relieved about was having decided not to laugh.

"Haliand, are you asleep?" Skyhawk's voice came from where he lay behind me, soft with the effort not to intrude. "If you're awake, there's something I need to talk to you about."

"You don't have to sound so worried," I said without turning, and some of the satisfaction I'd been feeling faded. "There's nothing at all wrong with my hearing, so you needn't think I might have missed what you said. You told me you wanted me, not that you loved me, so you have no ugly scenes to face or awkward excuses to make. I know you don't particularly like me, and I don't expect the sharing of bed games to have changed that."

215

"You sound like an old and cynical woman rather than a young girl," he observed, the relief I'd been expecting conspicuously absent from his voice. "You also sound like someone who has been taken advantage of so often, she's come to expect nothing else. You make me feel lower and more worthless than I feel on my own."

"It's nice to know you enjoyed yourself so much," I said, not understanding why I was beginning to feel terrible. "Aren't you going to ask if *I* enjoyed *my*self?"

"Haliand, listen to me!" he grated, and then a hand came to my arm to turn me toward him. He sat in the grass beside me, still unclothed, and the expression on his broad face was far from happy. "I've done a really terrible thing, and before I leave I want to explain it to you."

"Leave," I echoed, the only word I seemed able to speak. He'd done a terrible thing and suddenly was no longer insisting that we stay together, and that was what he was going to explain. Obviously I'd been very wise to decide to forget about laughing.

"The first thing I want you to know is that I *did* enjoy myself, even more than I'd expected to," he said, his somber expression and tone making it a tragedy that he described, not a pleasure. "It's never been the same for me with any other woman, and I'll never forget it. Unfortunately there's something else to be remembered at the same time, and that makes me wish I'd never come anywhere near you. I told Jentris that he and I were friends, and I gave him my word that I would keep you safe for him."

I looked up at him with all the lack of understanding I felt, and he smiled a faint, bitter smile as he smoothed my hair, and then he began getting to his feet.

"Your expression tells me you don't know what it means when one man professes friendship for another," he said, bending for his clothes with his back to me. There seemed to be white lines of some sort all across that back, but since Skyhawk was going on I had no time to ask about them even if I'd wanted to. "When one man assures another that they're friends, he's telling that other that he doesn't have to worry about what's going on behind his back. One friend guards the back of another, he doesn't sneak around behind it, or at least that's the way it's supposed to work. I gave Jentris my word and he trusted me, and then I turned around and bedded the woman I'd told him I'd keep safe for him. That isn't the usual way a man keeps another man's woman safe.''

While he spoke he dressed himself quickly, his eyes coming nowhere near me even when I sat up. I wanted to say something to him, to ease the self-disgust so thick in his voice, but for once in my life the thoughts I wanted weren't instantly ready to be brought out. I hadn't realized his word really did mean so much to him, and before I could think of anything at all, he had strapped his swordbelt around him and was settling it in place.

"That, I think, should explain why I'm leaving," he continued, his gaze still touching everything but me. "I obviously can't be trusted to control myself as a man of honor should, and it's fairly clear you were a lot safer before I caught up with you. I'll be the one to tell Jentris, of course, and I'll be sure he understands the fault was mine rather than yours. Please dress yourself as soon as you can, and use this episode to remind yourself that strangers can't be trusted no matter how honorably they speak.''

He turned and strode away toward his horse with that, and despite the fact that I called to him to wait, he was mounting by the time I stood, and riding away before I had taken more than a few steps after him. I watched him disappear into the forest, and then I turned and walked slowly back to sit again in the grass where I'd been.

"That was really nice, Hali," I muttered to myself, the terrible feeling beginning earlier now fully grown and completely with me. "Your sisters would either be very proud of you, or indignant because he told you a wild story and then left. But it wasn't a wild story, was it, and you didn't tell him that everything was *your* fault. You set out to seduce him, thought you'd failed, then succeeded in spite of yourself. Isn't success wonderful?''

No one and nothing came rushing forward with an answer to that, not even my own thoughts. All I could think of was that he'd done it because I'd been so upset, that he hadn't even laughed at his victory afterward as he could very easily have done. I'd been the cause of his breaking his word, not innocently but deliberately, and then hadn't even had the courage or the decency to tell him the truth. I was a princess and he was an ephemeral outlaw, a nothing, and wasn't *that* obvious from the way we'd both behaved.

I sat there in the grass for a short while, calling myself every nasty name I could think of, but not only didn't that help, it was also wasting more time than had already been wasted. I really did have to get after those thieves, no matter what sort of person I'd proven myself to be. I sighed as I got to my feet again, looked at the clothing I'd thrown in Skyhawk's face, then went to pick it up, but not to put it on. With my draperies dry there was no reason to wear anything else, even if the anything else *was* more comfortable. I didn't deserve to be more comfortable, most especially not in *his* clothes.

It wasn't long before I was dressed again and mounted, with Skyhawk's clothes folded and put away in my saddlebags. In with the clothing were the packages of food he'd left behind, forgotten in his haste to get out of there. As I guided my horse back in the direction from which I'd been brought, I had to admit there were some aspects of what had happened that I really didn't understand. Even for an ephemeral, Skyhawk had been behaving strangely, and I couldn't seem to think of any reason for it.

Like his being so attracted to me, for instance. I shifted in my saddle as I considered the point, but no matter what angle I looked at it from it still refused to resolve itself into a logical picture. It was certainly true that I didn't have much experience with men and their ways, but no one I'd ever met had seriously tried suggesting they were irrational or mindless. I could understand why the outlaw had found me attractive to begin with; there was nothing wrong with his eyesight, and we were strangers to each other. That, however, didn't explain why he'd continued to find me attractive, despite everything I'd said to and about him. When someone makes it very clear they don't like anything about you, the normal reaction is to quickly begin feeling the same about them.

But not the man called Skyhawk. Not only had he tried again and again to smooth things over between us, he'd let his concern over my being upset cause him to break his word. Why? Because he'd rather experience whatever pain was involved himself instead of letting me suffer with it? Why would he care? And why, after he'd already broken his word and had what might be considered what he wanted, had he mounted up and ridden away? That didn't change what had been done and could even be seen as making things worse, so why had he left? I didn't know, and the more I thought about it the more my confusion grew.

When I reached the point of feeling as though I were trying to pass into the side of a mountain in full daylight, I realized I had to find something else to think about. Since the thieves I was supposedly chasing were the best choice as the something else, I began by checking on their position by asking the trees. The answer I got seemed to indicate they were just as many hours ahead of me as I'd been afraid of, and the fact that I was gaining on them slowly wasn't much consolation. The only bright spot was knowing it wasn't necessary for me to catch up with them until after dark, when I'd be able to do something other than simply watch them from a distance.

Once I was settled down to traveling I ate some of the bread and cheese left behind by Skyhawk, but I wasn't really all that hungry. I felt . . . distracted, I suppose would be the best word, and I didn't quite understand why I should be. What had happened between Skyhawk and me was trying to take my attention, just as though it had been something important rather than the inconsequential pastime I'd always thought it was. My sisters had never seemed impressed or distracted . . .

I made a very rude noise and threw some long strands of

hair back over my shoulder in annoyance, remembering again just exactly how much my sisters' opinions were worth. Most of them played bed games with any man who came along, just as long as they found something faintly interesting about him when they first met. After having finally had the experience myself I couldn't understand how they could do that, casually and uncaringly, with almost anyone at all.

Or with someone they didn't really like. My horse snorted and shook his head, possibly commenting on my thoughts as he kept to the easy lope we'd been using everywhere the forest let us. Personally, I didn't know what sort of comment to make, about the experience or even about the man. I'd spent days hating everything about him, wishing he would disappear and never come back, but that wasn't what I'd felt when he'd held me in his arms. Maybe that was why my sisters did as they did, to stop themselves from hating someone who really hadn't done anything to them.

I shook my head hard, the way my horse had, trying to dislodge idiotic thoughts like the one I'd just had. It was true that looking back didn't show me much of a basis for the intense dislike I'd developed for the outlaw, but that didn't mean my previous feelings had entirely disappeared. I didn't quite hate the man any longer, but if I had it all to do over again, I didn't know for certain if I would.

I sighed as I looked around for some water to drink. What I really needed was a distraction from all those disturbing thoughts, and stopping for a drink just might accomplish that. I could smell water somewhere up ahead and to my left, deeper in the forest, so I turned my horse and headed that way. Since the thieves would most likely stop for a meal at midday, I could afford a brief stop for a drink.

It didn't take long to reach the small lake nestled in the midst of the forest, but once I got there I discovered I wasn't the only one to find it. I sat my horse a short distance back from the opening out of the trees, watching the woman who knelt at the lake edge, trying to figure out who she might be and what she was doing. From what I could see of her she didn't resemble the people in my own Realm, but she also wasn't so bad off that she looked like the man in the stable back at the inn, the one who had seemed to need fixing. She wore a long-skirted outfit that was a riot of colors, and there also seemed to be silver jewelry at her neck and ears. Her hands worked at doing something in the water, but with her body in the way I couldn't quite see what.

And then something happened that made it unnecessary for me to wonder or guess. I heard a splash that was so small the woman's exclamation almost covered it, and then she was reaching out into the lake for something that had fallen in. The small wooden bowl came to view as it floated just beyond her fingertips, and it really did seem to be trying to get away. The woman put a hand into the water and made small waves in her direction, trying to float the bowl back along with the water, but it didn't work. The water came toward her but the bowl didn't, and after a moment the woman gave up that line of attack. She got to her feet and watched briefly and helplessly as the bowl slowly floated farther and farther away, then turned from the lake and hurried toward the woods in my direction.

I had actually already decided to go elsewhere for my drink, and if I'd left as soon as the decision was made the woman never would have seen me. As it was she only took a few steps before her eyes found me where I sat my horse, and her reaction was somewhat on the strange side.

"Have no fear, child, I shall do you no harm," she said at once, having hesitated no more than a heartbeat before moving toward me again. "You find me in the midst of a small difficulty, yet shall I be pleased to seek out your fortune and fate as quickly as the difficulty is resolved. Tie your horse there, beside my cart, and I will join you before you have fully settled yourself."

Her hand had waved briefly to my right, indicating a small pony cart and the animal pulling it, and then she was absorbed in bending to pick up branches from the ground, examining their length, then discarding them to search on.

Her smooth-cheeked face was handsome rather than pretty, her very dark hair faintly streaked with white, and her dark eyes seemed warm and understanding despite the upset in them. Even fully erect, however, her sturdy body stood nowhere near as tall as my own, which led me to wonder why she'd thought I might be afraid of her. And what she'd said about seeking out my fortune and fate— I didn't know why she thought I'd want to do that, and I discovered that my curiosity had been aroused. Without stopping to think about it, I turned my mount toward where her pony cart stood.

Once I had dismounted and tied my horse, I looked around to see how far the woman had gotten in retrieving her bowl. I had heard her leaving the woods and hurrying back to the lake edge, and when I turned I saw she'd found a really long branch to chase the fugitive with. She stood at the lake edge with the branch in both hands, having a small amount of trouble keeping the far end of it from dipping into the water, and it was clear at once that that was all she would be able to accomplish with it. Her bowl floated just beyond her extended reach, bobbing a little as though teasing its pursuer, an impression the woman apparently shared with me.

"Ah, you misbegotten result of a proud and noble line," she was muttering as I came up behind and to her right, she having let the far end of the branch fall in order to glare more easily at the bowl. "You know well enough I cannot follow where you lead, and therefore do you mock me. Have you as little regard for me as you have for others that you do me so?"

"It's not saying yes, but it's not saying no, either," I pointed out, drawing the woman's startled gaze. "Does it make a habit of acting like that?"

"It, ah, does as it wills, as do all things in this life," she answered, her smile uncertain. "You must not think I truly spoke to the bowl, child, for I certainly did not. It was my anger and annoyance that spoke aloud, for my life-fate has decreed that I be unable to swim. The bowl is of great concern to me, for without it I will have considerable difficulty in reading the answers to the questions brought me by the troubled.''

"How could a plain wooden bowl help you with reading?'' I asked, privately wondering why she seemed so wary. "And what difference does it make whether or not you spoke to the bowl? Unless you were interrupting someone already speaking to it, why would anyone care?''

"Someone already speaking to it,'' she repeated with a sudden grin, and then she was laughing softly as she nodded her head. "Yes, best would likely be to consider it in just such a way, as the talkers clearly do not. The reading I spoke of is the reading of mysteries, child, and the carven runes must be spilled from a bowl precisely like that one, else will the message I seek be absent or unintelligible. It was used by my mother, and my mother's mother before her, and is meant to be handed down to one of my daughters after me. Should it not float away to an oblivion of warp and rot.''

She turned from me with the last of her words, real worry sending her sight back to the erring bowl, her upset increasing when she saw the thing even farther away than it had been. There were a number of clay pots and bowls at the lake edge, more than half of them filled with water, and somehow the escaping bowl must have gotten mixed in with the clay ones. I had no idea why the woman was filling so many things with water, but whatever the reason, she seemed to be regretting having started it in the first place. I thought about getting my drink and then continuing on, but there was really no way I might do that. The woman had a problem she wasn't able to solve herself, and now that I'd stopped I couldn't simply turn my back on her and ride away again.

"You know, I think I could use a brief swim right about now,'' I remarked, reflecting that it wasn't merely an excuse. The thought of a bath was suddenly rather appealing, and if at the same time I could be of help to the woman, so much the better.

"Ah, child, I shall ask the Great Ones to smile upon you,'' the woman said at once, turning to me with delight and gratitude warming her face and forming the smile she now wore. "In truth I should not hear of you taking the trouble, yet my need is so great . . ."

"It's no trouble at all," I assured her with a smile of my own, already beginning to get out of my draperies. "I do have to be moving on rather quickly, but this shouldn't take long and that water looks very inviting."

Which it did. As soon as I had my clothing off I sat down at the lake edge and put my legs into that lovely blue water, and found that I was being welcomed by sun-warmed wetness that was exactly right for the heat of the day. From the bank I slid into the water, and in that way discovered why the woman hadn't made any attempt to follow the bowl away from the bank. Even that close the lake bottom was nowhere to be felt, at least not for the short distance I'd gone down, but that distance was short only for a swimmer. A nonswimmer would find the lack of bottom terrifying, and for her sake it was a good thing the woman hadn't tried going in.

When my head broke the surface again I shook the water out of my eyes, then began swimming slowly toward the bowl. The thing bobbed with more agitation now, most likely due to the movement of the water my swimming was causing, but someone watching it might have thought it was seriously trying to escape. I couldn't understand that until I got really close, and then the strange way the bowl had been acting became more reasonable: the thing was made of wildwood. Wildwood trees grow in forests, but they're never a part of those forests the way the other trees are. Only ephemerals would be silly enough to make something out of the wood, and because of that deserved what they got. Even if they managed to hold on to whatever it was they got.

Two more strokes brought me in reach of the bowl, and once I had it in my hand I turned back toward the bank. As I swam I noticed that the bowl was more sullen than unhappy, more put out over not having escaped than miserable over being recaptured. If it could have pouted I was sure it would have, and that got me annoyed enough to whisper to it in the language of trees. It wasn't so young that it had an excuse to act the way it was doing, so I told it what the water would have done to it if I hadn't caught it. The sullenness dropped away leaving nothing but shock, and by the time I got it back to the bank it just about leaped into the hands of the woman waiting for it.

"Oh, so now you regret your escapade, do you?" the woman murmured very low as she held the bowl to her, turning somewhat away from me as she tried to comfort it surreptitiously. "We'll speak of this later, when other ears are no longer about." Then she quickly turned to me with a smile. "You certainly have my gratitude for the fine effort you made, child. Should you wish to leave the water now, I will give you a reading as a gift in exchange. There is little I cannot . . ."

The woman's words ended abruptly at the sudden disturbance coming from the edge of the woods, and as she turned I looked over to see four men emerge from the trees. Old, tired-looking horses had been left tied behind them, and the men themselves weren't of much higher quality than the horses. They wore old and faded shirts and trousers, their boots should have creaked or fallen apart from overuse and lack of attention, their dark hair was raggedy and unevenly cut, and to one degree or another they all had hair on their faces. It may well have been the grins they showed that suggested they rarely remembered to wash their hands—or faces—or bodies—but whatever it was, I knew immediately that I didn't care for the look of them.

"Hoy, looka there, brothers, it's th' old witch," one of them said to the others as they all strolled nearer, spiteful anticipation filling their expressions. "I wouldn' a believed she'd show up agin after th' last time, but there she be."

"That's 'cause she ain't yet learned what's good fer 'er," a second said, more than a small glitter to his grin. "We told 'er we din't want 'er comin' 'round no more, but that's all we done. This time we gotta do more 'n tell."

"You have no right to threaten me!" the woman said to them in an unsteady voice, her hands clutching the bowl as she took a very small step backward. "The folk of your village wish to hear of the old times, just as the folk of other villages do. Should we forget the old times, we will never find an opportunity to regain them! You move not at your own urging but at the urging of another, and I cannot—"

"You ain't listenin', old woman," the first ruffian interrupted, his expression as undisturbed as it had been. "We don' want ya talkin' t' our folk, tellin' 'em lies 'bout what usta be, an' then tellin' more lies 'bout what's to come t' prove th' first lies. There ain't nothin' we usta be that we ain't right now, an' yore sayin' there is jest makes folks hot fer what they ain't gonna get. We gonna see t' it you don' do that no more."

"Your master fears that his slaves will take heart and attempt to free themselves," the woman said as she watched the men draw quite a bit closer, her voice now steady and filled with contempt. "You four do his bidding for you fear that you cannot be more than you are, and would not see your kith and kin rise to a place you would be unable to reach. Can you not see that your beliefs arise from the very man in whose cause you labor? His words convince you of your worthlessness, and then does he use the feelings fostered within you to—"

"Enough!" the first man growled, the hardness in his eyes saying he may have heard but refused to listen. "Ya ain't one uv us, so we'd be fools t' listen t' what jest ain't so. Y're gonna—"

The man's words broke off as he stopped in front of the woman, but she had nothing to do with the action. From where he then stood he was finally able to see me past her shoulder, something he hadn't been able to do earlier. I'd been trying to decide what I might say to let the men know I was there and wasn't about to stand idly by while they hurt the woman, but that consideration suddenly changed. The man stared at me for about three heartbeats worth of time, and then his grin was abruptly back.

"Well, well, looks like this's gonna be even more fun 'n we figured," he drawled, possibly speaking to the others who were now behind him. "Folks gotta learn whut c'n happen if'n they's found in th' wrong comp'ny, an' there ain't no time better t'start 'n right now. Come on outa there, girl, an' take whut you got comin'."

"Why don't you come and get me?" I suggested, really beginning to be angry. Any thought that the man had a legitimate complaint was totally gone by then, and not just because of the way he'd been talking to the woman. He'd very quickly decided to take advantage of my being there, presupposing misconduct on my part to justify what he meant to do to me. I wasn't completely sure what it was that he did mean to do, but it really made no difference. Whatever it was, he had no right even thinking about it.

"Y' think I ain't gonna come 'n get ya?" the man asked with a snort of ridicule, his renewed good humor unbothered by my lack of cooperation. "I don't take no sass frum females, 'specially not frum females who go where they ain't 'sposta be. After this, ya'll listen good t' them as talk t' ya, not give 'em lip like y' knows better'n 'em. You boys get started teachin' th' old witch, an' by th' time yore done I'll have th' girl outa there."

The woman tried to keep him from going past her, an agonized glance in my direction showing she feared more for me than for herself, but the man simply brushed her aside and moved quickly to the edge of the lake. The next instant he was going to one knee and reaching for me, but that just showed how thick in the head he was. By then I was already moving backward through the water, avoiding his grasp the way the wildwood bowl had avoided the woman's hand, but his reaction was somewhat different from what hers had been. Rather than growing upset he muttered something under his breath, quickly yanked off his boots and his shirt, then dived into the water.

The woman on the bank cried out something that sounded like a plea for mercy, but since the other three men seemed more interested in what was happening in the lake than in starting to do her harm, she was obviously not asking for leniency for herself. I didn't hear much of what she said as I was already on my own way underwater, and the one thing I really regretted was that I didn't have time to reassure her. I wasn't the one who would soon be in need of mercy, and I had no more intention of granting mercy than the man who was coming after me would have if he'd heard her.

I was somewhat surprised that the filthy ephemeral didn't dissolve into a mud slick as soon as he hit the water, but that was just a passing thought. His dive was supposed to have brought him straight up to me, but my own dive took me around and below him, further out and deeper down. With my hair floating all around me I looked back at the man over my shoulder as I glided away from him, and opened my mouth in a silent laugh. I was absolutely certain a gesture like that would bring him after me, and it certainly did. His expression said he wanted to snarl, but underwater wasn't quite the place to do it.

I don't think the man noticed just how deep we were going until he caught up with me. I'd been deliberately swimming slowly enough to lure him on, and when his hand closed around my ankle I could almost hear the shout of exultation ringing in his head. I'd tried getting away but he had me now, and he would pull me back up to the surface and then do whatever he pleased with me.

Except that that wasn't what I had in mind. When his hand closed around my ankle I used the grip as an anchor, and swung around quickly to lock my arms about his waist from behind. That put my leg over his shoulder in a very awkward position, but he soon discovered the position was more than simply awkward. I was using my hold on him and my free leg to turn him, and suddenly we weren't heading for the surface any longer.

I'm told that those who can't breathe underwater begin to panic when their lungs start running out of air, and the man who had been chasing me did nothing to disprove the contention. His new position showed him just how far we'd come, just how dark the water around us was, compared to what was just below the surface, and that started it for him. He tried to move us both back up toward the light and air, found to his dismay that my efforts were moving us more in a circle, then abruptly gave up on the idea of taking me with him. His hand left my ankle as he began using both arms and legs to propel himself upward, but freeing my ankle gave me back the use of both of my legs. I kicked away from the surface, negating most of his effort to go toward it, especially since I was bigger than him. He had caught me just the way he had wanted to, but suddenly it wasn't the victory he'd expected.

The end came a little sooner than I thought it would, most likely because of the abrupt frenzy the man went into. He began struggling violently against the hold I had on him, his feet trying to kick back into my head, his elbows stabbing toward my body, but his feet couldn't quite reach me and the water muffled the swing of his elbows down to nudges. It wasn't until then that he thought of trying to force my fingers open, and although he did manage to do that he was far too late. He clawed twice toward the surface, desperate to reach it, but he had run out of time. I hung in the water and watched his body spasm, shuddered as the spasms subsided to stillness, then began making my own way upward. You can usually find the balance in things if you look for it, but the sight is never guaranteed to be a pretty one.

When my head broke the surface I shook it to clear the water from my eyes, then had to spend a moment treading water while trying to understand what I was seeing. I'd expected the woman to be having trouble with the three men left on the bank, but the woman was simply standing there, peering anxiously out over the water as though looking for something. The three men were some distance behind her, beating a hobbling but hasty retreat to the horses they'd left tied to trees, two of the men having a bit of difficulty supporting the third between them. I might have wondered what had made them so anxious to leave—if I hadn't been able to see the probable reason balancing on one foot, in the middle of pulling off one of his boots.

"Skyhawk, she has returned to the surface!" the woman

called, causing the man to look up as he stopped wrestling
with the boot. "She also appears completely unharmed,
thanks be to the Great Ones. What of the last of them,
girl? Does he continue to pursue you?"

"The last of them pressed a little too hard on the
balance of things," I called back, beginning to swim
slowly toward the bank. "His last effort at advantage-
taking flipped the scales entirely against him, and now
he'll never take advantage again. I'll be out of this water
in just another minute."

I put my face down and began swimming faster, but
hurrying didn't accomplish what I'd thought it would. By
the time I reached the bank the outlaw was already mounted
on his horse, and even as I watched he rode off after the
three he'd apparently bested with his hands alone.

"By the First Ancestors, wait!" I called after him, the
sudden frustration I felt making me angry rather than
upset. "There's something I have to tell you!"

"I fear he has no wish to give ear to whatever you would
speak of," the woman said with sympathy in both face and
voice as the miserable outlaw simply rode away. "Have
you need of assistance in quitting the water?"

"If I did, *he* wouldn't care," I grumbled, crouching low
and then jumping upward with a boost from my hands,
which got me out of the water with no further effort. "I'm
beginning to think he's avoiding me for a reason other than
the one he told me of, and I don't like that possibility even
a little. Innocence is a disease you can be cured of,
sometimes faster than those around you expect."

"He seemed not only quite the gentleman, but also
rather concerned for your safety," the woman observed, a
small smile bending her lips. "You had only just slipped
beneath the water when he appeared in great haste, and
those three ruffians considered him someone who might be
easily halted. He taught them better with not too large an
amount of effort, introduced himself to me as they limped
off to find easier pickings, and was nearly to the point of
entering the water when you surfaced. When you began
swimming toward the bank he bid me a polite but hasty

farewell, then took himself off. For what reason he failed to remain and speak with you I know not, especially as you two seem acquainted."

"It's just possible he knows how dangerous I am, so he's afraid of me," I answered sourly, just about done with squeezing my hair out and ready to get into my draperies. "I hadn't realized he would be watching me from a distance, but now the point seems obvious. He promised to protect me and he's going to keep that promise, even if I don't want his protection. The only thing he *won't* do is talk to me. I think I'll try to lose him in the forest."

"Such a course of action might perhaps prove unwise, child," the woman said, looking up at me with continuing amusement. "To have a protector such as he would be the delight of many a maiden, and perhaps there is a reason for the oddness of his behavior. We will sit together for a short while, and I will do a reading on the matter."

"I appreciate the offer, but I really am in something of a hurry," I began, quickly smoothing my skirts before bending to my sandals. "I don't mean to sound ungrateful, but . . ."

"Now, now, gratitude is more mine to offer than yours, child," she interrupted, her dark eyes filled with sudden determination. "Should it be possible for me to ease your mind upon the questions now roiling about within you, I will have repaid your efforts on my behalf. Do you mean to deny me the opportunity of squaring the debt between us?"

I straightened with my sandals in my hand and just looked at her, the impatience I felt to be on my way again overcome by her quiet question. I didn't need any thanks for the little I'd done, but the situation seemed to be considerably more important in the woman's eyes. Balance makes itself known in many ways throughout one's life, sometimes appearing as a demand rather than a suggestion, and this seemed to be one of those times. The woman felt herself in debt because of my actions, which meant the only thing I could do was let her repay me.

"Of course I'll let you help me," I said with a smile. "Let's go sit down over there, and you can get started."

"Excellent!" the woman pronounced, brightening immediately. "Seat yourself where you will in the grass, child, and I shall join you in a moment. I must fetch the runes to be spilled from my darling wildwood bowl."

"Why don't you call me Haliand?" I suggested as I watched her move briskly toward her cart before paying attention to where I wanted to sit in the grass. "If you're going to help me, you're at least entitled to know my name."

"And you mine," said the woman from where she stood searching through some of the contents of the cart. "Wissa of the People is greatly pleased to make your acquaintance, Haliand."

I said some pleasantry in return as I slipped into my sandals and began tying them, but I was more satisfied than most introductions tend to make someone. The woman hadn't been trying to insult me by calling me "child," I knew, but the habit had annoyed me more and more the longer it went on. I left my sandal ties briefly to reach behind me and spread my hair out to give the warm sunlight a chance to dry it, and then I went back to tying. It was pleasant there at the edge of the woods, warm and bright and fresh and clean, and it suddenly became clear that I would do well to enjoy the stopover, before it became necessary for me to take up the chase again. Following the thieves' trail wasn't all that unpleasant—but the end of the trail could well bring more instances of the balancing of things, like the recent one in the lake. There were times when I really didn't like being an instrument of balance, but I'd been raised to know there was nothing I could do to change the state.

"And now we are prepared to begin," Wissa said as she joined me where I sat, a beautifully carved wooden box held carefully in the crook of her left arm, the wildwood bowl in her right hand. "This will take no more than a short time, child, therefore will your kind patience be put to no great strain. Within this box lie the runes that are able to see the past, the present, and the future. Have you ever encountered their like?''

By that time she was seated on the grass and opening the wooden box, and I bent forward a little to see what she was talking about. Inside the box were quite a number of small, light brown oblongs, each one carved with even more intricacy than the box that held them. The small wooden runes were certainly pretty, but their odd shapes were like nothing I'd ever seen before.

''No, few have encountered the like of these runes, for there are no more than three of us who are privileged to guard and use them,'' Wissa said with a smile when I shook my head to indicate unfamiliarity. ''My sisters in blood and I were given these by our mothers, who were also sisters in blood as were their mothers and grandmothers before them. I was told that the first of our lines were close blood sisters, and each of them produced daughters who were then chosen among to find the next who would guard and read. In such a way do we continue to be sisters in blood; all derive from the line of the first three, who began the thing for us.''

Her hands had been busy while she spoke, moving among the small carvings in the box, choosing one here, two there, four beyond a rejected six. I'd lost count of the exact number she'd chosen when she ended the search, closed the box, then lifted the wildwood bowl into which the chosen carvings had been put.

''And now are we truly prepared to read the meaning of what most concerns you,'' she said, spreading one section of her multi-colored skirt out in front of her. ''These runes are those which show the taste and shape of you, those which fairly resonate to your presence. All folk now living are here in my box, represented by one combination or another, as well as those who are gone before and those who are yet to come. We are all of us so easily reduced to symbol, and yet so complex in our individuality.''

She was holding the wildwood bowl in both hands, her dark eyes seeing something other than me, and then the bowl tipped forward without warning, spilling the carvings all over the section of skirt set out to receive them. They were strangely easy to see against their multi-colored background, and they settled in meaningless groupings that were certainly completely random. I had the time to notice that there were eleven of the small carvings, and then Wissa made a sound of deep satisfaction.

"Ah, now do I see," she murmured almost to herself, her eyes darting here and there among the runes as she smiled. "A position of great discomfort and considerable indignation, to be sure, yet not without eventual worth. You are a fortunate child, though there is little doubt that you feel differently at present."

"I don't feel particularly *un*fortunate," I told her smile, at a loss as to what else I might say. "A number of odd things have happened to me lately, but as soon as I return home I'll be done with them."

"Perhaps," she allowed, more amusement briefly entering her smile. "It strikes me that a few words of explanation are in order, to allow you to understand. You must know that there are any number of old tales passing down from mother to daughter and father to son, tales which speak of times long past and what was done in those times. Many of the tales are no more than dreams put to words, wishes for better during times that are harsh, yet some few are full truth no matter the sound of them. One of these truths is that once men and women were more than they now appear to be, enough more that they were capable of wonders beyond even the grandest dreams we now speak of to soothe the pain of our dreary, work-filled lives. How the ability to do wonders slipped through our fingers we know not, yet do some of those wonders occasionally return to those who do not fear their presence, those who see them as the gift they truly are."

Wissa was staring at me soberly now, her calm urging me to believe the wildly outrageous things she was telling me. I wanted to tell her in turn that I knew she was speaking the truth, that I knew the reason behind the loss she and her people had suffered, but somehow I couldn't do it. I had the strangest conviction that hearing the rest of the truth would make things worse for her rather than better, especially in her relations with her people. Suspecting something doesn't bring the same anger as knowing, and the anger of knowledge can be dangerous to the one it holds in its grasp.

"You may now perhaps see why the talkers of the villages so dislike my visitings with their people," she said after a moment with her smile returned, apparently taking my silence for a willingness to believe. "Were I to merely speak the truth to their villagers they would be unconcerned, for freely given truth is taken by most as being worth little or nothing. I, however, charge coppers for what readings I give, and as the readings prove sooth so too do my words take on a similar weight. The talkers would have their villagers believe all people are naught when compared to the shining magnificence of the Highest Lord, therefore should those people humble themselves as the talkers demand. I see no reason for humility other than their speaking of it, and seldom fail to mention the point whenever I may."

"Which makes you popular enough to attract visitors like the ones we're so recently rid of," I said with a laugh, really beginning to like the woman. I still didn't know who the talkers were that she kept referring to, but they didn't sound like people I would enjoy meeting. "It's satisfying when you're given proof that you've gotten to the people you don't care for, but it can also be painful and very dangerous. What if I hadn't been here, or Skyhawk hadn't been watching from the woods?"

"It matters not what *might* have occurred," she answered with a small shake of her head, her smile now filled with secret knowledge. "Others have come before this, more than a few, yet do I remain unharmed. They have not the power to silence the truth completely; all they may do is label it lies. Those I guard, guard me as well, to ensure the continued speaking of the truth. Which shall now be given to you, as it has in the past been given to others."

She was looking at me with an odd directness, as though she knew I wouldn't care for what she was about to say. The wildwood bowl she had put aside was silently humming in a smug sort of way, and that bothered me even more than the look I was getting from the woman.

"As I said, child, there are those in whom the ability to do wonders reappears," she went on, giving no indication she saw the faint frown I could feel myself wearing. "Once I heard it said that the folk who came first were able to know their life-mates at first glance, an ability which allowed them to avoid the heartache we most of us experience in the absence of such certain knowledge. At the time I found myself unsure of the truth of the claim, yet do I doubt it no longer. The one who calls himself Skyhawk—the ability is his without question."

"But what could that possibly have to do with me?" I asked, still trying to decide whether or not she was right. The Talents we of my mother's Realm had were in many ways different from those of the people in Jiss's Realm, but I'd never heard of a Talent like the one she'd described. It was possible the ability was restricted to the Earth Realm, but even if that was so I still couldn't see why she was bothering to tell me about it.

"Child—Haliand—you listen to my words, but fail to hear them," she said, her voice as calm and patient as it had been, her warm, dark eyes matching. "It disturbed you that the man came to what he believed was your rescue, yet failed to remain to speak so much as a word to you. I have seen clearly what passed between you and therefore understand the upset you feel, yet must you understand the true basis for his actions. The first moment he laid eyes on you he knew you for his life-mate, but knew as well that another had claimed you before him. He has not yet found a true path through the swamp of present circumstance, therefore does he avoid discussion with you upon the point."

"That has to be the most ridiculous thing I've ever heard," I stated when she was through, too outraged even to consider being diplomatic. "If anything happened from the moment we first met, it was instant detestation of him on my part, and a complete willingness to argue with me on his. Not only don't he and I get along, most of the time we don't *care* that we don't get along. If those carvings of yours claim otherwise, I would suggest looking into the possibility of getting a replacement set.''

"Peace, child, peace," the woman said with calm soothing, her hand coming quickly to my arm as I began the first movements of getting to my feet. "All differences of opinion shall be settled to your satisfaction, else you need not pay my fee. Is such an offer not acceptable to you?"

"I don't find this discussion as amusing as you seem to," I answered, making no effort to respond to her smile. "And since you're having difficulty remembering, let me repeat what I told you earlier, but this time I'll say it a little more clearly: my name is Haliand, not 'child,' and I believe your 'reading' is over."

"Haliand is quite fitting a name for one such as you," she said, her continuing amusement making it clear she was ignoring the rest of what I'd said. "Legend speaks of the name as belonging to the daughter of a great, high lady, a daughter who was herself a force to be reckoned with. Think you one bearing such a name would simply accept the man chosen for her by circumstances which are unfamiliar to her, those over which she has no control? Instant dislike is the least of what would assail her, for she too would know the man for whom she was meant. The knowledge might well be so deeply buried she would not be openly aware of it, yet would the woman in her know, and by cause of that knowing, rebel. As you fought the binding so did he, my girl, yet were his efforts less effective than yours. Soon he will cease the struggle against what must be, and then will there truly be discord between you. When your struggles cease as well, then will you discover the brightness in the dark.''

"The brightness in the dark," I repeated flatly, meeting the steadiness in the woman's gaze, and then I rose so abruptly to my feet she had no chance of trying to stop me again. "If that fitting a description can be bettered, I'd rather not stay around to hear it. You've done your reading and I've heard it, and now I'll be on my way. I do hope the rest of your journey is more pleasant than it's been until now, just the way I expect mine to be. I always have preferred traveling alone."

"The runes show you as one who is closely acquainted with the truth," the woman Wissa persisted as I turned and started toward my horse. "You should know, then, that the truth may be struggled against yet never entirely denied. Remain here and continue on with me, and I shall endeavor to aid you in finding an acceptance of that which may not be avoided. The debt I owe—"

"Wasn't that large to begin with," I interrupted as I untied my horse in preparation for mounting. "Since I'm the one who supposedly has to be repaid, I'm the one who gets to say when enough has been reached. You've done more than enough, Wissa, and I simply won't hear of you helping any further. I bid you a good day."

By then I was already in the saddle, so I nodded to the woman and then headed my horse back into the forest I should never have left. The woman called after me, something about my being supposed to stay with her, but I wasn't interested enough to really listen. As soon as I could I kicked my mount into faster motion, already leaving behind monumental nonsense, beginning to leave behind an unwanted shadow I hadn't known I was casting.

Chapter 10

MY HORSE'S BEST PACE seemed to be a slightly hurried
canter, and he couldn't keep to it for very long. He began
a determined forward rush when I urged him on, making
me think the motion would have my hair dried before he
even considered stopping, but after only a short while I
discovered we weren't putting as much ground behind us
as we had to begin with. When I urged him on again he
made another valiant effort, but the second effort lasted
even less time than the first, and wasn't even as fast. At
that point I began suspecting I had a very long afternoon in
front of me, especially since my horse wasn't in any way
tired. Lazy was what he was, and obviously used to getting away with putting out minimal effort, nothing like the
mounts I was used to in my mother's Realm. I muttered
nasty things under my breath as I kicked the beast again,
and that time got a little more in the way of speed. Once it
got dark I could leave the stupid animal behind and move
at a much faster pace, but full dark was still a couple of
eternities away.

The very long afternoon continued on and on, but I
found a distraction for myself while I waged the constant
battle of keeping my horse moving faster than he wanted
to go. There were places in the forest that were more
tangled or overgrown than others, places where a rider
would be completely blocked from the view of anyone

watching her. We usually had to slow down in places like that, so I used the time before we reached one to decide which way I would go while I couldn't be seen, which direction I would take to completely change my route through the forest. I was still heading in the same general direction, but every shift was designed to put me a respectable distance away from anyone who might be following.

Not long after the fourth or fifth change of direction, I checked with the trees again to make sure I was still on the proper line for catching up with the thieves. I was told that the wagon was still keeping to the same pace it had been, which meant that I was closing the gap between us faster than I'd been doing earlier in the day. The trees couldn't quite decide whether or not I would catch up to my quarry by the time it grew dark, and I was given the arguments supporting each side of the controversy to consider. I had also intended asking about the presence of any enemies nearby in the forest, but the argument I'd inadvertently started got in the way. Before I could lure one of the trees away from opinionating and back to listening, a mounted figure rode up from behind and slowed to pace me, answering my question in the worst possible way.

"I want you to stop trying to lose me," the outlaw said, the evenness of his voice attempting to mask the annoyance in his eyes. "I can understand your not wanting me near you, but that's one of the reasons I've been staying back out of sight. If you don't spend your time deliberately thinking about it, you'll be able to forget that I'm even there."

"I'll be able to forget a lot more easily if you *aren't* there," I responded, taking my attention away from him and giving it instead to where I rode. "If I'm going to be alone I want to *be* alone, not just think I am. Why don't you go and check out the road, to see if there are any helpless but wealthy travelers in the vicinity? That should give you something to do while making both of us happy."

"Why *are* you alone?" he demanded, the near-growl in his voice showing he was only ignoring the rest of my remarks, not deaf to them. "I thought Wissa said you would be traveling with her for a while, to discuss something you would need someone to talk to about. If I hadn't come right back after making sure those three pieces of garbage weren't going to stop before they got back to where they came from, I would have missed seeing you leave her camp.''

''Your friend Wissa doesn't know as much as she thinks she does,'' I said, now even more annoyed with the woman. If I'd left even the second time I'd wanted to, I would have been entirely rid of my noble protector. ''And if you need someone to look after to make your life worthwhile, why don't you make it her? That way you won't be wasting your time, and she'll have someone around to do readings for. I doubt if anyone she charges is silly enough to come to her twice.''

''Why, what did she tell you?'' he asked, and now there was less demand and more—dread, possibly?—in his voice. ''I've been in this area long enough to have heard of her, but this was the first time I met her and she's never done a reading for me. Most people seem to think she's gifted with a special kind of sight, and I've never come across anyone who could say they'd caught her in a mistake.''

''Well, now you can say it,'' I pointed out, taking my own turn at ignoring things I didn't care to answer or comment about. ''She told you I'd be traveling with her for a while, but she was wrong. It just goes to prove no one can be right all the time, not even people who play with pretty wooden carvings.''

''You still haven't said anything about what she told you,'' he pointed out, apparently understanding at once that his answer wasn't going to be coming on its own. ''If it was all that wrong, why don't you tell me about it? Then I'll have two examples to mention around.''

''Since the reading was supposedly done for me, it's none of your business what she told me,'' I returned, keeping the words cool and impersonal and as distant as my attention. ''If you're all that interested in readings, go and have her do one for you. I'm sure she thinks she owes it to you for having saved her, so it won't even cost you anything.''

"You really do sound as though you don't believe a word she said,'' he remarked, and again his tone had faint shadows of uncertainty, and frustration and upset. "I'm curious to know what you consider so impossible, but if you won't tell me then you won't. How about telling me instead what it was you twice wanted to talk to me about? The first time you called me I was too disgusted with myself to want to do anything but be alone, and the second time I had to make sure those three I'd chased off were going to stay chased off. Since I was so rude to you twice, the least I owe you is to listen now.''

"I thought I made it fairly clear that you don't owe me anything,'' I said, still keeping my eyes well away from him. "If there was a chance you'd be curious about what I wanted to say to you those two times, you should have used one of the opportunities while you had them. At this point I've already forgotten whatever it was, so it couldn't have been very important.''

He didn't come back immediately with an answer to that, and it almost seemed as though he were trying to decide what to say. For my own part, I didn't have that problem; as soon as the man had raised the question, I'd known I no longer wanted to tell him what I'd been going to. I'd been so sure that I'd been the one who had seduced him, that everything happening between us had been my fault rather than his. After spending the last few hours trying not to think about it, I was no longer quite as sure. I was beginning to feel faintly embarrassed and possibly even stupid, and would have preferred talking about almost any other topic there was.

"So you've forgotten what you wanted to say,'' he responded at last with a sigh, weariness rather than anger or annoyance coloring the words. "I spent some time speculating about what it might be, but if it was as unimportant as you claim, then my guesswork must have been wrong. I'm—sorry I didn't ask sooner, and now it's too late. Which seems to be in keeping with the rest of my life. Just keep moving in this same general direction, and you won't have anything to worry about. There are areas to avoid around here, but they lay deeper in the woods than you need to go. It shouldn't be much longer before you and Jentris are together again, and I'm sure *he* won't make the mistake of not listening to you until it's too late. He's a good deal brighter than I am in more ways than one, and now I'll stop inflicting myself on you."

With that he urged his horse into faster motion, quickly pulling away from me as he angled right, toward the road. He was going back to hiding in the forest, I knew, out of my sight and sensing but not completely out of touch, and was probably also on the alert for Jiss. He was going to deliver me back to the man he thought I belonged to, most likely together with a full confession concerning what he'd done, but probably with no mention made about how he felt. Jiss had been right in thinking he was attracted to me, and that attraction was undoubtedly the basis for the nonsense Wissa had tried convincing me of. He was attracted to me even though he shouldn't be, and that had to be because he'd recognized me as the one fated to be his life-mate.

I made a very rude sound, loud enough to cause my horse to turn his head in curiosity. Skyhawk and his friend Wissa must have spent more time talking than either of them had admitted, but the man's wishful thinking, backed by the woman's supposed talent, wasn't going to be as convincing as they'd hoped. I still didn't know why a man would chase after a woman who loathed the very sight of him, but the reason didn't really matter. What neither he nor Wissa understood was that I couldn't be Skyhawk's true life-mate, simply because I wasn't the Earth Realm ephemeral they considered me. I wasn't struggling against a contention that I feared would prove true, I was flatly refusing to share the man's obvious self-delusion and the woman's mystical catering to it. They were absolutely dead-set on fooling themselves, but that didn't mean I had to join them in their fantasy.

Or even go along with supposed nobility. I moved in

annoyance in my saddle, thinking about the way I was going to be turned over to "the man I belonged to." I wasn't riding the forest looking for Jiss, I was chasing a bunch of thieves who had taken something I meant to take back. It really annoyed me that that foolish ephemeral had decided he knew what was best for me, and was going about seeing that it was done. I would take care of what was best for me, and the first step in seeing to it was easy. With no more than a glance for the direction in which the outlaw had gone, I turned my horse deeper into the forest.

My first concern was in not getting too far away from where the thieves would be, but after a few minutes of riding I decided the advantages of being deeper in the forest would outweigh the drawbacks. Skyhawk had to stay fairly close to the road so that he didn't miss his good friend Jentris, and if he did that he couldn't keep playing shadow for me. All I had to do was get far enough away from him by the time it got dark, and I'd never have to be bothered by him again. It had finally come to me that he'd found me the first time by locating the camping place of the thieves, and then had seen me before I had seen him. This time I would be well aware of the possibility and would make certain it didn't happen again.

The afternoon sunlight was still brighter than I really cared for as it slanted down through the trees, and occasional birdsong broke the silence as I rode along at a fast walk. The pace was the best one I could get out of my horse without constantly kicking him, and for the moment I was willing to settle for that. I had to get as far away from my pursuer as I possibly could, which meant I wouldn't be taking time out for rest stops. My body was beginning to wish there was time for rest stops, but if I intended pushing my mount for as much as he was worth, I couldn't do less with myself.

No more than a short amount of time went by, my thoughts taking most of my attention, when I suddenly noticed that the brightness of the light around me had changed in some way. It was no longer the brightness of sunlight, more like what would come from uncounted numbers of candles, the golden aura of the first sort erased and replaced by a shadowless flatness. I could still see the trees and bushes I rode through, as well as glimpses of the sky, but it felt as though an invisible curtain were dropping silently between me and everything I looked at. I could still hear the birdsong faintly, and my horse was still moving along at his favorite pace, but there was *something*—

And then a distraction came that made me forget all about strangeness, and brought me back to current necessity. I heard a shout somewhere behind me, and when I turned to look I could see that miserable outlaw, galloping through the forest a good distance back, his arm waving as though he were trying to get my attention. Since the last thing I wanted was to give him my attention, I knew immediately what I had to do instead. His horse was faster than mine but mine was carrying less weight, which made it just possible that I might outrun him. I also knew that I had to try, *had* to even if I failed, so I didn't waste an instant. With a yell I began kicking my horse, and the urgency inside me must have been stronger than I knew. For the first time that day my mount took off with enthusiasm, and the race was on.

Riding through a forest at a speed like that can't possibly be considered safe, but there are some things more important than safety. Or comfort. The parts of my hair that weren't streaming out behind me kept getting caught under me, and my body was protesting the extra exertion, but I simply had to get away from the man who was chasing me. Tree branches and small clearings went by in a blur, but every time I turned to look, Skyhawk was a little closer. I began feeling a perfectly understandable desperation and tried to get even more speed out of my horse, the refusal to give up the plans I'd made so strongly in possession of me that nothing else seemed to matter. I couldn't let him catch me, no matter what I had to do to prevent it, no matter how many chances I had to take.

I remember noticing how firm my resolve was and how completely unswerving, and then so many things began happening at once that I barely had time for noticing. Just as it came to me that the forest all around had gone through some radical change, I also became aware of the reddish tinge the light had somehow developed. Confusion barely had time to touch me before sudden fear shouldered it aside, for I looked up to see a—crevasse—of some sort directly ahead of me. My horse was heading for it at breakneck speed, but it wasn't possible to see the far side of the opening! That was when I tried turning the beast, tried at least to slow him down enough for us to stop, but he was no longer interested in being slow and lazy. He galloped toward the crevasse as though he couldn't even see it, totally ignoring the way I pulled back on the reins with every ounce of strength I had. On and on he went, faster and faster—and then he launched himself off the ground in a jump, no more than an instant before he plunged over the edge of the crevasse.

That jump was probably the best thing the stupid beast could have done—for himself, but not for me. As totally unexpected as it was, it threw me off balance completely, and as my horse sailed over the crevasse, I fell off his back right into it.

When my eyes blinked open I knew I was awake, but nothing more of a usual awakening routine began at the same time. Rather than getting up I just lay where I was, on some oddly dry grass, hurting almost everywhere it was possible to hurt. By then I knew I'd fallen off the idiot horse I'd been riding, but I couldn't quite remember hitting the ground. Not that I really wanted to remember it, I admitted silently as I stirred and then began forcing myself to sit up. I usually preferred to remember more pleasant things.

And more pleasant scenery to look at. I turned my head slowly as I rubbed at my neck, at first wondering if the fall had affected my vision, quickly deciding no fall could account for what I was seeing. The trees all around were black and twisted, branches and leaves included, the grass on the ground was dry and gray but still not dead, and the bright light all around was reddish in its overall hue but didn't seem to be coming from the obscured sky. The light apparently came from everywhere at once, and somehow erased the details of what was more than a few feet away rather than illuminating them. It also produced no shadows of any sort, and that bothered me more than all the rest of it. The lack of shadow seemed to say there would also be no dark, and I wouldn't have cared for that idea under any circumstances.

Even though I was still hurting I got to my feet, brushing at my draperies and trying to untangle my hair from around my arms. I seemed to remember falling into the crevasse, which meant I had to find one side or the other of it and then climb out again, despite the fact that I couldn't see any sides. The strange landscape appeared to stretch out in all directions, and even though I couldn't see anything clearly behind a ten- or twelve-foot radius, there wasn't even a suggestion of walls anywhere around me. I was sure that couldn't be, that I was confused or missing something obvious; it wasn't possible for there to be no walls, or even none close enough to reach quickly and easily. I'd fallen into the crevasse, so it had to be possible to climb out again.

I nodded firmly to show how completely I believed that conclusion, but if it hadn't been warm to the point of actually causing me to sweat, I might have shivered. I didn't want to ask myself what all those trees were doing growing in a crevasse, or where that strange, reddish light was coming from, or why the heat was so much higher than it had been before I'd fallen. I especially didn't want to think about finding my horse's body somewhere ahead, his jump ended in a way he hadn't expected it to be. When he'd leaped into the air I'd had the distinct impression he knew where he was going and intended landing safely—which made me wonder briefly what I would do if I walked a short way and didn't find his body. I didn't know what I would do and also didn't want to think about it, any more than I wanted to think about how long I'd been unconscious. It somehow felt as though it had been longer than just a few minutes, but if it had been more like an hour or two, why wasn't it closer to getting dark—?

"Stop asking all those stupid questions!" I hissed at myself, letting my eyes move all around as I tried to decide in which direction to go. "You can worry about finding answers once you're out of here, and by then you might even know what this place is. Are you imagining things, or does that spacing between the trees over there make it look as though there might be a path?"

I may have asked the question out loud, but I wasn't so bad off that I answered it in the same way. The spacing of the trees did indeed give the suggestion of a path or aisle, and even as I started for it I automatically asked the trees if I was going in the proper direction. Or at least I tried to ask the trees. Two attempts got me as much response as speaking in the language of spiders would have, and I was forced to admit that I couldn't even hear any conversation among the trees themselves. They weren't like any trees I'd ever come across before, which meant I was completely alone in that very strange place.

"Well, it's not as if I've never been alone before," I muttered as I reached the aisle, still looking around. "I've been alone lots of times, once or twice even without Sahrinth and Greaf. Like now. And back at that inn. But this place doesn't even have spiders."

Which was something I knew without having to look around any more closely than I was already doing. Spiders were intelligent life forms who stayed away from really strange places, which meant I was as alone as it's possible to get. *All* alone, completely on my own, in the most solitary of circumstances, almost exiled forever, absolutely cut off from every—

"Haliand, wait!" a voice called suddenly from behind me, a voice I wouldn't have wanted to hear even if it were the last voice in the entire universe. I'd managed to forget all about him no matter how close behind me he'd been, and when he hadn't been there when I'd come around, I'd been sure I'd avoided him entirely. I was seriously considering running no matter how much I hurt, but before I could come to a definite decision a big hand came to my left shoulder.

"Girl, are you all right?" Skyhawk demanded, then immediately pulled his hand back when I flinched at the touch of it. "No, you aren't all right, that was a stupid question. How badly are you hurt?"

"If you're trying for more intelligent questions, you still haven't made it," I responded, keeping my eyes away from him as I gently flexed my shoulder. "Since I'm up on my feet and walking, it should be obvious I'm not yet ready for the journey to the next level of existence. And I thought you were going to stay so well hidden that I'd have no idea you were there? If two steps behind me is your concept of staying hidden, I have something rather deflating to tell you."

"Yes, I can see you're all right, but you have nothing to complain about," he came back, the words very dry as he moved around to face me. "If you'd stayed out of the deeper woods the way you were told to, I could have stayed back out of your sight. When I saw you heading for this area and called to you to stop, you ignored me and rode ahead even faster. By rights I should have let you go through this alone, but I—couldn't quite bring myself to do it."

"Well, of course you couldn't," I agreed, still not looking directly at him even though he stood right in front of me. "Your good friend Jentris wouldn't have been pleased if you'd done something like that, so you had to change your mind. Would you like to tell me now what it is I won't be going through alone? I've never seen a forest that looks like this, so . . ."

"So you do know," he interrupted suddenly, and I had no illusions about it being the forest he was referring to. "I thought Wissa might not pick up on it if she didn't do a reading for me, but apparently she doesn't always need a deliberate reading. She saw what was going on and told you about it, expecting you to be so shaken and confused that you'd stay with her for a while to talk about it, but you didn't. You decided instead not to believe a word she said, got on your horse, then rode away. Do you really think refusing to believe will change what is?"

"Only when the *is* part exists solely in someone's imagination," I answered, finally looking straight at him to show I wasn't quite as young and credulous as he seemed to consider me. "Just because *you're* suffering from a delusion doesn't mean I have to do the same, not even to protect your friend Wissa's reputation. You may have noticed you and I don't get along very well, and there's a definite reason for that: I don't like you any more than you would like me if you hadn't decided it was 'fated' that there be something between us. Once you understand the only something is pure revulsion, we may begin getting somewhere. Now, about this forest . . ."

"You're right about our not getting along, but you're wrong about the reason for it," he persisted, his dark eyes showing the beginnings of his usual annoyance with me. "When two people meet they always have some idea about how attracted they feel toward one another, but once in a very great while it happens that they share something more than a vague like or dislike. I thought I was imagining things when I got my first look at you, but rather than fading my feelings began getting stronger and more certain. You were the one meant to be my woman, no matter how unlikely the idea seemed."

"*Unlikely* isn't the word I would have chosen," I came back, intent on showing him just how little interest I had in the discussion. "*Totally impossible* would be a good deal closer to the mark, so why—"

"And then I noticed how really set against me you were," he plowed on, once again deliberately ignoring what I'd said. "I tried to figure out exactly what I'd done to make you feel that way, but looking back showed I'd only been responding to your attempts to start arguments, not deliberately starting ones of my own. From everything I could see, you'd apparently begun hating me almost from the first moment we met."

"Now see that, you *did* notice," I told him with a small

smile and a warm nod of approval, my hands clasped behind me as I looked up at him. "If you were totally beyond help you wouldn't have been able to see that, but you did so you aren't. Now all we have to do is get you to understand that you really are imagining what you think you feel, and then we'll be free to hate each other in peace."

"So you still insist I'm imagining things?" he asked in a very mild way as he folded his arms, apparently all through with pretending he hadn't heard what I'd said. "If that's true, then maybe you'll answer a question for me. We both agree you hate me and have been doing it for some time, but I haven't heard a reason as to why that might be. Would you like to mention your reason now, just so I'll know it, too?"

"Why—there are lots of reasons," I answered, suddenly very much aware of the dark, unwavering gaze he held me with. "Not only do you have the manners of a badly raised rock, you're inconsiderate and deliberately rude and always insist on everyone doing things your way. And besides all that, I don't have to have a specific reason for hating someone. The fact that I do hate them is more than enough in itself."

"Is it?" he said in that same mild way, still staring down at me with the same look in his eyes. "I agree a person is entitled to hate anyone they care to, but most people have definite reasons for their hatred even if the reasons are irrational. The list you just gave me is pure nonsense, nothing more than after-the-fact rationalization of an already existing condition. What I'm trying to find out is the reason the hatred started in the first place— especially since I'm the one who helped you and Jentris escape from the outlaw camp. Most people would have been very grateful, but all you felt was intense dislike which turned into hatred. Why?"

He sent that last word in my direction and then just stood there waiting, almost daring me to come up with something he couldn't simply brush out of the way with a shrug. I wanted very much to prove to him how wrong he

was, to show him incontrovertible proof that I had a right
to feel the way I did, but nothing in the way of reasonable
argument would come to me. It also didn't help that I
could remember thinking at one point that I had no real
reason for the hatred I felt toward the man, nothing that
could be trotted out and paraded in front of others. I knew
how I felt, but I couldn't think of anything to say to justify
the feeling.

"Now that's a hopeful sign," he remarked after I'd
stood silent a moment or two, undoubtedly noticing that
I'd looked away from him again. "Instead of coming up
with your usual flood of words, you're taking some time to
think about the question. When it finally comes to you that
you have no real reason for hating me, you might start
thinking about the reason I've come to accept: You realized almost as soon as I did that you were meant for me,
and *that's* what you've been fighting against. It isn't me
you hate, just the idea of having no choice in the matter,
and that's something I can understand. I think it's safe to
say I've spent more time looking around than you have so
I don't see it the same way, but I do understand how you
feel."

"That's really very generous of you," I couldn't help
saying, looking at him again with all the annoyance and
exasperation that was suddenly inside me. "You understand how I feel, so you aren't holding my unreasonable
behavior against me. What you also obviously aren't doing
is thinking, something your last speech made very clear.
Most people would love to know who their fated life-mates
are, to keep them from having to spend years searching
and wondering, if nothing else. I don't pretend I think of
myself as being just like everyone else, but I do happen to
be human. If I was supposedly meant for a man I would at
least want to get to know him, and at no time have I felt a
desire to do anything but be rid of you. If that's your idea
of me seeing the same thing you did, one of us has a
terrible vision problem."

"Getting smart won't do anything to settle the disagreement," he said, the mildness in his voice touched very

faintly with impatience. "It's beginning to get tiresome repeating myself, but you had no reason to want to be rid of me. What you want to be rid of is the demands of the situation, one you weren't even aware of on the conscious level. That's why you didn't want to 'get to know me'; I was part of the thing you were trying to avoid. What you have to understand right now is that it can't be avoided. It's a fact that won't stop being a fact, so all we can do is deal with it."

"What do you consider 'dealing' with it?" I demanded, really disliking the entire idea. "Shall we sit down together in this lovely woods and have a picnic? Stroll together hand in hand while we exchange inane dialogue? Or was it something else entirely that you had in mind?"

"As a matter of fact, it was something else entirely that I had in mind," he said as he suddenly began looking around, apparently not noticing the cutting edge I hadn't been able to keep from my words. "The situation between us is very complicated, but now that we're both aware of it we can talk about it. While we try finding our way out of here, that is. This isn't anything like a good place to be, and the faster we get out, the better off we'll find ourselves. The path we have to follow is right there, so let's get started."

"You seem to know this place awfully well for someone who won't answer any questions about it," I said, more than happy to change subjects as I began moving toward the path he'd gestured to, the aisle I'd already noticed. "If it's that much of a secret, you shouldn't be able to get into it so easily."

"It isn't precisely a secret, and it's designed to be easily gotten into," he answered, moving with me as he continued looking around. "This is a special area created by the Highest Lord, made at the request of the village talkers in this neighborhood. The talkers said they weren't being listened to by their villagers the way they should be, and they wanted something the villagers could be shown rather than simply told about. Dozens of villagers have been sent through here since it was first made, and those who came out swore they'd never again do anything that would get them sent through it a second time. Its purpose is to show people what they can expect to look forward to if they aren't good, meaning if they don't do what the talkers tell them to.''

"I don't understand any part of that," I said with a shake of my head, beginning to look around the way he was. "I keep hearing about these talkers, and no one who mentions them seems to like or approve of them—but most sound afraid. What makes them so important, and why would the Highest Lord create something like this for them?''

"People should know better than to raise their children completely sheltered from life," he muttered. "Haliand, the situation behind the talkers is too involved for me to go into it in detail right now, so let me put it as simply as I can. Talkers are men who tell everyone how wonderful the Highest Lord is, and how people have to spend their lives living the way the Highest Lord wants them to. Since many people don't enjoy the idea of lives as restricted as the ones the talkers insist on, they try to do things to make them a little easier and more pleasant. If they were left alone to do those things the talkers would lose their control over the people, so they aren't left alone. Places like this are created to send people through, places to frighten people into doing as they're told. Even though most survive to get out again they aren't safe places, so we'll have to stay very alert until it's well behind us.''

"*We'll* have to stay alert," I repeated flatly, feeling as though I were in the middle of something I'd been through before. "This place isn't safe, so *we'll* have to protect ourselves. I wonder if that means one of us will do all the protecting for both of us—as it has up until now.''

He was silent for a moment, giving me the chance to decide that the question of the talkers really was one to go into at a better time, and then he made a soft sound of agreement.

"Yes, that was exactly what I meant," he admitted, and

now he was sounding faintly curious. "Why does the idea
of being protected bother you so much?"

"It's not a matter of its *bothering* me," I corrected as I
looked down at the grayish grass, surprised he would ask
something like that. "It so happens I can take care of
myself, and constantly being around people who insist on
doing it for me has been very annoying, not to mention
insulting. When I say I can do it myself and I'm ignored,
it's like being told I don't know what I'm talking about."

"You know, it hadn't occurred to me to look at it like
that," he said in so thoughtful a way that I looked up at
him again. "If someone ignored what I was saying or told
me I didn't know what I was talking about, I'd get more
than insulted. You would prefer it if I really did do nothing
to protect you?"

"Why, yes, I would," I responded, close to being
stunned by what I saw in his dark eyes. He wasn't asking
just for effect, or to see how I would react; he really meant
it! "I would not only prefer it, I would love it, but I don't
understand why you would ask. You can't mean you
intend doing something so reasonable, can you?"

"Reasonable isn't what I consider it, but why shouldn't
I do it?" he countered, faint amusement now shadowing
his expression. "I may be of the opinion that you need my
protection as much as anyone else who can't fight as well
as I do, but that's all it is—an opinion. If you want the
chance to prove me wrong, all I can honorably do is give it
to you."

"Yes, that would be the honorable way," I agreed, not
about to lose so unexpected an opportunity. "And when I
prove your opinion wrong, will you apologize?"

"I certainly will," he assured me a shade too solemnly,
that drop of amusement increasing. "I try to make it a
point to apologize when I'm wrong, which does happen
every now and then. Do you by any chance follow a
similar practice?"

I looked at him more closely for a moment, trying to
decide if he was seriously waiting for an answer or was
just trying to be clever, then concluded it didn't matter. I

had no interest in answering something like that no matter why he'd asked, not when my response was most likely to start another argument. It so happened I did believe in apologizing when I was wrong, but admitting it could have reopened the topic of how badly I'd misjudged him. It remained to be seen whether or not I'd misjudged him; once I learned how well he kept his word, then I'd decide if reconsideration was in order.

After that we moved along the path in silence for a while, the eyes of the man beside me constantly on the move. The aisle between the twisted black trees was wide enough for four people to walk abreast, but that doesn't mean we walked comfortably along a road that gave us the feeling of having elbow room. The reddish mist clinging to the trees and blurring the landscape only a few steps beyond where we walked was very confining, as though it were the solid walls of a cage rather than nothing but brooding vapor. Walking made the air feel even hotter than it had, but it also began loosening up some of the aches in my body. By the time I had to prove I could take care of myself—if I did get the chance to prove it—I would be back in good enough condition to succeed.

"Speaking of apologies, I feel as though I already owe you one," Skyhawk said suddenly, just as if there hadn't been a large gap of time since our previous conversation had ended. He was still looking around rather than specifically in my direction, and his left hand rested on the hilt of his sword.

"This whole situation wasn't in any way my doing, but I can't shake the feeling of being responsible," he said, and I knew he wasn't referring to our being in that place of twisted trees. "When I realized you'd already been claimed by Jentris I wanted to turn around and ride away, but that would have meant abandoning you two in an area you didn't know, leaving you vulnerable to recapture. I couldn't do something like that no matter how hard it was on me, so I gritted my teeth and just stayed with you. That episode at the inn made me glad I had, but once we won I decided it was time for me to be gone. There are people who enjoy constant pain, I'm told, but I don't happen to be one of them."

I nearly asked him why he was still around then, but I couldn't seem to do it. His voice was so toneless it was almost like listening to his thoughts, and the intrusion would have been inexcusable.

"I mean, I'm not a child," he continued, a short, mirthless laugh emphasizing the contention. "I know there's no guarantee that a man who finds his life-mate will end up being able to claim her, not if someone else has claimed her first. If nothing permanent has been done yet he may be able to hope, but as far as walking up to her and announcing that she's destined to be his—especially if she's made it very clear she wants nothing to do with him—and the man who'd claimed her had openly given his friendship and trust—"

"How could someone be destined for someone else without some sort of guarantee?" I asked, needing to interrupt as well as honestly wanting to know. "If it's possible for me to avoid a situation you say I find too confining, why would I react as though it weren't avoidable? I mean, either I'm meant for you without having the least say in the matter, or there's a way for me to get around the demand. It can't be both, so which is it?"

"I don't think you want to know," he said, his expression faintly pained, but my own expression made him sigh. "All right, so you do want to know, even if it starts another fight. The truth of the matter is—if one of us refuses to accept defeat in the matter of claiming, our mating moves more and more toward being inevitable. The very fact that I didn't ride away after getting you out of the outlaw camp started it, and that's what I wanted to apologize for. My presence was the direct cause of your having felt the way you did, and even though I couldn't have done anything but stay, I still wish it hadn't been necessary."

"There's still something wrong with your explanation," I said after the briefest hesitation, noticing that he'd no more than glanced at me before going back to being alert. "I can't quite put my finger on it, but somewhere there's a line of logic being chopped in half. I'll figure it out sooner or later, but right now I have another question. If your being here started my dislike of you, does that mean once you leave for good I'll suddenly realize what a wonderful person you were?''

"Do you mean will you stop feeling trapped?" he asked in turn, some of the amusement returning to him. "That all depends on whether you really believe I'm gone for good, and whether or not there's still a chance of my coming back. Haliand, two of the biggest problems between us are the facts that you think Jentris is your choice in a man, and you unfortunately haven't had much experience in life. Being with a man of your own choice lets you feel that you're in control of what's happening around you, making you believe that if you decide you don't like him after all, you still have the option of going off to find someone else. You don't want to be told I'm the man you think you'll be looking for, the perfect man for you to be the perfect woman with. You want to do your own looking around, and find it out for yourself.''

"And what's wrong with that?" I asked, the words coming out as stiff as I felt. "Why should I take someone's word for something, when I'd much rather find it out for myself?"

"There's nothing wrong with it, and there's no reason why you shouldn't do your own looking," he said quickly but gently, his tone now soothing. "That's why once I have you back with Jentris, you really will see the last of me. I wanted you to know that I won't force myself down your throat no matter how destined we're supposed to be for each other, and I won't take unfair advantage ever again. Jentris was the one who found you first, so he has the right to try to make you happy. Once I'm gone, I hope you'll give him the chance.''

There still seemed to be something wrong with what he was saying, but even beyond that I found myself very upset. He was beginning to get me confused, and the fact that he still didn't know there was really nothing between Jiss and me somehow made it worse. His apology and his

willingness to leave—would they still stand unchanged if
he found out I wasn't as claimed as he thought? I didn't
know and couldn't take the chance, not with the safety of
the Great Flame at stake. I'd have to live with my confusion until I had the time to work everything out—after the
reason I was in that Realm in the first place was success-
fully seen to.

We lapsed into silence again, his even more brooding
than mine, the reddish mist all around us coming in a poor
third. I didn't know what Skyhawk was thinking about,
but I was forcing myself to notice how much ground we
were covering without really getting anywhere—and how
there wasn't the least sign of the body of a horse. If the
Lord of the Earth had had a hand in creating the place I
was no longer surprised at the strangeness of it all, but that
still left a number of questions unanswered. Either the area
was narrow enough to jump over, or it wasn't; if it was
narrow enough we should have already crossed it two or
three times over, and if it wasn't there should have been a
dead or crippled horse. That we hadn't crossed it and also
hadn't found my horse simply added to the disturbance I
felt over everything else.

I know I didn't consciously start lagging behind the
outlaw, and that was probably one of the reasons he didn't
notice it any more than I did. We were, of course, very
involved with our own thoughts, so when I looked up to
find him half a dozen steps ahead of me and still going on
like that, I wasn't particularly surprised. I thought about
hurrying to catch up, decided against it almost instantly,
then looked around with the forlorn hope of finding a
different path I could take all alone. That was when I saw
it, and it was so unexpected I stopped short where I was.

There, in the midst of dead-looking trees and grass and
sullen red mist, was a pile of golden coins, the sort that
Skyhawk had said were necessary for getting things like
food and shelter in that Realm. With that area so rarely
frequented and no one else in sight I couldn't imagine
where the coins had come from, but there was no doubt
that they were there. In my mother's Realm they wouldn't

have been necessary, but that was because my mother's Realm was civilized. The Earth Realm obviously was not, and since there was no telling how much longer I would have to stay there, it didn't seem wise to simply pass the coins by. As I began moving toward them I knew I would give them up if I found whoever they belonged to, but until and unless that happened I would keep them against need.

The coins were in a casual pile on the grayish grass, their color so bright each of the small round shapes seemed to be gleaming. As I bent down and reached for a handful of them, I wondered if I needed them all; there seemed to be quite a few, and it might be more considerate if I left some for the next person in need who came along. My fingers scooped up a handful, which I transferred to my left palm, and then I cried out at the pain and let the coins scatter wildly as I shook my hand. The metal was *hot,* and holding the coins had burned me.

"The talkers insist that money is evil, and only they can be trusted to have it and not be corrupted by it," Skyhawk's voice came from behind me, mostly filled with calm. "I would say that was the reason that gold was put there, to burn anyone who tried to touch it against the teachings of the talkers. Are you all right?"

"How could I be burned and still be all right?" I demanded, turning to glare at him with all the anger I was feeling. "And what sort of stupidity are you trying to tell me? *Nothing* is bad or good all by itself, it all depends on what's done with it. And if people don't know how to handle something properly, you don't take it away from them, you teach them what they *should* be doing, otherwise they'll never learn. If you treat people as responsible human beings, they tend to *become* responsible human beings."

"Hey, don't look in my direction for a fight, I happen to agree with you," the outlaw protested, one hand to his chest and an expression of innocence on his face. "I was only trying to tell you what the talkers claim, not the way I consider it. It also happens to be the reason I kept going even though I saw the gold.''

"But you still let me touch it,'' I pointed out with no lessening of anger and maybe even a small increase, the throbbing in my palm making it happen. "It didn't matter to you in the least that I would be hurt, just as long as you continued on unburned. Would you like me to thank you now, or shall I wait until later?''

"Right now will do,'' he allowed judiciously, folding his arms across his chest as he looked down at me. "I gave my word to let you take care of yourself, and that's what I did. If I'd stopped you before you touched the gold and told you what would happen, you would have been within your rights to accuse me. Since I didn't protect you, I'd like to hear you thank me for keeping my word.''

His dark eyes were very serious as he said his piece, and I could feel that all amusement had gone out of him. I was very close to saying something nasty in return, mostly at the urging of the pain in my hand, but he was right about having kept his word, and was entitled to have it acknowledged—even though I still thought he'd done it on purpose.

"You're absolutely correct, and you *are* due my thanks for not having protected me,'' I allowed with all the stiffness that refused to leave me, meeting his unwavering stare. "Thank you for not protecting me.''

With that I turned and walked around him back onto the path, then continued briskly in the direction we'd been going before I'd spotted the gold. Although I'd said what was necessary, I hadn't liked doing it and didn't care to add anything else.

It didn't take long before the man had caught up with me, but his silence was a full match to mine. We just kept going through the unchanging reddish light, seeing nothing but the twisted black trees, and after a few minutes I became aware of a different tenor to my thoughts. The pain in my left hand was almost completely gone, the angry red of the burn faded to no more than pink. I stared at the final traces of injury on my hand, surprised that I had healed as quickly as I always did even in that Realm, and then I had to admit something. For someone who supposedly knew the proper meaning of balance, I hadn't done anything to prove it.

"I . . . think it's my turn to apologize," I said without looking at my companion. "You really did keep your word about not protecting me, but the thanks you got were somewhat on the surly side. I'd like to say the words again, but this time put a little more feeling into them: Thank you for not protecting me."

"This time you're welcome," he answered, sounding a good deal less grudging than I had. "I was hoping you would understand the point I was trying to make, and now apparently you have. Since we're in this together, we'll do better as friends than as enemies."

"I didn't say anything about wanting to be your friend," I told him as quickly as I could, finally looking up to see that he was watching me with a faint smile. "You were due an apology so I gave you one, but that's as far as it goes. Nothing else has changed between us."

"Oh, yes, ma'am!" he responded almost as quickly as I had, the intensely serious expression matching his words coming just as fast. "I'll be certain to remember my proper place, and won't step out of it again. Just consider me your abject slave, and command me as you will."

I shook my head to show I was ignoring his nonsense for the idiocy it was, surprised that he hadn't asked me again to have him whipped, and then I suddenly remembered the marks I'd seen on his back. The way the memory felt said that those marks had been bothering me, and I just had to ask.

"After the—time—we spent together, I couldn't help noticing that something had been done to your back," I tried, looking up to his face. "With all the times you've mentioned slavery, I was wondering if—you ever really were a slave."

"My back," he echoed, his expression this time going completely blank, his eyes seeing something other than me. He stayed distracted for what seemed like a very long time, then he pulled out of it with a shake of his head.

"No, I was never what most people would consider a slave," he said, his lips turned up in a mirthless smile. "I might have been treated as though I wore an invisible collar, but I was never formally declared a slave. Now you don't have to be afraid that my presence will taint both the ground and the air."

"I was just trying to find out if you ever really had been hurt with a whip," I returned, back to feeling as stiff as I had earlier. "If the question was an intrusion, I apologize; you can be certain the same won't happen again."

"No, wait," he said immediately, his hand suddenly on my shoulder to keep me from increasing my pace and walking away from him. "What I said was uncalled for, and it wasn't your fault that it was said. I tend to get a little—bitter—when I think about that time in my life, and I've got to learn to control it. The answer to your question is yes, I *was* whipped, and I think my not being a slave made it hurt twice as much. I sometimes believe it was done for that very reason, to hurt me worse than the lowest of the low, and the rage I feel is the kind you're best off never experiencing."

His hand had begun tightening on my shoulder, but then he seemed to realize what he was doing and quickly took it away. I hadn't looked back at him at all, not with the way his voice had sounded, not when I had been stupid enough to bring up the subject in the first place. Getting my original question answered had only generated more questions, but after what had happened with the first, I couldn't quite bring myself to ask them. The sullen red all around us seemed very fitting for that particular topic of conversation, but then Skyhawk sighed and shifted to another topic.

"You mentioned the—time we spent together," he said, sounding as though he were trying to force himself away from remembered agony and back to normal feelings. "By rights I should be apologizing and telling you how much I regret it, but the truth is I don't regret it. I shouldn't have done it and it won't happen again, but not because of regret."

"I think you've lost me," I said, looking toward my

left, where he now walked. I might not have answered if
he'd mentioned the subject at a different time, but after
what I'd done I owed him something else to talk and think
about. "You seemed regretful enough just before you left,
so I don't understand why you've suddenly changed your
mind."

"I haven't changed my mind," he said with a small
shrug, glancing at me in between watching all around us.
"Just before I left you I was upset over having betrayed
Jentris by breaking my word, and was certain I couldn't
trust myself to stay with you and not do it again. This walk
has given me time to think, and I've got most of it
straightened out in my mind now."

"By deciding you don't regret what happened," I said
with a nod, doing some of my own looking around. "I'm
glad you've come to that conclusion, because the truth of
the matter is it wasn't your fault. For reasons of my own I
encouraged you, but not because I wanted to hurt you. I
didn't know you'd think you'd broken your word, or that
you would be bothered quite so much. I think this is the
place where I get to say I'm sorry."

I'd hurried through my speech to make sure I got it out
before I lost the opportunity, but once it was said there
didn't seem to be anything to add to it. I began expecting
another long silence or an explosion of anger from him,
but what I got instead was surprising.

"If you're trying to take the blame for me making love
to you, I'm afraid you don't understand how it works," he
said with a small sound that was very much like a swallowed laugh. "I'm not a young boy lacking all experience
with women, and therefore lacking self-control. I couldn't
keep myself from taking you in my arms, though, because
you're the woman who was supposed to have been born to
be mine. I was willing to use any excuse just as long as I
had you, and didn't understand how unfair it was to you
until it was all over."

"You didn't hurt me, so why was it unfair?" I asked,
finding myself even more confused than I had been. I had
the feeling I ought to have been insulted over the way he'd

laughed, but it seemed wiser to try figuring out what he was talking about before getting insulted.

"It was unfair to you because there's really no chance that we'll ever be together the way we're supposed to be," he said, and now the words were gentle and totally devoid of all amusement. "It was nice to believe for a while that because we're destined for each other, there was a faint chance of its happening, but there really isn't. You and I come from two different worlds, and to expect you to share the life I live would be more than ludicrous. Truthfully, I can't even expect you to understand it, so why bother worrying about sharing? You're a sheltered young woman and I'm—who and what I am; it's necessary to remember that any number of people live their lives without their perfect opposites. I said I don't regret what happened and for my own part I don't, but you can be certain I won't try getting between you and Jentris ever again."

That time the heavy silence did resume, and for some reason I felt worse than I had when I'd first been told about his beliefs. I'd been sure he was mistaken and had been determined to prove it to him, but now I didn't have to bother. There was no chance we'd ever be together, he'd said; we come from two different worlds. That part was true enough, more so than he knew, and as far as who and what he was, I was completely aware of that as well. He was a backward primitive from a crippled Realm, an ephemeral who would not live long enough to realize even a fraction of whatever potential might have been his before his heritage had been stolen from him. No, we couldn't have spent our lives together even if we'd both wanted to, not with the disparity in our age spans. He would be dead of old age in the blink of an eye, while I—

I would have to go on all alone, with nothing but the memory of something I would never know again. Even if he'd been right, and was also somebody I could be interested in, how would it be possible to get involved with him knowing the terrible pain that lay ahead? Wouldn't it be better and easier to avoid something like that completely, to find someone who would be no more than a companion and never an ache deep within? Wouldn't it be better never to know—

"Did you hear that?" Skyhawk asked abruptly, stopping short to frown ahead. "I thought I heard something, very like a—"

The scream cut through his words, clear enough this time for there to be no mistake. Somewhere ahead a woman was screaming, and Skyhawk paused only long enough to be sure I was still with him before leading the way at a run toward the sound.

Chapter 11

THE DEAD-GRASS PATH wasn't hard to run on, and soon we caught sight of the woman who was screaming. There was a man with her as well, but he was too busy to scream. The two people were under attack by a number of strange-looking beasts, animals I'd never seen the like of before, and the man was defending himself and the girl with a branch from one of the twisted black trees.

The animals were really ugly, with wrinkled, leathery hides that looked red in the surrounding light, heavy hooves at the bottoms of their feet that made them move awkwardly, pointed talons at the ends of their clawlike hands, dangerous-looking horns on their foreheads, and long, barbed tails. Their teeth were also sharp and pointed, something that could be seen from the way the beasts snarled as they tried to attack past the swinging branch in the man's hand. The girl stood screaming behind him, her eyes on two of the beasts who were working their way around the man toward where she was, and Skyhawk paused only long enough to take in the scene before drawing his sword and plunging ahead into the fight.

I have to admit I was left standing and staring for a moment, but only because I knew I needed a weapon of some sort to use against the animals. For the same moment I didn't know where I would get one, and then I happened to see another branch like the one the man was using. This second branch was a little shorter than the one the man had, but I still hurried over and picked it up, then did my own running toward the fight.

By that time Skyhawk was already swinging his sword, working with the man who was trying to drive the animals toward a weapon capable of ending them. The animals, however, seemed to know what a sword could do to them, and were therefore rather uneager to face one. When I arrived with my branch and tried beating at them the way the man was doing, they snarled a final time and then turned and raced for the woods. Ungainly or not, it didn't take long before they were gone from sight, and as Skyhawk lowered his sword the other man dropped his branch, then turned to take the now-sobbing girl into his arms.

"There, there, my love, them cowardly things is gone and it's all over," he said to the badly frightened girl, holding her tight while stroking her hair. "They ain't gonna hurt you none with me still livin', an' that no matter who wants it different."

"Those animals are cowards; fighting them was the best thing you could have done," Skyhawk said to the man as he resheathed his sword, his gaze flickering here and there to make sure the beasts weren't sneaking back. "As long as you're too afraid of them, they can win against you. If you can manage to fight them despite your fear, they don't stand a chance."

"Then it was me who d-done wrong," the girl said, still badly shaken but trying to pull herself together. She was a small girl with brown hair and light eyes, a plainly pretty face, and a good figure under the faded yellow, long-skirted dress she wore. "I got so scared I din't even thinka fightin', but I ain't gonna do it again, Domil. Next time you won't be standin' alone."

"Wasn't standin' alone this time, Grenna," the man Domil answered, his smile softening the square lines of his face. He was a fairly large man, almost my size, and his old blue shirt and dark trousers covered the sort of heavy body produced by hard work. His brown boots were no newer than his clothing, but like them they seemed as clean as possible and gently cared for. "I knowed you was with me even though you was scared, girl, an' then I had this lord 'n lady helpin'. It likely don't mean much, sir, but you got my thanks f'r helpin' out that way. I ain't one t' ferget."

"Helping was our pleasure," Skyhawk said with a smile, surprising me quite a bit by including me in what he was saying. "The lady is Haliand, you can call me Skyhawk, and this would be a really good time for all of us to move on. The sooner we get to the end of this path, the sooner we'll be out of here."

"I'm Domil, this here's my intended, Grenna, an' we're right behind ya," the man said at once, shifting to keep one arm around the girl. "Woulda been past here awready, 'cept we stopped t' see if'n summa that could be had. Me an' Grenna feel like we ain't had nothin' t' eat in days."

The man Domil gestured to the left side of the road with his chin, showing with the gesture the "that" he'd been referring to. For the first time I noticed the food spread out on neat blue and white cloths, plate after plate of meat and vegetables and soups and desserts, all of it looking fresh and ready for eating. The sight made me realize how long it had been since I'd had anything to eat worth mentioning, but I wouldn't have touched any of it even if Skyhawk hadn't shaken his head.

"You're better off going hungry than trying to eat something you find in this place," he said, using his right hand to gesture us all into beginning to walk with him. "The talkers feel their followers should eat only what they're told they can, and not even much of that, or there might not be enough left over for the talkers to take. Even if you'd been allowed to eat that food, chances are it would have made you sick."

"Slaves, that's what them talkers want, nothin' but slaves," Domil muttered while the girl Grenna looked upset, his arm tightening around her shoulders. "They say it's the Highest Lord as wants us t' do all them things, but our doin' 'em don't do the Highest Lord no good, only the talkers. They like tellin' folk what t' do, like seein' 'em listen, an' purely love sayin' no t' them as don't quiver when they talk. You shouldn'a told 'em what we planned on, Grenna."

"I wasn't thinkin', Domil," Grenna said with a sigh, shaking her head. "When you said they wouldn' let you marry 'cause you ain't one a their goodies, I din't wanna believe it. When th' talker told me I hadda find a different man 'cause you was a follower a evil, I told him you was no such thing an' I was gonna marry you no matter what. Never thought they'd take us an' throw us in here, else I'da kept my mouth shut an' just walked away the way you wanted."

"We live t' get outa here, that's what we're gonna do first thing," Domil said to her, his voice firm with assurance. "There's gotta be someplace them talkers don't run things, an' that's where we're gonna go. You wait an' see, girl, we're gonna make it."

The girl smiled up at him as he looked down at her, their gazes meeting and clinging, their feelings for each other more than obvious. I turned away from them to give full attention to where I was walking rather than looking back to listen to the conversation, my stick still firmly and deliberately in my hand, and Skyhawk chuckled very softly.

"The talkers also try to control their people by telling them who they can and can't marry," he said just as softly, obviously talking to me alone. "Too often their people actually listen to them, which makes them think they can get away with it with everyone, even people like Domil and Grenna. What they've really done with those two is turned them into enemies, opponents who will become part of the group that will ultimately destroy the talkers and everything they represent. I truly believe that, more deeply than anything I've ever believed in my life."

"It's a comforting idea to believe in," I said very quietly as I swung my stick, feeling more subdued than I could remember ever being. He'd spoken to me about something very important to him, but I couldn't keep myself from pointing out what he wasn't seeing. "The only problem with comfort is that too often it gives false hope. What will Domil and Grenna and any others like them do when they find out the Highest Lord is solidly behind the talkers? Right now they don't believe it, but what will happen if they ever find out the truth?''

"You're remembering what I said about the Highest Lord creating this place," he stated, and I could feel the way he turned his head to look at me. "In a way I'm sorry I told you that, but in another way I'm glad. You now know the truth, so let's put the question to you: Will you live the life of a slave, simply because the Highest Lord wants you to? Before you answer, remember how really powerful he is, and how far above us all he stands. He could undoubtedly end our lives any time he cared to, so will you bow down and give the total obedience he wants?''

"No," I answered without the least hesitation, turning my head to meet his warm, dark gaze. "I don't care who he is or how powerful he can be, he still has no right to tell people they belong to him because they're less than he is. Any compassionate, truly self-assured being tries to help those of lesser ability, encouraging them to grow and flourish and become as much as they can. He doesn't force them to the ground and put his foot on their necks, telling them he's keeping them down for their own good. All that means is that he's afraid of them, afraid of what they could become if he leaves them free to go their own way. You want me to remember he can end me? Okay, I remember, and I still say, so what? Ending things doesn't make you special; keeping them alive and happy does.''

"I wonder how I knew what your answer would be even before you spoke it," he said, his smile of pleasure a full match to the look in his eyes. "That's the decision I hope our new friends will come to, they and the others like them. I'll be there to help as much as I can, but the ultimate decision has to be theirs. And once we're out of this place, you forget what you said. You still have to live where the talkers rule, and you don't need the kind of trouble they can give you.''

"I'm not afraid of the talkers," I said, gesturing aside what he'd told me with all the annoyance I was still feeling toward his "Highest Lord." "I can take care of myself, and anyone who tries giving me trouble will find that out."

"You intend making sure Jentris has his hands full?" he came back, his tone showing he'd found some annoyance of his own. "They'll start by going after him, you know, and their attacks won't let him reply with a sword. They'll consider him responsible because he'll be your husband, and there won't be any way for him to—"

"Will you stop that?" I almost shouted, suddenly so furious I was having trouble controlling it. "My being with Jentris is your idea, not mine, and I'm tired of hearing how well he'll do if I only let him! No matter what he is or isn't allowed to do I won't be marrying him, so stop wasting your time worrying on his behalf. He won't be in a position to need that worry."

I gave my full attention to marching along on the path, but speeding my pace didn't leave that miserable outlaw behind the way I hoped it would. He had no trouble keeping up with me, and after a moment or two he cleared his throat.

"You may have gotten the impression that I think Jentris needs me to speak for him, but that isn't so," Skyhawk said, now sounding half diffident and half firmly convinced. "Jentris can do well enough speaking for himself, which he'll prove as soon as I get you back to him. He'll make you forget about everything that's happened, leaving nothing but the way you felt about him before this all started. He does want you, Haliand, and you have to honor whatever vows there are between you."

I almost snapped out there were no vows involved, most especially since he was so sure there were, but instead simply clamped my jaws together and stayed silent. His nobility in stepping aside for the man who had claimed me first was almost more grating than his deciding he and I were meant for each other, and I really didn't care to discuss the subject any longer.

The two villagers caught up to us shortly after that, and we all walked along without speaking. Without the distraction of conversation it finally came to me that the heat of the place had been steadily rising, and by then the simple act of walking was enough to cause trickles of sweat. Despite that we all continued doggedly on, but after a time the man Domil suddenly spoke.

"Skyhawk, we gotta stop fer a bit," he said, sounding unhappy but in no way unsure. "My woman needs t' rest some, an' I don' mind sayin' I c'n use the same. If'n you an' the lady wanna keep goin', we'll hafta catch up later."

We stopped and turned to look at the two, and to say they appeared completely wilted was like saying the place we were in was slightly unpleasant. Domil's arm around Grenna seemed to be the only thing keeping her off the ground, and that despite the way she was fighting to stand straight.

"I think we can all use some rest," the outlaw told him, clearly refusing to abandon them even though he sounded no more tired than I felt. "We'll stop here for a while, and then we'll continue on together. There's no way of knowing how much farther we have to go, so splitting up makes no sense."

"Don't understand how this place c'n be even this big," Domil said, helping Grenna to sit on the dead grass before lowering himself to sit next to her. "I don' know how long we been walkin', but it surely feels like days 'n days."

"That's the way it's supposed to feel," Skyhawk told him, choosing his own place in the grass and folding down onto it. "If you don't listen to what the talkers say you'll be punished, and it doesn't make much difference if the punishment lasts forever, or only feels like it does. Either way, you end up suffering for quite some time. Aren't you sitting down with us, Haliand?"

He looked up at me with mild questioning in his eyes, and rather than answer I simply moved closer to the villagers and settled onto the grass. I had no argument with stopping for the sake of the people we were with, but getting even distantly friendly with the outlaw was something I meant to avoid. Everything he said seemed to set me off, and a little of that went a very long way.

My personal silence seemed to spread out to cover

everyone with me, and we sat for a number of minutes with nothing but the breathing of Domil and Grenna interrupting the quiet. I thought things would continue like that until we were ready to move on again, but suddenly Skyhawk stirred and got to his feet.

"I think I'll walk a short way ahead, to see if we have anything more interesting than this same dull landscape to look forward to," he said, glancing around rather than at us. "Domil, you stay with the ladies and keep them company, and I'll be back in just a little while."

Domil had stretched out flat on the ground, but he raised himself up on his elbows when he was spoken to. For a very brief moment it looked like he was going to argue the order to stay behind, but his obvious weariness and a glance at Grenna quickly changed his mind. He nodded once, then watched Skyhawk walk away before lowering himself to the ground again. The outlaw had almost looked at me before leaving, but instead of turning his head he'd squared his shoulders and then had marched off. I didn't realize I'd made a sound to show my opinion of that, until Grenna forced herself to sitting and moved closer to me with a smile.

"Men ain't any too smart no matter who they be," she said, amusement riding on top of her tiredness. "Ain't nobody in these parts who don't know Skyhawk an' his doin's, an' there ain't many who don't trust him even with his bein' highborn. You mind if'n I say somethin' that ain't no way my business?"

I suppose if she hadn't asked I could have ignored her, but the look in her light, friendly eyes said she really would pass on commenting if I wanted her to. Under other circumstances I might have gotten huffy and standoffish, but just then acting like that didn't make much sense.

"Everyone else has been giving me their opinions, so why shouldn't you?" I asked, actually finding the situation faintly funny. "Most especially since you seem to be a woman who really knows what men are like."

"How hard is it knowin' what men 'r like?" she asked in turn, sharing the joke with a quiet laugh. "Even my man Domil tried bein' like that, an' him usually better'n most. What I wanna say is, anybody with eyes c'n see Skyhawk's got it bad over you, so don't you pay no mind to what he says about goin' with somebody else. He don't like the idea no more'n you do, but f'r some dumb man-reason he feels he's gotta push you away. Could be he wants t' see if'n you'll come back anyways an' that's why he's pushin', but likely he thinks he's doin' it f'r you.''

"Yes, he does think he's doing it for me," I answered, immediately feeling the heavy annoyance rise in me at the idea. "He knows he doesn't have a chance himself because I've told him so, and not only does he accept my decision, he agrees with it. That's why he's decided someone else is going to be my husband, and he's working very hard to make sure it happens even if I don't want it to."

"Now, ain't that strange," the girl mused, her mind obviously working behind the distraction in her eyes. "That man wants you so bad I c'n taste it, but all he does is tell you you gotta go to somebody else. Somebody you don't wanna go to, an' you say he knows it?''

She waited for my nod before nodding herself, and then she shook her head.

"When Domil up and decided he din't want me havin' none o' his trouble, he come and told me t' find another man," she said, back to looking straight at me but still working on the problem. "Even he knowed how dumb that was, an' th' way he said it showed he din't want me doin' no such thing. Listenin' to 'em, you'd think he din't know how to get somebody t' do what they din't wanna. That make any sense t' you?''

"As a matter of fact, it does," I answered slowly, suddenly remembering the way I'd done many things I hadn't wanted to—before I got old enough to understand how I was being maneuvered into them. If Skyhawk had really wanted me to find someone else, he would hardly have kept pushing me at someone I'd said I had no interest in. And he would have been a lot less reasonable about the rest of it, just to make sure I didn't suddenly decide I liked him after all. What he'd been doing was trying to get me to insist on giving *him* a chance, a plan of action he must have considered his only option. He was going to see to it that I was absolutely free to decide on a man of my own choice—which would just happen to turn out to be him.

"Grenna, I'd like to thank you," I said when I finally noticed her frowning because she didn't have the facts she needed to see what I did. "With your help I think I now understand what's going on, and all that's left is to figure out what to do about it. Without getting mad."

The girl smiled and shook her head again, showing she still didn't know what I was talking about, but the real question was whether or not I knew. My very first reaction had been to wait until the outlaw got back and then start screaming and yelling, but too much of that whole situation still didn't make any sense. If I simply got mad I'd be throwing away any chance I might have to get to the whole truth, which meant I had to control my temper. And while I was controlling it, there were one or two things I could do to test the theories I'd just come up with . . .

"Look out, they're comin' in again!" Domil suddenly shouted, immediately beginning to struggle to his feet. I looked up to see those leathery red animals racing out of the woods toward us, delight in their burning eyes, and made my own effort toward getting to my feet as fast as humanly possible. The heat of the air was so oppressively heavy, it made even breathing difficult; jumping up and fighting with attacking animals was almost too much of an effort to consider. I tightened a dampened grip around the branch I still held and ignored the way my sodden draperies clung to me, then began making the effort that had to be considered.

When the animals reached us they slowed to keep from being struck by the stick I swung, and at the same time tried slipping past me to get at the man and woman behind me. Domil and Grenna were frantically searching for branches of their own to use, Domil cursing the fact that he'd left his previous weapon behind after the first attack. The two were still not completely rested and the heat was taking even more strength from them, but neither one made any excuse about not being able to do what had to be done. Grenna made small sounds of extreme fright and Domil cursed in a low, furious voice, but both of them searched frantically and without hesitation.

For my own part, excitement had thrown me quickly into the fight, but once I was in it I seemed to have more time to think than swinging hard in all directions should have allowed. The leathery animals were close enough for me to smell their awful odor, a rotten-eggs stench that nearly turned my stomach, and I suddenly found myself wondering what would happen if one of the beasts got past my weapon and closed with me. Their talonlike claws kept raking in my direction, thirsting for my flesh and the freeing of my blood, and realizing that made me even more ill than the stink did.

Domil and Grenna finally found branches they could use and came to join me in our combined defense, but after no more than a minute or two both villagers were panting heavily and I could see Grenna's swings didn't have enough strength behind them to stop a spider. That, I think, was the point more of the beasts began coming out of the woods, joining the first group and trying even harder to get at us.

If the animals hadn't been cowards, we wouldn't have stood long even without their reinforcements. They cringed back from my weapon even as they tried to evade it long enough to lunge forward, and every now and again one misjudged its chance and came forward only to be hit. When that happened the animal howled in pain and threw itself back out of the fight, usually to crawl away to supposed safety, but after the arrival of the new beasts a place vacated by a wounded one wasn't left empty for a short while the way it had originally been. One of the newcomers edged in immediately, snarling as its eyes burned with twisted anger, and whatever had been gained was immediately lost.

After what seemed like an endless time of battling with the larger number of animals, they suddenly changed tactics. My strength had already begun draining out with my sweat, and I hadn't dared turn to see how Domil was doing. I was sure he and I were fighting alone by then, Grenna having the will to stand with us but not the endurance, and then I found out I was right in a way I would have preferred avoiding. Without any indication that the animals were gathering themselves, they abruptly began attacking almost simultaneously, the majority of them driving in to my left, toward Domil.

I know I shouldn't have allowed myself to be surprised by the attack, but I was already stumbling to the right before I realized I should have stood my ground. The animals' ferocity had startled and frightened me, and because of that Domil and I were cut off from each other. I had a glimpse of him frantically swinging in all directions in an attempt to protect Grenna and himself, and then I was too busy doing my own protecting to have time to look at anything else. I just kept trying to hit those ugly beasts to keep them away from me, the illness of fear struggling to rise in my throat almost to strangling, and then—

And then the animals were screaming and throwing themselves away from me and toward the woods, any number of them trailing smears of thin, yellowish liquid that seemed to be their blood. Skyhawk made no effort to go after the fleeing beasts; as soon as he'd cleared the attackers away from me he went on to the ones around Domil and Grenna, and in another moment that batch too was on the run. I waited only long enough to see that none of them intended an immediate return, then let myself collapse to sitting on the spot where I'd stood.

I spent some time doing nothing more than breathing in and out, and that was another activity Domil joined me in. The poor man was so spent he really had collapsed once the animals were driven off, and right then lay flat on his back gasping as though he were going to explode. Grenna was there beside him, holding one of his hands in both of hers, more concerned about the man she loved than the many talon cuts she'd sustained. Skyhawk, down on one knee, was examining those cuts, probably in an effort to see if any of them needed immediate attention, but his continuing calm seemed to indicate they didn't. That let me take a minute to close my eyes, mostly in an effort to get my thoughts straight.

I opened my eyes again at the sound of approaching bootsteps, just in time to see the outlaw come up and then seat himself on the grass beside me. He was covered with sweat the way we all were, but he didn't seem nearly as tired.

"Domil should be all right once he gets his breath back," he told me, adjusting his scabbard with his left hand to make himself more comfortable. "Grenna is pretty badly scratched, but as long as she wasn't bitten she should be all right—as soon as we get her out of here. I'm none the worse for wear, so that leaves only one of us unaccounted for. How are you doing?"

"I'm tired and hot," I answered, still unable to resolve the confusion and upset I felt. "Aside from that, nothing has changed for the worse."

"Good," he said with a smile, the look in his dark eyes warm and satisfied. "It was stupid of me to go off and leave the rest of you, but I thought they would choose to attack one sooner than three. By the time I realized I had the weapon they were most afraid of and hurried back here, it was almost too late. I don't much care for 'in the nick of time' rescues even if I'm the one doing the rescuing."

"Then you weren't scouting ahead, but trying to lure them into attacking you rather than us," I said, for some reason not terribly surprised. "Is that all you have to say?"

"What more is there?" he asked with brows high, looking seriously at a loss. "If you want me to apologize for the miscalculation I'll be glad to, but I don't see why—"

"That's not what I meant," I interrupted, using both hands to push sopping hair back from my forehead. I didn't really want to say what I was about to, but difficult or not, it had to be done. "You—haven't mentioned anything at all about the fight itself. If you hadn't gotten back when you did they would have had me, which means you saved my life. Why aren't you pretending to apologize for having broken your word about not protecting me, or pointing out that I can't take care of myself as well as I insisted I could? That's the very least you have the right to do.''

"It took something to say that to me," he observed with the same quiet smile, his satisfaction apparently increasing. "I knew you were the kind to criticize yourself as ungently as you criticize others, and you just proved me right. What you're overlooking, though, is the fact that you *had* to insist on what you did, just the way I had to keep my word to the point that I did. Neither of us had any other choice.''

"If you expect that to explain anything, you have some rethinking to do," I said, feeling the frustration rise up next to everything else inside me. "Not only don't I have any idea what you're talking about, I'm wondering if you know.''

"Well, let's find out," he said with a sudden grin, looking as though he were enjoying a game. "There's one infallible way of telling whether someone has been allowed to make his or her own decisions to a particular point in their lives. If you tell them to do something and they calmly consider the order and then just as calmly agree or refuse, they have experience in running their own lives. If they get all bent out of shape and start arguing heatedly with you, they've most likely only just decided they're going to make their own choices no matter who doesn't like the idea. Does that tell you why you've been reacting the way you have?''

"Well, everybody's got to make that decision at one time or another in their lives," I said, for the first time glad that my cheeks already had to look flushed. "You can't spend forever letting other people do your thinking for you, but some people, primarily the ones who are doing your thinking, don't understand why not. And then there are those who try taking over the job from the first minute they see you.''

"Meaning me," he said with a nod, not nearly as insulted as I'd thought he'd be. "All I was trying to do was get you and Jentris to safety, and at first didn't understand why you kept fighting me. When I finally realized you were struggling to keep a brand-new independence, I also understood I had to step back out of the way and let it happen. That's why I seriously gave my word not to protect you, but never intended it to apply to a situation like the one you were just in. It's not easy to exercise independence if you're dead.''

He was still smiling, but the way he said the words let me know he was completely serious. He honestly believed I had the right to be independent, and wasn't hesitating to help me do it. Just like anything else, it takes time to learn to be your own person; he wanted me to have that time, and understanding that made me feel very strange.

"But that still doesn't mean you can't say how wrong I was," I pointed out, suddenly determined to see that he also got his rights. "I made a nonstop fuss over how well I could take care of myself, but when it came down to actually doing it, I needed to be saved. Since you had to put up with the boasting, you should now be entitled to make me put up with a horse laugh.''

"One of the things you're going to have to learn is how to make allowances," he said with a sigh, the smile now only in his eyes. "I also happen to be of the opinion that I can take care of myself, but you may remember that Jentris and I needed you to get us out of that cell at the inn. Everyone, no matter how competent, occasionally needs the help of someone else. When you know yourself as free and capable you'll no longer mind someone else helping out, but first you have to be convinced. An insult with truth in it is no insult at all.''

He waited to see if I had anything else to say, but although I made the effort to find something I wasn't very successful. Every point he'd made had touched me as truth, but his statement on insult wasn't complete. It's stilly to be insulted over something that's true, but it's even sillier to be insulted over an untruth. Going through life being insulted over things is an admission that you can't handle those things; if you can handle them, they don't bother you.

I suppose the reason it happened was my distraction with philosophy, coupled with the fact that I was still searching for something to say. I very much wanted to come up with words, and suddenly I stumbled over a set of them that I'd decided on a short while earlier. Of course, the reason I'd decided on them wasn't part of the package, only near it, which meant I didn't reach it until the damage was done.

"You know, I think it's time to admit you've been right more often than you've been wrong," I blurted, adding the smile I'd also decided on. "I've given you a lot of trouble when there was no need for it, so I'm going to make amends by finally taking some of your advice. Once I'm back with Jentris, I'll give him as many chances as he wants."

Once the words were said I naturally remembered why I'd decided on them, but it was very definitely too late. I'd wanted to know if Skyhawk was pushing me at Jiss only to get me mad enough to reject Jiss entirely, and the ploy worked better than I'd imagined it would. The warmth in Skyhawk's eyes turned instantly to desperate panic, and it became his turn to reach for words which simply weren't there. His lips parted as his mind groped for a way to erase what had happened, but that wasn't what he managed to find.

"That . . . *was* my advice, wasn't it?" he said, suddenly looking younger and more vulnerable than he ever had before. "I've—heard it said people don't regret it when they take my advice. You probably won't regret it either, but I don't think I'll ever give advice again . . ."

His voice sort of trailed off, and then he was rising to his feet to turn and walk away from me. I simply sat where I was, feeling wounded in a way I didn't completely understand, no longer searching for what might be said.

There wasn't anything else *to* say, and that would hold true for quite some time.

After a few minutes of staring at nothing, Skyhawk roused himself from distraction and went to see how Domil and Grenna were doing. The two villagers were fairly well recovered from the fight, but the draining heat was taking more and more of their strength. It was clear we had to move on again before they were no longer able to stay on their feet, and even they were able to see it. When Skyhawk told them it was time to go they struggled erect without argument, and that impressed me in a way that was very odd.

We continued on in the same direction we'd been going, but at a slightly slower pace. I'd been worried that our two new friends would have trouble keeping up, but they plodded along behind us, as grimly determined to get out of that place as Skyhawk and me. After a while we were surprised to see our path grow a branching off to the left, one that disappeared into the twisted black woods. We ignored the branching and just kept going, but after another short while there was a branching to the left and to the right. It was then we noticed that the side paths looked more attractive than the one we were on, brighter and cooler and somehow prettier than what we were trudging along. It was also then that we saw even more branchings up ahead, but Skyhawk anticipated anything any of us might be thinking about those enticingly offered alternatives.

"The only way out of here is along this original path," he said, turning a little to show he spoke to Grenna and Domil as well as to me. "Since curiosity and exploration of something new can weaken the hold talkers have over people, they want to discourage those things in every way they can. If we took one of those paths that look better than this one, we'd end up not only lost but probably attacked again as well. Hopefully it won't be much longer now before we're out of this place."

"How do you know so much about it?" I couldn't help asking, the question seriously bothering me. "Everything you say makes it sound as though you've been through

here before, but not being certain about how far we have
to go suggests the opposite. If you know as much as you
obviously do, why don't you know all of it?''

"I don't know all of it because I've never been through
here," he answered, showing a faint, forced smile. "I've
spoken to a number of people who *have* been through, and
from the things they told me I was able to figure out the
points the talkers were trying to make. It isn't hard if you
know how they think."

Domil and Grenna made disgusted sounds of agreement,
and then we all lapsed back into the silence that made
walking easier. Paths kept branching off to both sides of
us, but since we knew we had to ignore their growing
attraction, we did. What wasn't quite as easy to ignore was
the uninterrupted opportunity for thinking, something I
discovered when my thoughts took an unexpected turn. I
suddenly knew why I'd been so dead set against accepting
the idea of Skyhawk as my life-mate, and it wasn't for the
reason he thought.

I sighed as I looked down at the tree branch I was still
carrying, distantly noticing how smooth and untreelike it
was. That's the way Skyhawk's explanations had been, too
smooth to be real, too slick even to get a good grip on. I'd
gotten started on that particular thought-track by again
feeling terrible over the way I'd ruined the plan he'd been
counting on to work, and then I'd asked myself why I felt
terrible. If I had no interest in him, if I truly believed there
would never be anything between us, what I'd done couldn't
be considered all that bad.

Which meant I did have some interest in him, and there
was already something between us. The better I got to
know him the more attracted I felt, and that despite my
trying to resist the feeling. I could also feel myself looking
forward to learning even more about him, on and on until I
knew everything there was, until I had also told him
everything about me.

On and on to the very end of his life. The twinge I felt
then in the middle of my chest was almost painful, the sort
of ache that makes you wish the cause of it was imagina-

tion or a mistake. *That* was the truth I'd been trying to avoid, the thing that had made me reject him the first moment I'd seen him.

He was my destined life-mate, but his life and mine would not be of the same length.

Once I really understood, my first impulse was a willingness to trade places, to make me the ephemeral and him the one who would live on, but that just wasn't possible. It had taken a while to admit it, and then I had realized something else as well. To live with someone you really love while the years fall heavily on their shoulders, to watch them grow old and bent while you stay young, to finally hold them in your arms while they whisper goodbye with their final breath—that was an agony it wasn't possible to wish on another, even if you didn't care anything about them. It was horrible to consider no matter who had to go through it, but when the victim was yourself—

And that was the reason I'd tried to refuse acknowledging Skyhawk, the reason I'd tried to run away from the truth. The fate I would find with him would be horrible, an unavoidable agony, a hurt that would never, ever leave me. I'd considered it the worst thing that could possibly happen—until I'd thought of one thing worse. Losing the love of your life is unbearable pain—but nothing when compared to never finding him in the first place.

I shook my head a little at the dead-grass path I walked, wondering how I could have been so childish and shallow. Of course it hurts to lose your love, but once the sharpest of the pains fade far enough, you find the memories standing behind them. When life is gone memories remain, and the true agony comes when you think about having no memories to fall back on.

Nothing but a gaping hole deep inside, a place that's never filled, an aching hollow that can never be eased no matter how long you live. Could that possibly be better, to save yourself the agony of loss by never having anyone to be lost?

"No," I whispered fiercely to the path, knowing I was

right. A short while was better than no time at all, and if anyone had to go on alone afterward, I wanted it to be me. When you love someone you're happy to take pain in their place, delighted to know they'll never have to experience it.

"Did you say something?" Skyhawk asked me, and I glanced up to see him looking at me curiously. "I thought I heard you say something."

"It wasn't anything important," I answered with a smile. "Anything I have to say can wait until talking won't cause exhaustion."

"A wise decision," he said with a nod, a softened look now in his gaze. "You're picking up the knack of independence even faster than I thought you would. We can both save what we have to say until the sweat no longer makes us look as though we're crying."

I matched his nod with one of my own, but my smile couldn't help getting even wider. I didn't love him, I hardly even knew him, but I would give him his chance and help with it a little, and maybe our future would be soft with the shadows of mutual love.

Not long after that we found something else that improved the picture of the future: the end of the path. We rounded a curve to suddenly see harsh brown and gray rock ahead of us, and none of us needed Skyhawk to point out that the talkers were undoubtedly making another point. The only time discomfort and an acceptance of the unpleasant are positive acts is when someone else benefits from your doing those things, and usually they're the only ones who consider it positive. We would have a hard time climbing out of that place, but were supposed to believe the end results wouldn't be just as rewarding if we were to have an easy time.

We did have a hard time getting out, and that despite the fact that as soon as we started climbing the heat began to recede. There were enough hand and footholds in the rock to make an ascent only slightly dangerous, but we had to let our two friends rest a while before they felt up to trying the climb. Skyhawk went up first beside Domil, watching

the man carefully to be sure he didn't fall, and then I did
the same with Grenna. Climbing in draperies was only
somewhat difficult, less than what Grenna had with her
dress, but once the girl was helped over the top edge of the
crevasse I didn't mind being given help of my own. At
that point all four of us took some time out to rest, but
after a few minutes, when I began looking around, I made
a number of surprising discoveries.

"Can that be the same midafternoon it was before all
this crevasse nonsense started?" I wondered aloud, sitting
up as I looked around even more. "I don't see how it
could be, but I also don't see how it could be another day
entirely. And look at what we just climbed out of. Am I
seeing things, or is that crevasse no more than five or six
feet wide?"

"If you're seeing things, then so are the rest of us,"
Skyhawk answered from where he sat, inspecting the crevasse with a shake of his head. "That's the place we just
climbed out of, but six feet wide is all it is. And from what
other people have told me, there's never any time elapsed
out here, no matter how long you spend down there. You
find everything just the way you left it—and maybe even
a thing or two you didn't expect to find."

He nodded in the direction to my right, and when I
turned my head to look I was more shocked than surprised.
My horse stood no more than fifteen feet away, grazing
calmly, Skyhawk's stallion doing the same about six feet
further on. That was the reason we'd found no dead or
crippled bodies, then. Why would any healthy horse have
trouble jumping a mere six feet of trench?

"If our horses are over there, what are we doing sitting
here?" I demanded almost immediately, the shock fading
to nothing. "I have food left in my saddlebags, and hopefully so do you. Do Grenna and Domil have to pass out
before we remember they're even hungrier than I am?"

"If we'd kept going after that climb, we'd be the ones
who passed out," he retorted, but there was a grin on his
face to take the sharpness from his words. "It so happens I
do have food left in my saddlebags, and a waterskin to

keep the food company. Shall we do a little foraging the quick and easy way?''

He rose to his feet and held out his hand to me, and I hesitated only an instant before taking it. The hesitation I'd felt had been over just how I was going to take it, but that wasn't very hard to decide. I gripped it moderately tight as it pulled me up, but once I was erect I didn't make any effort to free myself. I watched as confusion entered Skyhawk's eyes, undoubtedly over the fact that I wasn't pulling my hand away, and then it came to him that he was the one who would have to let go. A brief struggle showed in the eyes looking down at me, and then his fingers opened to release me.

''Yes, I think we're definitely going to have to talk,'' he said, looking determined but not very happy. ''Let's get everyone fed first, and then we'll have our discussion.''

''What are we going to be talking about?'' I asked, as if I didn't know, following along as he started toward the horses. I was also smiling faintly, but since he was no longer looking at me, he didn't see the smile.

''We'll be discussing the details of certain vows, and assessing just how binding they are,'' he answered, the words definitely on the grim side. ''If there's a way out of this mess that isn't totally dishonorable, I intend to find it.''

I almost asked what mess he was talking about, but that would have been pushing things just a little too far. He deserved a bit of agitation for the way he'd tried fooling me, but I didn't really want to torment him. He'd have enough to contend with once we started our discussion.

The food in our saddlebags wasn't a feast, but we all attacked it with undiscriminating appetites as soon as we'd passed around the waterskin. Once we were happily filled Domil mentioned there was a stream nearby, and there wasn't one of us who wasn't delighted to hear it. Skyhawk and I brought our horses and Grenna took Domil's arm, and it wasn't long before we were all slipping into the water.

Without soap all we could do was rinse off most of the

sweat that had covered us, but that was considerably better than nothing. Domil and Grenna had a problem in that they had to get back into the same clothes they had taken off, but I had Skyhawk's outfit that he had given me back at the inn, and he had another change that kept me from feeling guilty. I would have given him his clothes back if he hadn't had anything else to put on, but as I closed the shirt I was very glad I didn't have to. There was an odd satisfaction in having his clothes to wear, one that would have been there even if they had been as stained and aromatic as my own.

"I'm glad to see you didn't waste any time getting dressed," his voice came suddenly from behind me as I stuffed my filthy draperies into a saddlebag on my horse. "Now we can take a few minutes to talk."

I finished the stuffing and turned to look at him, letting my gaze move up and down the length of him. While we were bathing we had all taken the trouble to be courteous, which meant we hadn't stood around inspecting those we bathed with. Now that we were all dressed again there was no reason not to look directly at him, especially since he looked so awfully good in the dark green pants and rust shirt he wore. I expected him to notice my inspection and comment on it, but he proved to be much too distracted.

"Let's sit down over there," he said, gesturing to a patch of grass near a tree. Since it was normal, living grass near a normal, untwisted tree, I joined him in sitting down. Once we were settled he hesitated a moment, then forced himself to look directly at me.

"All right, let's get the most important question asked first," he said, forcing the decision out through quite a bit of resistance. "Just exactly what have you promised Jentris, and what vows did he give in return?"

"I think that's going to be a hard question to answer," I said with what I hoped was an attractive frown, not about to let him get off quite that easily. "And I don't understand why you would want to know. I've already told you I'm going to take your advice about giving Jentris a chance, so—"

"Wait a minute," he interrupted, holding up his hands. "I can see I started in the wrong place, so let me begin again. I know I advised you to give Jentris a chance, and I have to apologize for deliberately trying to confuse you. I thought if I convinced you I was giving up all intentions of pursuing you myself, you might relax and give me a chance I would otherwise have no hope of getting. Part of that seems to have worked in that you aren't screaming at me any longer, but the part about Jentris, the part that wasn't supposed to work, hasn't faded away as planned. What I'm trying to say is—Haliand, am I wrong in thinking you're not trying to run from me any longer?"

The look in his dark eyes was so open and vulnerable I wanted to put my arms around him and tell him everything would be all right, but I couldn't do that yet. He was still skirting part of the truth, and I needed to know how long he would continue doing it.

"No, you're not wrong in thinking I'm not running from you any longer," I allowed with a small nod. "I thought about everything you said to me, and you were right about me needing to believe in my own independence and freedom. Now that I do believe, I don't have to run from anyone. I can take all the time I like to look around and find my own choice in a man."

"You know, I've never before noticed what a big, flapping mouth I have," he said with a sigh of self-disgust. "If I were right as often as you claim, I would be the wealthiest and most influential man in these parts. Look, Haliand, this is probably going to be enough to ruin whatever I might have accomplished in the way of getting closer to you, but I have to tell you I'm not going to just give you up. I said you were entitled to your choice in a man and I meant it, but what I didn't say is that I intend being that choice. You'll be saving yourself a lot of effort if you consider me first, before you go riding off in search, so what do you say? Will you at least try?"

The look in his eyes had more desperation than any sort of hope, and I was very glad I no longer had to go on pretending disinterest. I'd been waiting for him to admit his exact intentions, and now he had.

"All right, I'll be glad to try," I said, keeping the words sober and casual. "It does make more sense starting with those nearest you, to save yourself a long ride if nothing else. You know, you really do give good advice."

"You said yes," he stated, sounding as though he wasn't sure about which to doubt, his hearing or my voice. "You didn't argue or flatly refuse, or even try to insult me. You simply said yes."

"Were you hoping I'd say no?" I asked, very seriously concerned as I leaned toward him. "If you were, I'll be glad to change my mind. After all, you're the one who saved my life, so if you—"

"You try changing your mind, and I'll beat you!" he growled, but couldn't keep a grin covered as he shifted across the grass to sit closer to me. "But that's an empty threat, because you're not about to change your mind, are you? I'll bet you decided to give me my chance even before I asked for it."

"Well, you really are rolling up a score of being right, aren't you?" I asked with a laugh as he put his arm around my shoulders. "I would have mentioned my decision sooner, but I was mildly annoyed over the way you tried to make me forget Jentris by throwing me at him."

"Jentris!" he exclaimed, the grin dying as his arm froze where it lay around me. "I forgot all about Jentris. Haliand, this time you have to answer me: what sort of promises have you given him, and what sort has he given you?"

"This time I *can* answer you," I returned, "but I suggest you get a good grip on your temper. The only thing between Jentris and me is an agreement to cooperate in the retrieval of what was stolen from us. The situation is rather complex and I'm not free to go into details, but except for the fact that Jentris promised my mother he'd protect me, there aren't any promises involved. If you'd like the absolute truth, we're barely even acquainted."

"But—Jentris told me you were runaway lovers!" he

protested as he withdrew his arm completely, his expression mostly confusion. "You were right there when he said it, and you made no effort to contradict him! And what about the way you kissed him? If that's your idea of there being nothing between you, I'm fairly sure Jentris uses another definition."

"If you'll make the effort to think back, you'll find that the idea of our being runaway lovers was yours," I said, trying not to notice how much anger there was in with his confusion. "Jentris let you go on thinking that in order to protect me, the theory being the stranger we'd just met would be more likely to stay away from me if I belonged to someone with Jentris's size and ability. As far as that kiss goes—well, it seemed like a good idea at the time."

"To you two, maybe," he growled, and this time there was no joking around in the reaction. He rose to his feet and began pacing, his thoughts obviously black, his good humor entirely disappeared, not far from the point where smoke would begin curling out of his ears. I was trying to decide if it would be better for me to keep quiet or attempt to calm him down, when he stopped pacing, stomped back to where he'd been sitting, and dropped down next to me again.

"Have you any idea what I've been going through all this time?" he demanded. "I've been feeling like an absolute rogue for having betrayed Jentris's trust, and now I discover he had no right to expect anything more. I couldn't understand why I had to keep prompting him when it came to you, but now the answer's obvious: he had no interest in you at all until I pointed out how desirable you were! *He* doesn't have first claim on you, *I* do, and I think I owe him a little something for having tried taking advantage of the situation. I wasn't sneaking around behind his back, he was sneaking around under my nose."

"If you look at it that way, then I was sneaking around, too," I pointed out, needing to say that truth even though he wasn't likely to enjoy hearing it. "With that in mind, you have to owe both of us something."

"It's very fairminded of you to admit that," he said with a slow nod, his expression neutral, and then he shifted even closer to me. "Are you ready for some of what I owe *you*?"

As I looked up into his dark, steady gaze I almost told him my mother would get him if he hurt me, but then I realized how silly that was. If he hurt me I would look for and find a way of revenging myself, but somehow I couldn't quite picture him doing that. It was possible I was being a naïve infant, but if so it would be best to find that out as quickly as I could.

"I suppose I'm as ready as I'll ever be," I answered after the briefest hesitation, wondering if I should be feeling frightened. "Why don't you go ahead and . . ."

He didn't even let me finish. One minute he was sitting there listening, and the next his arms were around me, his lips lowering to mine. Being kissed like that was startling, but the surprise passed so quickly I was nearly surprised a second time. And then I realized I had better things to do than be surprised. Enjoying the feel of Skyhawk's arms around me and the touch of his lips were two of them, and kissing him back wasn't difficult at all. In some strange way his kiss was better than Jiss's, something I had time to be certain of before he let it end.

"Let that be a lesson to you," he said, smiling softly while continuing to hold me. "I owed you that and still owe you a lot more, and I'm a man who believes in paying his debts. You're going to have to take every bit of it, no matter how unpleasant you find it."

"I guess I'll just have to suffer," I answered with a sigh, but that time I was the one who couldn't hold back a grin. "It was horrible, awful, almost more than I could stand, but I'm brave enough and strong enough to stand firm in the face of the rest. Go ahead and try to make me back down, I *dare* you."

"That's nothing but bravado, and we both know it," he said with a grin of his own, pulling me closer to his chest. "You're terrified of me, practically frozen in place with fear, but that means nothing to me. I'm absolutely and completely heartless, and I'll prove it by ravaging you unmercifully—as soon as your hair dries. I hate ravaging women with wet hair.''

"You mean I have to wait before I can be ravaged?" I demanded in outrage, something that made him chuckle. "You weren't lying about being heartless, not to mention cruel and mean and totally unfair. How can you let a little wet hair delay your nefarious intentions? Do you want people to be ashamed to call you evil?"

"A *little* wet hair?" he repeated with a laugh, trying hard to look scornful. "You have the longest hair I've ever seen on a woman, and every inch of it is wet. Besides, I may be thoroughly evil, but even those who are evil are entitled to be shy. I prefer privacy for my ravagings, and that's something we don't happen to have right now. Wouldn't *you* want complete privacy if you were into evil doings?"

"I suppose so," I grudged half-heartedly, making him chuckle again, and then I leaned up to briefly touch my lips to his. "But the least you can do now is take conscienceless advantage of me the way you did a minute ago. We have enough privacy for that, don't we?"

"I think something like that can be arranged," he answered with his grin still strong, a definite twinkle in his eyes. "Small amounts of awfulness can always be squeezed in, just as long as you make the effort to try hard enough. Here, I'll show you how it works."

He lowered his head to me, not missing the fact that I was already raising my face, but before our lips could meet we heard the sound of very loud throat-clearing, which naturally caused us to look up. Domil and Grenna stood only a few feet away, both of them trying to look contrite rather than amused, and once our eyes were on him Domil added to the throat-clearing he'd just done.

"We din't wanna butt in, but Grenna and me's gonna start back t' th' village now," he said, his arm comfortably around the girl who stood beside him. "We ain't gonna stay long, only long enough fer a meal an' t' get what we wanna take with us, an' we thought we'd like t' ask if'n you wanna have that meal with us. If not, we gotta say our thanks now."

"Consider them said," Skyhawk answered with a smile, but then he grew somewhat thoughtful. "You know, our accepting your hospitality would really be you doing us a favor. We have a friend we have to meet, and there's an excellent chance he's already somewhere around your village. If it's not too much trouble, we certainly would like to accept your invitation."

"Trouble?" Grenna asked with a laugh, a delighted Domil obviously agreeing with her. "Since we all know what real trouble is, I ain't even gonna answer that. What I'm gonna do is cook you two a real good meal, an' then I'm gonna take Domil t' my house f'r the night. We's gonna be gone long b'fore sunup, but you two c'n stay long as you like."

She gave me a wink with that, very likely saying Skyhawk and I would soon have the privacy we wanted, but I had another consideration to bear in mind. The reason Skyhawk expected Jiss to be somewhere around the village was because the thieves would also be in that area, which meant it was someplace I had to go, too. As I let Skyhawk help me to my feet I wondered if I should tell him what I was involved in, but it didn't take long before I rejected the idea. I didn't want him involved right along with me, not when being involved could also get him hurt. Once the Great Flame was safe I would tell him everything, but not until then.

Domil and Grenna had intended to walk back to their village, but with two horses available it wasn't necessary. I rode behind Skyhawk on his stallion, and our new friends used my horse. Since I had to hold tight to the man I rode with, the time was more fun than I'd had in quite a while, but that doesn't mean I wasn't also thinking about the thieves. The sooner I got the Great Flame and Greaf broken free, the sooner

I'd be able to get on with what I wanted to do, which meant I had to do some serious planning. I hadn't had much luck with planning the last times I'd tried, but this time I wasn't prepared to accept anything but success.

The ride disappeared behind the tossing around of any number of ideas, and by the time we reached the village I felt I had more than enough to work with. I'd have to wait to see what the overall situation was before I made any decisions, but I did feel well prepared.

Domil brought us to a stop outside the village, and we dismounted and made a careful approach from there. From comments made during the ride I'd gathered the talkers would be on the lookout for the two they'd sent through their punishment place, so we'd be best off having no one knew we were there until we were gone again. We would all hide out, and then we would go our respective ways.

The village was an ugly place, so filled with wooden buildings painted colors wood was never meant to be that the whole place looked unreal. If I'd had the choice I would have stayed in the forest rather than enter the village, but I didn't have the choice and also didn't really have to go in. We skirted the village until we were close to Domil's house and stable, and then we rushed up to get inside before someone spotted us. Grenna entered the stable first to do something or other that Domil asked her to, and then the two men hurried the horses inside. I waited by the stable door, ready to take my turn once the horses were clear, which meant I had a moment or so to look around. That was when I saw it, the last thing I'd expected to see, a thing that filled me with a surge of elation.

Not all that far away, behind a stable just like Domil's, stood the wagon belonging to the thieves! There seemed to be two or three men guarding it, but whatever horses had been pulling it were no longer in sight. With the help of my mother's luck it looked like I'd found the place the thieves intended passing the coming night, and once it got dark there would be nothing that could keep me from them. The end of the chase was already in sight!

Chapter 12

❦

THAT IS, THE END of the chase was *almost* in sight. Skyhawk had to hiss at me before I realized I had the room to enter the stable, which I did as quickly as possible to keep him from seeing what I had. He'd been really angry when he'd caught me near the wagon in the woods, and the best way to avoid an argument on the subject was to avoid the subject itself. When the time came I'd find a way to leave without mentioning where I was going, and that would take care of that.

The stable wasn't very big, but it was neat and clean and seemed to satisfy the horse already in it. Domil's horse turned its head to see what was going on, but by then the goings-on were just about over. The horses we'd led in were unsaddled and mine had a halter put on it, then we were ready to leave them alone with their hay while we went into the house.

Grenna had gone ahead, but when we walked inside there were no lamps or candles lit against the late afternoon dimness. The girl was busy moving around gathering things together, and a moment after we appeared she put a final item in one of the two sacks she'd filled, gave us all a smile, then carried the sacks back out to the stable.

"Grenna's goin' t' get our meal started," Domil told Skyhawk and me as we watched her leave, both of us undoubtedly looking as confused as I felt. "If'n she does th' cookin' here, they'll be down on us faster 'n vultures on a carcass. We got somethin' they don't know about, a place we fixed up where we could be t'gether 'thout havin' 'em lookin' over our shoulders, an' that's where Grenna's goin'. Won't be too long b'fore she gets back, but meanwhile I got somethin' there's no use in savin' no more. C'mon over here an' sit y'rselves down.''

Domil ushered us over to a sturdy wooden table and chairs, then went into another room. Skyhawk sat down in one of the chairs and made himself comfortable, but I had to force myself down while pretending I had nothing else on my mind. What I really wanted to do was go to the curtained window that looked out in the direction of that wagon and stare out, but if I'd done that I couldn't very well have expected Skyhawk not to notice. I had to exercise patience as well as caution, and everything would work out just fine.

I occupied myself with looking around while we waited, and although the little house didn't have much, looking at what it did have wasn't a waste of time. What was there was well made and nicely kept, and some of it, principally the decorative carving, was out and out beautiful. It occurred to me that being able to speak to the trees would have been a great handicap for these people; with the amount of wood they needed in order to make things, they would have had a big problem if they'd had to find a substitute. I didn't condone the situation, not with the way I felt about trees, but I certainly understood the problem.

Not long after I came to that conclusion Domil was back, carrying a waterskin and four bronze goblets. The goblets were beautiful work that looked very old, and the man put them down proudly in the middle of the table.

''Them goblets was passed down t' me by my paw,'' he said, enjoying the way Skyhawk and I obviously admired them. ''He got 'em from his paw, an' him from *his* paw, an' so on, back so far we don' even know anymore. Grenna's got a necklace that come t' her the same way through her ma, an' things ain't never gonna be so bad that we sell 'em. They's the biggest reason we come back here, 'steada takin' off straight. Now you gotta taste this here wine."

He unslung what I'd thought was a waterskin and opened it, then began carefully pouring into two of the goblets. At that point I wanted very much to tell Domil that he and Grenna owned proof of the greatness that had once been their people's, but I wasn't Wissa and it wouldn't have been the same coming from me. If I said anything I would have to tell them how I knew it was true, and then they would be depressed and disillusioned rather than heartened. Wissa's words brought hope of a return to better things; mine would have brought a destructive resentment over what had been lost. Looking forward is always better than looking back, which meant I just had to sit there and keep quiet.

"Why are you only pouring wine for two, Domil?" Skyhawk asked, pulling me out of introspection to see that he was right. "Right now there are three of us, and when Grenna gets back there will be four."

"I ain't gonna be drinkin' till Grenna gets back," the man answered, and then he showed the shyest grin I'd ever seen. "This here wine was bein' saved f'r her an' me, f'r our weddin' day, an' that's why it's in a waterskin. I din't want them talkers comin' by an' findin' it, an' then takin' it f'r themselves. I don't want none till she's here t' drink it with me, but that don't mean you two gotta do without. Go on now, an' lemme know how you like it."

Skyhawk and I exchanged glances, but it was fairly clear Domil really did want us to drink without him. I took one of the goblets and slowly tasted the wine, expecting it to be little better than that ale offered back at the inn, but my brows rose in surprise.

"Domil, this is excellent," I said, not exaggerating in the least. "Wherever did you get it?"

"That's somethin' y'r best off not knowin', Lady," he answered, amusement spreading across his broad face as he winked at Skyhawk. "The good stuff ain't 'sposta be f'r the likes a me and mine, but we got friends who see we get a taste now 'n then."

I looked over at Skyhawk myself, but the outlaw sat there with a very innocent expression pasted on his face. When he saw my eyes on him he raised his goblet to me with a smile of matching innocence, and that was the end of that particular conversation.

We sat around the table for a while, two of us sipping wine, all three discussing inconsequentials, the shadows in the room growing deeper and deeper as the daylight lowered toward dark. Finally Domil left the table to go toward the stable, but he was back rather quickly with two serving dishes filled with things that smelled unbelievably good. He went out one more time and brought back two more dishes, then went for plates and forks and serving spoons. By that time Grenna was there with serving dishes of her own, and although that wasn't the last of it, both she and Domil firmly declined all offers of help.

When all the food was finally on the table, we paused before eating to toast Domil and Grenna and wish them luck in their new lives together. Grenna blushed and looked radiantly happy and Domil looked proud and very determined, and then the two people drank to each other. That was about as long as any of us could keep away from the food, but even a wait three times as long would have been worth it. Grenna must have been one of those cooks who use magic as one of their ingredients; we all kept trying to tell her how good the food was, but talking is difficult when your mouth is stuffed full.

We all got quite a lot of enjoyment out of the meal, but we knew it was over when Domil rose silently and left the room, to reappear a few moments later carrying a filled sack and a waterskin. This time there really was water in the waterskin, and he used it to rinse out the empty bronze goblets before packing them away in the sack. When he was through he and Grenna each hugged Skyhawk and me, and then the two of them went toward the stable. None of us had said a single word, but that didn't mean we hadn't bid each other farewell and good luck. I stood in the dimness for a moment after the two village people were gone, admitting to myself that I would miss them, and then I turned to look at Skyhawk.

"It isn't fair," I said, not caring how uneven my voice sounded. "They're good people, and it isn't fair that they have to leave their homes because they refuse to believe what others tell them to. If those talkers really thought they were spreading the truth, they wouldn't care who didn't believe. Truth can take care of itself, and doesn't need people pushed into believing it."

"Not enough people understand that," Skyhawk said gently, coming over to stand in front of me. "The ones most rabid to force belief on you are usually the fearful ones, those who are afraid they might believe something wrong or foolish. If they force everyone into believing the same thing and it turns out they're wrong, no one will stand there laughing at them and calling them stupid, because everyone will be in the same position."

"There are also the arrogant ones, those who know what's best for everyone," I reminded him, the topic of discussion doing its usual job of putting a bad taste in my mouth. "They have no idea that what's right for them isn't necessarily right for everyone else, and that's because they have no imagination. Why do all those people have to be like that?"

"They're like that because no one took the trouble to teach them to believe in themselves rather than other things and people," he answered, reaching over to put his arms around me. "It's easier for *you* if you raise your children to believe they can't get along without your guidance, but that just sets them up to believe they can't get along without *someone's* guidance. Once they're grown and moved away they start looking for that someone, and it usually turns out to be the loudest talker with the most obvious confidence. When you don't have confidence of your own, you have to rely on what you can get from others. Are we going to stand here all night discussing something we already know we agree on?"

His last question was so quietly put that it startled me, and then I realized he was still indulging in being right.

The conversation I'd started was an attempt to keep other, more delicate topics from being broached, but it wasn't possible to ignore forever the fact that we were finally alone.

"Well, we can always stand here all night discussing something we don't agree on," I suggested lamely, suddenly very aware of his arms around me. "I'm even willing to let you pick the subject."

"In that case, my choice of subject is standing here all night talking," he came back, the ghost of a chuckle in his voice as he looked down at me. "You did a great job defending yourself against attacking animals out for your blood. You're not saying now that you're more afraid of me than you were of them?"

"Why not?" I asked in return, finding the question no more than reasonable. "*Having* to do something is always easier than choosing to do it, even if there's actual danger involved in the one and almost none in the other. When you choose to do or not do something, you can't blame circumstances if it turns out you've made a mistake."

"Which statement brings us right back to discussing philosophy," he observed, his tone having turned very dry. "Rather than simply say you can't go through life without making choices, as even the decision not to make any decisions is a decision, I'll tackle the point in another way. Come with me."

He let go of me to take my hand, and then I was being led to the other side of the room and past a curtain into the room Domil had kept going into. I'd somehow thought it was a storage area or a pantry, but it turned out to be a small, neat bedroom. As soon as I saw that I stopped short, and Skyhawk turned to look at me again.

"What's bothering you now?" he asked, the question so mild it immediately made me suspicious. "You said you didn't want to make any choices, so I chose for you. If you try disagreeing with me, that'll mean making a choice after all."

"All right, your point is taken," I grudged, only partially avoiding the bright, dark gaze holding me. "If I give up the right to choose, I also give up the right to complain about what happens. But that doesn't change the fact that I'm still afraid.''

The last of what I'd said had been little more than a whisper, but he'd still had no trouble hearing it. He came closer and folded me in his arms again, and didn't seem to need to be told that what had happened between us once before didn't mean I had no reason to be frightened right then. What had happened before had just happened, but this time it would be cold-bloodedly deliberate.

"You really don't have to be afraid, you know," he whispered in return, one of his hands stroking my hair. "I'll never force you to do something you don't want to, but even better than that, I'll never force you into making a decision alone. Any time you need help, or someone to argue a point with, or just a sympathetic ear, all you have to do is tell me. I'll give as much help or as little as you like, and in return all I ask is that you do the same for me. Is it a deal?"

I stood there with my cheek against his chest, feeling his words settle down comfortably inside me, filling the emptiness that had been the dwelling place of my reluctance. Choices are more easily made when you know you don't have to make them alone, but can if you want to. I was suddenly well prepared to make a decision, even if the decision did still make me the least bit nervous.

"I'm not sure I ought to be making deals with you," I said at last, standing straight in order to look up at him. "I agreed to one of your deals once before, and I'm still waiting for something to come of it."

"We made a deal once before?" he echoed blankly, obviously not understanding what I was talking about. "Why don't I remember it?"

"Oh, Skyhawk," I said with a sigh, making sure he got the idea that I was working very hard to be patient with him. "I know men like to conveniently forget things, but I was so hoping you would be different. I don't want to embarrass you, so all I'll do is ask one question. Isn't my hair dry *yet*?"

He immediately began chuckling as his frown disappeared, and then I was being held very close as he kissed me. It's frightening to take the first step toward something that will change your entire life, but once you've made up your mind that you really do want that something, you have to hold your breath and simply plunge ahead. After the initial fright things tend to get better, and it wasn't long before I was holding Skyhawk and kissing him as hard as he was kissing me. I wanted very much to share myself with him, and I knew beyond doubt that he felt the same way. He didn't want to use, he wanted to share, and that made all the difference.

I don't know the exact moment we began getting out of our clothes, but it was done almost before I realized it, and then we were on Domil's bed together. The old quilt was more comfortable than the forest grass had been, and once Skyhawk had folded me in his arms again he sighed.

"It's difficult understanding how it's possible to be supremely happy and utterly dejected, both at the same time," he said, his hands slowly caressing me. "I can't tell you how good it feels to hold you like this, but at the same time I can't help wondering if I'll ever be able to give you even as much as a shabby bedroom like this one. I want you to have the best of everything, but I don't know if I'll be able to provide it."

"You'll do your best while doing what you have to, and all the while you'll be doing those things with me," I answered, delightfully aware of the hard feel of him under my hands. "If I thought possessions were more important than people, I'd be out looking for Jentris right now instead of lying here with you. But if the problem is bothering you all *that* much, I can always change my mind. Just how interested did you say he was?"

"Never you mind how interested he is," Skyhawk growled, his hands coming to my face to raise it to him. "This is a jealous, possessive man holding you, woman, and until he gets used to the idea that you really are his, you'd better watch the suggestions you make. Even if we have to pitch a tent in the forest, I'm still the only man you'll be living with.''

"And don't you forget it," I said with a growl of my own, wanting him to know I wasn't joking. "If the time ever comes that a tent doesn't suit me, you'll be the first to hear about it.''

He blinked just a little at the no-nonsense tone in my voice, and then he laughed softly before starting to kiss me again. Our life together was hardly likely to be easy, but as long as we both realized that, the problems we had would be minimal. Right then I wasn't interested in problems, only in sharings, and my hands on his body let him know that.

I could feel his pleasure at being touched, the same pleasure I was feeling even though the touch wasn't the same. My hands and fingers stroked him everywhere I could reach, but he reached my everywhere more easily and the caress of his hands was more sure, more knowing. His breathing was still even when mine grew ragged, his lips moving slowly from place to place, his tongue teasing me with light flickerings that sent the shock of lightning racing through my body. It suddenly came to me that he was remembering the nervousness I'd felt, and was making sure I was as eager for what was to come as he. I took his hair in both fists and kissed him fiercely, trying to show him I was more than ready, trying to thrust against his desire with my own, and then—

And then his arms were like metal around me, and we finally and fully were becoming one . . .

Sundown was long behind us before Skyhawk finally fell deeply asleep. I'd been feeling the urge to sleep myself, but I was too satisfied and at the same time too filled with anticipation for sleep. My man had given me very deep pleasure, but I couldn't relax and give that pleasure my full attention until my obligations were seen to. The thieves still had possession of Greaf and the Great Flame, and my freedom of action depended on freeing the captured. Once that was done I could come back and begin my new life, but you don't begin something new on the bones of the unfinished.

I made sure to move very slowly and carefully while getting out of bed, then wrapped my feet in shadow before finding my clothes and sandals and carrying them out to the next room. Dressing really quietly takes concentration, but keeping the rustling and shifting down does pay off. By the time I was ready to leave the house, Skyhawk hadn't even shifted around in the bed.

The stable was silent with nothing more than the small sounds of dozing animals, specifically the sound of two animals. Domil's horse, the one that had been there when we'd arrived, was gone, but the stable door was latched from the inside. Under other circumstances I might have looked around for the alternate exit they'd all used, but there was something of more interest to me outside.

I took the time to do some very careful shadow weaving before unlatching the stable door, then slipped out with as little noise as I'd made in the house. Once outside I quickly incorporated moonbeams into the places in my shadow weaving that I'd left for the purpose, and then I was ready to begin my approach to the wagon. If any of the men guarding it looked in my direction, there would be no unexplained patches of darkness or suspicious shifts of light to cause uneasiness. I hadn't been careful enough the first time I'd tried reaching the wagon, and that wasn't a mistake I intended to repeat.

The night was very quiet all around, the silence coming from the rest of the village emphasizing the small sounds of movement made by the wagon guards. There were three men standing in a semicircle around one side of the wagon, the other side almost on top of the house it had been left behind, and between the two barriers no one should have been able to reach the object that was being guarded. As I moved forward in a soundless glide I thought about all the time I'd "wasted" in the night forests of my mother's Realm, learning to blend with the darkness even more completely than its predators, and smiled. The decision on its being a waste of time came from my sisters, and I was very glad I'd never been talked into agreeing with them.

The three men were trying very hard to be alert, but they were spending too much time looking randomly around. It wasn't hard to wait until two of them turned their heads in opposite directions simultaneously before slipping between them, and that way neither of them had an unexplained shadow to question. They heard nothing and they saw nothing, and three steps later I stood right beside the wagon.

My first impulse was to climb inside as fast as I could, but happily I'd been learning to resist first impulses. It took a moment to realize there might be a fourth guard inside the wagon, but once I did I stood up on my toes and stared through the opening in the canvas. Inside was darker than outside, of course, but there's always a difference between empty darkness and occupied dark—if you take the trouble to notice. I'd taken the trouble in the past, which saved me trouble right then. The wagon was as empty as I needed it to be, which meant I could go ahead and climb in.

But not in the way people usually climb in. Scrambling over a closed wagon tailgate would make enough noise to wake dozing grass, and I had more beings listening around there than all the grass in the universe. Silver silence was still the key, so I took the time to build shadow steps, fashioning and placing them carefully by hand. Steps aren't harder to make than shadow sticks, they only take longer, but I couldn't afford to rush no matter how much of a hurry I was in. Everything had to be done right the first time; at that particular place and time, there would be no second chance.

When the steps were firmly stacked I climbed to their top and stepped into the wagon over the tailgate, bending down to avoid the top of the canvas. I was almost afraid to let my full weight rest on the wagon bed for fear of its creaking, but a quiet groan was the only sound the bed produced. That encouraged me to move further into the wagon, while at the same time staring into the heavy dark.

If the thieves had taken the Great Flame's box into the house with them, there would have been no need for guards—or at least so I was hoping. Logic said the Great Flame was still in the wagon, so all I had to do was find it.

All. Despite the dark I could see the wagon was almost empty, nothing more in it than a rumpled shadow that was probably a blanket, and a long oblong shadow that could be just about anything. I moved silently to the oblong shadow and crouched in front of it, then ran my fingers over it to discover a box made of wood. With no lock it opened easily, but inside was nothing but what felt like tools. I took the tools out one at a time then checked again, but that's all the box held.

I replaced the tools and reclosed the box, then settled back on my heels to think. If the thieves had, as I thought, left the Great Flame in the wagon, there had to be a reason. The likeliest reason was that they didn't trust the people in whose house they were staying, and didn't want them to know about the Great Flame. At first they must have thought they could simply conceal it in their clothing, but they would have learned quickly enough that—

That the Song of the Great Flame can only be muffled, never stilled! Once it got quiet wherever they were, the Song of the Great Flame would reach everyone trying to sleep and the secret would be out! They had to leave it outside, probably heavily muffled, with men around it who were trying to stay awake rather than sleep. That meant the box was definitely there in the wagon, and I had just found the means to locate it.

Despite the pounding of my pulse I closed my eyes right there, then deliberately strained my hearing as far as it would go. If I hadn't noticed the Song sooner then the box had to be deeply muffled, which made me very grateful for the sort of hearing I had. I opened my senses wide, wide, searching for the sound I knew had to be there somewhere, blocking out everything else, straining, reaching—

And then I had it, the golden sound of the golden-boxed Great Flame. It was so faint someone else would have thought they were imagining things or would have missed it entirely, but I knew the sound too well to be mistaken. It was almost exactly like the silver Song of my own Realm's Great Flame, and it was coming from—

Some place under the shadowy blanket. I opened my eyes again and slid over to the blanket, pushed it aside, then began feeling around on the wagon bed. There had to be something there, something more than dirty, splintery wood, something to give me access to what I was looking for. I felt all over the section the blanket had covered, getting more and more anxious—and then I touched it. A small fingerhole, definitely more than a simple depression, and lifting carefully proved me right. With a soft scrape a section of the wagon bed moved away from the rest, and under it was what felt like a great wad of wool.

I didn't need to remove the covering of wool to know I'd found what I was looking for. What I did instead was pull out the wad and what it hid, recovered the hole with the section of wood, and then tugged the blanket back into approximately the same position it had had. With that done—and my heart beating wildly!—I wove shadow all around the wool, then got ready to leave. Finding the Great Flame was only the first part of what had to be done; the second part was getting out of there with it without getting caught.

If I'd thought I was moving quietly when I entered the wagon, on the way out I must have come close to matching mist. I slipped out onto my shadow steps and floated down them, waited a subjective half-of-forever for the guards to be looking away at the same time, then whispered between them and off into the night. I don't think I breathed at all from the time I left the wagon until I was well into the forest away from the village, and then all I wanted to do was tremble violently. I still kept expecting a hand to fall on my shoulder, or a large number of forms to suddenly appear in my path, but the further away I got the more the feeling faded.

When I finally stopped behind a large tree to lean against it and simply breathe, I was already beginning to regain a large measure of self-control. I had gotten the

Great Flame away from the thieves, but I still had to find Jiss and let him know. I didn't want him getting into trouble trying to recover something the thieves no longer had, but I didn't know where he was. I could either search for him alone or ask for Skyhawk's help, but didn't know which idea would be best.

As I stood and silently debated the points, I took the opportunity to unwrap the box containing the Great Flame. I wasn't worried about whether or not *it* was all right, but Greaf was another matter. I'd been avoiding thinking about him ever since I'd entered the wagon, not caring to consider the possibility that something might have happened to him, but I'd waited as long as I could. Right then I had to know, but my hands were definitely trembling again as I licked my lips before raising the lid on the box—

And probably would have fallen over backward in surprise if I hadn't been leaning on the tree. Greaf stormed out like a tiny, raging forest fire, his blue glow definitely savage, his attack stopping no more than an inch from my face as he belatedly recognized me. He immediately began blinking in apology, interspersing that with delirious greeting while he darted in to stroke my cheek, and I couldn't keep from laughing softly.

"I'm delighted to see you, too, Greaf," I whispered, raising my hand to give him my fingers to dart around. "Are you all right? Did they hurt you in any way?"

His still-angry flickering assured me he was fine, and not only fine but ready to take on any fifty enemies of my choice. I was more than relieved to learn that, but I hadn't been so distracted I'd forgotten to begin rewrapping the Great Flame's box. Greaf suddenly noticed what I was doing and tried to protest, but I shook my head at him.

"I used the Flame's Song to find you two, but we don't want our enemies doing the same to find us," I explained. "We'll keep the Flame's box wrapped tight until we're well away from here, and then we can—"

Greaf! Oh, Haliand, you've found Greaf! Sahrinth's thought came suddenly, and then our usual third was with us, greeting and being greeted by an ecstatic Greaf. Blue flame-body and mist-body danced intricate patterns in the air, flashing their delight to the deep black skies, which was really all we needed.

"Hey, you two, are you trying to get us caught?" I hissed, faintly annoyed with beings who were old enough to know better. "This tree is blocking us to a certain extent, but why take chances? The party can wait until we're through the Doorway home."

Hali is right, Greaf, Sahrinth sent at once, settling down out of the high air with a guilty roil to his body. *This entire episode has been a nightmare, and it's not over yet. Where in this world have you been, Haliand? I've been searching and searching for you, and only just got back from my latest effort. I noticed immediately that the Great Flame was gone out of the wagon, of course, and when I followed the faint trail of the Song it led me to you. Have you any idea how upset I've—*

"Sahrinth, disappearing wasn't my choice," I said, firmly heading off what promised to be one of my friend's longer lectures. "When we have time I'll tell you all about what happened, but right now we have more important things to discuss. Prince Jentris is somewhere in this area, and you have to help me find him. We don't want him trying to recover the Flame when I've already—"

Hali, that's what I've been trying to tell you, Sahrinth sent, taking his own turn at interrupting. *I couldn't find you, but I had no trouble locating the Prince. When I told him the thieves stopped early at this village because they discovered there was someone here they could ask for orders, he was very pleased. He said that would give him a chance to recover the Flame while the thieves were busy with other things, and all he had to do was take the first opportunity to come along.*

"But with three guards standing around the wagon, that opportunity never came," I summed up on my own, nodding thoughtfully. "That means you have to get back to him fast, to be sure he doesn't decide to try making an opportunity."

I wish it were that simple, Sahrinth told me with a

sigh, his body showing small shifts of agitation. *When Prince Jentris arrived here it was still light, and the wagon wasn't being guarded at all. The Prince decided that was as much of an opportunity as anyone could ask for, left his horse in the woods, then made for the wagon. Haliand, you have my word that I knew nothing about what had been done. They must have arranged it while I was gone, otherwise I would certainly have warned Prince—*

"Sahrinth, stop making unnecessary excuses and tell me what happened!" I ordered sharply, suddenly ill with the feeling I already knew. "Just say it straight out!"

They set a trap, my friend sent, the thought so faint it was virtually a whisper. *He climbed into the unguarded wagon leaving me on watch, and when I saw men coming out of the house I rushed back to warn him. I thought he would be searching carefully and that was why I hadn't heard anything from him, but that wasn't it. When I entered the wagon I found him lying motionless, not a single mark or wound on him. He was unconscious, Hali, and then the enemy climbed in and took him prisoner!*

"Do you have it all, Sahrinth, or do you want me to go over it one more time?" I asked, making sure I didn't look at any landmarks to let me know where I was. I'd hidden the Great Flame's box in the trunk of a very ordinary-looking tree, and once I was led away from the place I'd never be able to find it again. Sahrinth, of course, knew exactly where we were and would have no trouble getting back to it. His kind of life form saw in different ways than mine did, and therefore always remembered what was where.

Haliand, are you sure there's nothing else we can do? he fretted, Greaf blinking unhappily at his side. *Your idea sounds so dangerous, and I'm sure your Lady Mother would be most disapproving.*

"If you can think of something safer to do that will also solve our problem, I'm more than willing to listen," I said in return. "We have the Great Flame, but taking it back without making any effort to free Prince Jentris is something I can't live with. If my mother were here in my place I know she would feel the same, so that's not a consideration either. I have to try breaking him loose from capture, but at the same time we can't risk having the Great Flame fall into their hands again. Tell me what you're going to do once you've led me away from this area and back to the village.''

Greaf and I will watch carefully, but from a distance, he answered with a sigh of his own, his cloud-body drooping dejectedly. *If you succeed in freeing Prince Jentris, we four will meet in the forest, retrieve the Great Flame, and then go home. If you should be captured, Greaf will remain here to follow along and see where you're taken, while I head for the nearest Doorway to your mother's Realm. Once there I'm to tell her exactly what happened, urge her to contact the Lord of the Sun, then guide back those she designates so that they can retrieve the Great Flame. After that—well, it all depends on what your Lady Mother and the Lord of the Sun decide.*

"Exactly," I said, wishing again that there was some way of getting word to Skyhawk that I hadn't left him because I'd wanted to. It would hardly be fair to get him involved in something where he could be hurt when the problem wasn't in any way his, so I had to make sure he knew nothing of what I was about to do. Having him with me would have been better for me, but I preferred doing what would be better for him. And when it came time for him to be told where I was from, I wanted to be the one to do it.

What—what if it should be decided that you and Prince Jentris can't be rescued? Sahrinth asked, his agitation increasing. *These things do occasionally happen, Haliand, and I don't think Greaf and I could bear it if—if—*

"Oh, Sahrinth, we're not going to be held captive *forever*," I said with a laugh, trying very hard to reassure my small friends. "And there's nothing to say we'll be held at all. I'm trying to cover every possibility I can think of as a just-in-case, but I don't expect to be caught. Jentris and I have gotten away from trouble twice before this, so there's no reason to believe we can't do it again. Let's get going now, so I can reach Jentris before it gets light.''

The assent I got from my two companions was silent and reluctant, but it was still agreement. I closed my eyes and stretched my arms out in front of me, then began following Sahrinth's directions on which way to walk. He had me stop, turn, and circle so many times I lost all sense of which direction I'd originally come from, and once that was accomplished I was able to open my eyes again. If I didn't know where the Great Flame was hidden I couldn't be made to tell anyone, but that was one safety measure I sincerely hoped would prove unnecessary.

It took a while to get back to the village, but the night still wasn't ready to be over. Three men continued to stand in guard positions around the wagon, but they weren't the same ones who had been there earlier. I wondered what would happen to all those men when their superiors found the Great Flame gone, and then I deliberately pushed the question out of my thoughts. When you let yourself be bound to people who have no regard for you, you can't complain when they treat you badly.

I gave Sahrinth and Greaf a quick wave, and then I left them to circle around to the left of the house the wagon stood behind. There was a small stable on that side just like the one attached to Domil's house, and I thought I might be able to get inside from there. My weaving of shadow and moonlight still protected me from what I hoped would be all observation, except, of course, that of Greaf and Sahrinth. Those two should be able to see me clearly, going in and coming back out.

But in order to come out, I first had to get inside. I'd decided to try the front door of the stable to see if they'd left it unlatched, but as I passed the side wall I saw a small door, one made for people rather than horses. I couldn't remember if Domil's stable had a door like that, but it didn't make sense not to try it to see if it was unlocked. It was a little closer to the nearest guardsman than I liked, but if it could get me inside the chance was worth taking.

I reached the door and gently pulled on the latchstring,

then breathed a sigh of relief when the door opened without the least squeak or protest. I slipped inside quickly and reclosed the door, then glanced around before starting for the door to the house. It wasn't so dark in the stable that I couldn't see how crowded with horses it was, but happily there were no guards keeping the horses company. I made it to the other side without waking the dozing animals, and then I had the door into the house to consider.

Or, rather than to consider, to open. I listened hard at the crack for a moment or two, heard nothing, then realized I could either stand there all night or take a chance and just walk in. If the house had been as small as Domil's I might have wasted a little more time waiting and listening, but its outer lines suggested it was more than twice the size of the other house I'd been in and had a second story to boot. Unless they'd simply tied Jiss and dumped him in the front room, I was going to have to spend some time searching.

Which meant I didn't have the time to do nothing but stand there listening. I sighed unhappily at the lack of choice, but I was, after all, there to rescue Jiss rather than to play it safe. It was either leave without him or continue on into the house, so I pulled the latchstring and plunged on in—but slowly. As I eased the door inward I realized I'd been half hoping it wouldn't open, but luck still seemed to be with me. It opened as silently as the outer one had, and then I was peeking around its edge to see if I was as unobserved as I thought.

And I was. The lower floor was as dark and deserted as anyone could have asked, the air just short of ringing with the silence of a house asleep. I slipped inside and closed the stable door quickly but softly, then looked around to see where I was. Rather than being in a room like the one in Domil's house, I'd entered a narrow hallway that contained the front door and the foot of a stairway to the left, and three doorways in the wall opposite. The hall itself was neatly painted a lightish color but was otherwise unadorned, and also had no prisoners in it. I had the feeling I'd need to try the second floor eventually, but right then I had three closed doors to try.

The logical approach would have been to start with the door on my extreme right and work my way to the left and the stairway I'd be needing, but I wasn't in the mood to be logical. In an effort to avoid thinking about the second floor for a while I started with the door on the extreme left, and actually found it easier to take the disappointment of there being nothing behind it. The small room the door had hidden was as plain as the hallway, with nothing in it but a small table with a chair behind it, and another chair standing a short distance away in front of it. The lack of doors in the walls said there weren't even any closets, so that made one down and two to go.

The second door opened on a room that was a surprise even without Jiss being in it. It wasn't possible to see colors in the small amount of light available, but the carpeting on the floor couldn't have been more plush, the furniture couldn't have been made of better fabric or leather, and the wall hangings and decorations should have taken decades of work to earn. It seemed to be a room to relax in rather than do work in, and I couldn't understand why some of its contents hadn't been put in the first room to make it more attractive and comfortable. I thought about that while I checked the single closet in the left-hand wall to find nothing, then shook my head. It was almost as though the sparsely furnished room was there so the people of the house could pretend to be poor, but why they would do that I couldn't imagine.

I checked the hall before leaving the second room, but there was still no one out there to keep me from getting to the third and last door. I really didn't want to go up to the second floor, not when I knew I would find the enemy a lot sooner and more easily than I would find Jiss, but once again I was going to have no other choice. I reached the last door, eased it open, peeked around the edge to look inside—

And had to stare for a minute, to be sure I was seeing what I thought I was seeing. The single small candle burning in the room gave off more than enough light, but for some reason I was having difficulty believing in what it showed me. The room looked more emptied-out than bare, as though furniture belonged on the thick, dark carpeting, but right then there was only one thing in it. Beside the wall to the right of the door, lying totally unmoving on what appeared to be a blanket, was Jiss. Just like that I'd found him, and for some reason the discovery came as a total surprise.

But then I pulled myself out of it, slipped into the room, and closed the door quickly behind me. I had no time for silly things like surprise, not when I had an unconscious Jiss to contend with. I didn't care to think about what would happen if I couldn't wake him, not at his size, so I tabled the consideration as I hurried over to him, hoping it would never come up. I *had* to wake him, so the first thing to do was get started.

I threw my shadow and moonlight weaving aside and got down on my knees beside Jiss before taking him by the shoulders and shaking him, but the direct approach wasn't the right one. He was even heavier than I'd imagined, and his softly breathing body responded not at all to the small amount of shaking I accomplished. His eyes were closed and his face serene, and there wasn't the least flicker of awareness that anyone was near and trying to get through to him. I took his face in my hand and tried shaking that, but although it moved more easily than his body, there was still no response. I thought about hitting him rather than shaking, told myself that would be unfair, then did it anyway. I was beginning to feel the first shadows of desperation, but even being unfair didn't work. There was no reaction to the slaps I gave him, not even the mildest of protests, and that ended that.

I sat back on my heels to stare at Jiss and try to think of something else, but desperation was growing thicker and getting in the way. If I could have lifted him I could have gotten him out of there, but it would take someone like Skyhawk to lift him and Skyhawk wasn't there. I took a deep breath and let it out slowly, knowing I didn't want

Skyhawk to be there, but I was rapidly running out of other choices. I continued to think about it for another minute, then grudgingly admitted I could only give myself one more chance to wake Jiss. If that didn't work I'd have to go for Skyhawk, even if it did put the man in danger over trouble that wasn't his. If I made sure to be very careful we might even avoid trouble altogether, and—

I gasped low as I felt the sting on the side of my neck, and my first thought was to wonder how an insect had gotten into the room. There hadn't seemed to be any in the other parts of the house I'd seen, not even in the stable. My hand went to the place that had been bitten as I began to look around for the insect, and then I felt a very definite chill. In all the days I'd been in that Realm I hadn't been bitten at all, not even in the middle of the forest. Wasn't it strange that the first time should come *there*, right in the midst of my enemies?

And then my eyes found the insect that had found me, and everything became clearer as well as a good deal colder. The thing hovered in the air not three feet away, small but distinctly red, the gleam of what seemed like eyes watching me. It was obviously no ordinary insect that had bitten me, and I suddenly remembered what Jiss had told me, about how the Lord of the Earth had power over even the smallest of life forms. Fear arrived to lend me strength then, and I tried to use it to force myself erect and out of the house. If I didn't get away Jiss and I were both in it—

But I couldn't even push myself to my feet. My heart hammered as I strained to stand, but even as I tried I felt myself falling to the left, my body no longer under my control. Suddenly all I wanted to do was sleep, right there on the carpeting I'd fallen to, the lethargy flowing through me insisting that this was all I could do. In my head I strained against it, trying to fight, but it was far too late. The battle had been fought and lost, and then even my eyes closed.

* * *

I was so exhausted I couldn't force myself fully awake, but the fact that I was being held and touched brought me back to some sort of awareness. I couldn't move or open my eyes, but the murmur of voices resolved itself into words.

". . . can see what you mean, sir," a heavy male voice said with a chuckle. "How fortunate she delivered herself right to you, and after you thought her beyond your reach."

"I thought her beyond my reach until that troublesome redhead fell to us," another male voice said, one that sounded strangely familiar. "He and that blasted outlaw he was with ruined our arrangement at the inn, but at the time all I could do was slip away and ride for my life. If I hadn't stopped here, where those fools in the wagon could encounter me and ask for my help, I would have had to return to the Highest Lord in defeat rather than victory. One of those responsible for our loss of the inn is now available for the Highest Lord's wrath to fall upon, and this girl—even if he should decide to keep her with him for a while—eventually she'll be mine. The sight of her will ease his anger at me, and afterward, when he's done with finding interest in her . . ."

Rather than finishing the thought in words he laughed slowly and with great relish, a sound that bothered me even in the midst of sleep confusion. It sounded as though something was very wrong, but I still couldn't force myself any further awake.

"Yes indeed, sir," the first voice said with laughter of its own, obviously agreeing. "You've mentioned you knew the girl would come when the man fell into our hands, but I still have no idea what brought them in the first place. The man fell to your tiny pet in the wagon, and putting a guard around the wagon forced the girl to come in here. Do you know what the man was looking for?"

"I do, but it happens to be none of your concern," the second man answered, his tone only faintly stiff because of the presence of distraction. "Should you ever rise to a higher position than chief village talker, you may question others on matters of import. For now you have only to admire my acquisition, my soon-to-be bauble and pastime. Have you ever seen skin so delicately pale, or a body quite that beckoning? When the Highest Lord is done with her she will become mine, but she hasn't yet been given to the Highest Lord . . .''

For the second time his voice trailed off, but this time his words weren't replaced with laughter. The touch of his hand came instead, a touch I tried to refuse, an attempt that did accomplish its purpose in a way. It wasn't possible to do so much as stir where I lay, but the try sent me back to the depths of sleep.

Chapter 13

I HAD NO IDEA how long a time I'd been unconscious, but after only a few minutes of being awake I wasn't happy with any part of the situation. I sat on a stone bench to one side of a wide, brightly sunny courtyard, four men not only standing around me but also staring directly at me. I didn't know the four men, or any of the other people bustling through the courtyard, and it hadn't taken me long to decide I didn't want to know any of them. I didn't like the looks of the estate house that stood not far from me, and if I'd had the choice I would have quickly gone elsewhere.

But I hadn't been given the choice. I'd been very confused when I'd first been awakened, and by the time the confusion cleared away I was already out of the wagon I'd apparently been riding in and sitting on the bench. I'd watched the wagon being driven away around the far side of the very large house, and that had been it as far as familiar things and people went. I'd been left with nothing but strangers and strangeness.

Especially strangeness. Now that the wagon was gone fewer people hurried in and out of the house, and I felt definite relief over their absence. They had all seemed to be under a—cloud of fear, I suppose you could say, and if they hadn't exactly been trembling visibly, most of them hadn't been very far from it. Seeing this had put a definite shadow over the house I sat so near, despite the brightness of the sunlight, but it wasn't a shadow I could use. I moved around on the bench, trying to feel more comfortable in Skyhawk's clothing, wishing night would hurry up and get there.

For all I knew I had a wait of hours ahead of me, but suddenly that possibility was wiped away. Three men came out of the house and started toward the bench I waited on, and one of the three, the one who walked ahead of the others, was unexplainably familiar. Somehow I knew him as the man at the inn who had been so eager to have me captured, and as I stared at him I realized I had another memory of him as well. He'd been there after I'd fallen victim to that insect bite—and during the ride in the wagon—and suddenly I knew he'd done something to me during that time—

"Ah, how delightful to see you awake again," the man said to me as he came up, his eyes virtually glittering. "For myself you were quite acceptable as you were, but the Highest Lord will want you aware of him. He's here in this residence to see to important matters, but I feel certain he'll find a moment or two for the consideration of . . . leisure-time activities. I, of course, will do you the honor of presenting you to him."

His smirk was extremely offensive, but certainly not the only offensive thing about him. He was fairly tall and not in any way overweight, but there was something about his body and face that suggested softness and pampering. His light brown hair was more than neatly combed, and his clothing was made of what looked to be rather expensive material. The spotless gray trousers, white shirt, red outer coat and red ascot made him look as though he had just been unwrapped, a perfect match to manners that gave the exact same impression.

"Nothing your sort does on my behalf could possibly be considered an honor," I told the man as I stood to face him, using my mother's most deliberately regal attitude. "I demand that you release me at once, and show at least the pretense of being well-bred."

"Do you indeed," the man murmured as his eyes grew heavy-lidded, his lessened amusement reflecting the way my condescension had affected him. "You seem to consider yourself a highborn lady of station, when you are, of course, no such thing. What you presently are, my girl, is a slave, a fact you would do well to recognize as quickly as your naturally limited intelligence allows."

"You call that a fact, and consider *me* unintelligent?" I asked with distant amusement, trying to cover my rising repugnance toward the man. My skin felt as if it wanted to crawl and a faraway illness was trying to move closer, but I was prepared to do just about anything to keep him from knowing how really frightened I was beginning to be. "If it's facts you want," I continued with no noticeable hesitation, "let's consider the fact that it's rather easy to call someone something they're not. Just as easy, in fact, as pretending to be something *you're* not, and obviously never could be. If you need an explanation of what I just said, please don't hesitate to ask. I'd be more than happy to supply one."

"How very gracious of you," the man drawled, his dark eyes glittering again but in an entirely different way. "You would have no objection to explaining that you are being called a slave in error, while I am being represented as your superior when I'm not. You're quite correct when you contend these things are easily said, but I contend they're just as easily proven. Do allow me to make the effort."

His smile had turned as distant as my previous amusement, and it must have been that very distance that caused me to be caught so far off-guard. Without my having picked up the least sign of warning his hand was suddenly blurring toward me, and then I was stumbling backward to fall against the bench I'd been sitting on, my face flaring pain from the backhanded slap he'd given me. I lay on the bench on my left side for a moment, blinking away momentary dizziness and trying to fight my way through the shock of what had happened, but the moment was all I had. A hand came then to twist itself in my hair, and my head was forced around to turn my face toward the man.

"Do you see now how easily some things are proven?" he asked, that smirk completely returned to him. "If you were a high lady rather than a slave, someone would have protested my striking you. Do you hear any protests or see anyone rushing to your assistance? No? Then I think my contention can be considered proven. Bring her."

His final order was to the two men who had come out of the house with him, and as soon as he released my hair and stepped away they moved forward to obey him. I was pulled from the bench by the arms and taken along behind the man who had hit me, and everything he'd said had been absolutely correct. There had been six men who had watched him slap me, but not a single one had even begun a protest. My face and head hurt and I was trembling too badly to be able to stop it immediately, but I was also beginning to feel something besides fear. Those people had no right treating others as slaves, no matter how good they considered themselves. If I was given even the slightest chance to do something to get even . . .

The man who had proven a point led the way into the house, his two helpers forcing me after him. The men holding my arms wore the sort of trousers, shirts, and boots that marked them as beings of little or no importance, a circumstance that was emphasized as soon as we entered the house. The entrance hall was, despite its size, virtually clogged with paintings on the walls, intricately carved tables holding vases or busts, heavy carpeting, expensive drapes, much more than one would expect to find in that part of a house. I was hurried past those things and up a central hall, and that too was stuffed to overcrowding.

A few minutes of walking brought us to an area toward the back of the house, an area that was marked by the presence of armed guards. These men, six in number, stood about guarding a closed set of double doors, but made no attempt to challenge our approach to them. One of the men gestured most of the others out of the path of the men we followed, leaving two who opened the doors to allow us all entry. Once we had walked through the doors were closed again behind us, and the man who had hit me glanced around at the other people the room held, then turned and moved the few steps back to my group.

"Judging from the number of people here, we'll have something of a wait before the Highest Lord receives us," he said softly, his voice and expression showing his annoyance. "A pity I hadn't realized that sooner, or I could have taken you elsewhere to pass the time in a more . . . amusing way. I'm quite looking forward to having you awake while I pleasure myself with you, unlike the times already past. Asleep, you don't struggle very much at all."

He reached down with two fingers to touch me then, a truly hateful expression of amusement on his face, and although I tried to back away from him with a gasp, the two men holding me refused to allow it. I was shocked and disgusted by what he'd said despite having somehow already known it, but beyond that I couldn't bear the thought of being touched by him even with clothing in the way. I would have run if I could have, not worrying in the least about how cowardly I looked, but I wasn't permitted to run. I was forced to stand there while that vile creature touched me as he pleased, and then I was laughed at.

"What was that you said about not being a slave?" the man asked lightly as he finally withdrew his hand. "You *will* learn better, for that you have my word. Bring her over to stand behind my chair."

His two helpers obeyed just as promptly the second time, pulling me around to the back of the chair the creature chose to sit in. The two men seemed faintly amused by how hard I was trembling, an emotion shared by those of the dozen or so other people in the room who had see what had been done to me. None of them were bothered in the least by such an outrage, but the same couldn't be said about me. I felt pale and ill, but somewhere deep inside fury had given way to a growling flame of rage.

It took a few moments before I had control of myself

again, and then I was able to ignore the hands on my arms and look around. The room we had entered was clearly an anteroom of some sort, and many of the people in it were dressed like the man who sat comfortably relaxed in front of me. Most of them sat in their own chairs or on couches, and almost all of them seemed to be accompanied by those who were dressed less well and seemed to be servants. Or slaves. I didn't know how one told the difference, and I didn't want to know. I looked at the four guardsmen standing in front of another set of double doors, and let my curiosity about what they might be guarding distract me from the subject of slaves.

Quite a lot of time went by with no one else coming in and no one going through the second set of doors, and it wasn't difficult telling how impatient everyone was feeling—even though they tried not to show it. I was faintly surprised that none of them walked out in disgust or demanded to know what the delay was, but it wasn't really difficult remembering that that wasn't my mother's Court, and those waiting weren't her people. The Lord of the Earth obviously preferred doing things his own way in everything, including turning his followers into beaten-down flunkies.

When the inner set of double doors finally opened, one of the men waiting got immediately out of his chair, straightened his clothing and put a smile on his face, then began walking toward the robed man who had appeared. He was clearly the one who was supposed to have the next audience, but the man in the long red robe ignored him in favor of the man sitting in front of me.

"Lord Tirfin, the Highest Lord will see you now," the robed man said smoothly, paying no attention to the anger showing briefly on the face of the man who was being displaced. "Follow me, please."

Lord Tirfin rose from his chair with smug insolence, glanced at the envy shown by the other men in the room, then gestured the two holding me into following before heading toward the robed one. I think the creature would have laughed aloud if he'd dared, and the bland gaze coming from the man in the robe said he suspected the same thing. Rather than commenting, though, he simply turned and led the way back through the doors, knowing without doubt that we would follow.

Once again the doors were closed behind us, but it wasn't precisely a room we'd come into. About ten feet beyond the door were heavy red drapes curtaining what lay beyond, and the man in the robe walked to them, stepped through holding one side open, then gave Lord Tirfin a sardonic bow. The robed man did well hiding his amusement at how nervous Lord Tirfin had suddenly grown, but I don't think the man we followed would have noticed even if the robed man had laughed aloud. His smug insolence was completely gone, and he led the way forward with what seemed to be faintly trembling hands.

The area before the drapes had been totally undecorated, but once we passed into the main chamber that no longer held true. The room was very large, paneled in fine wood and hung with gleaming drapes, and had guardsmen standing along both the left- and right-hand walls. Possibly all those guardsmen were there to protect the objects the room was decorated with: more silver and gold and precious gems than I had ever thought to see in one place. Golden statues and silver urns, jeweled weapons and inlaid wall and floor patterns, all of it gleaming and shining in the light of uncounted candles arranged about the room. Toward the back was a fairly wide dais that rose two steps above the floor, and on the dais, in a gleaming bronze throne, sat a man. Lord Tirfin led the way toward that man, and needless to say, I was pulled after him.

Lord Tirfin looked as though he would have enjoyed moving slowly toward the man on the throne, but with the way the man was staring at him, he didn't dare. The Highest Lord was a big man, almost as big as Jiss, with dark hair and eyes and dressed in casual clothing that must have been worth twice what Lord Tirfin's was. From halfway across the room he looked very familiar, but the closer I got the less familiar he seemed. By the time we all stopped a handful of feet in front of the dais, he wasn't familiar at all.

"Greatest Lord, you summoned me," Lord Tirfin said with a bow, then didn't add anything as he stood with his head down. He appeared to be waiting to be recognized after having reported his presence, but the recognition wasn't immediately forthcoming. The man he'd spoken to was paying no attention to him or to the bows of the two men holding me; his eyes were inspecting only me, and didn't seem to care for the idea that I hadn't bowed. He stared at me for a very long moment, his face expressionless, and then I was totally dismissed.

"Tirfin, you've failed me," the Highest Lord said abruptly to the man who awaited his pleasure, the words hard and cold but at the same time distantly delighted in a way that was chilling. "I presume you're aware of what happens to those who fail me."

"Greatest Lord, the fault wasn't mine!" Tirfin cried as he looked up beseechingly at the man on the throne, more than his hands trembling now. "I was not responsible for safety arrangements at the inn, I merely oversaw the operation! But rather than return empty-handed I brought you one of those who was responsible for the disaster, and look, look here!"

He turned abruptly, knocked away the man holding my left arm, took the arm himself, then pulled me out of the grip of the man on my right. None of it was carefully or gently done, but he didn't care about hurting me.

"This girl is one of them, and I brought her here for you!" Tirfin continued desperately, his fingers digging hard into my arm. "Between the man and this girl, your revenge may be taken in full! My lord knows I am ever loyal to him, and would sooner die than fail him. Allow me to continue serving you, my lord, and let your wrath fall on those who truly merit it."

The Lord of the Earth leaned back in his bronze throne, his arms on the throne's arms, his gaze distracted into consideration of what he had just been told. Beside me Tirfin was almost holding his breath, his terror so close to the surface of his actions that he was all but mewling aloud. He very much wanted to be absolved of all guilt, but he couldn't quite bring himself to believe that he would be. That, of course, showed his true stupidity, for his hand was still wrapped firmly around my arm.

And I was a balancing force.

What he believed, I reinforced, the touch of his hand to my arm making that state of affairs unavoidable. If he hadn't touched me he might have had a chance, but he'd been so eager to see me sacrificed in his place that he'd pulled me forward so that he might hide behind me. What he'd done instead was seal his own fate, and I felt not the slightest trace of guilt over that. Under other circumstances I might have tried to escape the grip that was becoming more and more painful, but just then I did nothing more than stand there accepting it—with the faintest of smiles on my face.

"Tirfin, you've made me stop and think," the Highest Lord said abruptly, nearly causing the man beside me to jump. "I listened carefully to what you said, and I find myself amazed. I can't recall the last time I was so amazed."

The man holding my arm began trembling harder, a reaction to his allowing himself to hope, but he should have known better. His lord was clearly someone who enjoyed torturing people.

"Yes, I was positively amazed," the Highest Lord continued, and now his eyes were directly on the man he spoke to. "I find it difficult to understand how I could possibly have allowed someone with your stupidity any power of any sort. You haven't even the intelligence to understand *how* you failed me, and that's the most unforgivable part of all!"

Tirfin's trembling had come to an abrupt halt, just as though the blood had frozen inside him and had therefore frozen the rest of him as well. He knew suddenly that he faced eternity, and the sight was not one he was prepared for.

"I don't care about that inn, you fool!" the Highest Lord shouted with blazing eyes, leaning forward to emphasize his words. "What was in that wagon was worth a thousand thousand inns, and its protection was given over to you! Leaving a stinger inside the wagon as its only guard was done at my command, before they started out, and that was what netted us the man. When you saw him you recognized him, knew he hadn't been alone, but you still *had the last stinger moved to the house!* You were so eager to capture that girl you forgot about what the wagon contained, ignored it entirely in favor of baiting your trap with the body of the man. How is it possible for anyone to be that stupid?"

"Bu-but my lord, I considered the sort of p-people we were dealing with," Tirfin stuttered, desperation forcing him to speak. "I knew the girl would never be smart enough to abandon the man, and I was right! She came into the house after him, and we *caught* her!"

"But not before she took what was in the wagon, you absolute fool!" the Highest Lord screamed, half out of his seat with near-insanity blazing from his eyes. "You put guards on the wagon when you took the stinger, never once stopping to wonder why *I* hadn't ordered guards! The reason was that I expected them to be useless, and they were! If you had left my arrangements as they were I would have done no more than have you whipped, for failing at the inn when you should have triumphed. But because of you the girl took what was meant to be mine, and *that* is what you will pay for! Guards! Get him out of my sight!"

Tirfin's fingers finally left my arm as he stared at me in horror, his body backing away as though it were trying to escape without benefit of guidance from his mind. His mind, of course, knew that escape was impossible, something quickly proven to him. Half a dozen guardsmen from the wall to our left came over to circle him, and then he was being dragged toward a small, undecorated door to the left of the throne. The man began screaming when he was only a few feet from the door, and the sound didn't stop until he disappeared through it and it was closed again behind him.

"So much for that," the Highest Lord said, drawing my eyes back to him, the words sounding as though they referred to a piece of paper he had read and was therefore able to put aside. "Now you can tell me where you hid the Great Flame. I'll have the location from you in one way or another, so you might as well save yourself the pain and give it to me now. And do bear in mind the fact that even if you care nothing about yourself, we also have access to your friend. If the thought of your own pain won't move you, you really must consider his."

"I've discovered that pain and hurt come in many different forms," I answered, distantly amused to see that the first person to treat me as a complete adult had turned out to be my most hated enemy. "Most people will do anything if you hurt them, or someone close to them, badly enough, even if what they do will eventually cause them even greater pain and harm. For that reason I made sure not to know where the Great Flame was put, to save myself from needing to depend on courage. I don't know how much of that commodity I possess, but now it really doesn't matter. Ignorance does a much better job of it."

"And you expect me to believe that," he said, a faint smile of amusement creasing his face, a fist supporting his chin as he stared down at me. "If you were one of these lower life forms I might consider the possibility, but with you being who you are? Tell me where you put my property."

"*Your* property?" I repeated in disbelief, but I could see the man meant exactly what he said. "You think stealing something makes it yours? Yes, I see you do, but what do you want with the Great Flame? What use can you possibly imagine you have for it?"

"I mean to allow it to serve me," he surprised me by answering, that faint smile still very much there. "When the Great Flame is combined with mine, the resulting gift will make me invincible. Or more invincible than I already am. As soon as it's done my forces will march, and once we have our two victories I'll also have the third Great

Flame. After that—who knows how far my fortunes will take me? As far away, perhaps, as the other end of eternity?"

I stared at him without understanding what he was talking about, but that was just as well. He wasn't expecting an answer from me, not with the way his glittering stare was turned inward. He saw things in the burning red light of madness, and it wasn't possible for the sane to view the same landscape. He dreamed in silence for longer than was comfortable for those around him, and then suddenly his eyes were on me again.

"You and I are of the same sort, girl, which means you'd know well enough the value of certain information," he said, as though our previous conversation hadn't had any interruptions. "You would have known you might have to bargain with me, and would not have left yourself nothing to bargain *with*. Tell me where the Great Flame is, and I'll have you taken directly to my apartments. Serving me is something you won't be getting out of, but you'll find that service much more enjoyable without having first been put to the question."

"You're very used to having people bargain with you, aren't you?" I said, finally having had enough of him. "You have everything and they have nothing, so they bargain their lives and essences and dignity for some of what you have. It obviously hasn't occurred to you that there may be people around who don't *want* anything you can offer, not if they have to pay for it in your choice of coin. You and I are about as far from being the same sort as two members of a species can be, and I can't tell you how pleased that fact makes me. I have nothing to bargain with and no interest in bargaining, and if that makes me a lower life form, I accept the calling with enormous satisfaction."

I got through the speech before the steadiness of my voice failed, a circumstance that made me very grateful. I knew what I'd said would enrage the Highest Lord, and I wasn't wrong; he stiffened in his throne with the madness back in his eyes, but I simply didn't care. If you keep silent with those of the Highest Lord's sort you may stay safer than speaking out would make you, but that's really only prolonging the agony. Madmen can only be counted on to be mad, never to be rational.

"So you have no interest in bargaining," the Lord of the Earth Realm snarled, his eyes burning into me. "The choice is yours, my dear lady, and I, as your host, am constrained to abide by your decision. If you should change your mind, do let me know as quickly as possible. If I should still be in the house, I'll most certainly intervene."

He snapped his fingers toward the guardsmen standing at the wall to my right, but it wasn't a group of guardsmen alone who came to surround me. The red-robed man who had led us into the room was there as well, and as soon as two of the guardsmen had my arms he turned and walked toward that small door the man Tirfin had been taken through. I had decided not to struggle against what would be done to me, to maintain as much of my dignity as possible no matter how afraid I felt, but losing face in front of my enemy quickly became very unimportant. I was five feet short of that door when my struggling began almost by itself, but it didn't do any good. I was still taken through the door, and not long after that it began.

I came to still strapped to the rough wooden table, the pain in my body so great that a moan was forced out of me. The man in the red robe smiled when he heard it, his amusement clear in the light eyes looking down at me. He'd enjoyed himself quite a bit over the last few hours, and still seemed totally uninterested in finding something besides me to entertain him.

"Welcome back," he said in a soft, easy voice, his hand coming to gently smooth away some hair from my forehead. "Are you ready to start again?"

My breath began coming harder with the question, terror freezing my throat closed, and the man laughed lightly before patting my head.

"Now, now, I didn't say we *would* start again, I only asked if you were ready," he told me, obviously enjoying his little joke. "The Highest Lord has gotten tired of waiting for you to change your mind and has left the house, so I thought I'd give you something of a rest until he gets back. I'm under orders not to stop in the middle of a session even if you decide you're finally ready to tell him what he wants to know, and the next session should bring you to that point. If he isn't here to listen to you you'll have the chance to change your mind again, and then we'll have to go all the way through yet another session. Normally I'd have no objection to that, but Lord Tirfin is waiting for my attention, and I've really been looking forward to the time. Lord Tirfin isn't expected to survive, and those sorts of sessions have always been my favorites."

"Blackfire take you, why won't you believe she's telling the truth?" Jiss said hoarsely from the other side of the room, pain in his voice along with frustration. "If she knew where the box was hidden, she would have told you by now!"

"Not necessarily," the robed man denied without turning, his stroking hand on my hair making me shudder and close my eyes as I turned my face from him. "She isn't the first woman I've given my attention, and a surprising number of those I attended held out longer than many men. One held out so long I found myself in love with her, and I've always regretted that she died not long after she finally spoke. Stay here, pretty girl, and I'll fetch those who'll take you to the place you'll wait for the Highest Lord's return."

He chuckled at his cleverness before moving away from the table, and when I opened my eyes to see him actually leaving the room I let myself feel a small amount of relief. He seemed to be telling the truth about letting me rest for a while, but I couldn't bring myself to believe it completely until I saw if it would happen. The man so loved to give pain that I wouldn't have put it past him to lie and get my hopes up, just to see them come crashing down.

"Hali, can you hear me?" Jiss asked, his voice struggling to stay low while at the same time trying to reach me. The stone room we were in was rather large, and Jiss was chained to the wall at the other end of it. When I

turned my head away from the door to the left I was able
to see him, way down on the right beyond my feet, and I
still found the sight extremely strange. The stone of the
room had any number of decorations, but most of them
were made of black iron partially stained with reddish-
brown smears like rust. The chains on Jiss were a rather
obvious exception, because the chains on Jiss were made
of diamonds. His bare body was bruised and cut from what
had been done to him, but his wrists and ankles were
bright with the faceted reflection of torchlight.

"Hali, I can't burn through these chains the way I did
through the leather, and could have done with iron," he
said when he saw my eyes on him. "I've tried more than
once, but it just isn't any good. Do you—think you'll be
able to hold out when he starts again?"

If I hadn't been in so much pain I might have laughed,
but there wasn't anything of laughter left inside me. The
man who had hurt me had been told I knew the location of
a certain "box," and hadn't believed me the times I'd
screamed out that I *didn't* know where it was. I'd come
very close to telling him about Sahrinth and Greaf, but
even when wrapped in a cloud of agony I'd realized he'd
never believe me. He didn't know I came from another
Realm, and hadn't known the reason why Jiss had been
chained with diamonds; telling him why I didn't know
where the box was would have been worse than not telling
him anything at all.

"Hali, girl, you have to try your best to hold out," Jiss
said when I didn't answer him, his tone gentle with support and understanding. "This won't go on forever, you
know, and once it's over the Great Flame will be safe."

Someone listening to him might have thought he was
being generously noble with my pain, but the man in the
red robe had given his attention to Jiss for a while, and
probably would do the same again. We'd both been whipped,
Jiss more than once, but the shock of being treated like
that had quickly passed when less spectacular but much
more painful attentions had been paid me. I'd always
known sharp objects could cause hurt, but had never dreamed

so much could be done with dull ones, and rounded ones, and raspy ones . . .

Jiss's eyes had closed where he slumped against the wall, and I thought he might be trying to fight off some of his own pain so that he could talk to me again. His wrists were set shoulder-high against the wall, and his ankles were also linked to the stone; he hadn't once been allowed to change position in the hours we'd been there, and I couldn't quite imagine how bad it had been for him. It had to be fairly terrible, though; he had spoken about the pain not "going on forever," and I didn't for a moment believe he thought we would escape or be released. He was ready to move on to the next level of existence, and I wasn't far from feeling the same myself.

"Oh, what a good girl, still right where I left you," the voice of the robed man came suddenly, and I turned my head to see him coming back into the room with two others behind him. The others were armed and uniformed guardsmen, and when the robed man gestured, the guardsmen came to the table and began releasing me from the straps.

"Since a wait is necessary before I can have another session with you, I've decided to make use of the waiting time," the robed man said pleasantly while the guardsmen worked to release me. "I'm having you put in a very special place, a place I've used any number of times before, so I know exactly how it will make you feel. The others all ended up begging to be let out of there, but the amount of time it took varied from person to person. I'm curious to see how long it will take with *you,* but I haven't gone so far as to hope you'll outlast the others. Females don't seem to do well there at all."

By that time I was being forced from the table and to my feet, and the movement, although increasing my pain, did well in covering the shudder that took me. When you're really afraid you tend to believe your fear can't possibly increase in strength, but I'd learned that capacity tends to adjust to changes in the situation. I'd feared the time of the next "session" with the robed man, but now I feared the time before it even more.

"Do enjoy your rest, my sweet," the robed man said
with a chuckle as I was pulled out of the room past him.
"Afterward, you and I will meet again."

The sound of his amusement followed us into the stone
corridor, and a few feet beyond the room. I wasn't walking very easily, and because of that it took me a moment
to realize that the two guardsmen supporting and directing
me were no more sharing the robed man's delight than I
was. They were also looking at me as little as possible
even though I was entirely naked, and that led me to
wonder if Jiss and I and those like us were the only
prisoners in that place.

The corridor we moved along wasn't very well lit, but it
did have torches stuck in sconces every ten or fifteen feet.
I didn't know where we were going and would have been
happier not ever finding out, but when my escort paused
so the man to my right could take a torch from the wall
before we continued on, I began feeling faintly more
curious than afraid. If our destination was all that terrifying and horror filled, wouldn't it be kept well-enough lit so
that the victims left there could see every frightening bit of
it? That was the way I would have done it, but possibly the
Lord of the Earth and his helpers looked at the matter
differently.

When we finally reached the place where we were
going, I found that my captors did indeed look at matters
differently. The torches had stopped appearing on the walls
a number of minutes before we stopped, and the two men
with me were glancing around nervously, as though they
expected something with large teeth to jump out of the
shadows at them. I could have told them there wasn't
anything in the shadows *to* jump out, but it didn't seem to
be my place to do that.

There was a heavy, greenish metal door on the left
where we'd stopped, and the guardsman on my left let go
of my arm to push a bar and then pull on the door. When
he finally got it open wide enough to make it possible to
see inside, the one on my right tightened his grip.

"Don't go gettin' wild an' screamin' with us, girl,

'cause it won't do ya no good," he said as he began to force me toward the open door. "We gotta put ya in there an' then we gotta leave, an' all the screamin' in the world won't get ya out again 'fore Lord Craver says ya c'n come out. Prob'ly won't be too long no matter how it feels t' ya . . ."

The last of his words were muttered as he shoved me forward, and then the other man was closing the heavy door behind me and sliding the bar back in place. I stood stupidly in the thick darkness for a moment, my bare feet mostly on the filthy straw I'd seen in the light of the torch, and slowly, unbelievingly, it came to me that that *was* the horrible, terrifying place they'd been talking about. The small, filthy, empty cell shown me by the brief presence of the torchlight was the place meant to break me down even more than the pain I'd been given.

The confusion I felt then was very thick, and all I could do was half fall, half sit on the scattered straw as I shook my head, trying to understand what they could possibly think they were doing. The heavy darkness was wrapped comfortingly around me, soothing away some of my more minor aches, and when I heard the scrape of tiny feet at the back of the room I was even able to smile faintly. It was nice having the company of other darkness dwellers even if they couldn't help me, which unfortunately was the case. They might come over to commiserate with me, but unless I could make myself small enough to use their way out of the room . . .

Despite the fact that I was in no real condition to do any logical thinking, it suddenly came to me that the guardsmen who had brought me there were not standing outside the door, waiting for orders to take me back. "We've got to put you in there and then we've got to leave" was what the guardsman with the torch had said, and the way he'd said it made me believe him. There was no one watching from the outside, and they would have needed the torch to find their way back to the place where light began again. Darkness inside, darkness outside, no one watching—

Without thinking about it I immediately began standing

up, which means I just as immediately fell back to the straw again, the pain so bad it almost sent me into unconsciousness. The two guardmen had supported me most of the way here, and the last of the surge of fear had kept me standing once I'd been put into the room. Without the results of fear to lean on I had nothing to counter the hurt I'd been given, but I knew I had to find something and as quickly as possible. If my guesswork was right I could get out of that room, but first I had to be able to stand.

I lay in the straw for a string of very long minutes, unmoving and with eyes closed, drawing every bit of strength I could from the darkness around me. The strength of darkness is soft rather than hard, but that only means it's easier to absorb, and you have to be careful not to trade with it the way you're used to doing. Darkness is always willing to trade strength for consciousness, something anyone who has ever fallen asleep in it knows, but I couldn't afford that trade. I needed the strength without giving up my consciousness, and the kind, gentle darkness understood and allowed it.

There finally came a point when I simply couldn't wait any longer. Moving was still painful but not as impossible as it had been, so I got slowly to my feet, found the front wall of the room, then made my way over to the corner on my right. The door leading in was in the same wall to the left, but the door held no interest for me. Doors are very restricted creatures in that their purpose is to either allow or disallow exit and entry, and which they do depends on the firm decision of someone who doesn't have to be the one wanting to use it. Walls, on the other hand, and most especially corners, aren't the same; people tend to build them and then walk away, all the while assuming they'll stay as they're built. Assumptions are weak things, not at all like decisions, and someone with strong belief backing up trained talent can usually overcome them.

Which is what I intended doing. Once I found the corner I wanted I grasped the deep shadow it was made of, then began unraveling it. The opposite of weaving is unraveling, of course, but there's a slight difference between the two processes. I'd learned it was possible to weave and shape less-than-heavy shadow, but no one had ever managed unraveling anything but really deep dark. At that point objects are virtually made of shadow, which is why I'd been so pleased to learn the guardsmen were gone with their torch. If there had been any light left out in the corridor, I wouldn't have been able to complete the unraveling.

But I *was* able to complete it. With my mother's luck and blessing sustaining me I was soon out in the corridor, and it was definitely none too soon. The strength I'd gathered was strictly limited, and I needed to use it to get me back to the room Jiss had been chained in. If they'd moved him the way they'd done with me I'd have a very large problem, but that was a problem I could worry about if and when it came up. The first step was getting back to the room, which might not be done quite as easily as said.

I had to use the right-hand wall to help keep me upright, but I reached the area of the first—or last—torches with only minor difficulty. Walking barefoot on that stone hurt my feet, but a return to light brought me the worry of something more serious than sore feet. Someone coming the opposite way up the corridor couldn't miss me, and the number of metal and wooden doors I passed led me to wonder just how soon a someone would appear on his way to one of those doors. I worried about the problem and fretted over the answer—and only just managed to notice when I began passing the door I'd been looking for. It was closed rather than standing open, a change from when I had last seen it, and it wasn't hard convincing myself that that was the reason I'd almost passed it by.

Leaning on the door helped me get it open, but it swung inward much faster than my ability to follow. I stumbled a little as it slid away from me, regained my balance, then went to get it where it had stopped. I'd had a glimpse of Jiss as I'd half-fallen into the room, and he was still in the same place. With that problem taken care of, closing the door behind me seemed the next most important thing to do.

When I leaned on the closed door and finally looked around, I found Jiss's eyes resting on me from the middle of a vastly disbelieving expression. Only a single torch had been left burning in the room, but that was more than enough to let me see again the things that would probably make me shudder for the rest of my life.

"Hali, how did you get loose?" Jiss demanded in a rusty whisper as I shuddered, his body trying to straighten up against the wall. "And why didn't you just keep going? You won't be able to get me out of this, and trying will simply waste your escape time."

"Jiss, I *have* to get you out of that," I said as I pushed away from the door, hoping the impetus would carry me all the way across the room. "It was all I could do to make it *here*. If I have to try going on alone, I'll never get anywhere. At least if you're along, we can lean on each other."

By that time I'd reached him, and the way I had to hold on to the wall for a minute to catch my breath kept him from finding any amusement in what I'd said. What he seemed to have found in its place was worry, and considering his own probable physical condition, I couldn't really blame him.

"These chains of diamond were set into the stone by their Highest Lord," he said after a moment, trying to sound as if he were explaining rather than disagreeing. "That's the reason they had to leave me here, instead of moving me elsewhere the way they did with you. That animal in the red robe was annoyed over that, and for a minute I thought he would take the annoyance out on me. Are you sure you can't make it on your own?"

"Positive," I muttered as I raised my eyes to the jewels clasping his left wrist, seeing the way his hand had turned to a fist above them. Since I didn't have much strength left, I didn't waste any of it adding that I wouldn't have left him even if I *could* have made it on my own. Jiss and I had had a strange sort of friendship, but I didn't believe in deserting people I'd agreed to call friend.

Jiss had said he'd tried using his father's heat to burn

himself free, and it hadn't worked. If the Lord of the Sun himself had tried it would have been another story, but Jiss was only his father's son, not his designated heir. He could only use a part of his father's talents and abilities, just as I could use only a part of my mother's—

I had to stand free of the wall when I raised my hands and cupped them around the scintillating jewels holding Jiss in place, but it was necessary so I managed it. My hands shielded the diamonds from the only source of light in the room, and when I felt the shadows form beneath my palms I shifted them over every part of that obscene bracelet. The Lord of the Earth had linked together a number of smaller gems rather than use one single large one, maybe to torment Jiss into believing it would be possible to break free, but I was hoping he'd outsmarted himself by doing that. I didn't have heat to use, or even the strength of absolute darkness, but my time in that Realm had given me something else.

Cold. The cold I rarely ever felt in my mother's Realm, the cold I had too often felt over the last few days, a reservoir of special strength I hadn't realized I was building until it became necessary to use it. My mother used cold the way Jiss's father used heat, and I, as her daughter, could use some part of that ability. I fed cold into the shadows under my hands, and made myself believe it would be enough.

And abruptly it was. Jiss had frowned as he watched me, but as soon as he felt the cold he seemed to understand what I was doing. He waited a moment, giving the cold a chance to penetrate the jewels, and then he jerked his wrist hard against the restraint that had held him so well. The diamonds, having grown really brittle, cracked at their link points and scattered to the floor, and Jiss now had one hand free.

I had to stand mostly unsupported when I freed his second wrist, but at least I was able to sit on the floor while I did his ankles. It seemed to take nearly forever before he collapsed to the stone beside me, but at last it was done and we could rest for a while. Jiss lay stretched out on his right side, his face a mask covering what had to be a lot of pain, his eyes closed while he fought to regain control of himself. I knew he was very strong, much stronger than most, but there's a limit to even the greatest amount of strength.

Even though Jiss had stretched out I continued to sit where I'd been, my head hanging and my eyes closed, but still in a seated position. I was fairly certain that if I lay down I'd never get up again, and I didn't want to put that sort of burden on Jiss. When he was ready to go I had to be the same, but I'd underestimated the amount of recovery time he would allow himself. After what couldn't have been more than fifteen minutes I heard him grunt as he forced his body into movement, and then faint footsteps followed him across the room. Another few minutes went by without more to be heard than faint scuffling, and then there were suddenly bootsteps coming back to me from the other side of the room.

"I thought I was wasting my time noticing where they put our clothes and my gear, but I still took the trouble to notice and remember," Jiss said, going down to one knee beside me to put a hand to my shoulder. "Do you think you can get dressed on your own, or would you like me to help you?"

"Right now I'm having trouble breathing on my own," I whispered, finding the effort to keep my eyes open almost more than I could do. "I know you're more used to handling the matter the other way around, but if you can help me get the clothes on I'll appreciate it."

"If I simply reverse the procedure in my mind, I shouldn't have any trouble," he said with a chuckle, then began easing me flat to the floor. "I can get your trousers on more easily if you're lying down, and then I'll help you sit up again. And I think we ought to do something about those wounds that are still bleeding."

"No, Jiss, it will take too much time," I disagreed, knowing the wounds I'd been given by the man in red were more painful than serious. "They're not bleeding so hard that I'm likely to find the next level because of them, so let's just concentrate on getting out of here. Once we're free, we can take as much time as we like."

His expression said he didn't want to agree with me, but he knew we really had no other choice. He worked as fast as he could getting my trousers and sandals on while still being gentle, and then he helped me back to sitting to put my shirt on. The clothing brought me memories of Skyhawk, which in turn seemed to add warmly to my store of strength, so when Jiss finally began helping and urging me to my feet, I was able to mix my own effort with his. Once erect I had time to notice that Jiss also wore his sword, and then we were heading for the door out of the room.

Every step of the way back to the room with the bronze throne I expected us to suddenly run into guardsmen at the very least, but we reached the door leading to it and nothing like that had happened. Jiss was moving considerably better than I'd thought he would, but I was moving worse and he almost had to carry me. I didn't want to think about how it would be, getting through the rest of that very large house with its equally large numbers of guardsmen, but I didn't expect it to be anywhere near as easy as it had been up until then. At some point or other there would be a fight, and all I'd be able to do would be to stay out of Jiss's way.

Jiss opened the door a crack and peeked out, then opened it the rest of the way and got us both through it. The throne room was still as magnificent as it had been, but just then it was also completely deserted. As we moved at the fastest pace I could manage toward the drapes and the double doors leading out, Jiss made a faint sound of amusement.

"If I had to guess, I'd say the high and mighty Lord of the Earth doesn't know you're a balancing force," he told me in a very soft voice that nevertheless also showed his amusement. "If he had known he would have had his tame sadist do more than simply hurt me, just to be sure I'd be useless if I somehow did manage to get free. Right now I'm almost back to full strength from having touched you, and I expect it to get even better than that. The Lord of a Realm has no business also being a fool.''

I smiled at what Jiss had said, and not only because I appreciated the joke the Lord of the Earth had played on himself. I had been so much around Earth Realm people that I'd forgotten Jiss would know about balancing forces, and he was absolutely right. By firmly believing he would get stronger rather than weaker he did exactly that, showing the benefit in the proper upbringing. If you're taught from childhood to believe in yourself, you have much less trouble as an adult.

The thought was a comforting one, but the comfort lasted only until we were halfway to the drapes. That was when the drapes parted and the red-robed Lord Craver appeared, followed by half a dozen guardsmen. Jiss and I stopped short immediately, but the group coming toward us continued on a few steps before doing the same, and then Lord Craver chuckled.

"Well, well, what a happy chance meeting," he said with his usual delight, his pale eyes glittering. "If we'd been a few minutes later or you a few minutes earlier, we would have missed each other. Now my companions and I can keep you two company on the brief journey back to the interrogation room, where we'll all have a lovely chat about how you happen to be here. Will you gentlemen please help our guests?''

The last of his words were directed toward the six guardsmen behind him, but Jiss hadn't waited for them to be spoken. He let me move back and away from him, and then he drew the sword I'd known he would need.

"She and I won't be going back to that room," he said flatly, watching as the guardsmen drew their own weapons. "And if you want to know how we freed ourselves, ask your Highest Lord. If you put the question right, he may even be able to tell you."

For once it seemed that Lord Craver had something to frown over, which he did while the guardsmen moved out and past him to my and Jiss's left. Lord Craver hadn't liked what Jiss had said and wasn't pleased with the—

unhurt—way he moved, and then the first of his guardsmen closed with his former victim. Steel rang in a quick flurry of attacks and parries, a series that made the guardsmen frown exactly the way Lord Craver was doing, then he was beyond all frowning and fighting. Jiss's point found the center of his chest, and even as he fell the other five came forward together.

If the surviving guardsmen thought Jiss would fall quickly to their concerted attack, they found out instead how wrong they were. Jiss went to them rather than waiting for them to come to him, and an instant later all six of them were engaged, Jiss outnumbered but certainly not overmatched. I felt a surge of pride inside me that this, rather than the so-called Highest Lord, was one of my own, and then pride and gladness disappeared as a hand closed on my right arm.

"They'll wear him down eventually, my pretty, but we don't have to stand here waiting for it," Lord Craver said, his other arm coming to circle my waist. "You and I will go back to our room, and pass the time with more interesting diversions. Let me help you around that confusion of fighting."

He began trying to force me to the left, around where Jiss stood holding off five blades to his one, and once we were past that there would be nothing between us and the door I would rather be ended than go back through. Fear added to my meager strength and allowed me to struggle, but despite my being larger than Lord Craver the fear alone wasn't enough. He grew annoyed with my attempted resistance and moved his hand higher on my side, knowing exactly where the worst of what he had done to me could be found, and pressed hard enough to make me cry out and double over. The pain was terrible, bringing waves of dizziness and nausea that were difficult to resist even from my position on all fours; I had healed some small amount from when I had first been savaged, but not nearly far enough.

"And now you've been reminded how stubbornness is rewarded," Lord Craver said as he bent over me, his hand stroking my hair. "Once we have you on your feet again, there won't be any more of it, will there? Come now, up on your feet."

His stroking hand suddenly closed in my hair, and his fist began trying to pull me erect. I cried out again at the added pain, knowing Jiss was too busy protecting his own life to help me, knowing there was nothing I could do to help myself. There were times like that, I had learned, times when you're helpless to protect yourself no matter how competent you are. You have to depend on the help of others, understanding all the while that there's no shame in something like that, but there wasn't anyone there to help me. I understood, and felt anger rather than shame, but no one was there—

And then Lord Craver made a choking sound as his hand withdrew from my hair, and that was something I didn't understand. It took an effort but I twisted around to look up at him—then sat on the floor with my eyes wide. Lord Craver was now the one struggling, specifically against the wide arm wrapped around his throat, an arm that belonged to—Skyhawk! My beloved's face was twisted into a mask of fury, and his arm closed tighter and tighter around Lord Craver's throat, choking the life out of him. I watched in silence as he accomplished his purpose, and when he was able to let the lifeless body drop, he left it and hurried over to me.

"Haliand, are you all right?" he demanded, going to one knee so that he might put a hand to my face. "Hold on, it won't be long before you're out of here."

"Right now I'm perfectly all right," I said with the most foolish smile I'd ever managed, taking his other hand in both of mine. "As soon as we *are* out of here, I'll show you exactly how all right I am."

"I'm looking forward to that," he answered with a smile of his own, and then he took his hands from me. "Don't try to get up by yourself, you'll have help in another minute or two. Right now I'm needed elsewhere."

As I watched him get to his feet again I had the urge to say I needed him just as badly, but it wasn't really true.

Skyhawk drew his sword as he turned from me, and then he was hurrying over to help Jiss, who wasn't doing as well as he had only a few minutes earlier. Jiss hadn't regained all of his strength, and the five men were beginning to tire him.

Skyhawk stormed into the fight from Jiss's left, and the two fought together for a few moments while they exchanged some words I couldn't quite hear. Then they stopped talking and concentrated on nothing but fighting, but that didn't last long either. Skyhawk suddenly went into a flurry of action that ended one of their five opponents and drove the other four back, and then Jiss was disengaged and sheathing his sword as he left the fight, turning away before hurrying over to me.

"Come on, Hali, we've got to get you out of here," Jiss muttered as he bent, and then he had lifted me off the floor in his arms and had straightened again. "The others don't know what's going on yet, but it's only a matter of time before they find out. When that happens, we want to be gone."

"But, Jiss, what about Skyhawk?" I protested, trying to find the strength somewhere to resist being carried toward the drapes. "We can't just leave him here!"

"It was his idea," Jiss answered, paying more attention to where he was going than to my feeble efforts to stop him. "He's guarding our retreat, and as soon as we're clear he'll follow. He also told me to turn right once we're out in the hall."

By then we were through the drapes and up to the first set of double doors, one of which stood open. Jiss carried me through it into a deserted outer waiting room, through that to the second set of doors, and out into the hall. Jiss barely paused as he made his way through the unmoving bodies of the guardsmen who had been guarding the outer doors, but I couldn't help staring and worrying. Skyhawk had done that on his way in, I knew he had, and we had left him all alone to do the same again. He had to be tired from having fought at least once already, but we had still left him alone.

Jiss made the turn right and continued up the hall, watching ahead of us while I watched behind. It was Skyhawk I was watching for, trying to will him into appearing in the hall behind us, but we reached the end and abruptly turned left and he still hadn't appeared. I glanced ahead to see where we were going, and really began feeling ill. Another two bodies lay beside a small door that seemed to lead outside, and the man who had undoubtedly done that as well still hadn't caught up.

Outside the door it was almost sundown, and although there were no more bodies I was certain there should have been. The door we left by was at the side and rear of the very large house, and although we had to cross a wide, open area that passed in front of stables, we made it to the woods beyond without anyone seeing us. Jiss was breathing heavily by then and I, without having done anything strenuous at all, was feeling dizzy, but at least we were clear and into the woods.

"Jiss, now we can stop for a while," I urged, still looking over his shoulder back toward where we'd come from. "You need to regain your strength, and Skyhawk needs time to catch up with us."

"Can't stop yet," Jiss panted, working hard to stay on his feet and keep moving, unable even to glance at me. "Need more distance between us and them. He'll catch up."

"But he may need us to help!" I whispered, trying again to fight my way free of the arms holding me up. "Jiss, we have to stop, and maybe go back, or he could end up being—"

I couldn't bring myself to say the word, and then I realized I couldn't say any word. The dizziness and pain I felt were increasing with every step Jiss took, and I didn't know how long I could hold off unconsciousness. Things began blurring and growing unreal, and then, suddenly, someone was taking me from Jiss's arms into his own. For an instant I was certain it was Skyhawk and my joy surged through everything else, but then my vision cleared and I saw I was wrong. The man holding me was one of my mother's Guardsmen, and others of them were working to keep Jiss on his feet. We were both being taken to where a large number of horses were tied, Sahrinth and Greaf waiting agitatedly beside them, and I tried to cry out that they couldn't take me away. I couldn't leave Skyhawk, couldn't leave my beloved, but awareness left me instead and it was done anyway.

Chapter 14

I STOOD IN THE SHADOWS and stared out over the marble balcony balustrade, trying to reach the peace of the night. Behind me was a pleasant murmur of voices coming from those who partook of the High Moon meal, but they were further back on the main part of the terrace. Where I stood I was alone, but even that wasn't bringing me closer to the peace I searched for. Truthfully, I didn't think anything would ever bring me to it again, but in a very short while I would try the only thing I could. I had to know for certain, no matter how painful the knowing was.

"Hali, why are you all the way over here and all alone?" my mother's concerned voice came suddenly from behind me. "The meal is just about ready to be served, but when we looked around you weren't there for it to be served *to*. Aren't you feeling well?"

"I'm feeling fine, Mother," I said with a smile as I turned to her, and the statement was even mostly true. "If you need someone to worry about, I'm afraid you're going to have to look elsewhere."

"I'm delighted to hear that," she said with a smile of her own as she smoothed my hair with a hand, the relief immediately turning her radiant. "To tell the truth, I was getting a little tired of having to worry only about you. It's much more fun worrying about a variety of people, and you're obviously too far recovered to need worrying about.

Even Prince Jentris remarked how well you looked after only a 'couple of days' worth of healing, and he said to tell you it wasn't fair. He still needs taking care of, and since he's bigger than you are, that shouldn't be, he insists.''

"All he really needs is rest," I said with an amused shake of my head, wondering if Jiss would ever learn not to call the passage of time in my mother's Realm "days." "And the last time I saw him, he didn't look to be in that much of a hurry to end being taken care of. He seems to enjoy having Felissa fussing over him."

"As much as she enjoys doing the fussing," my mother answered, and then her smile faded. "Hali, I've had the strangest conviction lately, one that shouldn't be true but refuses to go away. I feel that you'll soon be leaving again, but that isn't right, is it?"

"I'm afraid it is, Mother," I said with a sigh, reaching out to take one of her nervously moving hands. "I was waiting only until I was back to full health and strength, and now that I am I'll be leaving. I have to go back to the Earth Realm, to find out what happened to Skyhawk. If they captured him and he's still alive, I've got to try getting him out of there. If they ended him instead . . . well, I need to know that, too."

"The Earth Realm ephemeral who helped you and Prince Jentris to escape that madman's capture," she said with a nod, obviously having gotten the story from Jiss. "I can understand your concern and your need to repay the debt, but Haliand—are you sure *you* have to go?"

"I'm very sure, Mother," I answered, squeezing the hand I still held. "If you need your own doubts laid to rest, I'm willing to stand before the Scales of Judgment with you again."

"I wish I could convince myself it would do some good," she said with a sigh like the one I'd produced, tightening her own grip on my hand. "Before you left for the Earth Realm you were still a child, doing things mostly on impulse and hoping you were right rather than being sure of it. Now—now you're a grown woman, able to see

for yourself the proper path to follow, and I no longer have
the right to make you accept my help in formulating your
decisions. I knew that would happen sometime, but it still
seems so soon! You *will* be very careful, won't you?''

"Much more careful than last time, I can tell you," I
assured her, then gestured her into walking back toward
the couches with me. "The man who hurt Jentris and me
so badly is gone, but I don't for a minute believe he was
the only one of his kind in the Lord of the Earth's employ. I
want to get Skyhawk out of there, not join him for more of
what I went through the first time. The idea of going back
really frightens me, Mother, but it's something I need very
much to do."

"You really have matured, haven't you?" she said,
glancing at me as we walked with the smile that had
returned. "Not long ago you would have preferred being
ended to having to admit to being afraid of something, the
way you were of Prince Jentris. He frightened you on
purpose, of course, to teach you not to play those silly
tricks again, but you didn't know that. As far as you were
concerned, he was serious."

"I was also silly enough to believe you didn't know
what I had done," I said with a laugh. "Since I hadn't
been yelled at I assumed I'd gotten away with it, not
realizing that Jentris had probably asked you not to make a
fuss over it. He really is a very decent man, as my sisters
will find out when he chooses one of them to marry."

"You knew right from the beginning that you and he
would never make a couple," she said, pausing beside a
tray to help herself to a cup of wine before turning to study
me. "I should have seen that as a sign of your approaching
maturity, but I was too involved with everything else. You
didn't . . ."

"I do beg your pardon for this intrusion, my Lady," a
dryly courteous voice interrupted, causing my mother and
me to turn to see Feledor and his precisely correct bow. "I
haven't as yet had an opportunity to welcome the Princess
Haliand back to our Realm, and assure her how greatly
missed she was. I would like also to request a private

moment or two of your time, to discuss a matter directly concerning the Princess."

"You'd be wasting your time, Lord Feledor," I said before my mother could answer, reaching over for my own cup of wine. "Telling my mother you want to marry me won't get you the agreement you think it will, because she won't give you an answer without checking first with me. I have no interest in marrying you, now or even sometime in the future, so you'd do well to begin looking elsewhere."

His light eyes had come to me condescendingly, the way they had always done, and I wondered briefly how I could have feared him. The man was so taken up with his own importance that he paid little or no attention to those around him, assuming them to be inferior and therefore good for nothing but dismissal. He was right in believing his support was important to my mother; where he was wrong was in believing his support was more important than her daughters.

"My dear Haliand, I have no desire to look elsewhere than you," the man said smoothly, clearly showing amusement at what I'd said. "In your youth and innocence you undoubtedly expect to be immediately smitten with the man you're meant for, touched by the lightning of love, so to speak. Allow me to assure you that such things are no more than fantasy, child, and that you'll certainly soon come to appreciate the benefit of being paired with a man mature enough to give your life a proper direction. One cannot merely float or grope one's way through forever, you know."

"Why, Lord Feledor, how delightfully poetic," I exclaimed, making it necessary for my mother to use her wine cup to camouflage her expression. "The lightning of love, and floating one's way through forever. And you're quite right, you know: one isn't always smitten at first glance."

"You agree?" he said in surprise, at long last beginning to look at something more than my face and figure—or my youth and innocence. "I hadn't thought . . ."

"You most certainly didn't think," I interrupted, taking

immediate advantage of his choice of words. "If you *had* made the effort, you might have managed to understand that normal people most need someone to teach them how to direct their own lives, not someone to do the directing for them. Since it's a puppet you seem to want, Lord Feledor, try a toymaker's shop. Even if you managed to get me instead, you'd hardly be pleased with your prize. I've already learned how to pull my own strings. And now, if you don't mind, my mother and I were in the midst of a private conversation."

The man frowned just a little, turned his gaze to my mother as his lips began to part, then finally noticed she was looking at him with the same dismissal I'd already put into words. Wearing an expression that said he was confused and taken aback he bowed instead of speaking, then turned and hurried away. He seemed to need some thinking time, an awareness I hadn't thought he was capable of.

"And that should solve your problem with him," my mother murmured, watching as the man disappeared back in the direction of his couch. "Feledor was never one to find interest in a woman who was confident enough in herself to dismiss him, which you weren't before your trip. I'm looking forward to the time you feel ready to talk about your experiences. When you *are* ready, just let me know."

"I will, Mother," I said with a smile, then joined her in a hug before we separated to go to our respective couches. I took my cup of wine with me, but my interest in it didn't last any longer than my smile. Smiles were only for reassuring those you loved and those who loved you; they did nothing to warm the empty places deep inside which most needed warming.

I ate every bit I could stuff down during the meal, but not simply to reassure my mother. I intended to leave as soon after the meal as possible, and starting the journey on an empty stomach wouldn't have been very smart. I left my couch with the first of the guests to do the same, slipping out while my mother was in the middle of a conversation with Jiss, whose couch still stood close to hers. I wanted to be gone before Jiss decided honor demanded that he come with me, even if he still wasn't back to where he should be healthwise. That second time he really would be more of a burden than a help, especially since I intended moving around only 'at night. I'd learned to know where my strengths really lay, and wasn't about to ignore that knowledge.

My suite was as empty as it should have been, which meant Greaf and Sahrinth were off taking care of their own affairs in preparation for leaving with me. My last instructions to them before going after Jiss had worked out well enough that my mother's guardsmen were already there and waiting when Jiss and I reached the forest, a different contingent of them having previously retrieved the Great Flame and taken it back to my mother. If those guardsmen hadn't been there Jiss and I could have been recaptured, and we would definitely have had a much harder time of it even if we'd stayed free. Greaf, Sahrinth and I made a nicely effective team, and there was no sense in not taking advantage of that.

I packed the trouser outfit I meant to take with me and laid out a similar outfit I intended to wear, but sat down to study my map before changing out of the draperies I'd worn to the meal. The map showed the best route to and from the Doorway we'd used returning to my mother's Realm, a true, actual Doorway rather than the Realm Threshold we'd been forced to use the first time. It was situated near the house in which the Lord of the Earth had held us prisoner, and it hadn't taken us long to figure out why the more distant Threshold had been used rather than the nearer Doorway. Anyone going across the Threshold would be rendered unconscious, but with servants or slaves waiting for the thief, only those pursuing, if any, would be at a disadvantage. Chance had seen to it that it didn't work out that way, but that had almost certainly been the plan.

I sighed as I sat and stared at the map, beginning to hate the word *plan*. Everyone had made plans, including me, but we none of us were having our plans work out the way we wanted them to. I remembered how I'd felt when we'd left Skyhawk behind, how every ache I'd had had hurt worse at the thought of possibly never seeing him again. Even if he was still alive and I managed to free him, I'd be facing the exact same thing again one day, the pain of losing him before I was ready. Somehow I knew I'd never be prepared for losing him, no matter how long or short a time we spent together.

I sat back from the map I really wasn't seeing, feeling a Wish trying to rise up inside of me. Revered Ancestors, I wanted to say, please make him the way he was supposed to be, the way I am. He's an ephemeral, you see, and I'll have to watch him grow older and older until he reaches his ending, watch him watching me while I don't. If you can't make him like me then make me like him, so the two of us can face together the same happenings. I don't mind ending before my time, if that's what's going to happen to him . . .

But you can't make a Wish like that alone, you have to be joined by the other person involved, and I was absolutely certain Skyhawk would never agree. Oh, he would probably have no objections to being made like me, but the other side of it, the possibility of me being made like him—I just couldn't see him agreeing to that. He'd refuse to let me give up anything for him, would refuse to see how much more I'd have to give up if he didn't agree— stupid, stubborn men, who only wanted the best for you . . .

I left my chair to walk around a little, determined to try talking him into Wishing with me even if I had almost no chance of succeeding. I'd first have to explain about Wishing, of course, and everything else he didn't yet know, and bring him home with me to give us a chance to really get to know each other—

But what if he didn't want to come home with me, or didn't believe what I told him? What if he simply laughed at my silly flights of imagination, and gently but firmly refused even to try a Doorway? I couldn't very well drag him bodily, and if all he did was laugh . . .

"Hali, please come here a moment," my mother's voice

suddenly came from the room's sphere of water, her image too small to be seen clearly from that distance. I moved closer to the sphere, wondering why she sounded so odd, and once I was near enough for her to see me she tried to smile.

"Hali, would you come to the entertainment room, please?" she said, the smile not quite making it. "There's— someone here from the Realm of the Earth, and he asked to see the woman who was held captive by the Highest Lord. I think he may—have word—about the man we were discussing. He's . . . obviously a close blood relation to the Lord of the Earth."

I think my heart came close to stopping still at that, and I finally understood why my mother was so upset. If the Lord of the Earth had sent a member of his family to speak to me, then Skyhawk was as good as lost. The Lord of the Earth would demand the Great Flame in exchange for Skyhawk's freedom, and when he was refused he would lose no time ending my beloved. That, of course, was why my mother was so upset; she knew we would have to refuse, and that decision, no matter how necessary, would still be a betrayal of the man who had saved my life, and Jiss's. I wanted to shiver violently, and maybe even become very ill, but all I did was nod woodenly at my mother's image.

"I'll be right there," I said, the only thing *to* say, and then I turned away from the sphere and headed out of my suite. At first my mind was having trouble thinking, but once I was in the hall and moving toward the entertainment room, I began considering the possibility of using the man who had been sent as a lever to free Skyhawk. He was surely in our Realm under a flag of truce, a flag he was certain to believe we would honor. It was hardly likely he understood how my mother felt about that, how she was of the opinion that to let those without honor do you harm through your own sense of honor was downright stupid. You behaved honorably with those who did the same, and simply defended yourself against those who couldn't be trusted. The Lord of the Earth and his people couldn't be trusted, but there might be a way they could be used.

Again the lights were bright in my mother's entertainment room, but the guardsmen standing in the shadows outside were not as relaxed as they'd been when Jiss had been the guest in there. I didn't need to tell them to stay alert as I passed, and they knew they didn't need to warn me to be careful. If my expression was half as grim as it felt, it would be left to others to be careful of *me*.

My mother looked around as I entered the room, her expression a study in neutrality, but her guest was too engrossed in staring at the mirror table to have heard me come in. He was dressed all in blue leather, light blue shirt, medium blue trousers, dark blue boots, and even his swordbelt was a bluish gray. He had dark hair and was fairly tall, and I hated him so much my mother made a small sound of shock as she looked at me. That sound finally caused the stranger to shift his gaze away from the table and to her face, and when he saw her staring beyond him he quickly turned.

"I can explain," he said at once, wincing just a little at what he too saw in my expression. "I know I said I would follow as soon as I could, but those guardsmen were better than I'd expected them to be, and by the time I finally reached the woods you were gone. Then half the guards in the house started chasing me, so—"

"Skyhawk, you idiot, what are you doing here?" I demanded in what was pure shock, suddenly so deeply buried in confusion that I was seriously in danger of smothering. "I thought you were still back at that house, and I was just getting ready to come after you—!"

"I thought you might be, and that's the real reason I tried to hurry," he said very softly as he closed the distance between us, and then his arms were around me. "I wanted to follow as soon as I reached the woods, but if I had I would have led the pursuit right into your lap. I had to draw them away in another direction first, and once I'd lost them I tried picking up your party—and found that I couldn't. You and the people who had apparently been waiting to help you had simply disappeared.''

"Was that when you were taken captive by that madman?'' I asked, still more confused than thinking clearly. "Did he send you here with that member of his family, trying to make it harder for us to refuse his demands? Does he think we'll honor a twisted truce like that, letting him take you away again to be ended instead of breaking truce and freeing you? If he does, he's even more insane than—''

"Haliand, Haliand, calm down,'' Skyhawk soothed, his face now more sober than it had been. "You're upsetting yourself for nothing. I'm in no danger, and there's no truce you have to worry about breaking. I wasn't captured, and I came here alone.''

"But—I don't understand,'' I managed to get out, and then I looked over at my mother. "Didn't you say there was a member of the Lord of the Earth's family here? I'm certain you said that, so where did he go?''

"Hali, I think there's been a misunderstanding,'' my mother said slowly as she walked over to join us, her expression now thoughtful. "This is the man who saved you and Prince Jentris, the man you intended to go back for?''

"Of course he is,'' I answered impatiently, and then I understood what must have happened. "You thought he was a member of the Lord of the Earth's family?'' I laughed in relief and shook my head. "No wonder we've all been so confused, thinking we had an enemy in our midst. He's not an enemy, he's the man I—''

"Haliand,'' Skyhawk interrupted again, and this time *sober* was too pale a word to describe him. He not only looked grim, he had taken taken his arms from around me, and simply stood there staring down at me.

"Haliand, before you say something you might regret, you have to know that the Lady of your Realm has seen something you haven't,'' he told me, his tone just short of absolute neutrality. "As a child I learned there were easily identifiable resemblances between members of a Realm Family, and anyone familiar with the resemblances will know a Family member on sight. My real name is Arrik, and I'm . . . a brother of the Lord of the Earth.''

He said the words and then waited for me to respond, but I couldn't think of any response. All that came to me was the fleeting memory of what one of my sisters had said, when I first began learning how to Wish. Be careful of what you Wish for, she'd said, seriously enough to make me know she wasn't joking. If you aren't careful, you could get something you weren't expecting. It looked like I'd been Wishing a little too hard, while at the same time not being quite careful enough.

"Arrik is a name that's been in your Family for many generations," my mother said to Skyhawk, sounding casual and no more than faintly curious. "Is that why you used another name instead, to keep your own from being recognized?"

"Most of the people I associated with wouldn't have been able to recognize it," he answered her with a shrug, his dark eyes still unmoving from my face. "I took the name Skyhawk because I was ashamed of being who I was, a member of a Family too vile for anyone decent to stomach. It was the same reason I didn't tell Haliand or Jentris who I really was. All I wanted to do was help them, the way I always try to help as many of my father's and brother's victims as I can. I wasn't trying to mislead anyone—"

"Well, this makes for a very awkward situation," my mother said, just as though she hadn't heard the near pleading in the last of his words. "I hadn't expected something like this, and with a madman for a brother, I'm sure you can understand the difficulty. Under the circumstances, we none of us have any choice at all."

"You want me to go," he said, not flatly but with such utter-despair-fully-accepted that I felt the pain clear down to my core. "I can understand your not wanting a member of your Household associating with someone like me, and I can't argue the point. I'll just—"

"No," I interrupted, the decision so complete and sure that doubt simply didn't enter into it. "No one can blame you for what your father and brother have done, not when you were one of their victims yourself. You are not simply leaving this Realm, and certainly not without me.''

''Haliand, it's not that easy,'' he said with a sigh, my statements having barely cheered him. ''When we first met I thought you were from my Realm, the highborn daughter of some wealthy family. That bothered me for a little while for a reason I won't go into, but then I realized it didn't change anything about the way I felt. You were meant to be mine, and that's the way I wanted it. After I lost those guardsmen and then couldn't locate the party you were riding with, I spent a long time searching before it occurred to me to ask the trees. That was when I found out you were from this Realm.''

''You can speak to the trees, too?'' I exclaimed, at first surprised and then surprised I hadn't guessed sooner. ''So that was how you knew the outlaws were in the forest and riding after us, just before we hid among the thorns. And that was how you kept following me through the forest. I'd asked the trees to warn me of the approach of enemies, but they knew you weren't an enemy.''

''They certainly did,'' he said with a smile, but then the smile faded. ''Anyway, once I knew where you'd gone I was delighted. I got some clothes that were a little more presentable for the occasion, then made my first trip through a Doorway. Your Realm is very beautiful and the people friendly and helpful, but when I asked about the girl who had recently been brought back from the Earth Realm, they didn't know who I meant. The last of them suggested I ask the Lady of the Realm, since she was the one who knew about everything. I thought that was a good idea— until I discovered you were a member of her Household. With all the trouble going on between our two Realms, it would be very embarrassing for your Lady to have a member of her Household involved with the brother of her enemy. That's why I *will* be leaving. Alone.''

The look in his eyes was a perfect match to the way I felt, a sense of mourning for something that had died before it had ever had a chance to grow. I hadn't considered the position my mother would be put in because of my relationship with Skyhawk, but once it had been pointed out I wasn't too thick to understand. She couldn't support me here the way she had in the situation with Feledor, not when there was serious trouble involved. Skyhawk—Arrik—and I were meant for each other, but sometimes things that are meant still never come to be.

"I'm tempted to pull out my hanky and have a good cry," my mother said suddenly, her voice so dry that both Skyhawk and I were startled into looking at her. She stood gazing at us with an expression that said we were probably beyond hope, but she would still make one last attempt to reclaim us as normal members of society.

"I'm touched that the two of you are so concerned with not embarrassing me," she said, the words and her manner downright bland. "The only problem is, Prince Arrik, you've made a few mistakes, one of them being your assumption that Hali is a member of my Household. The truth is, she isn't."

"She isn't?" Skyhawk echoed with a frown of confusion, then his expression cleared and he laughed in delight. "But that's wonderful! It means there's no reason she and I can't—"

"Arrik, she's my daughter," my mother interrupted, now being very gentle. "You must have left your Family at a very early age, or you would have recognized her name as being one in *my* Family for generations. A Princess of my House is not considered a member of my Household."

"Then it's even more hopeless than I thought," Skyhawk said tonelessly. "It was always possible she might leave your Household someday and then we'd be able to get together, but now even that chance is gone. Unless I'm very much mistaken, she won't ever stop being your daughter."

"No, you're quite right," my mother said. "I'm very happy to say she never will stop being my daughter, but you're continuing to make those mistakes I mentioned. Rather than turning the situation hopeless, her being my daughter solves your problem. That's certainly clear enough to me.''

"Mother, if you don't stop tormenting him, I'll—I'll think up an escapade that the people of this Realm will talk about for the next century!'' I snapped, moving closer to Skyhawk to put my arms around him. "You have him in such a state he doesn't even know what to say, which you may consider amusing, but I don't!''

"Hali, dear, I'm not trying to torture either one of you,'' she answered, her expression gentle. "I'm trying to teach you not to jump to conclusions, especially since neither of you has enough information on how the Realms work to make those conclusions even faintly valid. You two don't have to worry about separating, and if you'll join me in getting comfortable on those couches over there, I'll be glad to explain why.''

"Mother, please, tell us why now,'' I came close to begging, knowing all too well what "getting comfortable" would consist of. First we'd sit down, and then we'd have to be served, and then— Skyhawk's arms had come around me as mine had gone around him, and I could almost feel him waiting to hear something that would turn out to be not quite as problem solving as my mother thought.

"The impatience of youth,'' the Lady of the Realm said with a headshake and a sigh, but rather than insisting, she gave in with her usual grace. "All right, you two, here it is. If Hali were a member of my Household, it would be improper for her to associate with anyone from what can be considered an enemy Realm, and that covers simply talking to them. She would be betraying my interests by transfering her loyalty to someone from an enemy House. Do you follow that?''

Skyhawk and I nodded together, having no trouble understanding the point. What I, at least, couldn't see was how our true situation was any better.

"Will you two please stop looking so tragic?'' my mother said in exasperation, her annoyance aimed at both of us equally. "I've already told you that the same thing doesn't apply to my daughter, and certainly not with a

Prince of what will soon be declared a tainted House. We weren't able to prove what we believed your father did to his people, Arrik, but your brother's recent actions are enough to condemn not only him, but his father as well. Your brother is clearly mad, a condition he's obviously been suffering from for many years, but your father named him Heir anyway, even with other sons to choose from. The only reason a Lord would do that to the people of his Realm is if he himself suffered from the same madness, and strove to perpetuate illness in place of sanity. Those Who Ruled Before have no choice but to declare your House tainted, and that means you're very important to all of us.''

"What could make *me* that important?" Skyhawk asked, trying not to sound as though he disbelieved everything he'd heard. "I'm nothing more than a renegade son of what was once an honorable House, and not even the only remaining son. The rest of my brothers have established estates as far from Trayron as they could get, and spend most of their time hoping he'll forget they're around. What I spend my time on is making as much trouble for Trayron as I can, with not even a small estate to show for my efforts. In most people's estimates, that would make me rather *un*important.''

"Arrik, you really must start spending some of your time associating with whole, normal people," my mother told him, now more upset than exasperated. "The fact that you alone are trying to do something to right your brother's wrongs, means you alone have no trace of the taint the rest of your Family suffers from. There isn't anyone in this Realm or the Sun Realm who would simply ignore the doings of someone like your brother Trayron, not if they weren't touched with the same illness. You're the only one not touched so, which means your original Family line can be saved only through *you*. In a situation like this, it's the duty of a daughter of another line to help save yours, and the question of disloyalty never enters into it. Now do you understand?''

"I understand the words, if that's what you mean,"

Skyhawk answered slowly, sounding very much like a man in a desert who sees what he knows can't really be water. "Your explanation does well in seeing to your daughter's happiness, Lady, which shows how deeply you care for her. The only thing that hasn't been shown is how someone not in your position will take all this, someone like the Lord of the Sun. With all due respect, I'm afraid you can't speak for him."

"But I can," another voice interrupted before my mother could protest what had been said to her, causing us all to turn. Jiss stood in the doorway with a faint smile on his face, and as he began walking toward us the smile widened to a grin.

"So your real name is Arrik, is it?" he asked Skyhawk, coming to a stop only a few feet away. "It's a good thing I didn't know that in the Earth Realm, or there might have been trouble. I wasn't feeling very happy with your Family just then."

"I can't imagine why," Skyhawk returned, the dryness trying to cover a good measure of uneasiness. "You have to admit it's hard finding elsewhere the sort of hospitality my brother likes to provide."

"Yes, there definitely is that," Jiss agreed with a laugh, and then his expression softened. "Skyhawk, my friend, the Lady wasn't indulging in Wishful thinking on Hali's behalf, she was telling you the exact truth. Everyone in our Realms sees it the same way, and that includes my father. If you need my word on that, you have it."

"Your father," Skyhawk said with a frown, staring at Jiss, and then he nodded. "Once I found out about Haliand, I should have realized— What my brother stole was important to both of your Realms, wasn't it? When you and she were taken away in the wagon she'd said belonged to the thieves, I suddenly understood that the two of you were involved with him in a way I hadn't guessed. There were too many guards riding with the wagon for me to be able to stop it alone, and once you'd been taken inside the estate house I had to wait for my brother to leave. He always moved around a lot, going back and forth between

things occupying his attention, and when he went he took
most of his guardsmen with him— Jentris, are you sure
your father will agree?''

"Positive," Jiss said with his grin back, ignoring the
way Skyhawk had rambled on before asking the question
most important to him. "And before you ask for a tenth
time, let me inform you that one Prince doubting the word
of another Prince is grounds for a fight. Since I'm still not
back to full health that would be taking advantage of me,
so you'd better give it up and start believing."

"Maybe it's just that he doesn't want me as badly as he
claims," I said to Jiss as I moved away from Skyhawk to
stand alone. "If he refuses to believe we can be together
then we won't be, and he'll be off the hook. At that point
I'll have no one to occupy my time, so I'll have to look
around for someone. Maybe Feledor . . ."

I let my voice trail off thoughtfully, aware of the amusement Jiss and my mother were looking at me with, and
then I was even more aware of a big hand coming heavily
to my shoulder.

"That name you just mentioned," Skyhawk said in a
voice that was much too soft, yet at the same time harder
than anything I'd ever heard from him. "I'm afraid I
didn't quite hear it, but I'm sure I know what it was. You
said Arrik—didn't you."

The last of it was definitely not a question, something
that made Jiss and my mother chuckle, but it did more
than that for me. I turned back to Skyhawk with a gentle
laugh, moving away from the hand on my shoulder as I
closed with him, then circled his body with my arms.

"Of course the name was Arrik," I told him with a grin
as I looked up at him, happily feeling his own arms fold
quickly around me. "If you don't know the name will
always be Arrik, you're totally beyond hope."

"Somehow, *I* prefer the name Haliand," he said, returning my grin with dark, glowing eyes. "The only trouble is I don't think I'm pronouncing it right, so I'll have to
keep saying it and saying it until I learn. My Haliand, my
Haliand, my—''

By then our lips were together, and it took quite a number of minutes before we noticed we'd been left alone in the room. That wasn't a bad arrangement, but taking him quickly back to my suite was an even better one.

Skyhawk—Arrik—and I had a quiet marriage ceremony, something we might not have managed if everyone wasn't in the middle of getting ready for a much grander occasion: the wedding of Prince Jentris of the Sun Realm to my sister, Princess Felissa of the Moon Realm. Jiss had found that he really enjoyed Felissa's company, her shy good humor, her gentle manner—and the way he never had to say, "Now, Felissa . . ." It seemed as though they were made for each other, and my mother was very pleased.

My husband and I spent our time getting to know each other, and we had such a good time doing it that the Grand Occasion was on us before we realized that time had passed. The Lord of the Sun arrived with his ladies for the festivities, and my mother and her lords got busy entertaining them. The only break in that was when Arrik was presented to Jiss's father, and the Lord of the Sun Realm confirmed what Jiss and my mother had said. Once the happy times were properly seen to, Those Who Had Ruled Before would declare the rest of Arrik's Family tainted, and most of the Doorways to their Realm would be closed until something happened to right the situation. I wasn't quite sure what that something was supposed to be, but everyone went back to celebrating before I could find out.

Jentris and Felissa were united quickly and happily, and then the two Great Flames were brought out for their part of the ceremony. We were all gathered on the largest of the back lawns, hundreds of people moving around among the food and drink tables and the couches and chairs, multicolored lanterns casting bright shades under the black sky to add to everyone's joy. When the silver and gold boxes were brought out, an expectant hush spread quickly over everyone, and even Greaf blinked with eager anticipation. I'd expected my friend to still be feeling something—awkward—for the Sun Realm's Great Flame, but he no

longer did. He'd learned they really were nothing like the
same kind of life form, and the only feeling he'd been left
with was respect.

The Lady of the Moon Realm and the Lord of the Sun
Realm each opened the boxes of their respective Flames,
then each moved forward to bring the boxes closer together. The Flames rose higher and higher as they neared
one another, their light growing brighter and stronger, the
colors so beautiful it was almost painful to watch. Arrik
and I stood hand in hand, the two of us having no more
idea about what would happen than anyone else—and then
we cried out at the sudden, blinding explosion of light as
the two Flames met. Other cries sounded all around us,
upset heard because it couldn't be seen, and then our
vision cleared to show us—

The most unbelievable sight ever conceived of, magnificent, glorifying, humbling, delighting, awing—

The sky, the all-black sky, was no longer all black. We,
each of us, stood and stared upward, struck silent by the
sight of how it had changed, hundreds of eyes wide and
mouths agape.

"Look at all those tiny points of light!" Arrik whis-
pered to me, the words almost soundless with shock.
"There must be millions of them, more than millions!
Where did they come from?"

I knew he hadn't asked the question expecting to be
answered—most especially not by me—but the answer
came anyway, strangely singing in our heads.

*Blessed children, take joy in the first of our Gifts to
you,* the voice said, the voice, we somehow knew, of the
combined Great Flames. *We have set a part of ourselves
above you, as a symbol of our love, as a guardian of your
safety. Should anyone attempt to do you harm our symbol
will come to stand your protection, outnumbering however
many your enemy may bring to harm you. No longer are
you alone, no longer need you fear the loss of hope. The
symbol of hope is now above you, and shall remain there
forevermore.*

There was another second or two of silence, and then

everyone began speaking at once, an uproar of excitement that seemed beyond being calmed. We babbled at each other, hearing nothing that was being said to us, and then we joined the mindless moving about that had started, everyone looking for even more people to babble at. I have no idea how long that went on, but I finally looked around to see that Arrik and I had somehow filtered out of the crowd. Just then we stood not far from my mother, who also stood alone as she stared upward with a smile, so I tugged at Arrik's hand and we walked over to her.

"Now I understand why the Lord of the Earth wanted the Great Flame so badly," I said to her, bringing her gaze out of the glorious sky and down to me. "If he'd had forces like that at *his* disposal, he would have become the Lord of Everywhere."

"To our eternal sorrow," she agreed with a smile, putting a comforting hand on my husband's arm. "But he didn't get what he wanted and now that wonderful Gift belongs to everyone, even the people of the Earth Realm. They won't understand what it really means, but they'll be able to see it."

"It may be possible, to *help* some of them to understand," Arrik told her, his smile warm and genuine. "I'll be making regular trips back there, to ruin as many of Trayron's plans as I can, and to tell everyone who will listen that there's hope for them all. There's never been such a glorious symbol of hope, and it doesn't even matter what you're hoping for. If there's something worthy of your hope, the symbol for it will always be above you."

"Yes, that's what we'll be telling people when we make regular trips back," I said mildly, looking and smiling only at my mother. "There are some Earth Realm people I don't like even a little, but there are enough good people to more than make up for the first sort. I'm looking forward to meeting more of them on our trips."

"I'll see about bringing some of them back with me when I return from *my* trips," Arrik said in the same mild way, also looking only at my mother. "That way you can all get to know them safely, and I won't have to worry about what's being done to anyone I care about.''

I opened my mouth to continue the one argument we'd had in our otherwise peaceful time together, just as determined to go as my husband was that I wouldn't, but my mother cleared her throat, then plunged in before me.

"There's hope for a good deal more than what you just mentioned," she said with swallowed amusement, gesturing to us to walk slowly with her. "I'm glad to hear you intend continuing your opposition to Trayron, Arrik, for the sooner he falls, the sooner the people of the Earth Realm will be restored, and the sooner you two can play your part in all this.''

"What do you mean, our part?" Arrik asked, beating me to it by no more than seconds. "I didn't know we had any special part.''

"Well, you certainly do," my mother answered with a twinkling smile, glancing at both of us. "Those Who Ruled Before can declare your Family tainted, but they can't do anything to remove Trayron from his place. The people of the Earth Realm must do that themselves, and only then will they begin being restored to what they once were. If and when that happens, you two will be able to complete the second half of your marriage ceremony.''

I knew it was my turn to question her, but I couldn't quite get a proper question formulated. Beside me Arrik seemed to be having the same problem, so she laughed gently and stopped to face us squarely.

"My darlings, don't you remember that I said your pairing was more than awkward?" she asked. "I also said there was no choice about what to do, but all that referred to the second half of a marriage ceremony between you. Haven't you realized yet that when any two Houses are joined, the same is done with their Great Flames?''

"But—we already have all those tiny lights above us," I protested, feeling more confused than I had in a very long while. "Where would the Great Flames find room to put more of them?''

"Hali, a second joining of the Flames would bring a

second Gift, not more of the first," she explained, smiling with greater patience than I really deserved. "I have no idea what that second Gift would be, any more than I had guessed about the first, but I know I can't wait to see it. The defeat of Trayron by the people he and his father wronged will mark the beginning of their new day, and on the dawn of that day we'll all have our second Gift."

"Our second Gift," Arrik and I murmured almost together, our gazes moving up to the no-longer-empty sky. I very much wanted to know what that second Gift would be, and could hardly wait for the dawn that would let my beloved and me give our own Song to the people of the Realms.

Whatever came it would be no less than magnificent, and would also belong to all those who knew how to hope.

And so, my children, the Lord of the Earth was set apart with those he wronged, defeated in his most cherished hopes, and left to rule in solitary madness. Those who would help the poor victims of his illness have already done what they might, and now must we do for ourselves before any further aid will be offered. We have only to stand straight and tall, knowing ourselves as not less than the one who calls himself the Highest Lord, and his tyranny over us will be done. We must believe, my children, believe in ourselves, and our hopes will come to be truth rather than fanciful dreams. We must never lose hope, never, never, never . . .

SHARON GREEN grew up in Brooklyn and discovered science fiction at the age of twelve. A voracious reader, she qualified for the school library medal, but didn't get it because the librarian disapproved of sf. ("If you want to press the point," she writes, "you *could* say Lucky Starr, Space Ranger, got me in trouble in junior high school. It would be the literal truth.") Later, she earned her B.A. at New York University, where she got rid of an unwanted admirer by convincing him that she was from another planet.

Currently Ms. Green lives in New Jersey with her sons, her cats, and her Atari computer. A prolific writer, she is the author of over a dozen books, including *The Far Side of Forever,* the Terrilian Warrior series, *Lady Blade, Lord Fighter,* the Jalav series, and *The Rebel Prince.* When she's not at her computer, she is engaging in one of her diverse hobbies: Tae Kwon Do (in which she has a purple belt), knitting, horseback riding, fencing, and archery.

RETURN TO AMBER...

THE ONE *REAL* WORLD, OF WHICH ALL OTHERS, INCLUDING EARTH, ARE BUT SHADOWS

The New Amber Novel

KNIGHT OF SHADOWS   75501-7/$3.95 US/$4.95 Can
Merlin is forced to choose to ally himself with the Pattern of Amber or of Chaos. A child of both worlds, this crucial decision will decide his fate and the fate of the true world.

SIGN OF CHAOS   89637-0/$3.50 US/$4.50 Can
Merlin embarks on another marathon adventure, leading him back to the court of Amber and a final confrontation at the Keep of the Four Worlds.

The Classic Amber Series

NINE PRINCES IN AMBER 01430-0/$3.50 US/$4.50 Can
THE GUNS OF AVALON 00083-0/$3.50 US/$4.50 Can
SIGN OF THE UNICORN 00031-9/$3.50 US/$4.25 Can
THE HAND OF OBERON 01664-8/$3.50 US/$4.50 Can
THE COURTS OF CHAOS 47175-2/$3.50 US/$4.25 Can
BLOOD OF AMBER 89636-2/$3.95 US/$4.95 Can
TRUMPS OF DOOM 89635-4/$3.50 US/$3.95 Can